Love, Chocolate, and Beer

THE
CACTUS CREEK
SERIES

NEW YORK TIMES BESTSELLING AUTHOR

VIOLET DUKE

ISBN-10: 1-941198-85-6
ISBN-13: 978-1-941198-85-8

Printed in the United States of America

10 9 8 7 6 5 4 3 2

Chapter 1

"*DANI!* WE'RE RUNNING low on top shelf tequila; I've been promising the cooks indecent favors so they'll run back to keep my red ale line on tap; and seriously, what does a girl need to do to get more ice? Where's that new barback and why the hell isn't he doing his job?!"

Rushing back from the brewery, Dani Dobson swooped under a waiter's tray of food and hustled over to keep her brewpub's best bartender from indulging in a little frustration-releasing attack on a now petrified barback and his apparently twice-forewarned bro-globes.

Not that she could fire the nutty hothead either way.

Aside from being her best friend, Xoey was a veritable bartending rockstar in these parts, a wild, glorious fun-magnet adored by all, replaceable by none.

Good lord, she could sell warm beer on a hot day. Seeing Xoey dial up the flirt-tending and begin basically grifting customers into switching up to pricier liquors, Dani knew the excess of empty liquor bottles on the shelves was the reason why. Cringing, she quickly sent a waiter to assist the new barback with his restocking duties before she jumped in to help catch them up on drink orders. "Give the poor guy a break, Xo. It's been a busy week."

"Oh please." Xoey snorted. "You hired me during Mardi Gras. I handled it just fine."

"*Ha!* Only because the tightly bound twins on your chest were mesmerizing the men into sucking up all the drink orders you botched."

"Slander!" she cried back with an indignant smile dipped in sin. "It wasn't *just* the men."

Amidst the resulting four-guy pile up that crashed into the bar at that declaration, it was the droll PSA one of them made on the dangers of driving with a stick near Xoey that caused a riot of laughter all around.

Amplified further when another went down on drunken knee to ask for Xoey's hand in marriage.

Dani chuckled. She loved this new crowd that had started coming into Ocotillos lately. They were a tad younger and rowdier than she was used to but the whole brewpub seemed to feed off their energy. That was reward enough for all the social media plugging she'd been doing the past few months, a collective undertaking by the area's entire motley crew business community to draw more folks to their little town of Cactus Creek.

Her custom-made heaven on earth.

While not without its addictive charms, Cactus Creek was...well, unique. Water-strewn desert backdrops and equally atypical residents made the town a far cry from the quaint tourist spots touted on Arizona billboards. Fancy lattes with warm slices of Americana they were not; hell, the only antiques they sold were antique arms. Instead, they boasted funky craft beers, oddball novelty shops, and down-home fusion eateries where culinary references to 'the south' were usually of a country between Mexico and Chile. More fun than sleepy, and comfy without being colonial, the only reason the town was often mislabeled 'eclectically historic' was because its stubborn-ass residents had kept all their favorite parts while still growing up with the times.

Over the years, most of Dani's time and money had gone to nurturing the same process of selective evolution for her brewpub as well. Sure, Ocotillos was now drastically cooler than the simple tavern with a simple name her dad had run it as, but its beer remained constant. Just as Dobson as the blood in her veins, born and bred exactly as her dad had taught her to brew.

Speaking of… Dani finished tying on one of the new bartending half-aprons Xoey had designed for them, all the while sending a belated apology over to the photo of her father on the wall for not having thought to put a leash on Xoey's creativity.

The girl was quite the dirty slogan savant.

Then again, it probably would've made him laugh his ass off, she mused, a wry grin tweaking her lips at the thought.

As if in confirmation, his jolly photo smiled back at her, mirroring the image she held onto of him in her mind.

It had been over three years now. Three years, but a part of her still expected to see him striding in that brewery door with the unconditionally doting smile he'd always had on reserve just for her.

She missed having someone love her like that.

The sudden burst of applause trickling down from the terrace had Dani silently cursing and ducking out from the bar—and her memories. She raced up the stairs to the rooftop deck she'd built a few summers ago, bobbing and weaving through the cram-packed sea of weekend Romeos on the prowl, trendy nine-to-fivers partying their hard week away, and co-ed clusters blithely kicking off the start of their winter break with a bang.

Thankfully, the musicians had thrown in an adlib bit to give her time to hop on stage and snag the mic. "*Let's hear it again for Rylan Grey and his band, everyone!*" she hollered, drawing forth a fresh wave of raucous hoots from the crowd. "Okay, it's time for me to feed these guys, so until they start their next set, the band break power hour starts right now: half price on tonight's food specials and BOGO on all your beers!"

Another round of merriment echoed into the night just as Rylan swallowed her up in his customary post-set bear hug. She planted a laughing kiss on his cheek and high-fived the rest of his guys, Vanna-Whiting her smartphone screen proudly for the single ones. "Tweets from girls wanting to jump you all right here on my deck? I'd say your fan base is evolving very nicely."

Rylan's drummer put his drumsticks up to his heart. "God bless higher education."

With a chuckling headshake, Dani waited for Aidan to tuck his never-leaves-his-sight drumsticks in his back pocket before walking the group over to the table she kept blocked off for them each week, already piled high with a hodgepodge of their usual dinner favorites.

Rylan pulled a chair out for her and flipped the one beside it around for himself before taking a swig from the mug of rye ale she'd eagerly slid before him.

Then she held her breath and waited.

Midway through his first gulp, his brows shot up. And then slowly drifted back down as his eyelids slid to an appreciative half-mast.

Next came the biggest compliment yet—he all but forgot she was even sitting there as he kept on drinking until half the beer was gone.

Finally, he let out a satisfied, rumbly sigh, followed by a low, slow whistle. "Damn. That is one *hell* of a beer, sweets. Best ale I've had in years."

Dani beamed, and proceeded to do a little victory dance in her chair. Rylan wasn't big on lavish compliments, so when one came along, it was definitely call for celebration.

He took another long swig, nearly finishing off the mug. "Seriously, this one's a winner. Tell me you're making this the official winter; it'll be a crying shame if you don't."

"I am. And it's all thanks to you. After what you said about the last trial batch, I added ginger to enhance the malty milk sugar and honey." She kissed her fingertips. "Voila, the Rylan Red was born. I'm the only one who calls it that but still, feel free to be completely honored."

"Well call me Rumpelstiltskin. I done taught you to spin straw into gold." He slung his arm over her shoulders, pulling out the country drawl he grew up with that usually only made an appearance when he sang. "Now that you've named one of your babies after me, what say you change your last name to Grey as well, love? Make an honest man outta me."

"Goofball." She swatted his hand away. "And risk the wrath of your rabid female fans?"

A teasing voice called out, "I'd be more worried about the male ones. Shoot, they'll yank your hair right out at the roots." When Xoey popped her head around the corner, the guys cheered and fist-bumped her in welcome.

Aidan waited until she made her rounds before quickly pulling her onto his lap.

Cartoon waves of steam were sizzling off the pair within seconds, until soon, Aidan's *drumsticks* were no longer the attention-gathering focal point where his rocker jeans were concerned.

Dani sighed. "You know, Xo, if you'd just seal the deal with the guy already, the rest of us wouldn't need a cold shower just from seeing you two say hello."

A chorus of '*amen*' sounded from the entire band.

Aidan's sounding the most reverent of them all.

"Tempting." Xoey hummed over the suggestion—for all of two seconds. "*Buuut* I wouldn't want to corrupt the poor man." She tossed a positively carnal wink Aidan's way. *"Yet."*

The guys hooted and hollered and elbowed their theatrically smitten drummer.

Dani joined the laughs for a bit before ruffling Rylan's hair and getting up to give a green light for the small group of band bunnies hovering nearby to swoop in.

Despite the guys' hard rule of never getting cozy with groupies, she still liked giving them space to enjoy the bunny attention.

Zigzagging down the crowded stairwell back to the bar, Dani greeted a few regulars before heading over to her usual tending area behind the bar and sliding a sideways glance over at Xoey. "I'm telling you, if you and Aidan keep up with this flirting to be the dating equivalent of each other's nicotine patch arrangement, you two are going to end up in bed."

"And I told *you* I'm not taking love life advice from a woman who doesn't have a life outside of this brewpub," maintained Xoey, before coming to an abrupt halt.

Whatever riveting thing she'd just spotted made her expression suddenly slow-melt into a pleased little smile. Highly suspicious. Dani's eyes narrowed as Xoey began chastising her with the same ole lecture, with seemingly new objectives, "The amount you've been working this year is obscene, Dani. Far worse than your usual recreational workaholism. You are simply too hot to be going through an *eleven-month* dryspell."

Dani felt color flood her cheeks as she shot a look around at everyone within earshot before sending Xoey a keep-talking-and-I'll-kill-you look.

Ignoring it, Xoey steamrolled on, eyes alit with best friend mischief. "I say we end your dryspell with that—" she stabbed her finger, ever so indiscreetly, at the criminally good-looking man a few tables down from them— "panty-melting chiseled goodness over there. He's back again. And he *definitely* wants you all kinds of naked."

———•———

LUKE BRADFORD DIDN'T KNOW why the almost irrationally sexy bartender was pointing at him and frankly, he didn't much care. It was the one with the killer smile beside her, the brunette he'd caught fleeting glimpses of the last few weeks while he'd been busy moving into town fully that gripped his attention yet again. She was tucking her sleek, dark chocolate hair behind an ear in seemingly shy reflex and he just sat there with the round he'd just bought the guys, unable to take his eyes off her.

"Holy shit." Isaac jabbed him in the ribs. "I'm pretty sure that insanely hot bartender is pointing at you. Do you know her?"

Luke could barely hear him. Or much of anything for that matter. His sole focus remained on the cute brunette— the hardest working bartender there by his estimation. Even as her friend was telling her something that for some reason, involved pointing at him, the woman hardly paused long enough to spare a quick glance his way.

Just as well. He wasn't sure he would've survived a lengthier look than that.

Though she'd doused it quickly, a sizzling, ultra-feminine awareness had flared in her eyes in the brief moment they'd met his. And now a sweet, honest-to-god farm-girl blush was pinking her cheeks right up.

Man, oh man, was he in trouble.

If the quintessential girl next door had an equally cute, but unpredictable, feisty twin sister, this woman would be her. With her adorably stubborn frown and quiet, kitten gaze still mulishly refusing to look directly at him again, she was drawing him in—hook, line, and sinker.

At that point, Luke stopped trying to hide his interest. He was doing a lousy job at it anyhow.

Instead, he decided to up the blatancy level of his gaze considerably, and *dared* her to play.

She ignored him for a full minute. To his growing entertainment.

Eventually, however, her gaze collided with his. And held. He immediately deployed his dimples, a tiny bit triumphantly, counting on that to rile her enough to make her drop her defenses just a little bit more.

It did.

She instantly went on the offense, covertly returning his stare head-on and dropping the checkered flag for the silent game of Chicken that followed.

Hot damn.

Another scorching, hard-fought minute later, victory was his.

Not just because she'd broken the connection first, but because a touch of humor had ghosted her lips when she had. Immediately following, the next hour found their gazes colliding across the room with increasing frequency. It was all more friendly than flirty but still, Luke was captivated.

And officially clueless as to what his friends had been talking about for the past twenty minutes.

The fact that the whole guys' night out had been his idea in the first place just made his bro-code infraction that much worse. The four of them hadn't hung out in months. He'd been stressed as hell relocating his chocolate shop to Cactus Creek, and Isaac had started practically living at the mixed martial arts gym he'd opened up in Tempe last year, trying to figure out ways to get it out of the red. Connor had the best excuse seeing as how his now two-month-old was apparently going through diapers on the hour every night, while Connor's brother Brian took second place honors having just gotten married a little while ago to a firecracker who was keeping life thoroughly interesting from what they've heard.

Yep, the guys were definitely going to ride him about this one for a long time. But, it was a decision he congratulated himself over when his continued lack of attention to his friends allowed him to catch his mystery bartender bending over to grab something from a floor shelf.

Unevolved of him? Absolutely. But doubly rewarding, seeing as how it prompted a nose-scrunching twitch of a smile that she tried really hard to hide behind a droll eye-roll.

Damn, she was cute.

No longer even pretending to pay attention to the guys anymore, Luke leaned forward in growing curiosity as he watched her face light up then as she fiddled with some buttons on her wristwatch, eyes now locked on the vintage clock above the bar. He could practically see waves of excitement ebbing out of her as she soundlessly counted down another few seconds.

Finally, at the top of the hour, she went over to the wall phone to make a brief call, after which, she hesitated, chewed on her lip in debate, and then slowly lifted her gaze to find...him.

He quirked a brow up in question.

And got one *heck* of an answer via the shy, happy smile blooming across her face.

Rippling with a deep pride obviously born from cherished memories, that incredible smile sucker-punched him, drove him crazy because he didn't know the meaning behind it.

The moment passed as soon as a customer grabbed her attention for a drink order.

She was still smiling at everyone around her, but it wasn't the same. Sappy as it sounded, he wanted to see that earlier smile again. Up close, this time. Hell, he wanted to learn everything there was to know about that smile.

And more so, the woman behind it.

A minute later, just as he was finishing off his Black and Tan so he could go order a second—from up at the bar—the music playing on the house speakers suddenly cut out, and was replaced by the sound of loud, boisterous, blissfully off-key singing.

Weird.

Weirder still was the eruption of ecstatic cheers and wolf cries echoed all around the brewpub as a result.

All eyes flew to the glass picture window looking into the Ocotillos brewery, where its workers—whom he'd never seen working in these large numbers at night—were lined up, arms linked and beer mugs sloshing as they crooned out the lyrics to an infectious old school British drinking song. Then, as if this were some sort of musical, the entire joint was soon joining in and rocking out. A few beer-happy dudes even ran to the brewery glass like super fans at a hockey game.

"What is all this?" he hollered with a smile over the deafening good cheer, directing his question at the Sullivan brothers, since he knew they were both friends with the owner of Ocotillos.

The waitress lowering a platter of food onto their table beat them to it. "It's a tradition here," she said with an affectionate smile. "The whole thing started about fifteen years ago with Vince, the original Dobson brewmaster." She pointed to the big, framed photo of him in its place of honor on the wall. "For every new seasonal brew he created, he'd have customers try it for a night on tap before he launched it officially. And if folks didn't fall head over heels during the tasting, the crazy man would scrap it and start from scratch, throwing months of work down the drain."

She paused her story when a perfectly harmonized singing of the chorus rang out from the staircase, courtesy of the musicians who'd been performing upstairs. Everyone in the brewpub spun around to see the four rocker guys holding their beer mugs up in salute toward the bar; and like a surge of thunder, the crowd stomped their feet and raised the singing decibels in the place even higher.

"But in the cases like tonight," she continued with a grinning shout, "if the customers downright loved the new beer, he'd call back to his guys and tell them to 'have a drink' to celebrate the birth of a new Dobson beer." Tucking her food tray under an arm, she nodded her head over at the animated brewery workers who'd all removed their caps in respect while singing the drunken lyrics. "The singing part started one year when the brewpub had been at the tail end of financial crisis. Good ole Vince decided he wasn't gonna go down without a fight. So, bless his heart, he poured every bit of his soul into one more brew...that ended up winning the biggest craft beer award around."

She smiled with the far-off look of someone who'd been there. "When we found out, he and the brew boys broke out in song right there in the brewery. And this was the song they sang. From that day on, the song became an unofficial anthem, a tradition the baby of the Dobson clan, the new brewmaster here, still carries on whenever a new beer is born."

Right on cue with the story, his mystery bartender hopped up on the counter behind the bar to write *Warm Winter Rye [Red Ale]* on the chalkboard with all the other Dobson beers listed on tap.

A symphony of applause rippled across the brewpub and the look of pure joy on her face vaulted straight into Luke's chest—surprising, considering he'd never even had a conversation with the woman.

"Wow, you've got it bad," murmured Isaac, thoughtfully evaluating the emotions running across Luke's face with annoying accuracy. He didn't comment further, however, which Luke appreciated. Like all his close friends, Isaac knew all about Luke's take on love. It was a mirage.

Always just out of reach.

Blinking back the unwelcome demons from his past, Luke shrugged and quietly admitted to himself as much as Isaac, "There's something about her." Like a first-time addict going from zero to sixty on a rush, he immediately swung his gaze around to find her again.

God, she was pretty. And intriguing. And so impishly sweet a person couldn't help but smile upon seeing her.

Of course in his case, it was growing painfully obvious that smiling wasn't the only visible reaction he'd be having to the woman.

Hell, anyone with eyes could see the hard time he was having keeping his reaction to himself. And it didn't help one bit when her lips parted on a soft breath at just that moment when their gazes collided.

Good grief. A brain simply couldn't be expected to function with *all* its blood racing to command central south. His brows dipped low in reflection as he adjusted his jeans. Had anyone ever affected him this way before?

This wholly, this swiftly?

He shot to his feet. *Nope, never.*

Eyes locked on hers, he cut a path straight for her.

…Only to have his ego take a sizeable hit when she abruptly tapped in another bartender and started edging away from the bar.

Undeterred, he picked up the pace.

Equally stubborn, so did she.

And this round went to her.

She vanished behind a door to the back just as he reached the spot she'd vacated beside the exotic bartender Isaac had been staring at earlier.

With a grin of amused approval, the bartender said simply, "Took you long enough."

The unexpected comment caught him off guard. And not in a good way. "What is this? Some kind of game or something for you two? Is that why you were pointing at me earlier?"

That made her expression sober quickly. "My friend isn't into games." She spoke now in full protective-BFF mode, staring him down. "Competitive? Ridiculously so. A player? *Hell* no."

Luke felt his frown dissolve into a smile, liking both that compelling character profile and oddly, the bold bartender as well, in all her strange and candid glory. "Unlike *you*, you mean."

A pleased laugh bubbled out of her. "God, you're perfect for her. As sharp as you are blunt."

She studied him for a second before coming to some sort of conclusion. "She's lugging liquor boxes out from storage, back near the brewery pass-through. You should go help her."

He squeezed her forearm in thanks and set out to do just that.

When he opened the storeroom doors at the end of the back hall, he was greeted by the sound of his mystery woman's voice...softly cursing up a string of *very* creative expletives.

Oh yeah. He grinned. *This is going to be interesting.*

Chapter 2

"*HOLY HEFEWEIZEN...*" Incredulous, Dani yanked open a box of mid-shelf tequila and pulled out two bottles as she attempted to get her pulse rate in check. Though she was now a closed door away from the man who'd been scrambling her brain with those scorching hot looks of his for the past hour, she was still buzzing from the potent currents that had passed between them throughout.

And fighting the impulse to go back out there for another hit.

Heck, it felt like every female cell in her body was ganging up on her, defiantly urging—demanding—she do the reckless for once and give in to each promised temptation that had been radiating from that man.

What in the world? She'd seen the guy in passing, what, three or four times in the last couple of weeks? They'd chatted briefly—about the weather, if memory served—for maybe thirty seconds that one time he'd come in to pick up a food order. He was just a random guy who visited Cactus Creek once in a while on his lunch break as far as she could tell.

She shook her head, thoroughly mystified. This wasn't her. Dani Dobson did *not* get weak-kneed for a guy without getting to know him first, and most times, not even then. She didn't flirt with strangers from across the room. And she sure as hell had never felt like a cat in heat before tonight.

Taking a calming breath, she fanned her suddenly overheated skin. Clearly, she was just plain losing it, cracking finally under the mounting stress she'd been under lately.

In a few weeks, her brother Derek would be home from his honeymoon and she still didn't have a clue on how to buy out his half of the brewpub—the one thing making it impossible for him to pursue the dreams he'd patiently put on hold for her years ago.

The day she'd royally screwed up.

And for every day he didn't complain, pressure, or do any less than give her support and praise for her successes—while never mentioning that one epic failure she never let herself live down—she hoarded another guilty reminder of how badly she was letting him down.

It was an impossible situation she had little to no control over. So yeah, she was going a little crazy.

…Crazy enough to consider maybe, *possibly* doing something about a situation she *could* control.

Namely, her 'dry spell.'

A jolt of awareness instantly charged her skin as she

recalled every memorable thing about the stranger from the bar Xoey was insistent on nominating for all the sex-having.

Dani was certain she'd shared a moment with him out there, right before the new-brew celebration had started, not too long after the sexy staring contest he'd challenged her to that was *still* making her blush. Across every inch of her body.

"Xoey's out of her mind." She shook her head, at a loss for words to match her blistering hot thoughts. "That guy out there can't possibly… I mean he was just so—"

"I was so…what?" prodded a deep voice from directly behind her.

"You!" she gasped, spinning around. She gripped the rum bottle she'd just unboxed and poised it before her like a fencing sabre. "What're you doing back here?"

"Whoa, easy." He shot both his hands up in the air, amusement curving his mouth into a lopsided grin. "No need to bottle-bash me. Your friend, the other bartender, sent me in to help you."

"Of *course* she did," Dani muttered in exasperation.

Mental note: Xoey was *so* fired.

When she retracted her weapon, the man efficiently slid next to her as if she hadn't been poised for assault with deadly bottle, and began opening liquor cartons like he was being paid to. "Now what were you just saying about me?"

She balked. "How could I've been saying anything about you? I don't even *know* you."

His pupils flared. But not in annoyance at her well-worded, bald-faced lie. But rather…in hunger.

She took a step back.

"Sorry." He tore his eyes away from her and focused on the whiskey bottles he was lining up behind the older bottles in accordance with the labeled restocking instructions on each shelf. "The thoughts in my stream-of-consciousness just went to dangerous waters," he added in that malt-rich voice of his. "I went from thinking 'pants on fire' to thinking about your pants." His voice graveled, heated for a second as if teased by his own words. "Then, well, you can follow the breadcrumbs."

Lordy, the man was lethal to the female population.

She did in fact follow those crumbs, right over to her backside. Unconsciously, she took a compulsive swipe at her jeans with her free hand—nope, no flames engulfing her butt—and felt the temperature in the room spike dramatically.

Dammit, if he didn't quit looking at her like that—all steamy eyes valiantly glued to her face rather than her fire snuffing efforts below... She shivered. Not wanting to even mentally voice the trouble that would ensue from that train of thought. It was bad enough that the faint scent of one of her dark ales was lingering on his lips in that sexier than sin sort of way, but candying it atop a gentlemanly sweet center to boot was just playing unfair.

Of course, like a masochist, she tipped her head back to meet his gaze anyway.

"Hi," he rumbled gently, a soft smile flirting with the corners of his lips.

It was a content murmur more than anything else and somehow he managed to make that one word, the mere act of greeting her, meeting her for the first time sound so...special.

Oh, hell. The moment her fingertips began gravitating to his chest, the rest of her couldn't help but follow. His hands settled lightly at her sides and she watched, spellbound, as the simmering heat in his eyes burned hotter. Deeper.

An unexpected sigh of pleasure seeped out of her and instantly, his fingers flexed against her hips in response. It was the only warning she got. In one sultry swoop, he strapped a steel arm around her waist to pull her flush against him before he caught her jaw with his free hand and just exploded past all her defenses with one slow, soft brush of his lips against hers.

Then just as quickly, he pulled back.

Seemingly shocked at his own actions, eyes fixed on hers as if to gauge her reaction, he dragged in ragged breath after ragged breath. To try to slow things down probably.

One second, two seconds...

On three, her lips found his racing pulse just above his collar. A timid tongue swipe was all it took to get her shoulders pinned back against a wall, his hand speared through her hair, and the sensitive skin along her neck schooled on how turnabout was so far beyond fair play.

Breathing became barely a memory as his mouth decimated any hope she had of control. Before she knew it, she was undoing her shirt, daring him to follow suit. She wasn't normally the bold instigator type but with him...she couldn't think, couldn't wait, couldn't—

She gasped. *I don't even know this guy's name.* She jerked out of his arms and leapt a few feet away from him.

"Are you alright?" He held a startled, worried hand out to her like a forbidden apple.

Yes please. She shook her head hard, sidling farther away from him. "I don't do that…this. Ever."

"Well then, you're one of those who are just phenomenal without needing practice," he teased lightly, the concern in his voice evident. "Hey, it's okay. Why don't we just sit and talk for a bit?" He perched atop a nearby liquor crate. "I promise not to pounce on you."

He meant it, she could tell. He just sat there waiting, patiently giving her the time and space she needed. Slowly, she sank down onto the crate directly in front of him.

"Are you?" he asked softly, gently smoothing her hair back to study her expression.

Feeling like she'd lost all her marbles, she looked up in confusion. "Am I what?"

"One of those who doesn't practice much? At this?"

Dani gasped again, this time in anger. "Did Xoey bribe you to end my 'drought' or whatever she calls it?!" She jabbed a finger in his chest. "Because I'll have you know—"

"Hey, calm down." His hands curtailed her efforts to drill into his sternum. "Your friend didn't tell me about any, um, drought." The corners of his eyes crinkled slightly.

"Don't you dare laugh at me, you ass!"

"I wasn't laughing. I was smiling." The glare she shot him could've leveled a city.

His hand halted an inch from sliding into her hair again, or rather, an inch from her now fully visible teeth. "Why do I

22

get the feeling you're thinking about biting a hunk of flesh out of me"—he blinked, fascinated—"Did you just growl at me?"

While he was now showing her the same caution one would a feral cat, his heated gaze said he found her ferocity inexplicably sexy. "Yes, I was smiling about your drought; so sue me. I like the thought of you not remembering any kisses but mine." His eyes roamed her face. "To hell with it, I don't need all ten fingers…" He caressed her cheek and she felt her eyelids drift closed at the touch.

"Dani, you in there?" bellowed Javier, one of her cooks from the kitchen. *"Can you bring out the—"* His severed request morphed into a muffled howl, a high octave just below soprano. *"Never mind,"* he reneged in a squeaking gasp of male agony shortly after.

Dani winced, recognizing the audible footprint of Xoey's handiwork. The mental image of Xoey de-balling poor Javier threw Dani back to the here and now. As reality rushed in, she could once again hear the bar noises sifting in under the door, smell the savory aromas from the grill, and see— even in the semi-darkness—that she'd been minutes from rounding a few of the bases with a perfect stranger.

Avoiding his eyes, she fiddled with her bar apron. "I should probably get back to work."

"Right, of course." He stood and helped her up. "Sorry, I never lose my head like that. Not sure what's up with me…huh, that sounded a lot dirtier than I intended—" He stopped and grinned when a ripple of amusement tinkled past her lips.

She couldn't help but chuckle. This was fun; *he* was fun.

As she rolled the liquor cart to the door, Dani racked her brain for a sexy comeback to keep the banter going. Not exactly her forte.

Luckily, she was saved from making a conversational ass out of herself when he abruptly stepped in front of the cart and said, "I know you have to get back out to the bar but I'll never forgive myself if I let you walk out this door without getting you to agree to have dinner with me."

He cringed in sheepish male hindsight. "Though I'd probably settle for at least getting your name."

Right, names. Or the lack there of, in their case. The whole reason she'd stopped kissing him to begin with. She stuck an awkward hand out in belated greeting. "My name's Danica. But everyone calls me Dani."

He intertwined his fingers with hers and drew her in close, turning an awkward moment into an insanely sexy one in a few seconds flat. Lowering his head slowly as if to give her a chance to say no, he laid a soft, barely there kiss on her lips when she didn't.

"Nice to meet you, Dani." His two dimples flashed as he said her name. "I'm Luke."

Their magical, movie soundtrack moment was interrupted, however, by a dread-filled, hushed voice on the other side of the door. "*Dani?*" Javier's whisper was tinted with panic. "*I'm really sorry but we need to get more coriander.*" A low murmur joined his. "*And cooking tequila too.*"

Dani screwed her eyes closed in embarrassment and

called out, "I'll bring them out, guys."

She was barely through her sentence when she heard the two of them scrambling away from the door. There was definite cursing in Spanish. Along with some praying.

The sound of lethal pointy-toe boots stomping after them was the obvious reason why.

"I really ought to get out there," she groan-laughed. "Cooking with one hand while protecting their crotch from Xoey's wrath probably isn't all that safe. Or sanitary."

"As a protective guardian of the same anatomy, and an avid non-fan of any variety of jockstrap cuisine, you have my sincere appreciation." His earnest look caused another round of mirth to unwind through her. "Just so we're clear," he added quickly, "you do know a kiss after a dinner invite is a universal ironclad yes, right?" His tone was matter-of-fact, his eyes adorably optimistic.

"That so?" She let loose a grin and tossed out, "Did I agree to anything else?"

"Just a few other things I won't be able to stop thinking about until our date," he teased right back.

She stared at him for exactly one missed heartbeat before that whole bout of temporary insanity she'd been worrying about earlier flared up and caused her to do the most un-Dani thing ever.

She tackled him.

Well, she sort of just pushed him back into the storage room but in her mind it had been far more primitive. Hands on the ridges of his torso, she tugged him in for a final kiss.

And released him a long minute later with a whispered, "I'll be thinking about those things too," as she basically floated to the door.

"*Jesus Christ.*" Luke's tortured breath trailed close behind her.

By the sound of the rustling at the small of her back, he was attempting to adjust the fit of his jeans. When that resulted in apparent failure, he muttered in her ear, "You had to wait till *after* I finally got my soldiers to stand down from earlier, didn't you?"

If there was a complaint in there somewhere, it was altogether undetectable.

And Dani was entirely unrepentant.

She did, however, manage to keep her giggle contained to a tickled grin when a quick glance at his 'problem' revealed that yes, his southern post was indeed at full attention...in a *very* impressive call to arms.

After one gentle, but nerve-firing farewell slide of his hand down her back, she made her way to the kitchen to deliver the items she retrieved for the cooks before grabbing the liquor cart and heading back out front as well.

Thankfully, her bartenders appeared too busy to even notice how long she'd taken to return with the liquor bottles. So far, so good.

With ninja stealth, she slinked warily past them on the way to—

Bam. A shiny black designer boot clacked on the floor before her to block her escape.

Busted.

Stretched sideways like Gumby, and apparently with eyes on the back of her head, Xoey topped off the triple sec on the kamikaze she was pouring before tossing the customer a wink and twisting around to throw an arm over Dani's shoulders. "I'm impressed. And frankly, a little jealous, boss. Even I've never 'passed the earth's stratosphere' during *Seven Minutes in Heaven* at work." Her thoughtfully up-raised eyes showed her adding it to her things-to-do list.

Oh geez. Dani sighed. Xoey was nothing if not goal-oriented.

"So, spill," pressed Xoey. "Was he good?"

"At what?" Dani's liquor bottle restocking took on a new, extravagantly deep focus.

"At whatever's telling everyone you know what Victoria's secret is."

Dani swore and spun around to button her top back up. Luckily, it'd only been a fairly chaste peek, but the disappointment echoed by two guys awaiting drinks—and a gleefully smug Xoey—still served to mortify her. She cast Xoey a blistering glare. "We didn't 'travel' that far in there," she hissed. "By the by, since we're on the subject, remind me to fire you later."

Xoey pranced back to her 'tending spot to salt the rim of a mug for an agave citrus lager. "Okie dokie. My drought-ending skills are far more vital to the human race anyway. Yours will be the Cinderella story to launch my career."

Dani hurled a bar towel at Xoey's peek-a-boo midriff,

laughing despite herself. She never could stay mad at her crazy friend for long. The reason why that was escaped her, however, when not a moment later, Xoey cheerfully threatened, "From you or from him, either way, I'm getting the sordid details, Dani."

The pest.

Relenting with a fierce blush, Dani admitted, "I didn't learn much more than his name."

But *of course* that just made Xoey put a dramatic hand to her heart. "I am *so* proud."

Dani rolled her eyes. "You measure these things with a very short, very strange yardstick."

"Quite proudly, yes. Because it's the only yardstick that measures what truly matters in life." She raised an eyebrow wisely. "Feel free to borrow it anytime."

It was a dare.

Profoundly grounded, but a dare nonetheless. Dani snuck another peek over at Luke. Could she really do it? Risk her heart the way Xoey did so often? So fearlessly?

Just then, the target of her rapt attention glanced up and caught her looking at him. He and his buddies looked to be getting ready to leave and as if he could hear her silent question from where he stood, an encouraging little smile brought out one of his two dimples.

He was out the door before the whispered '*I don't know*' to her own question quietly passed her lips.

Chapter 3

LUKE WAS LOOKING to score a multiple tastegasm today.

After finally tearing himself away from Dani last night, the first thing he'd felt impelled to do—well, after the cold shower of course—was to head to the random little nook between his kitchen and living room that his apartment realtor had insisted on calling a 'pseudo dining room.' Though the term 'pseudo' in this case meant just barely large enough to fit a two-person table, sans the chairs, the odd space design kept his rent cheap and actually worked for him.

Completely ignoring the still-taped moving boxes littering his apartment, he began arranging ingredients on the big granite remnant he'd found a few weeks ago at a recycled building materials store and thrown on his dining table so he wouldn't go stir-crazy without a shop kitchen to work in during the relocation.

Minutes later, he was hard at work creating a new

chocolate. But not just any new chocolate. *The* new chocolate he'd been struggling with all week.

His muse, clearly, had nothing on his feisty little bartender.

With pure inspiration hitting him from every angle, his mind pinballing between woman and chocolate, he'd ended up working straight through the night.

Come morning, it was faith, not cockiness that had him calling his shot like the legendary Babe Ruth. Revving on a no-sleep high and an entire pot of coffee, he pushed through the still papered-over storefront door of Desert Confections—past the never-disappearing renovation clutter that was weeks behind schedule, and the granite guys finishing up the counter that was supposed to have been installed days ago—heading straight to the back in search of his shop manager, Quinn, the self-named Wicked Witch of the West herself.

Though most days, she prided herself on upgrading one of those W's to a B.

Finding her in the office, buried in paperwork as always, Luke edged over to her desk and held his newest chocolate creation out about an inch from her mouth.

Then, he waited.

As he knew she would, Quinn didn't ask or even look before opening up for a taste. It was practically in her job description. Plus, though gorgeous, the woman had so many '*does not play well with others*' and '*may attack if provoked*' signs around her like a force field that she likely never had to watch out for a man waving anything else in front of her lips

Still glued to the shop's post-relocation spreadsheets she'd been analyzing, Quinn chewed the chocolate carefully, almost scientifically. So slow it drove him bonkers.

Then finally, he heard it.

A thoughtful murmur twirled around an intrigued throat hum. And then one tiny sigh. All the quiet reactive noises Quinn made when a chocolate was good. But of course it was *good*. After once getting a face full of what she called *constructive feedback* 'back' from her, he'd never given her anything less than good since.

The question today was if it was great. Change-the-game great.

He backed up a step and crossed his arms. "Well?"

"Definitely a home run."

He pumped his fist in triumph. No tastegasm this time but that was okay. At least she didn't fake it. He hated when women did that.

"Our first home run of the year." Grinning like a champ, Luke strode over to their whiteboard to log the new homer in on their chocolate chart, which was cross-referenced with 'base numbers' from the Quinn tasting scale.

Generally speaking, the bulk of the chocolate confections that made it from Luke's test kitchen to his shop's display cases took at least third base on the Quinn tasting scale. Aside from the customer-requested bridge mix by the scoop, Luke refused to sell anything that only got to Quinn's second base, and it'd been years since he'd created any single-basers.

Then there was his gold display case chocolates. His pride and joy.

The elite line of specialty creations made up of all his homers to date...and the one multiple tastegasm on record.

Not a myth. He'd seen it with his own eyes.

And just as he never uttered the words that would evoke baseball's no-hitter jinx, Luke *never* talked about the 'multiple tastegasm.' But his particular avoidance wasn't for superstitious reasons. It was far more sinister. He didn't even dare say the phrase aloud for fear it would clue Quinn in on the fact that the system he used to gauge her ratings wasn't even based on baseball. It was based on her. Or rather, the sounds she made during tastings...which happened to be the same ones she made in bed.

She had no idea.

Though he'd really only started the whole thing as a joke that had been all the funnier because she never got it, the system ended up being too perfect to get rid of. Of course, when their very brief 'benefits' in that area ultimately expired right before they agreed to start the shop together way back in college, so did his window to let her in on the joke. And breaking the news all these years later sure as hell wasn't an option, not with her being his best friend and the closest thing he had to a sister now.

No, the only way he'd tell her that the homers they discussed all the time were...errr, *another kind of home run* would be through a 'Dear Quinn' letter. A lovely posthumous one by certified mail.

In the meantime, Luke was just going to have to keep his reflexive chuckles at bay. Silent though they always were, each one was inching him up the will-call list for the bus to hell for sure.

Ignoring one such chuckle right now, he found himself humming MLB's seventh inning tune instead. That is...until he turned around and saw Quinn frowning. For cryin' out loud, the woman used to analyze things to death after sex too. He rolled his eyes. "Oh, just tell me."

"Don't get me wrong, the bonbon is fantastic—unique flavor, great texture. But..." She made another face. "White chocolate, Luke? Really? The lil' wallflower of the chocolate family? Isn't this against your religion or something?"

She knew him so well.

"I'm reborn." Despite the marked improvements in the purity and quality of white chocolate over the years following the added FDA regulations back in '04, Luke still generally never worked with the stuff. Until now. "Honestly, I've just never been a huge fan of the flavor before I tasted this *particular* white chocolate."

His eyes drifted innocently to the ceiling as he slid a rather large file of papers onto her desk. "Remember that chocolate festival I was at last week?" He flashed all his teeth and one of his dimples at her. "Well, I met a new chocolate maker from Japan who makes this insane couverture white chocolate recipe—"

As soon as Quinn snatched the file from him, Luke jumped out of her kicking range. "Hear me out before you knee me in the balls. I had to move fast to sign him. This guy uses only the best of the best: Venezuelan criollo beans, a mind-blowing Kamahi and Rata honey blend from New Zealand—remind me to order some for our fudge by the way—and gold-label Tahitian vanilla. Quinn, you know how picky I am about vanilla."

Oh lord, if her scowl was anything to go by, it was obvious she'd gotten to the money portion of the contract. To cut off her fit of objections, which promised to be way more voice than reason, he slipped a second bonbon in her mouth.

"You have to admit, it's pretty darn incredible, right?" It was. And the rich filling he'd made using a cloudberry liqueur from Finland was both an intense and sublime match. He didn't have to wait long for her besieged taste buds to start overruling her bullheaded sensibilities.

Another purr. "Hey, is that..." Her brows arched in surprise. "Is there coffee in this?"

Damn, she's getting good. Hiding the proud big brother grin he knew she hated, Luke marveled at how far Quinn had come since they'd first opened up his tiny, hole-in-the-wall chocolate shop in Mesa years ago—light years from the delicate daisy she'd been in college a decade back.

"That coffee note is in the chocolate itself," he explained. "Probably one of the secret ingredients in the flavor profile. I heard he uses a special Korean pine nut, too."

Quinn looked up skeptically. "Wait, *that's* the big new idea you wanted to run by me today? White chocolate?"

So saying, she did reach over to steal another morsel.

"Honestly, Luke, unless you're seeing a wave of folks flooding in to buy these for their dogs, this isn't 'revolutionary' enough to help us with all the overhead costs we're racking up leasing out this whole building. I mean I've managed to keep the hype going with our old customers via social media but I still think we need to worry about exposure and access since you've moved us out to the boonies." She jabbed her fingers into her temples. "How in the world did you ever talk me into this relocation again?"

Hell if he knew.

To Luke, the town of Cactus Creek was just plain special. Offbeat. Indelible. *Fun.* Kissing cousin to Scottsdale but separated by Black Mountain Summit, the one great divide between city and country, Cactus Creek was a quirky little world of its own, close enough for city folk to escape to and far enough in lifestyle to make the trip worth it. He'd wanted to move Desert Confections here the second he'd stepped foot into town.

Quinn? Not so much. Getting her on board had been a friggin' miracle, what with moving having been not just a gamble, but utterly unjustifiable. Of course, that little factoid, and all the rational sense he'd been taught in business school, had ceased to be relevant the moment Luke had felt *it*—the instant, blinding, finding-your-soul mate connection to the town of Cactus Creek.

Had he not been so bowled over by it, there was no way he would've pushed the issue; God knew Quinn had enough weighing on her shoulders being a single mom with inhumane medical bills from her son's terrifying first year of life spent in and out of surgeries. As such, suggesting the move had been a gut-roiling experience for Luke. He'd gone in ready to reluctantly give it all up following the anticipated hell-no response from her...to instead finding himself profoundly humbled when she'd shocked him with a nervously trusting 'yes.' Yes to follow him, despite all the reservations she had regarding the town.

That in itself made the decision that much more risky.

Because it meant failure simply wasn't an option.

Unfortunately, with their new shop already starting off to a rocky start with a one-week delay in their grand opening, Quinn was doing her best to stay cool-headed...a feat which left her legs nice and warm to act on a hair trigger, ready and willing to kick him in the ass as a see-I-told-you-so and now-what're-you-gonna-do-to-fix-it combo that historically generated quick results.

Today was no different.

"White chocolate is just one part of my idea," he added quickly before she had a meltdown. "Did you know that in Japan, they celebrate Valentine's Day *and* something called White Day?"

Her frown told him he only had mere seconds to get to his point.

"Basically, Valentine's Day isn't a day to *exchange* gifts between couples. Rather, only the women give the men gifts, namely dark or milk chocolate. The exact reverse holds true on *March* 14th, a holiday called White Day there since traditionally, white chocolate is what the men reciprocate with...although I've read that a gift worth three times more than the Valentine gift is an acceptable alternative."

A hint of a smile tipped her lips at that explanation.

Ah, he had her now. "You see where I'm going with this?" Adrenaline ran through his veins. "I say we bring the whole idea here to Arizona as a cool new two-part lovers' holiday custom."

He pulled out the gift bag he'd filled with basic confectionary tools and chocolatiering ingredients last night. "Since those traditions say it's customary for the chocolate the women give the men to be homemade, we could even create some hype to make that part of it as well with kits like these to help women make their homemade V-Day chocolates. Even hold classes to teach ambitious customers how to make fancier stuff their guys will trip out over—"

Quinn's jaw unhinged. "Wait, *are you high*?! You're actually suggesting we just hijack tradition and let men totally off the hook in February? You want us to *change the rules* for Valentine's Day?"

"Completely for the better. Just picture it: we market it as a new two-prong, equality-of-the-sexes holiday for love, with crystal clear parameters in February and March." Luke began picking up momentum. "Getting the men on board should be cake because these new rules help de-mystify the holiday a bit. Foolproof it even. All we have to do is make it fun and sexy for them to convince the women in their lives to embrace the change as well." His mouth twitched. "That wasn't supposed to come out in the plural sense, but you get my meaning."

"Charming." She eyed him stubbornly. "Okay, so the men will probably love it, but how about the women? You're *not* winning over the female population with *that* pitch."

His expression softened. Turning to look at the only photo he had on his side of the office—the one of his parents laughing at their recent anniversary party—he said simply, "For the women, we should just show the revamped Valentine's Day for what it is: a romantic day devoted to a woman making a thoughtful gift for the man she loves. I actually think a lot of women would like that. Moreover, I know I'd be lying if I said I wouldn't consider myself hella lucky to be on the receiving end."

Quinn blinked thoughtfully at that, visibly thrown off-kilter by his sensitivity on the matter. "So then in March, we offer a dazzling line of white chocolates for men to spoil their women with," she added slowly, her lips quirking up in approval. "We'd lengthen spring sales by a month."

"Exactly!"

Quinn looked at him as if he'd unexpectedly sprouted genius horns. "We could call it White Chocolate Day to corner the market as ours instead of splitting the focus with flowers and stuffed animals." Her eyes lit up even more. "Luke, this could actually work."

"It *will* work, Quinn. But with Valentine's just a few months away, we've got no time to lose. Since you're the social media whiz, you should handle all the web stuff. Twitter, blogs, online ads, contests—whatever will create an online firestorm. I'll take care of the new chocolates and setting-up the classes, along with on-site promotions and whatever else I can come up with."

She nodded but remained uncharacteristically quiet. A downright oddity.

"I think the words you're looking for are '*wow, you brilliant man*,'" he inserted helpfully.

She rolled her eyes and picked up the new white chocolate contract as if it were covered in acid. "And encourage more of this type of behavior from you?"

He grinned, knowing her well enough to see she was about to cave. "You know this could be our big break-out, Quinn. Just what we need to set ourselves apart. We'll finally be set. With the surplus sales this has the potential to generate, you could pay a chunk of your medical debt off, lower the monthlies and maybe get ahead of it enough to start saving for lil' Coop's future as well. And *I* could—"

He paused and waved a hand in front of her now-distracted face. "*Hello*, earth to Quinn?"

When Quinn broke her gaze away from the group of people outside who'd caught her attention, the look on her face was excitedly determined. "I'm in."

He dropped back against the wall, relieved. "So, we're doing this?"

"Yep, and I think I already have an ad campaign in mind." Her eyes shifted outside again.

Luke peered out the wraparound window of their shop

that overlooked the brewpub across the small alleyway the next building over. Nothing out of the ordinary. Just a bunch of twenty-something-year-olds filing in for lunch. Ocotillos was always busy this time of day. He certainly didn't see anything that warranted the engrossing inspiration she'd seemed so taken by.

"I'm going in," she announced before heading out the door toward Ocotillos, leaving him to watch in puzzled amusement as she began scoping out the brewpub through the window, all covert-like. When she slipped out of sight around the building, he shrugged and ambled over to his desk, easing back in his chair with a satisfied grin.

Life was good. His newly shop was about to embark on a venture his gut *knew* would succeed, his business partner was off being creatively weird—always a good sign—and just nine hours ago, his dormant love life had regained a pulse again. Amazing. Particularly the last bit, he mused, smiling as his mind began wandering back to last night.

Back to Dani.

Does the two-day waiting rule apply if a first date hasn't happened yet?

Seeing as how last night's storage room festivities was unlike anything he'd ever done before, he decided to deem it exempt from all standard dating—

And that's when it hit him.

He stared blankly at his cell phone's contact list, not even bothering to scroll to the letter D. *Can't look up a number you didn't get in the first place.* "You freakin' idiot."

Great. Now Dani probably thought he was some sort of player. *Shit.*

Immediately, he opened up his Facebook account to see if he could find her on social media…only to roll his eyes in disbelief a second later.

You didn't get her last name either, genius.

Man, he'd seriously been out of the dating pool for way too long. Jumping up from his seat, he began pacing as he analyzed the situation. Considering Dani had still been there when he and his friends left last night near closing, there was no way she'd be working a day shift today—unless her boss was a slave-driving ass, which was doubtful since everyone in town had nothing but glowing things to say about the owner of Ocotillos.

Okay, so casually showing up to 'run into her' at lunch wasn't an option, and heading back tonight was also out since he'd already promised Quinn he'd babysit while she had a long-awaited girls' night out with her friend from college.

He halted his pacing and frowned, instantly rejected the idea of waiting another few days to find her.

Grabbing his keys, he headed out to see if Cactus Creek had a town florist.

Chapter 4

ZERO MISSED CALLS.

Luke stared at his smartphone screen. The same taunt had mocked him ten minutes ago too.

Grouchy now on top of Monday-morning antsy, Luke started tapping his pen on the desk.

Irked, Quinn grabbed his pen and set it down with an exasperated huff. "Okay, what's her name?"

Huh. Isn't that the million-dollar question, thought Luke sardonically.

"Dani," he eventually answered with a blunt frown.

Quinn's mouth rounded into a surprised *O*. "*Wow, you're really crushing on this one.*"

Not really in the mood for any pseudo-sisterly torment, he remained silent, shuffling through the upcoming week's paperwork his eyes had been glazing over for the past ten minutes.

Reaching over, Quinn plucked the papers from his hands, refusing to let it go. "So what happened? Did she shoot you down?" She crossed her arms, wholly serious when she offered, "Do you need me to kick the stupid woman's ass for you?"

That was his Quinn—vicious, but sweet.

"No," he sighed. "This is all my fault. I didn't get her number the night we met. So yesterday, I left some flowers for her over at Ocotillos where she works, along with my number." He frowned at his phone. "But she hasn't called."

"Maybe she's just shy," reasoned Quinn. "Or maybe she's doing the 'wait two days' thing guys you guys do."

Or maybe he'd been way off about the type of flowers he'd selected for her, and now she thought he was a weirdo with crappy taste in gifts.

He resumed his pen-tapping.

"Go home." She packed up his things for him. "You pulled an all-nighter creating that new chocolate on Saturday, you babysat for me most of Sunday, pulled another all-nighter to get the shop kitchen set up, and somehow *still* managed to make more corporate chocolate batches for this week. You must be beat." She tossed his keys to him. "Go. I'll take care of the deliveries today."

Since Quinn had brilliantly suggested they make sampler baskets for several dozen big businesses in the area, they now had a ton of corporate accounts and new distribution arrangements that were going to hopefully defray the cost of the move, and negate the hit they were taking by having to move their grand opening to after the holidays due to renovation delays. It had been a nightmare making all those chocolates without a full shop kitchen the past two weeks but it had been worth it.

Luke rubbed his neck. "I guess I am pretty fried."

Yawning, he gave her a peck on the cheek in thanks and headed out to his car, feeling the exhaustion wall getting closer with each step.

It wasn't until he was halfway home, and barely awake, that he realized what he'd forgotten to do this morning.

Quickly grabbing his cell phone, he hit the first speed dial and didn't even wait for Quinn to say hello before he started in with the apologies. "I'm an ass. I completely forgot you wanted to discuss your video ad ideas for our V- Day campaign this morning. You want me to head back in?"

Quinn's voice grinned over the phone line. "Don't worry about it. You're exhausted, and clearly distracted. We can talk more about the video ads later. I'll just do some prep work for it today. Seriously, take the morning off. One day of you being a red-blooded man isn't going to kill us."

Wow.

What happened to the freaked out Quinn from the past few weeks? The mistress of doom and gloom that had been glowering over every unforeseen relocation cost and terrorizing six-foot tall contractors into giving her an extra-wide berth whenever she was in the shop while they worked.

Hearing her excitement today went a long way in easing the weight he'd been feeling on his shoulders the past few weeks. He didn't realize how much he'd been needing Quinn to go back to being the yin to his yang in his chocolate operation, the one whose belief in their success was based as much on loyalty and faith as it was good, sound business.

"Damn," he commented, now slightly more curious than tired, "your idea must be good."

"I'm going to start the ground work for the videos already," she responded, in her token all business, no ego way.

She wasn't asking, she was simply letting him know, which is how he *knew* she was back to her old self. Quinn being a step ahead of him had always been their status quo. Grinning long after she hung up, he pulled into his apartment parking stall and threw his car into park just as he felt his body quickly start to unravel.

All at once, every tired muscle in his body weighed on his bones like newly dried cement, the burst of relieved adrenaline he'd had a second ago depleting the last of his emotional reserves, causing him to hit the wall hard. Staying awake was nowhere in the realm of possible anymore.

Almost like he were drunk, Luke stumbled in his door, dropped everything in the hallway, and fell into bed half-zipped, eyes already glued closed.

Falling asleep at this time of day wasn't all that uncommon for him. His vampiric sleeping schedule began years ago when he'd discovered how much he preferred working on his chocolates before dawn. And thanks to the miracle of blackout curtains, the kind that didn't let a single ray of sunlight through, he was able to make a pitch-dark refuge for himself regardless of the hour, a necessity if he hoped to get a wink of sleep during the day.

Today though, even with the Arizona sun blazing through his open curtains, he was out cold. Unconscious to everything.

Even his beeping cell phone.

————◦————

AT THE LANDING OF the back stairwell that led from her little studio apartment down to Ocotillos, Dani attempted to stretch the aches out of her neck, calves, and everything in between. Even her hair hurt.

"Ugh, I'm getting old."

Not that she would dare repeat that in the brewpub.

She'd made the mistake once last year and just barely missed a lynching by her wait staff, half of whom had been like aunts and sisters to her for over a decade now, since the day she'd turned sixteen and had begun following in her dad's beer brewing footsteps.

They'd all rabidly decreed that she'd better have at least one sagging body part before she even thought of uttering those words again.

…Which *of course* morphed into a scolding discussion over how she wasn't making the most of said non-sagging body parts while she still had them.

Oy.

Between Xoey and her wait staff, Dani could hardly get

through a week without talking about her lack of a life outside the brewpub lately and/or a very scientific hypothesizing over whether or not her virginity has technically grown back.

The latter mainly consisted of Xoey busting out the strangest pseudo-science facts from the internet while referring to herself as Professor X.

To be fair, it's not like she *never* dated. She'd had a few short, lukewarm relationships over the years. That seemed to be her specialty. Nice. Safe. *Boring.*

Absolutely nothing like the very un-Dani tryst she'd had with Luke the other night.

God, that man could kiss.

Their brief but memorable few minutes in the closet had left her humming. Literally. As in she'd actually caught herself humming a sappy 80s love song up the illogically steep fire escape to her loft apartment above the brewery afterward.

Not that she'd been under the fanciful impression that the whole thing had been anything more than a beer-fueled flirtation gone wild. The guy hadn't even asked for her number. She'd seen it often enough in the bar business over the years.

But strangely, she didn't regret a thing. Those few hum-worthy kisses had been more memorable than the last two times she'd had sex. No contest.

Before she could replay one of those kisses and start humming yet again, a jaw-cracking yawn hit her hard.

Holy hell, she was exhausted.

Having her weekend day cook switch shifts with her at

the last minute yesterday had forced her to work back-to-back shifts cooking for the first time in months—brutal, since she'd both opened and closed the bar day before. To top it all, because the universe, or at least Arizona's jury system, didn't think her life was interesting enough, she was now covering her weekday day cook's shift as well.

It wouldn't have been so bad if today weren't a Monday. As it was, with the tight demands of her time each week, she'd had to turn today's regularly scheduled clerical duties into last night's blurry-eyed homework. She'd barely gotten in an hour of sleep before her alarm had gone off a few minutes ago.

Smothering back another whale song yawn, Dani waved to her mid-morning crew and began faxing out next week's vendor orders before filing the net calculation logs she'd finished at four this morning. She then spent a few minutes online before moving on to the part she'd been looking forward to today—writing this quarter's bonus checks for her assistant managers and brew managers.

It thrilled her to no end that the checks would be bigger than usual, courtesy of the great crowds they'd had through the holidays. Rewarding her management team sizably and giving her staff regular Christmas and anniversary bonuses were among the many business ethics she'd inherited from her dad, a luxury she was fortunate to have been able to keep up because of Ocotillos' growing success over the years.

After scrawling her signature on the last check, she rushed downstairs to fire up the kitchen grills for the lunch rush. Within a half hour, Dani was churning out food orders with little more than sheer caffeinated hope keeping her awake, a sad fact she was trying desperately to keep from showing in her food.

Dani never allowed herself to put anything less than her heart and soul into both her brewing and her cooking. She worked the way some people prayed, and reaped the same kind of fulfillment for her commitment.

That said, by the time noon rolled around, however, she was plum fulfilled out.

Not going to make it.

As far as bone-tired delusions go, the one of Xoey stomping in and yanking the tongs out of her hands was up there with fairy mermaids on unicorns. Entertaining, but all too unbelievable.

With a groan, Dani tried pinching herself to wake up from what was clearly an *extravagant* daydream resulting from her falling asleep at the grill.

She blinked. No cigar.

After another hard pinch, she finally realized that Xoey really was standing there, not only hours early for her shift, but in a *cooking* apron.

Dani's mouth gaped open in disbelief. Make that shock. The full apron was not a look Xoey ever rocked, nor was the kitchen an area she ever entered except to flirt with the cooks.

Craig, the kitchen part-timer who was carrying a pan of meat from the walk-in fridge came to a skidding stop with a quiet, "*What the—*"

Oh good, he saw it too. So this wasn't a hallucination.

They both stood there and watched Xoey efficiently check the order monitor to see what dishes she needed to get started on, and then hustle to grab the ingredients for a portabella salad.

"It's not *that* weird," snapped Xoey. "Craig, get over here." She slapped a spatula into his hand. "I called Javier and he'll be coming in to cover soon. Till then, you're gonna show me how much you've learned so far. Don't screw it up."

The wide-eyed college kid who'd been mostly limited to prep and appetizers until now just bobbled his head and got to work.

Turning back to Dani, she scowled. "You have to learn to ask for help, lady. The brew boys shouldn't have to call me to tell me you're like the walking dead in here."

Awww, her workers had called Xoey.

"Go up to your office and get some sleep. And don't even think about coming back until tonight, missy." With that, Xoey got to work throwing a flank steak on the grill, blending up some basil for their pesto dressing, and scooping hummus onto a platter.

Dani didn't even get to utter a word before her server staff promptly herded her out of the kitchen.

Up in her office, she saw waiting for her, a glass of icy strawberry milk and a warm cookie, her all-time favorite comfort food combo thanks to Elle, the veteran waitress who'd been the first to spoil Dani with this afterschool snack decades ago.

A faint mist gathered in Dani's eyes. *Crazy wonderful*

workers. Smiling sleepily as she sipped her milk, Dani shuffled to the couch at the back of her office and plopped down.

Halfway through her milk and cookies, a flash of color on the far table caught her eye and had her quickly heading over to investigate the source.

It was a beautiful Christmas cactus—one of her favorite desert blooms—with loads of volcanic, chlorophyll-green leaf strands and waxy, bright flowers in full bloom.

Touching one of the flame-red petals, unique to this variety, she smiled, curious as to who'd have brought it in. For all she knew, it could've been here for days. And since none of her workers saw the untamed beauty in all the local desert cacti flowers she chose to decorate her brewpub with—often asking why she didn't go with orchids or other 'normal' restaurant flowers instead—Dani knew this had to be a gift for her...but from whom?

Oh, mystery solved—there was a card.

She felt her lips curve up in a smile as she read it.

To: Dani

I've discovered that calling you to schedule our first date is slightly more challenging without your phone number...or a way to look you up without your last name. Sorry for my utter lack of game. My number's on the back of this card. Hope to hear from you soon.

She chuckled over the '*This is Luke, by the way*' signature.

So it *hadn't* been a onetime thing for him.

Blushing over that news and admiring the cactus with a touch of wonder, she marveled at Luke's choice of this prickly plant over the more obvious rose bouquet most guys would have opted for.

The unbidden appraisal of how un-cliché he was made her lace her fingers together to restrain herself from calling him right then and there. As she'd discovered more times than she cared to admit, making a call when she was this tired was about as bad as drunk-dialing.

Cat-yawning again, she dropped down onto the sofa. Nope, definitely a nap first.

Burrowing against the cushions, relaxation swiftly draped over her. Soon, she was drifting in and out as she peeked at the cactus one last time.

So sweet, she thought hazily before dragging her phone out of her pocket. The 'no sleep dialing' rule didn't apply to texting, she reasoned with drowsy clarity. Oh, or *sexting*. Even better. Blinking slowly, she sexted Luke the first wayward thought floating in her head and hit send.

A devilish grin tugged at her lips. She'd close her eyes for just a sec until he...

Dani was asleep before she even completed her thought.

Chapter 5

IT WAS ALREADY NOON by the time Quinn finished the last of the deliveries for their small but loyal list of grocery distributors and chefs who used their chocolates on their restaurant menu items.

She'd spent the entire morning deliberately detouring through every main bar district in the neighboring areas as her vision for the Valentine's Day marketing plan took firmer shape. But none of the establishments she saw fit the video vibe she had in mind for their ad launch.

Really, there was only one business that would do.

The inspiration for her ideas to begin with.

Driving past Ocotillos, she decided then and there to go with her first instincts. The brewpub had the exact look and patronage she was going for, even though it was a little more small town than she'd envisioned for the video. No matter, beggars couldn't be choosers.

With her mind made up, she quickly got the ball rolling by first calling in a favor to a friend who worked freelance as a video graphics designer. Evan was the perfect guy to handle the footage she wanted to squeeze in today.

By the time she finished coming up with the interview questions she wanted to ask during the video, Evan was ready and waiting with his equipment set up on the busy walkway as she'd requested. Twenty- and thirty- something year-olds were steadily filing in and out of Ocotillos for lunch. A pleasant surprise. Maybe the brewpub wasn't as small town as she thought.

Luckily, she'd worn one of her less severe skirt suits today—one that made her look less like a tired single mom and more like one of those reporters who did fieldside NFL interviews. Taking a breath, she spotted what looked like older grad students—cool, attractive guys in their mid- to late-twenties.

"Hey guys," she grinned conspiratorially. "I just have a few questions about Valentine's Day. You have a quick sec?" Their lukewarm reception, and silent groans, were totally understandable. It was, after all, still December. She'd be annoyed too, especially since she was one of those folks who hated stores that started pushing Halloween in the summer and Christmas in October. As her prime interviewees started politely walking away and toward the brewpub, she tossed out quickly, "My chocolate shop partner and I are actually thinking about doing a little V-Day overhaul. Changing the rules a bit for you guys. Even the playing field a little. And we could use some of your thoughts on the matter..." She flashed them a radiant smile and rolled out the kind of charm she'd almost forgotten she possessed.

And the answers began rolling in.

Almost an hour later, after finishing her tenth slam-dunk interview, Quinn decided to wrap it up. Each of the small groups of young business professionals and college students she'd interviewed had given her exactly the kind of answers she'd been looking for, along with fun bad-Valentine anecdotes she couldn't have scripted better herself. Plus, they were all genuinely enthusiastic about the concept of Valentine's Day and White Chocolate Day as well.

This was going to work, she was sure of it.

Whistling cheerfully and feeling better than she had in months, she tucked away the waiver forms she'd had each interviewee sign and beamed again at the volume of fantastic responses she'd been able to obtain in such a short time.

The pleased high she was floating on faded fast, however, when she glanced up from her bag and saw a woman in a black Ocotillos t-shirt stalking toward them in what could only be described as barely contained fury.

With the angry scowl she was wearing, the cute pixie-looking woman somehow managed to look like an enraged mama bear jolted out of hibernation. The paradoxical contrast should've been funny.

It wasn't.

"Why the hell are you videotaping out here without our consent?" demanded the woman.

Quinn went into damage control mode real quick. "We were just interviewing people for a short video ad for our new chocolate shop next door." She pointed over at their no-longer papered over storefront window the next building over while her eyes told Evan to start packing up the camera equipment like his life depended on it. Meanwhile, Quinn kept her all-business mask on, hoping the cool smile and no-nonsense reply would mollify the woman with murder in her glare and send her on her away.

No such luck.

The woman's eyes narrowed on the Desert Confections sign and then zoomed back on her. "So why are you harassing people coming into *our* brewpub instead of filming outside your own shop?" she asked finally, her voice now a little calmer. But still basically terrifying.

"Well, we had very specific questions to ask...for a very specific interviewee group—young business folk and older college students mostly," replied Quinn, surprised to hear the tiny stutter in her own voice. Her inner wicked witch was actually intimidated by the woman from Ocotillos. An impressive feat. If she hadn't been so busy watching the woman's fist to make sure it didn't come barreling her way, she would've complimented her and asked if they could be twitter friends, their kind needing to stick together and all.

"Give it a rest. The cooks and I overheard your interview," seethed the woman. "Those *very specific interviewees*? They're called 'our customers.' You specifically targeted them and asked them questions to use what they say against our business." Hostility filled her voice, holding nothing back. "Just so you know, insulting the way some folks like to spend a night out in our brewpub doesn't make your only-in-the-movies lame excuse for romance look any better than what our business has to offer couples. All it does is make you look like an ass. An ass trying to sell a load of fairytale bull."

Quinn was stunned. "We were just trying to show a contrast. We weren't trying to insult you."

"Well you did. Trust me when I tell you, my business is the last one you want to mess with in this town. Now why don't you pack-up this Reporter Barbie act you have going on, and get the hell out of here before I really get pissed."

Quinn backed up another step. The woman was saying she wasn't 'really' pissed yet, but her expression said a good ass-kicking was still very much in the realm of possibilities. "Look, maybe you heard some of the questions out of context, but they were harmless interviews. I wasn't trying to 'mess with' your business, I assure you. I don't do business that way."

The woman scrutinized her for a second and took a slow, steadying breath. "Okay, let's suspend reality for a moment and say I believe you didn't really mean any harm; you're kidding yourself if you think this was all so innocent. You used our customers, plain and simple. What's worse, you used them to try and make the nightlife that *we* provide them look unromantic in comparison to the cheesy night at home eating chocolate and drinking champagne in red lacy lingerie.

That's your fairytale portrait of romance, right?" She rolled her eyes. "Whatever, feel free. Just don't drag our customers or our business into it. If I catch you harassing our customers or making us look bad out here again, you'll be sorry."

With that, the woman spun on her heel and stomped back into Ocotillos.

Quinn quickly helped a mildly traumatized Evan put away his camera gear. She felt awful. Never had it been her intent to put down another business to promote Desert Confections. Had she really done that? That wasn't what she'd been trying to do at all. She detested commercials that used such petty marketing techniques. It was cheap and unseemly, and completely insulting to the standards she held to as manager of Luke's shop.

Completely flummoxed, she had no idea how to proceed. Desert Confections had clearly just made their first enemy in town.

An irate, pissed-with-a-sawed-off-shotgun one.

Alerting Luke of that fact was priority number one.

Stomach in knots, she went back in the shop to sound the Defcon 3 alarm.

———•———

YIKES. RAISE THE SIREN TO DEFCON 1.

Quinn jumped when the door of Desert Confections opened with a bell-jangling shove nearly a half hour later, courtesy of the same angry worker from Ocotillos.

Hell, even the big, buff granite counter guys jumped out of her way when they saw her. As the woman charged through the store, bee-lining right for the back offices with a glare penetrating the separating glass window partition like a bullet, Quinn automatically began fumbling for her cellphone. Who she was planning on calling, she had no idea. The Coast Guard was the fastest, but the Marines could probably take this five-and-a-half-foot walking powder keg.

Maybe.

It was fair to say Quinn didn't scare easy, or at all usually, but good lord, this woman was like a dainty little vial of dangerous chemical you just weren't sure about.

Quinn just barely resisted the urge to hit the deck when the woman came up and slammed a piece of paper onto her desk. With a deathly silent, spittin' mean glare and not a single word, the woman stormed back out the same way she came. Somehow, Quinn managed to maintain her composure. Until the bell on the door stopped quavering, that is. Then and only then did she allow herself to expel the breath she'd been unknowingly holding the entire time.

Hooooly shit. Feeling a migraine building, Quinn picked up at the furiously delivered letter and opened it slowly, cringing as if it had a ticking red clock on it.

Not quite. But close.

The letter, written on Ocotillos stationary, had a single, waspish paragraph, addressed to the owner of Desert Confections. It demanded that he or she attend to: 1) the unauthorized videotaping and resulting abuse of Ocotillos' patrons via underhanded advertisement goals that weren't fully disclosed to participants, 2) the insulting and offensive display of unprofessional business ethics, inclusive of but not limited to slander, and 3) the overall questionable treatment of a fellow business in the neighborhood that would be considered *actionable* with the town commission.

The sentences following went on to describe, in detail, just how hellish life could quickly become for them in Cactus Creek if they didn't take this official grievance seriously.

Quinn squeezed her eyes shut and unloaded a string of words she never got to use around her five-year-old son.

"Luke is going to kill me."

———

DANI PLUNKED DOWN into her office chair and stared at the Phoenix address business card in her hand. Rewinding the last hour in her head, she tried to wrap her brain around all that had happened since she'd stomped out of Desert Confections.

Did that really just happen?

In one impromptu meeting, did she really just find the missing key that would unlock a way to make her brother's dreams of a winery a reality? Her eyes widened in continued disbelief as she replayed the blur that had been the last hour with Harold Jameson, the devoted town business council member and longtime family friend who—together with his citified, intensely stoic son Noah—owned most of the commercial property in Cactus Creek.

Including the space currently being leased out by Desert Confections.

When she'd first barged into Harold's office in the town center, she hadn't even noticed the tall, dark, and foreboding Noah sitting off to the side throughout her entire just-to-be-heard tirade. But by the end of her rant, the small town boy turned bigshot Phoenix tycoon she'd known since grade school definitely made his presence known.

Mostly because the latter half of her complaints to Harold had ended up morphing into a heatedly pieced together suggestion for booting out the building's chocolate shop owner.

"Do you have a replacement business in mind? Or should the town just take a retail hit because the owner insulted you?" Noah's voice had boomed from the corner, startling the wits right out of her.

Surprised at the sight of him, and thrown off-balance by this valid question regarding much-needed town revenue, she spoke the first words that had come to mind: "We could open a new country-chic winery there."

...That her brother Derek could run.

Honestly, she'd been as surprised as the two men in the room by her suggestion. Mainly because she was shocked she'd never even considered the possibility before.

Since the tasty products of Derek's winemaking hobby had made its way to a number of town functions and local celebrations over the years, the winery idea hadn't exactly come as a surprise to Harold or Noah; both knew Derek's dream had always been to open a winery. But Harold clearly wasn't pleased with the turn the conversation had taken.

Noah, on the other hand, looked *very* interested.

"And would you partner in on this project with your brother?" he had asked curiously, in a way that made it clear he wasn't really posing a question.

Jedi mind tricks aside, she acknowledged in the affirmative because it was the truth. From there, Noah flat-out hijacked the meeting, explaining his hunch that a craft winery sister business next door to a craft brewery would be a solid investment idea. He went on to shower more praise over Dani's follow-up thoughts—unfiltered ramblings she'd simply forgotten to censor, really—of how adding a few wine-based dishes made with the proposed house-vinted wines could be added to Ocotillos' unique food menu, already well known for its entirely beer-based rustic fusion cuisine made with their own brewed beers.

Culinary gold, Noah called her idea.

A newly expanded menu to match the newly expanded business—the potential for success, he said, was vastly exciting and she'd practically passed out over the candid assessment. Coming from *Noah*, that was ridiculously high praise. The man didn't impress easily.

Truthfully, she was impressed herself. A brewpub-winery partnership between her and her brother had never once occurred to her, let alone a mutually beneficial real estate merger as well that would bridge her commercial property with the one next door. It truly was the perfect idea...

For everyone but Desert Confections, that is.

Desert Confections. Strange how hearing the name of her neighbor's business was now filling her with guilt instead of the blinding anger she'd felt an hour ago.

And the guilt was warranted.

She could've stopped at the persuasive brewpub/winery details.

She *should've* stopped after the part about how her proposed brother-sister team—a human-interest angle in itself—would never do the lowdown things Desert Confections had done today.

But no, like a possessed woman so close to finally fulfilling a long held dream, Dani simply hadn't been able to resist ending her spiel with one final bargaining chip: *"Derek and I will even lease out the space for more than what you're currently getting."*

That had effectively earned her a mildly disapproving look from Harold.

...And Noah's business card.

Replaying it all again, Dani leaned back in her chair and covered her face with unsteady hands. Whether it was to stifle a gasp of hope for Derek or a self-flogging condemnation for actually having suggested a means to shut down a fellow business, she wasn't sure.

Both probably.

The dreadful churning in her stomach was undoubtedly due to the latter though.

Don't get ahead of yourself, Dobson. That wasn't even a real sit-down.

It's not as if she'd presented a formal plan of action that would actually get *acted* on. No, that meeting had just been a hoop-dreamy little 'what if' talk.

…With her dad's old buddy and a veritable business genius she'd gone to grade school with.

Damn, there was that churning again.

Shaking her head, Dani tossed the business card in her desk drawer—she really was getting worked up over nothing. The chocolate shop had just barely started their preliminary half-year contract last month. And if her hunch was correct, they were going to do well for themselves here. She did *not* just lay the groundwork for ending their business dreams to pave the way for her brother's.

Had she?

It would take one phone call to clear everything up.

Unsure yet if she was pushing or pulling, she picked up the card again and started dialing.

Chapter 6

LUKE GOT UP around two pm, a few hours earlier than he usually did, mainly because the missed message alert on his cell phone was beeping the sanity right out of his head. He went into his text inbox and blinked as the words on the screen wiggled into his sleep groggy brain.

Before slapping him fully awake.

Dani had finally texted him.

The quick, flirty sentence was exactly like Dani, sweet at first glance, but enticingly suggestive below the surface. He shot up off the bed and quickly sent her back a red-hot reply.

Then he waited...and waited...and waited some more.

He finally understood why people sexted. The whole thing was wickedly hot fuel for fantasy fodder. The entire time he waited for her to respond, his mind ran through scenarios of Dani seeing his text message and blushing, right in the middle of bartending at Ocotillos. Or right in the middle of her bed as she thought of an even hotter reply to send him. He could just picture her biting her lip while she...

Seriously. Sexy. As. All. Hell.

By the time he figured out she was likely too busy to sext back, the rabid horndogs in his head were already howling. He groaned and tried to get himself to stop thinking about Dani.

Yeah, that was just a stupid idea. He let out a resigned sigh. Ice-cold shower, definitely. Followed by an earlier-than-usual return back to work as well.

What was that saying about idle hands and all?

———•———

ALMOST AN HOUR later, finally back to his normal non-blue coloring, Luke walked into the shop and sat down in his office to get some work done.

...Only to leap right back up when he read the short, scathing note awaiting him on his desk. He immediately ran up front to find Quinn.

She was busy by the door talking to a particularly chatty elderly woman who'd happened by to see how the grand opening plans were coming. Luke held his tongue and listened in frustration as the woman talked Quinn's ear off about something completely unrelated to chocolate. Allergy medication, it sounded like. It took nearly a minute for the customer to finally stop gabbing long enough to look at the gift box order brochure they were still continuing to hand out for corporate, phone, internet—and apparently walk-by—orders.

When Quinn turned to quickly look his way during the brief silence that followed, she glanced down at the letter in his hand guiltily, and mouthed a silent apology.

Good god, the note was real.

How the hell had Quinn managed to piss off the owner of Ocotillos? *This* badly? Each word on the handwritten note was like a lethal dart angrily stabbed into paper by a 'D. Dobson'.

Luke reassured Quinn with his eyes that he'd take care of it. Though he had no idea how he was going to accomplish that, or even what was going on, he thought it best to get over to Ocotillos to try and clear this whole mess up ASAP.

He sprinted across the lot between their two buildings and stepped foot into the brewpub a record ten seconds later. A quick request to talk to the brewmaster led him straight on over to the back of the brewpub.

Where he ran smack dab into a woman.

A bump and slide later, all his senses roared in recognition as they took in the sleek feline limbs, the faint smell of fruity lotion, and the breathy gasp that gave him a semi in an instant.

"Luke!" Dani sounded so pleased to see him, he momentarily forgot why he was there. "Sorry, I..." she began, her eyes dropping to his lips as if she was recalling his very vivid text message to her earlier. "Some craziness was going on so I couldn't..." Her cheeks pinked instantly. "That is, your, um, message was..." She cut herself off again and stumbled through a few more partial sentences before she eventually snapped her mouth shut.

No doubt in offense to the enjoyment that was surely lighting his face. "I take it you got my text?" He couldn't help it. The woman was so damn cute when she was flustered.

Her eyes narrowed over his teasing, then *gleamed*. That was a promise of retribution, definitely. "Sorry I can't catch up with you just yet, Luke. I have a quick *text message* to get out first." She smiled sweetly and began backing away, phone in hand like she was arming a bomb. "I sure do hope you're here with all your friends again today," she added with a fiendish grin that took all the standard brewpub hospitality right out of her statement.

He shot his hand out to stop her, chuckling all the while. Damn, she was fun.

"Play nice," he whispered, pulling her gently to a dark corner near the storage closet he remembered so very fondly from the other night. "You have me all tied up in knots too."

Her gaze softened at that. The frisky glint, however, remained. It was a nice little warning that said he'd better avoid checking his text messages in church...around relatives...or in public as a whole. Luke let out a hearty laugh. "Woman, you can't look at me like that while we're standing here, two steps away from my favorite room in this brewpub."

Another shy blush highlighted her cheeks again, even as a building heat ignited her warm whiskey eyes.

God, he could get lost in those eyes.

As if hearing his thoughts, slowly, she turned her eyes up to meet his fully.

A split second before his lips caught hers.

"Christ, you're addicting," he exhaled roughly after a spectacularly mind-numbing kiss that left him reeling. A mutual problem for her too, if her dazed look were any indication.

Brushing another kiss on her lips because it was just plain impossible not to, he rested his forehead against hers and threw himself out there. "I want to do this right, Dani. Take you out, subject ourselves to a few hours of semi-chaste flirting, maybe some high school just-over-the-clothes action if I'm lucky. The whole deal. No more of these brief backroom trysts."

The smile she laid on him was blindingly seductive.

"Or not," he wavered, barely stopping himself from kissing her right back into that storage room. "Jesus. I have zero control around you." He dropped a soft kiss on the side of her neck. "I swear, I'm really not usually like this."

She closed her eyes, absorbing the tender gesture. "Neither am I." She slid her hands up his chest before admitting quietly, "But I like it."

He let out a strangled breath.

His heartbeat sped up under the weight of her fingers as they went on an expedition of his back, each muscle in her path tensing and hardening from even the lightest touch.

Unable to be a passive bystander to her explorations for very long, he caught her chin and dipped down to claim another kiss.

But slowly this time.

As if they had all day.

That was the plan at least. Until her soft, unfiltered moan prompted an answering groan to rumble out from deep in his throat.

"I have to get out of here while my brain still has some semblance of control over the rest of my body," he muttered, his breathing staggered, heavy.

Looking at her with what he was sure was devastating disappointment, he caught the tiny hint of a grin threatening to appear on her lips. One of his eyebrows rose gamely as he stepped forward again to nip her earlobe. "Vicious woman. You're enjoying this, aren't you?" He then teased her lower lip with his teeth, his dimples creasing shamelessly when her breath broke on a shiver. When he felt just the very tip of her tongue flirting with his, he slanted one more searing, double-edged kiss on her lips before eventually exhaling another strained breath and taking a giant step away from her.

"Your kisses make me drunk." He reached for her hand while making sure to keep the rest of his body a safe distance from hers. "Just like they did the other night when I forgot to get your last name. I'm sorry, Dani. I swear I care enough to get your whole name. Hell, your whole life story even."

She gave him a smiling shrug. "I didn't get your last name either."

"Bradford," he filled in immediately. "I'm Luke Bradford. Gemini, recovering sports junkie, animal lover, bell pepper hater, evening news ignorer, and new fan of all things beer-flavored...particularly you."

At her startled, but softly pleased expression, he continued, "I want you to get to know me, just like I want to get to know you. Beyond how well you kiss."

At her continued lip-biting silence, his smile faltered. "Unless...that isn't what you're looking for?" He hadn't meant for the question to come out so gruff but the idea of her having casual no-name hook-ups with customers on a regular basis had him on edge. Especially since he knew that he was too far gone to bow out completely, even if that were her thing.

The brief flash of sadness darkening her eyes then had him pausing, and noticing for the first time that her hesitancy looked more like pained uncertainty than anything else. Concerned, he reached for her hand to ask her what was wrong. But before he could, a piece of paper fell out of his pocket and landed between them.

Her eyes zoomed in on the distraction and a gasp burst out of her a moment later.

She sounded...livid.

Jerking her gaze up to him, her blinking expression was the very definition of confusion when she growled, "*Why do you have my letter?!*"

Now it was his turn to gape at her. "*Your* letter?" Understanding dawned on him like a ton of slow bricks. "*D. Dobson,*" he remembered from the letter. He looked at her with a touch of awe. "*You're* the brewmaster and owner here."

"Don't sound so surprised." Irritation warred with lingering confusion in her scowl.

He met her glare thoughtfully. "You know, I'm not actually." He smiled as he turned and looked through the portal glass openings in the swing-through doors to the front of the brewpub. "This place is great," he said with honest appreciation.

Unmoved, she crossed her arms. "You didn't answer me. Why do you have my letter, Luke?"

Hearing her confounded tone drop in temperature with each word, he ventured forward a little more carefully, answering neutrally, "Well, because you wrote it to me, it seems."

Her hands balled up into two aggravated little fists. "*You're* the owner of Desert Confections?!"

"Don't sound so surprised," he parroted back to her, still markedly amused at the situation.

His grin died quickly though when he realized those were waves of pure anger rolling off her. He held the letter up with two fingers. "Look, I don't even know what all this is about. But that's no excuse. Quinn works for me so if she upset you today, I'll take full responsibility."

It was plain as day that Dani was reeling. She put a few more feet between them, closer to the door. But she didn't look like she was escaping, rather…re-arming.

Luke watched the emotions swirl across her face like a riptide while the rest of her stiffened, armored up cool and composed. Within ten seconds flat, a calm expression had settled on her face like a bulletproof shield.

What a transformation.

Luke could only assume it wasn't the easiest thing for Dani to be both a tough brewpub owner and adorably cute at the same time. He figured that's why and how she perfected the I-don't-take-shit-from-anyone stare.

The same stare she was using on him now.

"Mr. Bradford," she said politely. "In this neighborly business dispute, I think it best that you go back and learn all the details of this unfortunate matter from your worker first. We can then meet at a later time to discuss how to find an amicable solution, perhaps even one that is mutually beneficial." The murder in her eyes went down to third degree manslaughter. "Might as well make lemon ale from lemons, right?"

She took out her smartphone and opened up her calendar. "Though I'll be in the brewery tomorrow, I do have time to squeeze you in for a meeting in the afternoon." She gave him a borderline friendly smile while briskly putting her phone back in her pocket, as if it were already a given that he would accept her terms.

Whoa. She was good. She managed to be as professional as a ruthless CEO and as likable as the girl next door while consistently establishing the upper hand by 'inadvertently' making him feel like a slight nuisance on her time, both present and future. Masterful.

"*Ms. Dobson*," he replied without missing a beat, "that is very neighborly of you, and undoubtedly good advice. I'll go talk to my shop manager straight away. I do appreciate you fitting me in for a meeting tomorrow." He stuck his hand out cordially. "Until then, please know that all of us at Desert Confections are again, deeply sorry that we got off on the wrong foot with you. Maintaining a strong relationship with our neighbors is a huge priority for us."

She mutely accepted his handshake, visibly surprised. Or shocked, more like.

Geez, she must've done business with some real assholes in the past for her to be this unprepared for his eating humble pie. Wondering if she was given a hard time in the beer world because she was a female, suddenly, Luke was fiercely impressed by Dani, knowing she'd probably done her fair share of putting ego-tripped men in their place.

"Okay, well then, good day, Mr. Bradford. I'll see you tomorrow." Abruptly, she turned and pushed through the employee doors, presumably to leave him there to watch her walk away.

The woman was full of tactical moves.

Just one slight hitch. He was still grasping her hand, effectively tethering her to him with gentle but firm fingers. Reluctantly, she turned back to face him, her expression unreadable.

"Now that our business personas are done chatting, can you and I talk?" he asked quietly.

"About what?" Dani's professional mask was already starting to crumble. This time, her step away from him through the doors *did* look like an escape.

"About us." He joined her in the open doorway, uncaring that they were now standing in full view of everyone in the dining area. "If brewmaster Danica Dobson wants to march away from the owner of Desert Confections to show him who's calling the shots, that's fine. But don't use this as an excuse to walk away from me, plain ole Luke. None of this has to affect us, Dani."

He tapped the phone in her hand pointedly. "Or what we've barely gotten started."

Dani looked from her phone back to him, turning pink at the reminder of her sext message to him earlier. "Some women might go for this whole you-dom, me-sub action, but I'm not one of them," she sliced through her teeth. "Release my hand. My workers are starting to stare."

He didn't let go. Instead, he shook their joined hands in another handshake. "Hi, I'm Luke Bradford, Luke for short. I own the chocolate shop next door. Pleasure to meet you."

She frowned. "What are you doing?"

"Meeting you again. Seems to me, if we'd done it right from the start, you wouldn't be so mad at me, Luke, the man who hasn't been able to stop thinking about you since the other night."

That icy facade she had been using as a shield cracked before his eyes. He watched the chill slowly melt as she shook his hand back, albeit guardedly.

"I'm Danica Dobson," she said finally, "brewmaster and owner of this brewpub. I prefer to go by Dani. Nice to meet you too."

The relief that washed over him finally allowed him to let go of her hand.

Dani shoved that hand into her pocket like it might run off on her if she didn't. "You're absolutely right, Luke. We got off to a bad start, both professionally and personally—"

"Tricky start," he interjected. "Not a bad start. I loved how we met."

A moment of silence passed before she admitted, "Me too."

Her eyes gentled for a second before narrowing back on that frickin' note in his hand. "That doesn't mean this isn't going to take time to sort out. Your worker was way out of line this morning in her interviews."

"I already told you, I'll talk to her. Dani, I really am sorry, and I'm sure Quinn is too."

"Yeah, she looked it," replied Dani with just a touch of satisfaction in her voice.

He grinned, impressed. "If you managed to scare my shop manager then you're even more incredible than I thought. And here I thought you were already pretty darn awesome."

The direction of their conversation made Dani look around at the customers and workers around the room sliding curious glances their way. "Maybe we should talk later...on the phone."

"And by text?" he supplied helpfully.

Her eyes turned wary. "What?"

"I was thinking you could maybe follow through with

that threat of yours and reply to my text message first." Grinning, he teased just a little more. "I already have about a dozen more texts I want to send back to you. Each one admittedly a bit dirtier than the last."

She ducked her head, hiding the smile that was already curving the corners of her mouth. Rolling her eyes in that cute way he was starting to adore, she turned and headed to the brewery, leaving him standing in the dining area with the promise of a soft, "You asked for it."

"Can't wait," he called out to her retreating figure as it veered down a back hallway.

Without turning back around, she just lifted her hand and waved back at him in acknowledgement.

Knowing half the brewpub was now watching his exit as well, Luke made sure he was out of eyesight all the way around the building before he drew to a halt.

Jesus, he'd just gone all in with nothing but a pair of deuces; he was damn lucky she hadn't called him on it.

Now he had to corner Quinn and find out what the hell was going on.

Chapter 7

THE NEXT AFTERNOON, armed with all the information regarding the videotaping, and Quinn at his side, Luke walked up to the roof deck of Ocotillos for his meeting with Dani.

The moment he saw her, he took note of two things. One, Dani could light up the room when she laughed. And two, the gritty, tatted-up musician that sang there regularly—the one currently hugging Dani and tickling her ribs mercilessly—had just become the first person Luke had ever felt compelled to punch in the face in greeting.

"Are we early for our meeting, Ms. Dobson?" asked Luke with biting formality.

Dani gave him a strange look. "No, actually, you're on time. Rylan here was just finishing up a sound check with the new equipment for tomorrow night. I'll be right with you."

When Dani turned to exchange a few more hushed words with 'Rylan' before smiling sweetly at the way too comfortable kiss he dropped on her cheek, Luke bristled again.

"Don't get your panties in a twist." Quinn smacked him. "Those two are obviously just friends. Guys like *that* will kiss anything with legs and mean nothing by it."

Luke practically swallowed his tongue in surprise. Quinn *never* commented about men—good, bad, or otherwise. Moreover, she certainly didn't look at them the way she was looking at this Rylan guy.

And that was nothing compared to how Rylan was looking at her.

From where he stood on stage, Rylan was eating Quinn up with his eyes, gazing at her with such intensity, she eventually shifted her attention to an invisible piece of lint on her skirt.

At that point, Luke *did* notice that the way Rylan regarded Quinn was vastly different from the brotherly way he treated Dani. The sharp contrast finally helped Luke unclench his jaw and take a seat, removing his inner neanderthal—who he rarely saw—from the helm.

A few minutes later, Dani moved into the seat across from him at the table, deleting the smile she'd had while talking to Rylan before wrapping the regal business-Danica cloak around herself.

"Hello, Mr. Bradford." She nodded at him before turning to address Quinn. "I'm sorry. I was understandably upset yesterday so I didn't get your name."

Quinn shook Dani's hand. "Quinn Christiansen."

Out of the corner of his eye, Luke noticed that Rylan was still standing on the side, continuing to watch Quinn with more than just idle interest. Quinn clearly noticed as well, and couldn't seem to stop herself from sneaking covert mini-glimpses at him, while absently tapping her pen on the table each time.

Luke's eyebrows shot up in disbelief. Quinn *hated* when people did that.

By then, Luke didn't even attempt to hide his amusement. Lord, this was rich. Quinn had the hots for a tatted-up musician. Loudly, Luke cleared his throat in such a way that even a blind man would see the laughter behind it. Then, he reached over to pluck the noisy pen from her fingers and pat her arm with evil brother sympathy.

It was a grown-up *ha-ha-I-know-your-secret.*

Quinn turned bright crimson.

Now *that* just made Luke turn fully and stare. It was quite a sight. He'd always thought Quinn could've been cast as one of the *Lord of the Rings* elfin maidens. As such, seeing her flush all the way to her pale blond roots was, well, like seeing one of those ethereal elves turn beet red.

"Something you two want to share with the class, Mr. Bradford?" asked Dani frostily, having been excluded from the silent exchange between Luke and Quinn for a good half a minute or so.

He blinked. Dani's voice had gained a hard edge to it, laced with venom. It crackled with currents driving close to the unprofessional border, completely different from the warm, melodic voice he'd had on replay in his head since the night they'd first met.

Well, well, so jealousy wasn't an ailment that was singularly afflicting him.

"My apologies, Ms. Dobson. It was an innocent private joke, I assure you." He watched her stubborn chin refuse to budge an inch. Well shoot, he wasn't racking up negative points with Dani just because Quinn was lusting after Rylan. "If you're under the impression that I'm solely responsible for Ms. Christiansen's current state of embarrassment, please direct some of that blame to your musician back there who has been undressing her with his eyes for the last five minutes."

A choking sound mingling mortification with unholy hostility ripped out of Quinn.

Dani's lips twitched as she averted her now-understanding eyes.

Oh, that was nice. Even cool, I-collect-balls-for-trophies Danica Dobson didn't want to embarrass Quinn any further.

That prompted Luke to reel in his torture line as well. He patted Quinn's hand again, this time to call a truce...for now. He was nowhere near done teasing Quinn though. Not when she had a ten-year head start of annoying sisterly behavior under her belt.

While Quinn continued to glare at him, Luke flashed Dani a friendly smile. "Why don't we start again? Quinn and I would like to apologize for filming without your consent yesterday, and take this opportunity to explain our ad campaign."

He spent a few minutes going over the Valentine's and White Chocolate Day marketing angle, quickly highlighting the major points. "So you see," he concluded, "Quinn here was simply interviewing the twenty- and thirty- something year-olds because they are our target audience for these ads, not because we're targeting Ocotillos."

Dani's smile showed all teeth. "What you don't get, Mr. Bradford, is that saying things like, 'Oh no, do you think you're going to be stuck here with the guys for Valentine's or do you think your girlfriend will forgive you in time?' *does* target my business by turning us into the anti-Valentine place to be. Quinn is basically implying that if you're too much of a loser to have a Valentine date on this oh-so-precious holiday, you're probably going to be at Ocotillos!"

Quinn's eyes bulged, appalled as she swiveled her shocked gaze to Luke. "I don't even remember saying that part. I swear, if I did, it was just when I was joking with the guys to get them to open up more."

She swung her eyes back to Dani. "Until now, I hadn't really thought about how an exchange like that would sound from your point of view. I am deeply, deeply sorry. I will of course edit that part out of the video completely, and refrain from saying anything like that again in any of my future interviews."

"As I said yesterday," sighed Dani. "I know you don't *mean* any harm. But, it's inevitable that my business and other pubs or bars are going to be portrayed negatively in this idealistic ad campaign of yours. From what you've explained, you're establishing a very clear definition for the 'perfect' Valentine date and you're contrasting it to the nightlife, what you consider the antithesis of romance." Her lips tightened. "The two are not mutually exclusive."

Luke leaned back and let his cocky, business-savvy alter ego make a guest appearance. "Ms. Dobson, are you suggesting that for our first date, you'd find it more romantic if we hung out at some bar as opposed to a night in front of a warm fireplace, enjoying a great meal I cooked for you? You must admit, the two scenarios are quite distant on the romance scale."

Dani's eyes blistered in annoyance. Undoubtedly because he'd crossed their professional and personal lives together yet again. "That depends, *Mr. Bradford*. Are you asking me for market research purposes, or to get ideas on how to best get in my pants? With you, it's hard to tell."

Even Quinn flinched at that.

If Luke wasn't so turned on by watching Dani practically spark with fiery attitude, he'd probably have been more irritated at the verbal kick to his shins. Instead, he just arched a brow. "Now Dani, if this is how we're going to play, why don't we excuse Quinn from the table?"

Quinn was more than happy to oblige. She quickly exited her seat and moved over to the side, just out of the blast zone, watching like a bystander of a scheduled construction explosion.

Luke leaned in closer to Dani. "You haven't answered my question."

"Hmmm, would I rather suffer through a cliché date built on your lame, antiquated views of romance or go out and have some fun? Gee, tough choice there."

"Right. Because you prefer making out with strangers in storage rooms," he shot back, stung by her words.

"You *asshole!*" Dani shot out of her seat, shoving away from the table.

Luke swore and clamped his hand over hers to prevent her from stomping off. "Dani, stop. I'm sorry; that came out wrong."

"How the hell did you intend it to come out?"

"I just meant that it isn't exactly romantic when we're forced to steal a few quick kisses while hiding in a dark room with people nosing around outside."

"Are you saying you didn't enjoy it?" she asked silkily, inching so close he could feel her breath floating across the collar of his shirt. "Are you saying that you aren't wanting to feel me up against that storeroom wall again right now?"

She slid a light hand down his arm in an outwardly innocent act that made his heart rate double. "Wasn't it the *least bit* memorable?"

He circled around her lightning quick, stamping both hands on the table, one on either side of her, caging her in. "You damn well know the answers to those questions. And you know we share the same answers."

With a quick sidelong glance at the small audience that

was starting to eavesdrop openly around them, he added quietly, "But that isn't romance."

Dani shrugged impassively. "Then we'll agree to disagree. I thought it was romantic."

"Sweetheart, I mean real romance. All the good parts leading up to the fire—the kindling, the sparks, the maddening slow burn. That feeling of being swept off your feet?"

"Like I said," she repeated quietly, defensively.

Luke's eyes widened in surprise. A rush of adrenaline coursed through his veins. Hot, possessive. "Are you saying that so far, I've been the most romantic guy in your life?"

"Mr. Bradford, we're getting very off-track from the goals of our meeting."

"Screw the goals of our meeting. I'm looking at a different set of goals here." He slid his hands on her shoulders, eyes gentling with his voice, now low and tender. "Haven't you ever been romanced, Dani? Or were the men from your past relationships all total idiots?"

Her glare turned proud. "Get off your high horse; not every girl wants the white picket fence. I don't believe in fairytale romance and I don't do relationships. So no, the guys I date aren't idiots. Quite the opposite. They're smart enough *not* to try your kind of romance on me."

"Then consider me the inaugural dumbass who will," he growled lightly. "I'm not cheating us out of all that comes with a relationship, sweetheart—the falling, hard and fast and deep, without that invisible safety net you keep around you.

Ready or not, *my kind of romance* is exactly what you're going to get."

He was pushing her. A burst of wild rebellion eclipsed her eyes and he knew the instant she'd decided to pick up the gauntlet he'd thrown.

Her fierce gaze flash-cooled to a fired bronze so charged, so stunning, he felt punched in the gut by it.

"By all means, feel free to try and take a swing at that impossible pitch," she fired back with a measured calm that soon unraveled into a slow, deliberate smile.

Uh oh.

"Who knows? Arguing with you could be fun. I hear great things about make-up sex."

His neck muscles corded at the thought.

"As long as you know the score," she warned, arms crossed stubbornly.

Of course he knew the score—how else was he supposed to change it?

"You've made it abundantly clear," he replied drily.

"Well then," she tossed him a look just this side of dangerous, "while you're attempting to school me in your Desert Confections variety of romance, I guess I can take the time to show you how folks would have way more memorable connections without all your stuffy rules."

Instantly, the DNA in his Y chromosome went on high alert, reacting to her very clear, very female goading. "What exactly are we talking here, honey? Because it sorta sounds like you want to bring our businesses into this."

"Just following your lead, *honey*. You made that bed—you prepared to lie in it?"

"Are *you*?" His blood pressure spiked at the double meaning possibilities.

Now her eyes were really dancing. "Okay, smart guy. You do your little romance campaign for Desert Confections—whatever you want to do, however you want it. And I'll start one of my own for Ocotillos. We'll start when you have your grand opening and have a town vote on Valentine's Day to see which of us ends up on top."

With all her words sounding decidedly sex-inspired to his lust-hazed mind, it took Luke a few beats to realize she'd just issued a throwdown. "Wait, are you serious?" He jerked back to study her face. "You want to pit your brewpub against my shop? Beer vs. Chocolate. In the arena of *romance*?"

"You bet. You sell it your way; I'll sell it mine."

"You're on." Luke's grin turned positively wolfish. "I gotta say, I've never been more motivated to end up 'on top' on Valentine's Day."

"You make it sound so dirty." The slow roaming glance she slid over him was far from disapproving. "And here I thought you were such a tame gentleman the night we met."

For an unromantic suffering a dry spell, hot damn, the minx could do seduction just fine.

He didn't rise to the bait though. "I don't know about tame, but I am a gentleman. Outside the context of this little wager, I fully intend for you and I to take turns being on top, sweetheart."

Mentally girding his loins, Luke expected Dani to fricassee him with one of her token smart-ass replies. But when she instead just stood there at an utter loss for words, he knew he'd just taken her brain on a field trip her hitched breathing said she was enjoying.

Hell yeah—chalk one point up for him.

She snapped out of it an instant later, however, and the sexiest bedroom eyes he'd ever seen hardened to a glare of annoyance at the satisfaction in his grin.

"Shame only the loser will be kneeling for his," she flicked her eyes down his frame. Leaning in close, she dropped her voice to a whisper. "Because *my* idea of romance would dictate we take turns at *that*, too."

He almost fell to his knees right there. Then of course she just had to do that ball-busting signature walkout of hers, leaving him to stare hotly after her to try and get his pulse to stop racing away with his imagination.

A rough sigh shot out of him as he checked the score.

Okay, that was definitely one point for Dani.

One second later, his phone beeped.

A text from Dani.

Hell, he hadn't even seen her using her phone. Then again, his eyes had been glued a little farther south from her hands thanks to that sexy strut of her.

>> *To answer your earlier question, yes, I would prefer hanging out at 'some bar' instead of your fireplace.*

He winced and chose his return text carefully.

>> *Does this mean we're still on for our date? And if so, should I wear protective equipment?*

Her response took longer than he expected.

>> *Honestly, I don't think it's a good idea anymore. BUT I'm willing to...discuss it at another time, without all these prying eyes around.*

Another beep.

>> *And yes, protective gear would probably be wise. Chuckling quietly, he texted back with a grin.*

>> *You know I'm going to bring my a-game to wear you down, right?*

She replied instantly.

>> *Counting on it. Looking forward to it, in fact.*

Damn, the woman was a walking dare wrapped in a taunting red ribbon. And he just couldn't get enough of her. After a promise to call her later, he pocketed his phone and thought about the throwdown they had somehow managed to shove each other into.

By far the strangest start to a new relationship he'd ever encountered.

And he had a sneaking suspicion it was going to go down as his last.

———•———

DANI GRINNED, feeling Luke's eyes follow her as she pocketed her phone and made her way down the stairwell. *This was going to be fun.* As far as new neighbors went, Luke was certainly turning out to be—

That's when she nearly toppled headfirst down the steps as one extremely tardy, extremely important detail came crashing down on her.

Luke was the owner of the chocolate shop next door.

The one she'd basically thrown under the bus yesterday...

Chapter 8

"THE CAVE WHERE ROMANCE *goes into hibernation!*"

Dani Dobson practically spewed the water she'd been sipping on all over her computer screen as she repeated the insulting description of her brewpub—or 'beer joint' as it had been so asininely referenced in the article. "Holy shit, now the man is *deliberately* trying to piss me off," she muttered to herself as she quickly scanned the rest of the feature piece about the town's new chocolate shop having their official grand opening tomorrow.

Co-written by the aggravating shop owner himself.

"Is that the article on Desert Confections?" came a gum-snapping voice from the open doorway.

"Yes," grumbled Dani, glancing up at her best bartender, surprised—and peeved—to find amusement on her friend's face. "Why the heck are you smiling? Xoey, he's skewering us in this article."

The fact that he'd somehow managed to sweet-talk his way out of the standard interview the town did on newcomers for their e-newsletter, and instead *write* a short added editorial as a part of this week's combo 'Happy New Year and Welcome-the-Newest-Member-to-Our-Town' feature grated on her nerves even more.

Mostly because it was pretty damn good.

Xoey planted herself in the comfy corner chair and propped her feet up on Dani's bookshelf, immediately leaning back to tip the chair onto its hind legs as she replied with a shrug, "Actually, I thought it was sort of tame, considering."

"Considering *what?*" Dani saw nothing tame about anything she'd just read. Sure, they'd agreed to go no-holds-barred in their burgeoning little neighborly chocolate shop vs. brewpub feud—which most of the town had begun putting wagers on as soon as word got out last month about her not-as-quiet-as-she-thought throwdown the man had practically goaded her into issuing. But *this*...this article was deliberately worded to get under her skin, something the man was frighteningly good at.

In that make-it-so-you-can't-stop-thinking-about-him sort of way.

"Well," Xoey broke into her thoughts, "considering the intense, still clearly unfulfilled jump-your-bones chemistry you two have going, I think Luke kept it in check."

Dani felt her cheeks heat like a sun-ripened tomato. Not

just because the name Luke Bradford had the ability to make her blush like a teenager hearing her first decadently dirty word, but because Xoey had hit the nail on the head in her assessment of Dani and Luke's bizarre, completely unboxable relationship status.

Intense chemistry? Yep.

Unfulfilled in the bone-jumping area? Most definitely.

And that's how it was going to stay.

The chair fell back onto all four legs. "It's been what, three weeks since you two started dating?"

"Luke and I are *not* dating," Dani corrected quickly with a frown.

"Riiight. You're just sext-flirting acquaintances with*out* any benefits." Another gum pop. "I don't get you two. I mean you guys clearly hit it off before Christmas. That first night you two met, you were practically floating around on a bubble afterward. After one measly kiss."

It had been one heck of a kiss.

Dani sighed. "But then that bubble popped when I found out he was the one who'd taken over the shop space next door."

Thankfully, the holidays had hit immediately after they'd discovered that little detail. The resulting flood of winter break pub-goers had kept her so slammed she'd spent nearly every day that week too exhausted to obsess as much as she'd intended to over the mess with Luke and the winery pitch she's made to Noah.

Not that she'd heard a peep from Noah since.

And Dani was human enough to admit that her guilt over the situation didn't totally extinguish the tiny sliver of hope in her heart that something would in fact result from her impulsive business proposal.

It was oxymoronic and absolute hell on her sanity.

Ditto with the war between relief and disappointment she'd been feeling about Luke being out of town through the holidays and then unavoidably swamped while trying to get his chocolate shop ready for its grand opening.

After a week or so of sparse texts squeezed in during both of their impossible schedules, and with the outrageously fictitious town gossip that the two of them were practically scratching each other's eyes out every time they saw each other (small towns, gotta love 'em), Dani had been all set to start the new year pretending like the kiss had never even happened.

But *then* Luke had to go and send her another gorgeous potted cactus last week, just like the one he'd surprised her with after their kiss the night they'd met. Only this time, he'd sent a stunning and extremely rare white-flowered variety instead of red.

Along with a scorching hot full-blown *sext* message that had made her panties basically fall right off.

So *of course* she'd had to reply in kind.

...And here they were today.

Theirs was now the strangest question-mark-filled relationship she was still trying to keep in the strictly platonic flirting category.

Apparently, not very effectively.

"We've gone over this, Xo. I can't date anyone who could affect my business. It's a disaster waiting to happen."

"Says who?"

The universe's history books as far as her life was concerned. She flinched at the reminder.

Xoey's follow-up groan was sympathetic, but utterly exasperated. "You're over-thinking this. The guy hasn't even been able to pick up his lunch orders here the past few days without the two of you exchanging those stolen glances and burying those double entendres not *nearly* as deep as you both seem to think."

It was a weird Freaky Friday moment, being on the receiving end of that particular lecture for once.

Dani Dobson being borderline inappropriate at work. Oddly, it was also a little refreshing.

Her contemplative silence earned her Xoey's patent eye-roll. "Like I said, seemed to me like he held back a lot in the article…considering. It's clear he's willing to be patient until you come around. Which begs the all-important question. Is this about—"

Before Dani was forced to face the interrogation she could already see forming in Xoey's mind, she was rescued by the fourth ringing peal of the pub phone. "I'll get it," she called out gratefully to whoever was in earshot.

"Ocotillos," she answered on the fifth ring.

"So, did you like the article?"

Luke.

A badgered huff expanded in her chest at the teasing tone of his voice. It seemed to be her auto-reply to the man. And while she'd never admit this unless sworn under oath by the government, only about seventy-five percent of her impending growl in response to his chuckle was out of mildly entertained irritation. The remaining twenty-five percent was more a singing chorus of all the female cells in her body exalting in feral stereo to that low, perpetually grinning timbre in his voice.

It'd been that way from the moment he'd introduced himself weeks ago, really. It was unsettling, but strangely not unpleasant. Which, in itself, was all the more unnerving.

Because the truth of the matter was, he made her days a little more...fun. Not really something she'd had an abundance of in her life in recent years.

And that was precisely why she had to keep her guard up. To combat against all the dangerous charm and fun.

"*The cave where romance goes into hibernation?*" she quoted his line from the article belatedly, trying to throw herself back into the phone call, and out of her head. Luckily, the mere repeat of that sentence was enough to get her hackles rising. The pleased laugh she could hear muffled through the receiver helped a ton as well. "You said you were going to keep it civil."

"I did," he threw back matter-of-factly. "I was originally going to write 'the place where romance goes to *die*.' Hibernation is a totally different thing. It's temporary. Restful, even. A cuddly cave for teddy bears." The grin coming from his end of the phone line was thoroughly audible.

Jesus, it was like the man had a map of *all* her buttons.

As that twenty-five percent she'd been thinking about earlier was swiftly subtracting all the way down to zero, she heard the ding of his shop doorbell and a quick muted exchange in the background before he returned with, "Sorry, gorgeous. The delivery guys are finally here with the last of our delayed tables and chairs so I have to run. Do me a favor and save some of those sexy growls for when I'm there in person for lunch. I kind of miss them when I don't hear them at least twice a day."

And with that, he hung up.

Leaving Dani to sit there with a glaring half smile on her face and a now even fifty-fifty annoyance-to-attraction percent ratio.

The man was an unapologetic troublemaker.

Who was starting to grow on her.

The sound of an amused gum-snap popped her reflective bubble like a pin-prick. "If you keep distracting him with all this innocent 'non-dating,' Luke's going to have to push back his grand opening another week again. Or maybe that's your master plan to sabotage him," Xoey teased as she checked her watch and headed out the door. No doubt because her internal alarm had just told her it was time to go bat her lashes and harass a few early bites of today's lunch specials from the kitchen boys—a thoroughly unnecessary exercise seeing as how all brewpub workers ate for free, but one Xoey did daily anyway even on her days off like today.

To the cooks' enjoyment, of course.

Meanwhile, Dani was still attempting to breathe through the uncomfortable stab in the pit of her stomach over what Xoey had just said. Nothing more than a joke of course, but it rang way too close to home, and brought back the unwelcome reminder of the very thing eating her alive for the past few weeks.

Gnawing guilt of the worst kind—one that was getting worse with each day she wasn't granted an 80s-movie-style do-over for her hotheaded actions before Luke had come over to apologize for what Quinn had done.

Hell, Luke's business or not, what she'd done was just wrong and she knew it.

She'd been upset over what Quinn's interviews, yes, but that was no excuse.

Logically, she knew that Noah's lack of follow-up all these weeks was very a clear sign that she needed to toss her Dobson winery idea in the trash.

But she just…couldn't.

Because that dream had already been given up on once.

By her big brother.

Who'd shelved it away years ago so that she could live out *her* dreams. And live down her failures.

The latter being far bigger than the former.

Even though she truly would never deem it okay to throw Luke or any of the town folks' businesses under the bus, if one goal could cloud her vision on the matter, being able to do this for Derek would be the one.

No matter the cost.

Three weeks ago, there had been little *cost* to factor in. Three weeks ago, the owner of the business next door had been an unnamed stranger who'd royally pissed her off.

And now? With every day she got to know every aggravating, but still mostly sweet and charming thing about Luke, there was most definitely a steep cost to consider. In fact, she'd steadily begun convincing herself it was a good thing (sort of) that Noah had probably found some gaping hole in her winery suggestion.

But then there was the part of her—the part with two horns and a tail, for sure—which reasoned that while a Dobson winery tied to her Dobson brewpub would only work in that exact building next door, Luke could easily move his shop out and be successful anywhere. If by some far-fetched chance Noah did call her back about her proposal, she would of course insist it wasn't her intent to get Luke booted out of town. Just…relocated elsewhere in town.

Or maybe someplace better even. A bustling boutique area in Scottsdale, perhaps. It could be a win-win all around and Luke could—

Who're you trying to kid, Dobson?

She was scum. Plain and simple. Luke was a genuinely nice guy who deserved far better than Dani Dobson. In more ways than one. Her inner vacillations on the degree to which she sucked were interrupted, however, when Mr. Nice Guy himself approached with a knee-weakening grin. All niceness aside, the man was devastating to look at. Period. Handsome was too weak a word to even pair into the description.

He was ruggedly approachable, if that was even a thing. The strong, chiseled jaw and deep, dark eyes would drag you under his spell, but his gentle, laughing smile was what would make it impossible for you to escape. And his body. Good lord. He had one of those hard bodies that suits were tailored for, the kind that a loosened tie would look 'drop-your-panties-for-me' on. Combine it all with his soft, sun-browned hair and the rugged five o'clock shadow of a hard-earned day, and he was Dani's very definition of sexy.

Cowboy in the city sexy.

And he was looking at her like she'd just brought the first sunrise he'd seen in ages.

"Hey, beautiful. Quinn is manning the rest of the delivery so I thought I'd stop by a little early to get my Dani-fix with a side of lunch." His eyes crinkled at the corners affectionately.

There was that gnawing guilt again.

Dani contemplated running back to get his and Quinn's order herself. *Coward.* She sent a waiter instead.

"I don't suppose you've checked the brewpub's twitter feed yet?" he asked with a teasing glint that normally would've had her racing off on a Scooby search for answers. But not today. All her mind could focus on right now was the corrosive pit in her stomach, growing bigger the more the man kept giving her those sexy, eye-twinkling smiles.

"I usually check it at lunch," she replied absently, studying the cash register extra-closely to add the two lunch orders to his tab. Clicking on random buttons to avoid making eye-contact, she probably could have kept at it all day long if Luke hadn't stepped forward and leaned his elbows onto the counter.

Which made her jump back a good two feet away.

A purely olfactory response.

Her mood now spinning in a complete one-eighty, she stifled a laugh, mostly to keep from breathing in the stifling perfume smell that was clinging to him. "Let me guess, you signed up for a Farmer's Market booth today."

His eyebrows shot up in surprise. "Either you're psychic or very weird things get circulated as gossip around this town. I just signed up for a booth an hour ago."

She backed up another step. As did the sympathetic bartender standing next to her. "I take it no one warned you about the Carradine sisters?" Though long-retired, the two nearly identical women still ran the town center activities office as volunteers. Notorious flirts who weren't shy about broadcasting their fifty plus years of practice in competitive dating and professional marrying, they never missed an opportunity to hug it out with any of the town men who made the mistake of getting within arm's reach.

Understanding lit his eyes. "The two old biddies at the town center." He shook his head and lifted his shirt to sniff it. "I took off my jacket and stuffed it in a plastic bag as soon as they finally let me leave. Is the perfume smell really that strong? I thought I was the only one suffering through it."

Another of her bartenders reached under the back

counter for an Ocotillos shirt and slid it across the counter. "On the house, man. We've all been there. And trust us on this, laundry won't exorcise the smell. You need to take it to the dry cleaner. They'll give you a Carradine sister special."

Dani chuckled sympathetically. "On the plus side, this means you're now officially one of us."

His lips tugged up on one side. "Then it was worth it."

And just like that, the guilt she'd been feeling multiplied tenfold. His open pleasure over being part of the town just about gutting her.

Lordy, was it possible for a person to drown in guilt?

Flicking his wrist over to check his watch, Luke quickly gathered the bags of food the waiter had just brought up. "I'd love to stay and talk more but I have Quinn's order in here too. Hard as it is to believe, she is actually capable of getting, ahem, 'witchier' when she's hungry."

Dani tried to keep the tension from showing in her off-kilter smile as he gave her another warm grin on his way out. The very second he rounded the corner, however, her smile fell away and she reached in her pocket to look up her friend Connor's phone number. As Noah's lawyer, Connor handled all of his legal paperwork and corporate research. If Noah was taking her winery idea even remotely seriously, he'd have contacted Connor by now to handle the information gathering and proposal vetting.

Patience just wasn't a virtue she possessed.

"Dani?" came Connor's voice right after the first ring. The surprise in his tone was obvious, the concern as well.

Probably because she never usually called his cell phone. "Everything okay? You haven't gotten yourself thrown in jail have you, young lady?"

She almost laughed then. Connor was only about six or seven years older than she was but because he'd been friends with her father and most of the other brewpub workers from back when she'd still been in college, he always treated her like a niece.

"Hey Connor. No, nothing like that. I just had a quick question for you."

"Oh." The worry in his voice melted away. "Sure thing sweetie, fire away."

She tried to think of how best to phrase her question without breaching Connor and Noah's attorney-client privilege. Or bringing up Luke. That one was key because as she'd discovered a few weeks ago, Connor and his brother Brian were buddies with Luke as well.

"I was just, um, wondering if, err, Noah mentioned me to you at all in the past few weeks?" she ventured awkwardly. "Like, say, after the holidays?"

Yeah…a covert CIA recon specialist, she was not. The brief pause that followed had her holding her breath.

Just as he expelled a long, wary one. "Dani, tell me you're kidding about this."

Oh, crap. Was her plan really *that* bad? "I put a lot of thought into it, Connor. I really thought it was a good idea at the time…"

"You know I'm not one to butt into other people's

choices but babe, trust me, this *isn't* a good idea."

Her heart plummeted to her feet. "But he sounded so interested in the winery."

"Aw, Dani. I didn't mean it like that. I'm sure he's interested in you. You're beautiful and smart, and..." His tone suddenly turned incredulous. "Wait a minute. You went to a *winery* with Noah? As in the beverage you're practically allergic to because it doesn't contain any hops and barley? Did you get lost or something? Or were you already drunk before he got you to agree to that? Christ, Dani, tell me you didn't already sleep with him—"

"*What?!*" Dani shrieked, looking around to see if there were any hidden prank cameras around. "What in God's name would make you think *that?*" Not that Noah wasn't handsome as sin. He was. But he was also like a big brother. An overly intense, domineering, and grouchy as hell one at that.

Now, Connor just sounded confused. "So you're *not* calling me to ask if Noah's been 'talking' about you?"

"Good lord, Connor. What do you think I am? Twelve? No, I'm not calling to see if Noah likes-me-likes-me. I was talking strictly in the business-sense."

A relieved chuckle rang out over the phone line. "Do me a favor and lead with that next time. Noah's a great guy and all, but I would have hosted an intervention if you were actually sleeping with him." Sounding like his usual self again, Connor questioned curiously, "Okay, so what's this business talk you were asking about? Noah never mentioned anything about a winery at all."

Well, there was her answer.

Noah hadn't even brought her idea up to Connor, who he always ran *everything* past. "Never mind, Connor. Forget I asked. It wasn't a big deal."

Connor's voice sobered again. "I'm sorry I misunderstood, sweetie. Were you looking into some investments or something? Because I can have—"

"No," she interrupted, just wanting to get this phone call over with ASAP. *The winery idea is dead. Move on.* "I was just checking into something for a friend. But I think we have enough info. Thanks though."

"You sure?" he asked, clearly unconvinced.

"Yep. Listen, I have to get going. The lunch rush is starting. Come by and bring that beautiful new baby in with you sometime, you hear?"

That brought forth a proud-papa smile she could hear crystal clear over the phone line as they exchanged their goodbyes. She kept it light, even though she was crumbling a little bit on the inside.

At least now she knew. Her idea *was* pretty risky as far as investments go.

She put a hand to her belly to keep it from bottoming out as she exhaled slowly, dividing her focus between telling herself there would be other chances for Derek's winery *someday*, and trying to convince her guilty conscience that just forgetting all about this whole complicated mess was the best for everyone involved.

When the sad finality of it all sank in, however,

disappointment for her brother began blending confusingly with a supreme *relief* for Luke and his shop.

Which made zero sense.

She'd only known Luke for all of what, a few weeks?

Probably just the guilt over what she'd almost done to Luke's business, she kept reasoning when the internal accusations on where her loyalties were began pelting her with all-new pellets of guilt.

It was only a good while later that she remembered how bad she'd always been at fooling herself.

Chapter 9

DANI WAS STILL DOING her best to forget the whole winery idea and all her mixed feelings about it when Xoey returned to the office later that afternoon, falling into the corner chair and flip-topping her head back with a tired thud.

Xoey coming back to hang out here on her day-off wasn't all that unusual; her being *this* exhausted, however, was. Sympathetically, Dani sighed and suggested the unthinkable, "Xoey, you know you're more valuable than gold to me but I'd understand if you want to reduce your schedule here a bit to focus on your pilates and dance classes."

That made Xoey drag her head up with a start. "Why would I go and do a crazy thing like that? You know as well as I do that my students are ninety-nine percent female while my bar customers are seventy-five percent male." Her expression said there was no competition. "Like I tell my accountant, it's really all about the numbers."

Dani shook her head and chuckled. "Ah yes, I failed to do the math on that one."

"Besides, that's not why I'm beat. Like a crazy lady, I stayed up till dawn designing those T-shirts and tank-tops I told you I'd make for this throwdown." She tiger-yawned again. "I was going to finish up on my next day off, but after I saw Desert Confection's little twitter contest this morning, I figured I'd better power through the silk-screening today."

Twitter? That was the second reference today. Wait, didn't Luke mention something...

Dani shot over to her computer and opened up her twitter feed immediately.

Lo and behold, there *had* been a series of tweets from Luke this morning. Mentioning her. "Why that little—"

He'd called her out.

On Twitter. He'd actually gone and made the first official public strike. Up until now, it was just town talk and playful answers regarding the rumored Valentine's Day chocolate and beer throwdown. Well, besides that blasted article, of course. But this twitter bomb was a thrown gauntlet if ever there was one.

It started off innocent enough, beginning with a twitter link to his shop blog that gave a quick summary of how the throwdown came to be. Scanning the short blog, Dani read his detailed description of how she'd called his ideas about Valentine's Day "a load of fairytale bull born from antiquated views on romance, and parented by clichés."

Ouch, she had said that, hadn't she?

So chocolate wasn't 'as fun or even as sexy as beer,' he defended in the paragraph after. On the contrary, it was 'thoughtful, and sweet, and from the heart—the basis of romance,' he maintained.

Crap. She was in trouble.

The man even made cheesy sound charming.

And though he was a newbie in town and not the neighborhood darling that Dani was, he continued—oh no, he didn't...he played the *sympathy* card—he was still going to fight the good fight all the way until Valentine's Day when the town votes would be tallied to see who reigned supreme in promoting more romance throughout this throwdown, chocolate or beer.

Which led to the contest.

In the spirit of bringing back some old school, and celebrating this throwdown, he put together a little contest inviting folks to write the most creative limericks they could come up with on how and why chocolate was more old school romantic than beer in two successive tweets, both with the hashtag #chocnotbeer. He blatantly encouraged *'ruthless creativity'*—the punk. And the ten most heavily retweeted limericks would win a $50 box of their assorted premium chocolates at tomorrow's official grand opening.

But that wasn't all. He'd opened the contest up *nationwide*, warmly stating that all out-of-state winners would get their prizes promptly mailed to their doorstep via overnight mail so they could all still celebrate the grand opening together, even across state lines. Of course, that led to a tidal wave of new, now doting out-of-town fans who proceeded to gush about how dreamy and generous he was.

Before retweeting like crazy.

Dani felt her blood pressure rise even though a part of her was grudgingly impressed that he wasn't pulling his punches. Doing a hashtag search, not surprisingly, she found hundreds of tweet entries from townies and out-of-towners alike...including one from a very familiar twitter avatar.

"Xoey!" She swung a gaping glare at her friend. "*You* entered this?!"

With a sheepish grin, Xoey shrugged. "Gotta give it to the guy—it was a fun idea."

She read Xoey's frustratingly catchy entry. It had *a lot* of retweets. "Can't you *ever* use your wordsmithing for good instead of evil?"

Xoey beamed. "Hold that thought. You're going to love me for those very skills when you see my finished masterpieces," she sang out excitedly as she rushed over to the boxes stacked outside of the door.

Curious, Dani went over to peer into the giant boxes Xoey was shoving into the office with her feet. Seven in all. Incredulous, Dani looked through the stacks of novelty t-shirts and tank-tops that Xoey must've spent the entire day printing. "You aiming for a promotion, Xo?"

"God, no. I just figured we had to do *something*. After reading Luke's article, I looked up the added counterpart holiday to Valentine's Day in Japan he wrote about. Did you know that this 'White Day' holiday on March 14th is a *huge* thing there? Apparently, white chocolate is sold by like the fleet in the country on that day. And they celebrate the two linked holidays in Korea and China too. I'm telling you, this Feb 14th / March 14th holiday combo he's wanting to import here is totally going to take off. He may say he's old school, but his whole pitch about trying out their unique two-part holiday trend here—the one-way gifts between couples, one in February and the reciprocation in March—is freakin' new school genius. If he manages to tie all that in to the throwdown, we're going to have to watch our backs."

Agreed. Dani had thought the same thing when he'd first told her about his White Chocolate Day marketing plan the other week.

Beyond impressed with Xoey's work ethic and creative drive, Dani repeated her question, seriously this time, "Xo, I mean it about the promotion. I've been thinking I need a GM around here, and you've got the skills for it. You interested?"

Xoey shuddered. "Don't even joke about that! As you well remember, the only reason why I'm your *assistant* manager now is because I lost that frickin' bet to you." She shook her head woefully. "How could I have forgotten your freakish tolerance to tequila?"

Dani smiled at the memory, one of her more deviously genius moves to ensure the strongest management team for Ocotillos. With Xoey looking ready to cut and run at the mere mention of the bad p-word again, Dani put a pin in their promotion discussion and instead, bent over to pull a few shirts out of the box. Immediately, she fell in love with how

Xoey put 'I VOTE BEER' across the backs. "I gotta tell you, Xo, I know I teased you about your drunken three a.m. infomercial purchase, but that little home silk-screening machine has paid for itself a hundred times over in publicity the last few years for both Ocotillos and your classes."

Flipping the shirts around, she saw they had fun gender-specific slogans printed on the fronts. Classic Xoey. Grinning, Dani read one out loud.

AFTER A HARD DAY, THE ONLY THING AN ICE COLD *CHOCOLATE* WOULD CURE IS PMS.

Oh, that was so wrong. She could think of at least a dozen guys who'd wear it.

Xoey fished out some racerback tank-tops with the slogans strategically placed across the front, about boob high. "And for our college crowd..."

IT'S TRUE. BEER MAKES YOU SMART.

Ah yes, one of Xoey's more popular sales pitches from behind the bar. No doubt those tank tops were going to sell like hotcakes. Especially since the other side of the tank-top had a smaller tattoo-style design between the shoulder blades that read:

THE MORE I DRINK, THE SMARTER YOU GET.

Dani chuckled. "Don't tell me, this entire clothing line is made up of Xoey-isms."

"Pretty much." With a wicked grin, Xoey straightened up and peeled back her jacket to reveal the spaghetti-strap tank she had on today. "And the *pièce de résistance.*"

THERE'S NO SUCH THING AS CHOCOLATE GOGGLES.
I VOTE BEER.

Dani burst out laughing.

Xoey's eyes glinted with a playful sparkle. "Hey, if you like that one, what do you think about me kicking it up with a racier set of slogans? Of the borderline-inappropriate variety?"

"Uh, that would be a no. I draw the line a good distance away from *your* borderline."

Xoey pouted. "Spoilsport. C'mon. I wouldn't come up with anything terrible. Just funny, innocently dirty ones like: When I eat chocolate, my butt gets bigger. But when I drink beer, *your*—"

"Oh *hell* no." Clearly, Xoey couldn't even see where that line was.

She snickered. "Fine. I'll scratch that one." Still chuckling, Xoey hopped up to head to the bar for a drink. "Give me an hour to think up a few more tastefully naughty ones."

Dani's brain staggered, knowing her imagination couldn't even fathom whatever Xoey would likely be coming up with in terms of dirty chocolate/beer ads. There really was only one way to stamp out that kind of rampant creative energy. "Wow, Xoey. Keep up all this hard work and you'll be getting that promotion in no time," promised Dani sweetly.

Aghast, Xoey dropped the box of shirts like it was on fire and dashed out of the office, running right past Rylan, who jumped to the side as she bulldozed past him. His eyebrows sprang up. "Do I want to know how you managed to get *that one* scared?"

"I just made it clear that there was no glass ceiling for her here."

"Ah right, that'll do it. Pity. If she wanted, that woman could be running her own bar."

"Yeah, but she doesn't want it. Not yet, anyway." Dani leaned over and gave Rylan a peck on the cheek. "What's up, handsome?"

Rylan pulled out his smartphone and showed Dani what he and the rest of the band members had cooked up. A Facebook fan page flashed on the screen. "What do you think? Since you've done so much for me and the guys, we wanted to show our allegiance in this war between you and the chocolate shop guy with a three-night concert before, during, and after Valentine's Day. I know we didn't clear it with you first but we've already talked to a few other bands. Two were in nearby states for tours, and that last one is a local band that's been killing it in venues across Arizona. None of 'em have ever been asked to perform on Valentine's so they're stoked."

Dumbstruck, Dani stared at the vibrant 'WE VOTE

BEER' fan page before her.

"The concert won't be anything fancy," he continued, "so you can just pay them our normal rate and take care of their food and drink tab for the night. With the way I've been going on about your beer over the years, they were all plenty happy with that deal."

When she started to protest paying any of the musicians that little for a full-blown concert, he held her head in his hands to stop it from shaking right off her shoulders. "Sweets, these are my friends; they're not doing it for the money. They just want to hang out, have a good time, and jam a little." He then snuck in oh-so-casually, "And as for me and the guys, don't worry about paying us that week."

"Your band is *not* going to play here for free!" she crossed her arms and glared him down.

He not-so-subtly ignored her. "Hey look, the concert already has a few hundred 'likes.'"

His beaming pride had her all but tackle-hugging him. "You are too much sometimes. You do know you're getting too big to play in my lil' ole brewpub, right? You all should be on the road touring or something, not helping me with this crazy little wager."

"Aw, you know that's not us. We all love our jobs, and the half of us who're not already living the family life are trying real hard to get there." He kissed the top of her head. "So yes, we did have to do this for you because you've been with us from the start, letting us have our weekly rock star fun in the meantime."

As if on cue, the rest of his bandmates trotted in. "Well, babycakes, what do you think?" asked Aidan. "Did we overstep or are we all booked here for the concert?"

Dani stood back, teary-eyed as she lovingly pouted at each of the men who'd become brothers to her. "Fair warning, I'm about to break into a full-blown chick-cry in T-minus five seconds. You all may want to take cover."

The guys immediately feigned horror and pivoted on their heels to rush back out the door. She laughed and gave them each a big ole peck on the cheek as they exited. "I don't care what you guys say, I'm paying you all double your rate for this concert!"

The guys murmured placatingly and nodded in a way that assured her if she did, she'd find her checks 'accidentally' left behind in her shredder bin.

Rylan followed suit, giving her a grinning hi-five out the door. "Good luck, doll. And don't you dare hold back now. Any man worth his salt will be able to take his woman handing him his ass on a platter every once in a while."

Before she could so much as stammer a denial over his assumption that she was 'Luke's woman,' he was gone.

Dammit, now why in the hell was that one little repeated statement making her belly all warm and fuzzy?

———·———

In the quiet of the pre-dawn morning, Luke pulled out a couverture dark chocolate block from one of his top chocolate makers and carefully chopped it into thin slivers.

Only the best to start off their official grand opening day. Not that he was treating today any different from any other day. It certainly didn't feel any different. Because of the delays in getting the front of the shop done, coupled with the fact that they'd been working behind the scenes for the past month on corporate gifts, continued distribution orders across the county, and all their internet and phone gift box sales, today's grand opening in Cactus Creek wasn't nearly as exciting as their first grand opening back in Mesa. True, the town was looking forward to it, but honestly, he knew that most everyone in town had already tasted the chocolate samples they'd been giving out in the town square and at varied town events the past few weeks. Really, he knew the thing the town folks were most excited about was the official launch to the chocolate vs. beer throwdown.

He didn't blame them; that had been a primary focus on his mind the past few weeks, too. Damn near since the moment Dani threw down the challenge.

Scooping the newly serrated chocolate slivers into a steel mixing bowl, he gradually tempered it to a slow melt and then left it to sit for a bit once he got it up to the right temperature and consistency.

As his set timer ticked away, he wandered over to the pantry, figuring today was as good a day as any to try out a new flavor. After grabbing a few different Mexican chiles he'd picked up from the farmer's market down to a powder with his mortar and pestle, he threw in some jasmine tea leaves from a local grower and steeped the finished concoction in a cup of hot chocolate made from the couverture slivers.

Huh, not bad.

The taste was on the subtle side for him, but layered just right, it would probably be a good seller. He made a few notes and logged it as a win to perfect later. All in all, another successful experiment in the uncommon and unlikely department—the secret to his best creations. Honestly, his first shop probably wouldn't have thrived the way it had if not for his nontraditional flavors drawing in customers. From ingredients rarely paired with chocolate to unexpected flavor twists with their own unique kick were unquestionably his trademark.

Hell, that was probably why he was so into Dani. Unexpected and unique were practically that woman's middle names. She had complex layers, that much was obvious, all surrounding a sweet core that could either melt or burn red hot in two seconds flat.

…All the better to provoke her with.

Seriously, pushing her buttons to get that passion she kept bottled up to flare like Fourth of July fireworks was hands-down his new favorite past time now.

And judging by the past few weeks, the feeling was clearly—albeit grudgingly—mutual.

He grinned remembering how she'd issued that throwdown a few weeks back in that adorably piqued, fairy-fierce growl of hers.

Just when he'd thought she couldn't get any cuter.

While operating as he always did by sense and sight over measurements and thermometers through the next reheating and cooling steps to get the exact sheen, snap, and mouth feel that was his signature chocolate, Luke considered all the different ways he could truly enjoy this throwdown.

There were just so many possibilities.

Sure, the limerick contest had been fun and all, but he knew he could do better. He aspired for greater.

After swiping the fully tempered chocolate onto parchment paper to check its gloss and texture, he grabbed the refrigerated chocolate squares he'd made yesterday as samples for this morning's grand opening. Working his way through the first hundred, he pushed his imagination to dig deeper—what would Dani *least* expect him to do? That was the question. He pondered that as he did dipped the squares in the tempered chocolate and then stencil-sifted the ground chile and jasmine tea mix on top.

Pausing after a few, he decided to switch things up by putting the powder layer *under* the tempered coating instead of over. The surprise factor of that would likely create a new—

That's when it hit him.

Surprise factor. The perfect angle for the video ad they'd been planning for their campaign. It would also serve as a grand throwdown strike as well. Two birds, one stone.

Plus, it was so nail-gratingly aggravating, he was sure it'd drive Dani *nuts.*

He could hardly wait.

Chapter 10

A HUGE GRIN LIT Luke's face when he heard his shop door jangle open a half hour later.

"*Are you out of your freakin' mind?!*" barked Quinn, storming into the shop at ten to eight, phone waving at him like a weapon. "I almost crashed the car when I heard your voicemail over my bluetooth. You want to shoot a commercial inside of *Ocotillos?!*"

"Dani *did* say to do whatever we wanted, however we wanted."

Quinn erupted, questioning everything from his sobriety to his will to live.

Luke just laughed and stepped around her to start a batch of the pistachio whip white chocolate bonbon with honey crystals they were planning on launching this week. Remembering at the last minute that he did indeed have a will to live, he plastered on his yes-Quinn-I'm-listening look before pouring the molten white chocolate onto their marble slab countertop. Generally, he preferred this tabling method over using a bowl—it was almost meditative, mainly due to how silent Quinn got when he began smoothing through the rich chocolate puddle with his metal spatula and putty knife. It was a phenomenon often displayed by customers as well, a crowd pleaser for sure that justified his having Quinn spring for this second marble slab for him to use behind the counter, which was about half the size of the one back in the kitchen.

"You were saying?" he prodded amusedly without looking up.

She blinked. "I was saying you're crazy," she grumbled, her voice unconsciously hushed as if she were in a library while her captivated gaze watched the chocolate start to thicken and shine.

Funny, you'd think his spatula strokes were lulling a cobra.

Of course, nothing lasted forever.

Quinn was soon back to arguing all the many reasons *not* to do their video at Ocotillos while he deposited the now cooled white chocolate into a bowl to bring its temperature back up and ready it for the bonbon molds. As he stirred, Luke listened to each of her very valid points.

Well, sort of.

It was tough, what with Quinn starting to sound like the Peanuts cartoon teacher and all. When she launched into what he guessed was Part F of Reason Number Three, he moved on to brushing colorful honey crystals into the wells of the bonbon molds to make for a decorative tint on the finish. He threw in a very solemn wow-never-thought-of-that nod as he ladled in the tempered chocolate next, cooling and coating it so only a thin layer remained in the grooves. Lastly, he piped the pistachio cream filling he'd made earlier into each chocolate-lined crater and then poured a final layer of white chocolate over it to seal the bonbons shut.

All that was left was refrigeration and later their part-timer, Rissa, could pop them out of the mold trays. Checking the clock, Luke quickly washed up and went over to get the cordless, grinning all the while like a kid on April Fool's Day. "Perfect timing. Dani should be starting her shift now."

Quinn pinched her nose bridge. "You haven't heard a word I've said! I'm telling you, Dani's going to have your balls for this. She's going to rip 'em off, feed 'em to you first, and *then* kill you—"

"It's ringing." He held the phone up in the air. "Unless you want Dani to hear you hollering, you may want to..."

Quinn instantly pursed her mouth shut. Luke snickered; it was like he had a fun new app to torture her with. And when the hot little voice of that app greeted him on the line, his smile widened.

"Hi Dani, it's Luke. I know this is late notice but do you think I could book Ocotillos for a video shoot tomorrow? We want to film a commercial to get the word out about our Valentine campaign, something really compelling to help it go viral. And, no two ways about it, your brewpub would be the perfect site for what we have in mind." He stifled a laugh over the dead silence that greeted his enthusiasm, picturing steam blasting out of Dani's ears. "And hey, if you're free, maybe we can grab a bite after the shoot—you know, to celebrate this throwdown getting into full swing and all... What do you say?"

Oh baby, let the fun begin.

———◆———

DANI SAW RED.

Luke had the *audacity* to think she'd allow them to shoot their video ad at Ocotillos? Oh, she wanted to allow some shooting alright—a Glock at his big brass cojones sounded about fair.

"You've GOT to be joking," she finally managed to sputter through clenched teeth.

"No, I'm not. Your brewpub is the perfect site for our video. Unless—" he paused just long enough to make her bristle, "you don't want us to. I mean, you did say we should go all out but I'd understand why you'd be afraid...errr, I mean *uncomfortable*."

He was smiling now; she could hear it. A tide of anger blanketed her eyes. "You can't possibly think I'll let you goad me into allowing a competing marketing ad to be filmed here," she snarled back. His ludicrous request was insulting enough, but pairing it with his well-aimed taunting—and man, did he know how to piss her off—was a lethal catalyst.

"Trust me, honey. There's no competition. You'll see."

She almost threw the phone against the wall. Instead, she exploded into a curse-drenched outburst, showing off the extensive vocabulary she'd picked up over the years behind the bar.

Awed chuckling rang out over the phone. "Wow, I usually get to know a girl before we get into this kind of pillow talk," he provoked even more.

Okay, now he was just pushing his luck. Schooling her voice, she replied, soft and sugar sweet, "My real pillow talk is far more inventive, Mr. Bradford...or at least that's what I've been told." A tiny off-white lie to poke his green-eyed monster in the misters. Ire really was an excellent acting coach.

You could hear a pin drop.

Good, let him stew. Smiling now, Dani continued all business-like, "No problem, *Mr. Bradford*. You can do your little video shoot here. But, I will have to charge you double our normal fee because of the last-minute notice. And, you know, just because I want to."

"Fine," replied Luke with noticeably forced calm.

Oh, what she would've given to see his face. "Then I'll see you tomorrow, Mr. Bradford."

"For dinner as well?" he interjected quickly, his voice still gruff...but hopeful.

"*What?*" Seriously, a sackful of puppies could get exhausted by him.

He was back to sounding amused. "Were you agreeing to just the video or dinner too?"

"No, not dinner. The musicians are performing tomorrow night. I have to be here."

"Another night then?" His voice softened. "Soon? All

kidding aside."

A pregnant pause followed as she tried to reel in her reaction to the man. "Sure. Dinner another night sounds great," she replied eventually, her voice catching a tiny bit as unbridled thoughts recalling the events preceding the first time she'd agreed to dinner with him, probably all duplicitously sent *by* him via some alien telepathy, began swarming in her head.

When her pulse rate quickened to match his breathing, she shook herself and cleared her throat with an emphatic huff. "There you go again blurring the lines, mixing business with pleasure...err, I mean *non*-business things."

Searing hot embarrassment rushed into her cheeks. Her IQ seemed to belly flop a few dozen points around the man. "You can just bring your check for the rental fee tomorrow, Mr. Bradford. We'll see you then," she finished quickly, rushing to hang up the phone as if temptation incarnate were ready to jump out of it.

"Hey, Dani?" Luke's voice was quiet, but just loud enough that she could hear him.

She brought the cordless back up to her ear at the last second. "Yes?"

Lord, she should've known better. In an unfair payback for her reckless verbal poke earlier, and probably to ruffle her a bit since she insisted on calling him Mr. Bradford just to annoy him, Luke slipped her a short, steamy preview of just how good *his* pillow talk could be.

Dani blushed right down to her toes.

His quiet, "Until next time," signaled the end of the call. As well as that battle round for them.

Breathing shakily, she put the phone back in its cradle and put a cool hand against her ear, sure that it was singed from Luke's hot words. Honestly, the man should come with a warning label.

It wasn't until a full minute after she hung up the phone when it fully hit her.

He'd *totally* just goaded her into allowing them to shoot their video here!

. . .

FOUR MEN ARE AT A TABLE in a casual restaurant, engaged in a merciless three-on-one rag fest hailing the tallest in the group as king of the first-year scrubs due to the volume of grunt workload he's been getting lately in their law firm. Fittingly, the three ask their waitress to bring a double shot of Crown Royal for 'King Evan,' who just laughs and takes it all in stride.

A table over, a trio of women are eating and talking grad school research. As the men await their drinks, one of the women catches Evan's eye. And vice versa. Despite her shy but inviting smile—and his obvious interest—he plays the cool card, pulling his eyes away from her to focus back on his friends who are busy solidifying their plans to go to a concert this weekend.

When Evan casually slides his gaze back to the woman a little later, sadly, she's gone.

Outside, the camera catches her stopping outside of Desert Confections, looking thoughtfully at a flyer about their Valentine's Day chocolate-making class.

A few nights later, Evan and his buddies are on the dance floor amongst a packed house watching Rylan's band in concert at Ocotillos. The camera zooms in on Evan's eyes widening when he spots the same woman he saw the other day hanging out with her friends, not twenty feet away from him. This time, he doesn't hesitate. He heads right over to meet her.

But she gets swallowed up in the crowd. Evan searches every last corner of the deck until finally he frowns and gives up, turning around to head back to his friends.

Halfway there, however, someone taps on his shoulder.

It's her.

The camera circles around them, slowing as the two stare at each other. The people all around slip out of focus, and the music morphs into the sound of a pair of heartbeats.

Gently, she presses something into his hand.

He looks down and sees a carefully crafted piece of chocolate in a clear candy box. Pleasantly surprised, he turns the box around to survey the intricate features of the finely detailed truffle. It's striking. Beautiful in a masculine sort of way. Eyes soft with appreciation, he cradles the gift in his hand and looks up to thank her.

Only to find she's vanished.

He immediately shoulders through the crowd to locate her but she's nowhere to be found.

Frustrated, he inspects the truffle again, scanning the clear box all around and over to see if there's some mysterious clue he missed.

There is.

A slow, sexy grin transforms his features and he immediately pulls out his phone to dial the number written on a tiny slip of paper underneath the chocolate.

. . .

"CRAP," WHOOSHED XOEY, as she clicked off the Desert Confections' video ad on YouTube.

Dani shared her sentiments. The commercial was good—really good.

Girls would no doubt fall in love with it, and guys would secretly not hate it. *Damn.*

The production hadn't been extravagant—Desert Confections' lone employee, Rissa, had been the female lead, while the male lead was played by Evan, Quinn's friend who'd taken care of the videography for the shoot as well.

And truth be told, their adding a few clips from those dang street interviews that had started this whole thing actually gave it an artsy film school vibe with cool folks off the street giving their candid reactions to the idea of Valentine's Day and White Chocolate Day.

Already, the video had racked up an exorbitant number of hits. Clever girl that she was, Quinn had asked Rylan's permission to use one of the songs he'd sung during the concert scene as music for the entire commercial. She'd smartly put the band and song in the video description and in doing so, managed to piggyback off the band's popularity to steal some fan views.

What made the video hype take off from there, however, was her second genius idea of asking viewers to comment on the whole Valentine's Day / White Chocolate Day package deal.

That was all it took for folks to start debating the pros and cons. With way more pros. By this morning, the two-part holiday idea was trending on Twitter and headlining on Facebook pages and blog feeds. From teen lovebirds to silver anniversary couples, support for this holiday revolution was growing and spreading like crazy.

It was a holiday revolution in the making.

And it was all thanks to Quinn. Due to her enormous web presence, a ton of attention was being drawn to what was being dubbed 'the most unlikely romance battle of the season,' aka the Desert Confections vs. Ocotillos throwdown. Remarkable. Something that had begun as a little town wager between two business owners was escalating into a colossal showdown. With the cyberstorm Quinn was detonating across the internet, a frenzy of folks from all over were starting to declare their dogged allegiances between Luke and Dani, chocolate and beer.

Dani felt the excitement brewing in her. For her, competition was worse than chocolate and almost better than beer. She thrived on it. All this couldn't have come at a better time. A healthy battle like this was just what she needed to forget about failed winery ideas and the like.

Her eyes narrowed. *That* reminder provided the creative jolt she needed for a fun idea to take shape—well, fun by Luke's standards at least. Soon, a slow smile spread across her face.

Xoey's eyes rounded. "Tell me!" She sat down excitedly. "I know that look. It's your evil genius grin. What do you have planned?"

She simply raised her brows in a way that had Xoey doing a cackling fist-pump. Dani reached for the town phone directory to look up Desert Confections' phone number.

If she wasn't mistaken, Quinn would be the one manning the shop right about now...

———◆———

DANI HUSTLED AROUND THE deck of Ocotillos, rushing to add final touches for the last scene of the brewpub's commercial shoot.

Aidan, Rylan's drummer and the band's resident video guru, had translated her vision perfectly, capturing the fun, sexy marketing angle she was going for—first date romance, laid-back, non-cliche style.

And because his day job consisted of shooting and editing wedding ceremony videos on site in time to be viewed by the guests at the reception, he was *fast*. Aidan had the first half of the video edited within an hour, which allowed Dani to watch it while he set up the equipment for the second half.

Hitting play, she smiled when Rylan's voice crooned out her favorite love song to start off the scene capturing Rissa and Evan's first date:

. . .

EVAN FUSSES WITH HIS TIE, repeatedly adjusting it until the sound of quiet knocking at his front door causes him to nearly strangle himself. Thankfully, he's able to loosen the death knot cutting off his air supply as he races to open the door.

The moment he sees Rissa, his breathing is halted once again.

Mesmerized, he smiles and greets her with a gentle kiss on her cheek. Little bowl vases of red roses line every furniture piece in the living area of his bachelor studio, and tealight candles flicker on the romantically adorned coffee table. The ambiance is quietly elegant.

As is their conversation.

Stilted chitchat on current affairs segues to an awkwardly hushed wine glass clinking, followed by her faint cringe and his choking cough when they actually taste the fancy wine.

Evan runs a finger under his collar in growing despair at what's looking to be the most uncomfortable first date ever.

The kitchen timer dings.

With visible relief, he rushes off to retrieve the plates of food he left warming in the oven. They were plated to perfection, like something off a Food Network show. His brief smile of confidence quickly fades, however, when chirping crickets mock his return to the living room. Even more nervous than before now, he puts the two plates of risotto-stuffed Cornish game hens and seasoned baby vegetables on the low table.

Eyebrows raised, Rissa quietly compliments him on the meal.

And with that one brief, shining moment of promise, their sporadic dinner talk over tidy bites of the fancy food quickly goes from clumsy to nonexistent. They even begin a horrifically boring discussion about the unusual weather lately.

Then silence again.

Finally, one sterile, overlong minute later, Evan reaches for her hand. "You want to pack this up and go hang out at Ocotillos instead?"

Her eyes widen and a grateful smile emerges. "YES!"

They blow out the little candles and the room fades to black.

. . .

DANI WAS THOROUGHLY PLEASED as the first half of the video ended, and not at all surprised that Aidan had decided to follow Quinn's lead of using the band's music in the video. But he took it a step further by laying a great remixed track with a few of their most popular songs, edited to fit the vibe of the commercial and each of its scenes perfectly.

Turning around, Dani located the real-live Evan and Rissa standing off to the side of the dance floor on the roof deck of Ocotillos amongst customers who, since this was a closed shoot, were really just every spare friend Dani could wrangle at the last minute. Rylan was already belting out their newest song from the stage, and on Aidan's cue, everyone began dancing as the cameras started rolling, the live recording continued where the video had left off:

. . .

HANDS ENTWINED, EVAN AND RISSA walk through the crowd to grab an open pub table up front near the band just as a friendly server comes by to get their drink orders.

Not hesitating in the least, Rissa orders an Irish Car Bomb along with a dark lager.

Evan looks smitten. "Nice. I'll have the same."

As they wait for their drinks, they launch into an animated discussion filled with nonstop laughter. Their fun conversation flows easily as the music pulses around them.

Rissa shoots Evan a shy smile. "Do you want to dance?"

Grinning, he removes his stuffy tie completely. "Since the moment I laid eyes on you."

Out on the dance floor, Rylan's deep, heady alternative rock music is the soundtrack to their flirting, as their dancing turns into a fast, seductive ride. With her back against him, and their bodies fitted together like puzzle pieces, Evan lays his chin against her shoulder and murmurs something in her ear that makes her elbow him playfully in the gut. He chuckles and wraps his arms snugly around her waist as the music on stage strums to an end.

While everyone else is making their way off the dance floor, Rissa drops her head back against his chest, and this time it's her mouth at his ear. Her words were brief, but it's enough to inspire him to spin her around and draw her in close.

"We're not going to discuss the weather again, are we?" whispers Rissa against his lips.

Evan smiles and leans in.

For their first kiss.

. . .

"THAT'S A WRAP!" called out Aidan. "Thanks, guys. We got it. You all did great."

Dani beamed from ear to ear. Not just because the video was a slam dunk, but because from the looks of it, neither Evan nor Rissa wanted to finish their kissing scene. So cute. She'd seen their interest in each other grow throughout the shoot. They'd been inseparable all afternoon, flirting like no one else around them existed.

That's why, along with their paycheck for doing the video, Dani also included a rather generous Ocotillos gift certificate for them to use together. On a real first date.

Okay, so she enjoyed moonlighting as cupid from time to time. It wasn't a big deal.

It certainly did *not* mean she was a fairytale romantic like Luke.

Chapter 11

LUKE COULDN'T STOP staring at her.

While some might pass off Dani's girl-next-door looks as just 'sweet' at first glance, she exuded a simple, feisty grace that made her his specific brand of gorgeous. And in her faded *Dobson's* softball shirt and wash-worn capri jeans tonight, both tumble-dried to their current body-hugging fit, she was just the sexiest little thing to boot. All combined with that quick wit and room-stopping smile, she was easily the most appealingly wholesome, tempting woman he'd ever met—a whole-package-deal that had every bit as much to do with how attractive she was on the inside. Caring to a fault and so infectiously lovable. He simply couldn't get enough of her. Even when she was driving him crazy.

Speaking of crazy... After *weeks* of attempting to sneak past the defenses of the most stubbornly guarded, obsessively self-reliant woman he'd ever met, during which time, he'd given her a truckload of assurances that he didn't in fact have any grand expectations for some epic love story, he and Dani were finally out on their first meal outside of the brewpub— dinner at a Mediterranean café followed by a walk through town for dessert.

Their first official 'non-date.'

Which was what the sanity-stealing woman was insisting on calling it.

Ridiculous name for the perfect evening aside, he was having a great time. The best part was that even though they'd been getting to know each other for over a month now, it took this non-date for him to discover that his adamantly non-mushy brewmaster was an unconscious hand-holder. Squeezing said hand, he smiled. "Alright, I give. What's with the impish grin?"

Dani blinked innocently. "What do you mean? This is just what my face does when I'm having a good time. It's called a smile. Look it up."

"You know, I'd buy all that if I didn't already recognize that as your special little Dani grin that makes me crazy."

"Xoey calls it my evil grin. Figures it'd make *you* all hot and bothered." She smothered a cute nose-scrunching smile.

Yet another adorable turn-on for him. Then again, nothing about Dani seemed to turn him *off*. He smoothed a thumb along her knuckles affectionately. "Okay, so if you weren't flashing that insidious grin to raise my blood pressure, could it simply be that you've been thinking about the video you just launched?"

Dani's face was a mask of restrained curiosity. "Oh, so you've seen it?"

"I kind of figured you wanted me to. What with your blatant twitter taunt this afternoon."

When he provided no further comment, she jabbed him in the ribs. "C'mon! I gave you feedback on your video. Tell me what you thought of ours."

"Eh."

Her eyes narrowed to annoyed slits.

God, she was fun to tease. He continued military silence until she unleashed a piqued kitten growl. "Okay, okay." He kept a straight face and lied outrageously, "It was abysmal."

In disbelieving amusement, her lips quirked to the side. "That bad huh? And yet our *abysmal* video still managed to acquire nearly as many hits as yours already. Weird."

"Ah, but let's give credit where credit is due. That was mostly Quinn and you know it. When she turned this little wager of ours into the online frenzy linked to our promotional events and videos, she put us on the cyber map. With the amount she's been tweeting, facebooking, and blogging, the Arizona college population alone is putting in hundreds of views a day."

"You're right," admitted Dani. "I saw all the cyber buzz she's been getting out there. She's really firing everyone up for this throwdown."

"And you're providing some particularly flammable fuel." Humor colored his tone. "The shot of the Desert

137

Confections chocolate box just as Evan blew out the candles on their crappy date? Nice touch."

"Caught that, did you?" An effervescent giggle rippled out of her as she patted her back.

"Yep. And somehow tricking Quinn into practically demanding that you *allow* Rissa and Evan to star in your video? Very impressive. Superhero caliber, even."

"I remember you said she has a younger sister." She grinned. "Being one myself, I just dusted off the old techniques I used to annoy my brother with. Quinn never stood a chance."

He laughed. "So far, you're proving yourself a worthy adversary, Miss Dobson."

"Oh, you haven't seen anything yet." Her eyes danced.

The woman even made unrelenting competitiveness look sexy. Bewitched, Luke leaned over, eyes locked on her simpering lips in an I'm-about-to-kiss-you sort of way.

…Only to have her shift away at the last second.

Not without a spark of hunger in her eyes and a soft, frustrated sigh, however.

"I'm sorry," he apologized immediately, kicking himself for not holding to his own assurances that this wasn't a date. He wanted her trust. But dammit did he want that kiss, too.

"Don't be," she said quickly, quietly. "It's not that I don't want to. Believe me. It's just… Well, besides that first night in the storage closet… Basically, this would be our first *official*…even if it's not a date…" She trailed off with a frustrated huff—tongue-tied and gaze locked on her shoes.

His eyes widened in understanding. *She's nervous.* With first kiss jitters. The woman was just so unbelievably cute. Not allowing her another second to retreat back into her head, back over that wall she'd erected after their careers and the throwdown got in the way of what they'd started back in that storage closet, he circled his arm around her waist and drew her body flush against his. He drank in the tail end of her gasp as he bent down to quickly brush his lips over hers, nearly growling when she responded like a lit fuse.

Finally. He'd waited over a month to feel her in his arms again. And it was every bit worth the wait. Tilting his head, he deepened the kiss, knowing it was already far deeper, hotter, just...more than the ones they'd shared as strangers the night they met.

Christ, it was sweet.

When Luke eventually lifted his lips away—almost needing to see for himself that this wasn't just one incredible wet dream—an accidental confession slipped out from under her breath. It was quiet, but he heard it: *Best first kiss ever.*

With a groaned sigh born of pure tenderness, he leaned in to collect a second kiss. Then a third. Soon, he lost count.

Jesus. Every apple-scented square inch of her fit in his arms even better than his memories.

Breathing heavily, Luke looked down to see that her eyes were still closed and his imagination swiftly whipped to an image of her looking like that in bed. His bed. "You're killing me, sweetheart." Her shivery cat-content smile didn't help any. "Unless you want me to throw you over my shoulder

139

and head to my place—if we make it that far—you need to open your eyes."

She did.

And he swallowed another deep groan.

Pure pleasure mingled with unabashed desire in her eyes. He blindfolded her with his hands. "Never mind. Keep 'em shut. If you keep looking at me like that, I don't think I'll be able to stop myself from jumping you."

This time, when he peeked at her eyes, they were twinkling with amusement.

"You're forever amused at getting me all hot and bothered," he mock complained.

"About that," cut in Dani, hesitantly. "Errr, our hot and bothered tendencies, that is…"

"Yeah?" His voice sounded deeper now, just this side of gritty, even to his own ears.

"I know we've established that you're a recovering serial monogamist and I'm…"

"Not?" he supplied helpfully.

"Yes, thank you. I am enjoying this non-date, however. And I'd really love nothing more than to drop the 'non' part from the title…"

A smile stretched across his face. "Yeah?"

"*But*," she interrupted quickly. "I think you and I look at dating far differently. So, I've been thinking about some sort of casual, preliminary trial runs first. I mean we work next door to each other, so if things go sour, life would start sucking pretty quickly around here."

He frowned. "So...you're suggesting 'pre-dating' dates?"

Blushing scarlet, she shrugged and looked at the ground. "I guess so."

Cautious woman. He tilted her face back up so she could see his eyes when he answered her truthfully. As long as he got to be with her, he didn't care how they labeled their time together. "I don't need a trial run to know I want to be with you. But if you need us to go out on some friendly pre-dates to test the waters, I'm on board. Whatever you need."

Holding her hand up, she clarified, "Friendly, meaning no sex." She paused, avoiding his eyes for a second. "Just because I'm not into serious relationships right now doesn't mean I'm easy."

He jerked back like she'd smacked him. "Dani, I never once thought that."

She turned away. "Considering the way we met, I wouldn't blame you if you did."

He cupped a hand against her warm cheek. "I don't."

"Then you wouldn't mind being totally chaste for a few friendly pre-dates?"

"Few, meaning two?" he teased with a fair measure of hopeful seriousness.

Her shy laughter effectively shot that suggestion down. "I was thinking more like ten."

Ten?!

He blinked at her as if she'd gone insane. It wasn't about not wanting to wait, but rather, not being *able* to. After a beat, he sighed and kissed her lightly on the lips. Chastely. "However many you want to have is fine with me, sweetheart."

When he promptly stepped back to keep things from getting too friendly, he saw her frown. Her eyes were locked on his lips as she waffled, "Of course, I'm willing to negotiate…"

"Really?" A smile played at the corners of his lips as he pulled her in for another kiss. This one long and deep. His version of negotiating.

"Seven?" she amended breathlessly after that rather excellent rebuttal point.

Luke looked at her for a moment before stepping back again, this time to lift his hand palm up to show her the almost invisible tremor plaguing him. "See this? It's been happening more frequently lately. I'll be minding my own business, working on my chocolates, and find my mind wandering over to thoughts of you. Then *boom*, I get the shakes," he revealed quietly. "It's crazy. My hands didn't shake even when I first began chocolatiering." Seeing her concern, he let his voice warm affectionately. "Now don't go thinking this is the chocolatier's version of the blue balls defense because it's not—I don't have the shakes from lack of getting some. I get them because it's you." He cupped her cheek lightly. "Seven dates, ten—hell we can wait thirty. However long you need, Dani. I'm happy just being with you."

"Five dates it is then," she conceded with a wobbly smile, leaning against his chest and burrowing her face at the groove of his neck, as if she were made to fit exactly there.

His arms locked around her. "Looks like I'm going to have to make a new line of jagged chocolates until then," he muttered before sealing their deal with a kiss.

———◆———

GENTLY, DANI ROLLED a small lump of chocolate ganache into a ball, highly skeptical that the brown Play-Doh-looking sphere was going to turn out anything remotely similar to the beautiful truffles on display in the front of Luke's chocolatiering class.

Since her Thursday night had freed up at the last minute, Luke had suggested she crash his class. At least she let him think it was all his idea. Her hints had been pretty subtle. The chance to cross into enemy territory was one she couldn't pass up.

So far, she was kind of having a blast—a little factoid she'd only admit to out loud under a judge's order.

She couldn't believe how much she'd learned already, due in no small part to Luke being a gifted teacher. He took them all from tempering chocolate to starting on this ganache almost effortlessly, being patient and fun the entire time. Heck, in a short half hour, she went from not knowing what a ganache was to emulsifying chopped chocolate like a pro, gradually mixing in hot heavy cream until it was smooth enough to fold in the softened butter.

Honestly, left to her own devices, Dani would've probably just thrown fully melted butter in with the melted chocolate and cream, and whipped it all up in her blender. That's how she made her pesto mayonnaise, after all. But as if he'd read her mind, Luke showed them that doing exactly that would cause the ganache to break, and look more like something a diarrheic canine left behind. Nothing at all like the gloriously shiny, emulsified chocolate that good, creamy ganache made the slow and steady way should look like.

Look at her, talking like an expert.

While the ganache they'd just learned to make was their take-home batch that needed to cool and dry overnight, Luke proceeded to then announce to the thirty women who'd signed up for the class that he'd premade a small batch for them to practice making truffles, which, apparently, were just a modified ganache adjusted to a thicker density with flavors added to the mix at differing stages. Sounded simple enough.

That said, after surveying the lump of chocolate she'd been rolling around for about a minute—and making worse, if that was possible—Dani was starting to think her earlier thoughts on the lofty goal were accurate. The sticky 'truffle' ball did *not* look good. Dani glanced around and saw the other students frowning at their own lumpy spheres with the same disappointment. She made sure to keep an encouraging smile on her face though, wanting so much for this class to go well for Luke.

He noticed.

After giving her a small, affectionate smile back, he finally put them all out of their misery by revealing the trick to achieving the silky smooth, perfectly rounded truffle shape—

he used a fork to dip the balls into another bowl of hot ganache to make the iconic smooth outer layer. Sneaky.

Tickled, Dani followed suit with her own ganache ball, choosing the alternative he'd suggested of a decorative drizzle-coated finish instead of the traditional powdered cocoa for a different look.

Not surprisingly, the time flew by after that as they did increasingly cooler things, and designed a bunch of store-window-ready chocolates. Dani had finished four gorgeous chocolate creations, and was frankly, getting a bit addicted to the whole process.

A low, impressed voice feathered her ear in an almost-kiss. "Those look great. I'm sure whoever you're making that for will love it."

The possessive tone in Luke's voice made it pretty clear who he was referring to.

"Thanks," replied Dani, forcibly keeping herself from leaning back against him. "This class is really amazing, Luke." She kept her poker face on though. "Not that I'm saying this Valentine's Day 'chocolate for your man' idea of yours isn't still borderline barbaric."

The lips at her ear curved into a smile. "Well then call me a caveman because the thought of you making something special just for me makes me want to drag you back to my cave." His fingers gently brushed the backs of hers.

A warm feeling uncurled in her tummy. "Cut it out," she whispered.

He let out a very male sigh. "You're right. Wouldn't

want the others to think you're the teacher's pet. I better make sure to treat every woman in here the same way—"

His teasing was cut short by a perfectly round, cocoa-dusted truffle being rammed into his now laughing mouth.

With her jealousy making a rare but flagrant appearance, she looked around and thought back to some of the hushed conversations she'd overheard throughout class. Seriously, a man on the make was one thing, but a woman on the prowl? Downright scary is what it was. Though she couldn't figure out why it was riling her so much. It wasn't as if Luke belonged to her. He was a free agent in a sport she'd long retired from.

Relationships. Nope, not her game anymore.

So considering the fact that she was the one imposing all the road blocks to anything more serious between them, she absolutely did *not* like this feeling of powerless possessiveness. Not one bit.

She just needed to level the playing field again a bit. "Hey, that warm drizzling chocolate you use for decorations…you think you could bring some of it with you on our fifth pre-date? Or rather, for the *end* of our fifth pre-date."

His fingers flexed sharply against her waist. "Jesus, have some mercy, woman."

"Nope." She licked a bit of melted ganache off her finger. Slowly. "Suffer in silence."

Luke growled and spun around, gruffly muttering something about needing to go get something from the freezer to cool off...the chocolate.

With a satisfied smile, Dani hunkered back down and poised her hand above her last molded chocolate, trying to decide how to decorate it. The decision, it seemed, was linked to who she was making it for. Instantly, that warm feeling returned to her belly. She decided making chocolate for someone special really was a nice idea.

Highly romantic.

Not that Luke would *ever* get that admission out of her.

———•———

AFTER THE LAST OF THE chocolatiering students left, Dani leaned against the entrance of Desert Confections, contentedly admiring the lines of Luke's broad back as he reached up to lock the storefront door and set the alarm. He had the body of a guy's guy, the kind kept tan from running and playing street ball shirtless, and solid from regular lifting.

Distractingly sexy.

In fact, so intent was she on eyeing all those ropey muscles rippling beneath his polo shirt that she didn't even hear the whispered oath he muttered before he snagged her by the waist and slid her in front of him. With his body blocking hers from any nosy onlookers, he bent down and seized her lips in a roller coaster kiss that told her he'd been as eager for a kiss as she'd been all night.

Oh wow. She had to hold the door handles to keep from melting into a puddle.

"So, movie or dinner first?" he asked roughly, after finally taking a breath.

Eyes half-lidded from being so thoroughly kissed, she was sure the answer of what she wanted was written all over her face, and it wasn't one of the two choices he'd listed.

Her very responsible mouth answered, "Dinner," however, and his visible disappointment matched hers. She kept her resolve though. Just a few more of these friendly pre-date dates. She could do it. At least that's what she kept telling herself. "I need food," she told him firmly.

"You mean to tell me you didn't get enough to eat in class?" he teased then, planting one more soft kiss on her lips before taking her hand in his and walking them over to his car.

Her cheeks reddened. She'd been quite literally a big kid in a candy store throughout class, nibbling on all the ingredients they'd worked with as if the world's supply of chocolate were going to disappear. But who could blame her? If Luke hadn't wanted Dani to keep 'accidentally' smudging some on the truffle ganache on her knuckles and nails—which, of course, required her to promptly lick it off—he shouldn't have emulsified boysenberry cream and hazelnut oil into that batch. She was only human. "I was hungry! You try cooking for eight hours straight." Since her head cook was playing merry-go-round with his hours due to *personal matters*—aka love life drama—Dani had spent all day on the grill covering his shift. On the bright side, the flip in her schedule had finally given her an opening to squeeze in another long-awaited pre-date with Luke.

"I'm still bummed you didn't tell me earlier. I would've come in for lunch," said Luke with true disappointment in his voice. "Nothing against Javier or Dave but I always thought my lunches on Fridays and Saturdays at Ocotillos tasted just a little bit better than the ones during the week." He slid his arm around her shoulders. "Turns out *you* were that difference."

Dani grinned proudly at the praise. Back when Ocotillos had been her dad's cozy craft brew tavern, Dani had learned to be a good pub and diner cook. She'd enjoyed it immensely. Truth be told, if she hadn't taken over the brewpub, she would've tried opening an eatery with the same mixed-ethnic menu Ocotillos had. Maybe a bar and grill. Definitely not a restaurant though. Pretty, tiny-portions-on-giant-plates variety of metro fusion cuisine simply wasn't her.

That's why being the brewmaster *and* cook of Ocotillos was the best of all worlds in her book—rustic, family-style dishes made with the beer she brewed. What more could she ask for in a dream job? "Bet you didn't think a *gringa* was making your favorite food in the kitchen, huh?" she teased, eyes twinkling. Customers often flattered her with that remark.

Though the Latin American flavor profiles of her cooking was a mismatch with her fair, mostly Irish skin, she cooked the pedigree of food she grew up loving, courtesy of her dad and his favorite aunt, the two people responsible for most of the skillsets she possessed. Unlike a majority of her peers, Dani had neither a brew science degree nor formal culinary training, but she more than made up for both by pouring her heart into everything she made. It was how her dad had always done it for both his family and his customers—and how she *assumed* mothers did for their kids.

Not that she'd know firsthand.

"Un-classically trained *gringa* or not, Dani, you're amazing at what you do."

"You're not so bad yourself." She smiled as her taste buds began humming over the remembered taste of his chocolates. "Your Juniper Whip is seriously the stuff of fantasies."

His dimples flashed as he curled her closer to him. "That's my favorite too. It's not my fanciest or best creation but it's the one that first made me believe I could open my own shop."

The layered emotions in his voice did funny things to the rhythm of her pulse. Lately, just being near Luke could get her to this utopic place where smiles came for no reason and heartbeat irregularity was a constant state of being. As wild as it was comforting, it just...fit.

She faltered a step then, tripping over what was very likely her heart.

Luke caught her. "Hey, you okay?"

"Yeah." She jerked back and tried to school her features before they betrayed her emotions. "Guess my leg just gave out there for some reason."

And it was a big reason. In a word: Luke. Luke, who regularly dropped off chocolates for the residents of a nearby retirement community and care home...just because. Luke, who was great with children, generous and loving without limits or expectations, and so unbelievably patient with her that it boggled her mind sometimes. Luke, who made her weak in the knees from a kiss, sane after just a quick chat, and as safe as she'd ever felt with a simple hug. Luke, who had her seeing tiny glimpses of something she never allowed herself to see with anyone anymore.

A future.

If she wasn't careful, she was going to fall heartbreakingly in love with the man.

And at right this moment, she was struggling to remember why that was a bad thing.

Chapter 12

"I AM OFFICIALLY IN love with Dani."

Frowning, Luke walked into Quinn's office after hearing that bizarre announcement from her. "Why are you declaring your love for the woman I'm dating?"

Holy crap. He'd just barely checked the impulse to insist she not *steal his line* about the woman he was dating.

That couldn't be right, could it?

Granted, he and Dani had been talking on the phone every night for weeks now, but with their hectic schedules, they'd only really been on two official 'pre-dates.' He couldn't possibly be starting to have serious feelings for the woman could he? That was too fast, even for him. Plus, following his normal MO of falling hard and fast was a surefire trip to heartbreak city where Dani was concerned. She'd made it crystal clear that she simply wasn't looking for the white-picket-fence fairytale ending.

Seriously, his heart *had* to know better. It couldn't possibly be going stupid over Dani already.

Then Quinn went and said Dani's name again and the unmistakable gallop in his ribcage smacked the logicizing right out of his brain.

Well, apparently, it was possible.

Damn. When his heart set him up to fail, it evidently liked to swing for the fences.

Minutes later, his head was still spinning from this revelation when Quinn elatedly slapped a printout against his chest and turned her laptop around to demand his full attention.

Looking at the order on the screen he shrugged, puzzled at the degree of her excitement. "So Dani ordered some chocolates. Big deal. Most of our distributors get at least triple that."

"Yes, but the question is *why* she ordered that chocolate. She's planning something—a counter attack. And she's using our Desert Confections chocolate to do it. I repeat, I freaking love that woman."

"You do know that whatever she has planned will probably skewer us."

She dismissed that with a wave of her hand. "It doesn't matter. All publicity is good publicity. Any tactical maneuvers Dani makes continues to build the hype over both your businesses." She preened. "Our website and blog have been getting a ton of traffic since. Folks all across Arizona are weighing in...albeit, a lot for beer over chocolate, but who cares." She swatted her hand against the shop's financial tally paperwork she'd shoved at him. "Our sales quintupled this week alone, and that's not even counting the advance orders for our Valentine's Day home kits." Tapping her finger on her chin thoughtfully, she continued to leave the muzzle off all the lightning-fast inner workings of her mind, "Maybe I should slide a mention into a few local news anchors' twit feeds throughout the week? That might get them curious enough to look into it for a human interest story or something, get our foot traffic up even more."

Luke shook his head in amazement. When it came to marketing, Quinn left no rock unturned. "Sometimes you scare me."

"But most times you love me. Like now." She pulled open a box sitting on her desk.

He peered inside at its contents. "What are these?"

"You'd mentioned wanting something like it for women to personalize the chocolate valentines for their men. Well, I'm delivering. A week early. These are design transfer sheets similar to the ones you use to put our gold emblem on our elite chocolates. I had the same company make short little gold messages instead—just a few key phrases of our choosing. Sort of like a cross between M&Ms and candy hearts, with a provocatively sweet twist."

Luke's eyes widened. Provocative was putting it mildly for some of the messages.

"Oh, relax," she said in a rare display of identity swapping with him. "They go on the bottom of the chocolates like a hidden message so they'll be the couple's secret. Plus, since they're simple heat-transfers, customers can easily DIY them for their homemade chocolates. Or, for the women who'll be buying instead of making their valentine chocolates, we can apply whatever messages they want to anything here in the shop as well." She grinned. "I made sure to come up with a wide variety of messages—some sweet and heartfelt and 'old school,' others *descriptively* sexy. The extra racy ones that made your eyes pop earlier are courtesy of my sister's dirty mind; anything more, ah, *personal* would have to be custom ordered, of course." She looked at him expectantly. "So what do you think? If they get popular, we can do this all year round."

He was impressed. "These are perfect. I have to hand it to you. You always manage to take my ideas and give 'em a shot of steroids."

"Try nuclear steroids. Check this." She opened up their Facebook page, showing the small get-the-word-out contest she'd made.

Luke scanned the directions, impressed at both the simplicity and the sentiment of the contest. Folks just had to post to Facebook a photo of a place in Arizona they thought made a great romantic date site and then tag Desert Confections in the picture to get it to show in the Desert Confections album along with a brief description of what made the location romantic.

"We've already got hundreds of entries, some of places I never even heard of." Quinn's eyes danced with excitement.

"And it's all thanks to the 'Chocolate Foreplay for Two' kit we're giving away as the prize."

He arched an eyebrow in question, but before he could ask, she jumped up and grabbed the basket of assorted chocolates he'd started assembling yesterday...at least he *thought* it was the same basket.

"What's the 'Chocolate Foreplay for Two' kit you ask?" she offered animatedly. "Why, that's the new name for this product gift basket you were working on, which I took the liberty of spicing up. It now includes an assortment of bonbons with classic aphrodisiac fillings, a chocolate mint drizzle to be served first cold then hot, and a strawberry wine cordial / whipped truffle duo to be, errr, 'shared' creatively." She beamed. "I was thinking it's high time we show folks how chocolate can be sexy as well as sweet. What do you think?"

Luke whistled in admiration. "Geez, woman. Did you even sleep the last few nights?"

She leaned back in her chair like a satisfied cat. "I'm just doing my part since you've been working your ass off in the kitchen. By my calculations, you've made more chocolate in the last month than you used to make in four months at our old place. Oh, which reminds me—" She picked up a colorful brochure with several photos on it circled. "I think it's time."

Luke looked at the brochure, unsure whether to be surprised or stressed. Going into this relocation, he'd promised Quinn she could dictate when it was time to upgrade their equipment. And he'd keep from whining until then. While the scale of their new shop, in terms of both shop size and product output, dictated they get four new display cases specifically made for chocolate refrigeration, they'd been managing to get by with the two secondhand pie cases they'd used in their old shop in Mesa.

Even with their smaller output back then, which was a fifth of what they were generating now, the pie cases still hadn't been ideal for keeping the chocolates at the optimum temperature for very long. Luckily, they always used to sell the chocolates quickly enough that it wasn't ever really an issue. Now, however, with the volume of daily traffic and the number of distributors they now had, keeping the old equipment wasn't really an option.

In retrospect, Luke *was* thankful she'd had her reservations about getting new equipment right off the bat because though Quinn didn't know to what degree, the costs for renovating and remodeling had far exceeded the loan they'd gotten for start-up costs. To cover the difference, Luke had tapped into his savings…which was why he was now thirty grand poorer.

But now here they were, with the green light from Quinn to do that which she had been so against just months ago. This was huge.

Just one problem.

In attempting to secure a small-business loan for this very day—knowing without a doubt it was coming—he'd already gone to several banks after their current bank had denied his request to add an equipment loan of forty grand to their existing loan. Only four banks had given his application serious consideration, and only one of them had interest rates that didn't make him feel violated.

But even that was too high for them to afford.

Though they'd never kept things like this from each other before, Luke simply didn't have the heart to tell her. So instead, he just teased lightly, "If I'm not mistaken, I'd say it sounds like you're a little *pleased* with our relocation now."

Though her shrug revealed very little, her emotional expression held nothing back. When Luke saw the mist gathering in Quinn's eyes, he stopped the teasing and drew her in for a tight hug. Far as he was concerned, no one deserved financial security as much Quinn did.

He still remembered the night she'd shown up at his door after the jackass wanna-be-rocker she'd been dating disappeared without a trace, leaving her alone, scared, and pregnant. From there, the universe had decided to be really cruel, torturing her newborn son battle with fatal organ complications right from birth.

Thankfully, little Coop had survived it all, but when the hospital bills first began pouring in, the dollar amounts to repay had seemed impossible to pay back in a single lifetime.

But Quinn had rallied. She'd fought like a bat out of hell to manage the debts. And not a day went by that he wasn't grateful the business they'd created had been able to help her as he'd always hoped.

The reminder of all they'd accomplished, and how much faith Quinn had had in him was all it took for him to decide that Quinn was absolutely right. It was time. Their expansion and relocation was quickly proving itself to be a success. They needed that new equipment.

Then, as if fate itself had heard him, his eyes fell atop a the town newsletter on Quinn's desk. On the front page, he saw a feature article about their building's landlord, Noah, and some multi-million dollar project he was working on. That's when a faint memory snuck up on him. Dani had once mentioned Noah loaning some money to her friend to help with the start-up of her shop in town.

Maybe he'd consider doing that for us as well.

"So are you actually going to make me say you were right?" huffed Quinn, breaking into his thoughts. "Or will you just get the loan and order the damn machines already? I'm pretty sure the bigger one is on its last leg. I swear it's not staying cool the way it used to."

Smiling affectionately at the woman who'd become closer than a sister to him. "*Yeah*, I'm going to need to hear you say I was right."

As he blocked Quinn's assault with a deadly file folder, Luke made a mental note to call Noah first thing in the morning. He was going to get that loan no matter what.

———•———

"*JAMESON.*"

"Good morning, Mr. Jameson. This is Luke Bradford. I'm the one leasing—"

"Yes, hello. You're our resident chocolatier in Cactus

Creek," the voice cut in, no-nonsense and roughly cultured. "I've been hearing a lot of good things about your shop lately."

The man expressed a few more pleasantries that were clearly not rehearsed or fed to him. He sounded every bit the high-powered, hard-earned, and directly-connected business man he was reputed to be. The kind that didn't care one iota about prestige, and worked damn hard for his money. Luke had run into a few men like Noah Jameson during his business school days. A small and formidable few.

"What can I do for you, Mr. Bradford? My secretary said you wanted to schedule a meeting to discuss something regarding the property you're leasing. I'll be out of town for a few days; is this something we can discuss on the phone before I leave tomorrow morning?"

"Well, Mr. Jameson—"

"Call me Noah. Mr. Jameson is my father to everyone in Cactus Creek."

"Oh, of course. Well, Noah. I talked to Dani and—"

"Wait a minute, you talked to Dani?"

Geez, the guy sure did like to interrupt. "Yes, we're, um…friends." Man, he hated saying that. Every day, that measly description of his relationship with Dani was starting to rankle more and more. "She and I met over the holidays and hit it off, I guess you could say."

"I see."

"So as I was saying, I talked to Dani and she mentioned you'd helped one of her other friends who had a small start-up shop in town by giving her a small loan."

At the silence from the other end, Luke found himself missing Noah's interruptions.

"Because our chocolate shop has been doing so well," he trudged forward with confidence. He wasn't a Noah Jameson, but he knew how good his shop was doing as far as small businesses go. "We actually need to acquire new and larger equipment to keep up with our now booming sales. The cost for this equipment is quite substantial—"

"And no banks will give you a reasonable loan," finished Noah matter-of-factly. "I have to say I don't blame them, mainly because of how young your first loan is and how much you've levied in your personal savings account the past few months to cover renovation and remodeling costs."

"How did you know about my—"

"You're a tenant leasing out one of my bigger real estate holdings in Cactus Creek. It would be irresponsible of me not to know your financial situation."

Luke sighed. "So I take it your answer is no?"

The lack of an immediate response from Noah gave Luke a flicker of hope.

That was extinguished a second after that.

"Unfortunately, my answer *is* no, Mr. Bradford. That is, if you're asking for a simple business loan similar to the one I gave Dani's other friend Lia. I have the same reservations as the banks you've approached, I'm afraid."

He paused. "However, I *can* offer you a collateral loan."

Luke frowned, confused. "But we've already established I have little to no assets."

"You have your chocolates," continued Noah as if Luke hadn't even spoken. "They're good. I've tasted a few myself."

"You have?" Somehow he didn't see a Phoenix big shot like Noah eating truffles.

"Yes. I've had my assistant order several boxes from your premiere line. I try to support Cactus Creek businesses where I can. And in your case, you sell something I can actually give to my colleagues and business contacts without them thinking I'm off my rocker."

Luke chuckled at that. Cactus Creek wasn't exactly teeming with corporate-friendly gifts.

"The loan I'm suggesting is similar to a patent collateral loan, but instead of a patent to an idea or product, you'd put up a few of your premiere recipes for the life of the loan."

His *recipes?* Luke's stomach plummeted so fast he felt nauseated. He couldn't possibly do that. Not his recipes. No way would he ever—

The rising wave of objections in his head was squelched by a sudden chirp from his cell phone.

A text message from Dani.

>> *Guess what? We have your favorite on lunch special today! Saving you a plate.*

Instantly a grin split across his face. Soon, a second voice in his head, calmer than the one earlier, began reasoning with him. Was putting up his recipes for collateral really *that* great a risk? It was a necessary expense so he'd see the benefits from it not just in sales but in his taxes the following year. As long as sales kept up, everything would be fine. And it's not like he was going anywhere. He already knew he wanted to stay in Cactus Creek for the long haul; this was just one more firmly planted root to keep him here.

All good reasons.

And the follow-up chirp from his cell phone reminded him of another big reason that was surely rooting him there as well. Seeing Dani's avatar grinning at him on the screen alongside her second text, this one even more playful than the last, Luke felt his lips begin to move, seemingly independently from his brain. "Could you send me the collateral loan papers to look over?"

"By all means. I'll have my secretary email you some information and we can have a sit down sometime over the next few days. If you agree to the terms, we can get the process started after I get back next week."

While the extended timeline to think about this should have made him relieved, on the contrary, it left him unsettled. He didn't want the added time to talk himself out of this. He believed in his chocolates, and he had faith that their marketing plan for the shop was going to succeed. He didn't get this far in the business by *not* taking chances. This was a risky one, for sure, but no riskier than relocating to Cactus Creek in the first place. Shoving down the last of his doubts, he asked instead, "Actually, why don't I just come in later today? Then we can get the loan paperwork started immediately before you leave for your trip."

Luke finished up the call just as Quinn returned to the office from her meeting with the printers. Perfect timing. He didn't want Quinn knowing anything about the loan; there was no way she'd ever let him put up his recipes as collateral.

As far as his decision went, the longer the idea settled, the better it sat with him.

It was just a loan. And the shop was already doing well.

What could go wrong?

Chapter 13

Luke was halfway out of the shop when the sound of an elderly couple quarreling over which gift box set to buy gave him pause. "Hey Rissa," he called out to the ASU grad student who'd been with them as their one and only employee for the past year and a half, back when they'd just started to get really popular in Mesa. "Why don't you give this nice couple samples of..." he checked to see which box sets they were considering, "the Brulee Bonbon, the Dark Hazelnut Buttercream, and the Juniper Whip."

The couple turned around in surprise and came over to thank him personally.

"My pleasure," he assured them warmly. "Enjoy."

Now for his favorite part.

From the corner of his eye, he watched as the sweet old couple tasted the samples and began gushing over the unique flavors. Luke ducked his head and beamed a little. It never got old. Seeing folks taste his chocolates for the first time always made his day.

Luke entered Ocotillos from the brewery entrance a minute later and scanned the vast metallic maze in search of Dani. It took a while, but he finally found her with a few of the beer boys hosing down one of the larger beer vessels and looking pretty darn cute in those big rubber brew boots of hers. When her animated laugh echoed out over the quiet industrial hum of the giant machines all around, Luke couldn't help but smile. She really looked in her element back here.

So, rather than scooping her up and kissing her the way he'd been thinking about all morning, he instead decided to hang back for a bit to study another puzzle piece that made up the enigma that was Dani.

While Dani always displayed a vibrant joy for her work, whether she was tending bar or out front running the brewpub, when she was back here as brewmaster, she seemed to exude this deep, soul-refreshing passion that was inspiring to witness. He admired that type of dedication, felt a kindred bond with her for being as excited about her life's work as he was about his.

Plus, after another week of overloaded things-to-do lists on both their parts, thanks largely to the growing hype of the battle between their businesses, he was missing her something fierce. What could he say? He was addicted to the woman. But with their impossible schedules, they were now in a quasi long distance relationship of sorts, built mostly on phone calls, sexts, and jibing twitter fun.

At least they had their nightly phone ritual though.

Every night, for the one hour a day the stars in their chaotic schedules aligned after Dani finished her night shift and before Luke went into the shop at four a.m., they'd lie in the dark in their respective beds and talk about anything and everything on the phone until his work alarm went off. Luke had started the ritual simply because it was the best imaginable way to start his day; Dani said she loved having his voice be the last thing she heard before she fell asleep.

As great as these phone talks were, however, actually being in the same room with Dani was on the top of his agenda today. Preferably for a meal, ideally at a socially acceptable time for that meal. Not even for a date. Just a low-key power lunch so he could see the woman in between chocolate deliveries and beer-boiling schedules.

"Pop quiz time, Mikey," he heard Dani's voice call out cheerfully as she descended the brew vessel ladder and waved over the newest addition to the crew, the ASU student who'd started coming in once a week to train since the start of the semester. Luke knew Dani's love for outreach brew education had roots with her father. The man had been a pioneer in his time, a strong advocate for home and craft brew training. Hence the daily brewery tours for customers interested in the brewing process, and the internships they now had for anyone, young or old, wanting to learn more about the business.

She was a damn good teacher, too, from the looks of it. Luke watched the kid, Mikey, hang on Dani's every word, practically without blinking.

Luke stayed out of Dani's sightline the whole time so as not to interrupt the lesson as she led Mikey over to the small brew system. If he remembered correctly from the tour, this was the 'Baby D' system, the one used for recipe experimentation.

"Five correct so far, not bad." Dani smiled proudly. "Okay, next, which malts did we use for this batch and why?"

"The caramel and roasted ones," answered Mikey confidently. "For the richer flavor and redder color."

"You didn't even break a sweat on that one!" she praised. Tapping a thoughtful finger on her chin, she smiled and fired out, "Alright last question—you're on kettle duty for my newest brew today, so what's the hops schedule?"

Mikey's eyes floated to the ceiling to jog his memory. "I do the smaller first batch of hops at the start for bitterness, and then later add whole leaf hops for aroma and flavor."

"Gold star. There's hope for you yet, kid." She nodded proudly and stuck her fist out for him to bump. "Okay, you have my notes and brew log. When Jim gets back, I'm afraid it's more cleaning duty for you." She tapped his baseball cap bill sternly. "Until then, eat an actual meal today, will you? Chips and soda don't count."

Mikey hid his grin and sighed dramatically. "Yes, *mom*."

Luke grinned as he listened to the exchange. He'd used that same tone on his own mother many a time during his teen years. When he looked over to see Dani's reaction, he saw that her eyes had gone soft, mothering and doting over the six-foot-tall 'kid' even as she continued to bust his chops.

That right there sent an arrow of hope through his heart that maybe, just maybe she wasn't totally closed to the idea of at least an off-white picket fence in her future.

Suddenly, he could picture that fence so clearly—and the house on the other side of that fence with Dani in the kitchen wearing the same smile she had on now while spying on an adorable kid with her honey-colored eyes surreptitiously hiding his green beans under a napkin.

Luke blinked in surprise, scattering the wishful thinking into a thousand pieces in his mind. Well, this was a first. While admittedly he'd pictured all his serious girlfriends as his someday-bride, never had he found himself imagining one as the mother of his children as well.

Until now.

A rush of emotions coursed through his veins over that fact, intensified threefold when he caught the exact moment Dani discovered him standing there on the other side of the machine. Hell, he'd consider himself the world's luckiest guy just to be greeted with that smile of hers every day for the rest of his life.

Of course, in one of life's ironic moments of manifest reality, the first words out of her mouth after that were, "Hey, Luke. Sorry, do you mind waiting a bit? I'm almost ready."

Logically knowing she only meant that in the context of their lunch today, in his mind, he was nodding in reference to their relationship as well.

Yes, he'd wait for her until she was ready.

Literally and figuratively.

Luke grabbed a seat at the bar and noticed for the first time a list of all the past Dobson beers, carved into the wall off to the side behind it. After studying the long list, he started to see an interesting trend. "Hey, Sam," he called over to the bartender on duty. "How come your seasonal brews have only been in the summer, fall, and winter? Why not spring?"

Sam's answer sounded very...careful. "Fall, summer, and winter are all easy seasons for brewers—more robust beers for winter, light ones in the summer, and of course the malty brews during the fall months. Spring has less...brewing standards."

Luke frowned. What an informative way not to answer his question. Even more curious was the way Rylan, who was eating at a nearby table, was avoiding looking at him altogether.

Then Xoey, who'd been in the middle of dropping off more t-shirts, cupped a hand on the side of her mouth and stage whispered, "*We're not supposed to talk about it.*"

"Oh stop, you guys," shushed Dani, finally joining them. "It's not like it's an NFL superstition or something." She turned to Luke. "Folks around here call it the Dobson curse."

Luke's curiosity piqued. "Should I be wearing a vial of holy water around my neck?"

"Not that kind of curse, goofball. Just the unlucky kind. For as long as I can remember, my dad couldn't make a successful beer in the spring. They'd always flop. Pretty horrendously. The ones that came close to being decent would always run into problems during the trials—too flat, fermenting gone awry, etc. Eventually, he just stopped trying to make a spring beer."

"What about when you took over as brewmaster?"

"While I don't believe in curses, even I have to admit I've brewed up some stinkers."

Luke shook his head in amazement. "I find that impossible to believe."

Xoey put a sobering hand on his shoulder. "Oh trust me, she's made some awful ones." She gagged in memory. "Dani, remember that blackcurrant rum beer? And that bizarre lychee one you tried to make a few years ago? Blech!"

"Gee thanks." Dani's nose scrunched in consternation. "In theory, those two should've come out really good."

"In reality, one tasted like sugary spoiled malt vinegar and the other just tasted like ass."

She laughed. "I'll give you that. The smell and the taste didn't match up at all in that last batch; I can't believe you all even swallowed it. You should've just spit it out."

"*I* would've," assured Quinn as she walked in to join the tail end of their conversation. She passed an important-looking form to Luke—very 'official business'—even though the way she and Rylan were looking at each other pretty much outed her as a bald-faced liar regarding her visit here.

Luke scoffed. "You mean you would've spit it back in her face. Been there, wiped that."

Quinn shrugged. "If it was bad enough, sure."

"Wow, no one here would ever be *that* honest with me." Dani's eyes rounded in admiration.

"You hear that, Quinn? What a concept. They actually respect their boss enough *not* to spit in her face." Luke's comical look of shock was priceless.

"I respect you," assured Quinn. "But I also have certain expectations of you. Evidently, being able to duck in time to avoid my *feedback* is no longer one of them." She clucked her tongue disappointedly. "Live and learn…"

They all laughed, mostly at his expense.

Luke's laughing smile instantly turned into a hidden, incredulous grin when he saw Rylan slide his hand onto the small of Quinn's back as he whispered something in her ear. That was the type of thing that would usually result in a lost limb for most men where Quinn was concerned.

Discreetly, Luke signaled Dani with his eyes to check out the development.

When she looked over, her eyes instantly widened to the size of saucers right before she grabbed his hand.

"Hey, you know what? The lunch special isn't quite ready yet so why don't we go to your shop for a bit first? You can show me that new chocolate you created yesterday."

She shuffled swiftly toward the door, hollering out to her assistant manager on the way, "Sam, tell Jim I'll be back in the brewery in an hour. The recipe I'm trying on the Baby D system is on a hundred-twenty-minute boil cycle. I had extra time to rack the last Rylan Red in the Daddy V system so Jim won't have to condition at all today, but I do want him to check the valve on Ole Betsy, it's still acting wonky. Thanks!"

With that, Dani yanked Luke out of his chair and

dragged him outside.

Luke chortled the entire way. "Subtle."

Her shoulders lifted in a show of muffled glee. With one more peek at Rylan and Quinn still talking inside, Dani fluttered her fingers together in a tiny clap—a lovable rare habit she had when she delighted in seeing a happy couple together. "Those two look so good together."

Grinning adoringly, he shook his head. "I love your little Dani clap."

She went still. "My what?" She was genuinely befuddled.

"You, Ms. Tough-As-Nails Brewmaster, have one ultra girly habit whenever you're wanting to play matchmaker." He kissed the tip of her nose. "A peppy little cheerleader clap."

Now Dani looked truly horrified.

"It's adorable." He gathered her to him and kissed the frown lines on her forehead. "It shows you're just as much of a romantic as I am," he taunted a bit more, his lips now enjoying the challenge of coaxing her pout to stand down.

"It does not," she insisted, although the wobble in her voice said his coaxing was making her reach the point where she didn't really remember what 'it' even was anymore.

He smiled against her lips, using guerrilla tactics with his tongue. "Admit it, I'm right."

"This is blackmail," she argued, trying to catch his elusive lips.

"No, this is more me badgering the defendant on trial."

Her teeth gently caught his lower lip for an instant while

her hands smoothed over his abdomen in the way she knew made him crazy. "Should I plead the Fifth?" she asked, her breath nuzzling against his ear as she leaned in as close as she decently could on a public sidewalk.

"I'm pleading the fourth," he muttered as he swooped in to surrender.

She knew he didn't mean the Fourth Amendment, but rather their fourth pre-date. While the constraints of their perfectly rational agreement to have five casual pre-dates had certainly sounded good at the time, with their crazy schedules, the fruition of their agreement was nearing at a snail's pace.

He laid his forehead against hers and heaved out a rough breath. "The prosecution gives up. We'll let the defense keep deluding herself on her romantic tendencies."

"And here I was all ready to take your plea bargain," she fibbed teasingly.

When he just about fell against the wall at her implication, Dani laughed and dragged him over to Desert Confections before they did something in public they'd both regret. Or enjoy beyond consequence.

"You're going to have to walk in front of me when we get in the door," warned Luke.

Dani leaned back and brushed against him. "Or your customers will think you just really like your new 'Chocolate Foreplay' kits?"

He actually felt his ears redden a tiny bit. "That name wasn't my idea."

She laughed. "I figured."

"Speaking of Quinn." He tilted his head questioningly. "She told me you ordered some of our chocolate for Ocotillos. 'Fess up. Are you going to be playing nice?"

The look she gave him was all sass. "Never." She moved her hips against his to further support her declaration.

"Woman, behave," he growled as they entered his shop. Though they made it safely in his office without any more evil taunting from Dani, after taking one look at her still-thinking-about-it eyes, he had to exit right back out to the kitchen, muttering, "Not nearly far enough away."

Much to Dani's amusement.

A full two minutes later, he finally returned with a few pieces of the newest chocolate he'd created that morning, his hands still slightly unsteady.

Dani offered him an olive branch for his suffering. "You really want to know what we're planning for your chocolate?"

"Quinn's been dying of curiosity," he replied honestly.

Amusement tipped a corner of her mouth. "Remember how I told you I wanted a make-your-own-dessert thing at Ocotillos profiling beer-based desserts? Well, we're starting a weekly blind date mixer at Ocotillos where that activity will be making its debut."

"And our chocolate?"

"Is the enemy." Her teeth gleamed fiendishly. "Our customers get to cruelly liquefy it in beer fondue and blowtorch it in beer cracker s'mores."

Luke tipped his head back and let out a booming laugh.

Her grin relented. "No worries. It's not nearly as

sinister as it sounds," she reassured. "It just so happens I've used your chocolate to make fondue and s'mores at home, so like most of the Ocotillos recipes, I was just bringing a little bit of home to the brewpub. Completely innocent."

Her face lit impishly at his dubious expression. "Okay, so maybe it isn't *completely* innocent." Eyeing the piece of chocolate he was holding in his fingers, she licked her lips. "If I promise not to enjoy torching your chocolate *too* much, can I get a taste of that truffle?"

Smiling, he slid the roasted chocolate and huckleberry tequila bonbon into her mouth.

Watching the candid reaction swirl across her face as she bit into the shell of the rounded chocolate with a snap and savored the liquid burst of flavor inside, Luke found yet again that his favorite part of seeing someone experience his chocolates was infinitely more incredible when it was Dani doing the tasting.

He bent down to steal a kiss, wanting—needing—to capture the moment with as many senses as he could. In a bolt of awareness, his eyes dilated so fast he went dizzy when the touch of her tongue shared the flavors with him. Even through the chocolate, he could still taste Dani. The combination was sweeter than anything he could have imagined.

This was undeniably now his new favorite thing.

Chapter 14

LUKE WAS AN EVIL, evil fibber, Dani decided as she tiredly rubbed her eyes and tried to wrap her brain around the fact that she was sitting in Desert Confections, attempting to do paperwork for Ocotillos at four in the morning. *Four!* Somehow, Luke had pulled the brain out of her head, via her lips, and got her to agree to this demented idea of working before dawn like he did *after* tricking her by changing the clock in her bedroom three hours back.

She huffed. If she'd been more awake—and not kissed senseless—she'd have planted her butt right back in bed when the realization that it was still dark had seeped into her brain.

But then he'd kissed her again.

Now here she was.

Yawning again, she tried in vain to focus on the paperwork laid out before her but it was no use. She was simply too tired to function at this ungodly hour.

Luke on the other hand was not. Like a freakin' early bird machine, he'd been working intently on his chocolates for the last twenty minutes, pausing only to look up every so often to make sure she was still awake, giving her a supportive smile if she'd catch him doing it.

Okay, so it was kind of nice.

Plus, to be fair, he'd only been doing what she'd asked since the supervillainously boring insurance paperwork she was trying to get through did need to be done before ten am today. She glanced down at the forms again. Yup. Still as mind-numbing as they'd been two minutes ago.

Stretching, she got up, wanting a break after her fifteen minutes of strenuously avoiding work. Not wanting to disturb him, she tiptoed over to sneak a peek at the extravagant chocolates Luke was preparing for some swanky party. As she approached, not as whisper-quietly as she'd intended, he grinned and stepped aside to let her peruse the entire collection of chocolates.

She was awestruck. He'd done an intricate art deco design with crystallized fruit peels, metallic flakes, and bright airbrushed color. "You're an artist," she breathed, taking it all in. Pointing at the set that looked like crackled ice, she marveled, "I can't believe you actually piped those in. They look like they came out of a mold."

"I wanted something more haphazard." Wiping his hands on his apron, Luke rolled his neck and shoulders, wincing as he tried to stretch the bunched tension out of his muscles.

Dani shuffled behind him and gently kneaded his shoulders for him. His blissful groan pulsed through the air in the silent shop. She grinned. He let her spoil him for another minute before pulling her around to thank her properly on the lips. Arms circling her waist, he tilted his head sympathetically. "Need a snack to stay awake?"

She shamelessly popped open her mouth, not needing to be asked twice. Chuckling, he surveyed his premium chocolates in the display cases thoughtfully before selecting two complementary pieces. He reached over to tuck the first in her mouth.

Dani's lashes dropped partway as the two inner layers of loquat cream and saskatoon berry mousse hit her taste buds, mingling with the bittersweet chocolate shell. "Sooo good," she groaned as the flavors swirled around her mouth in a hidden dance, intensifying and changing, like all of Luke's gorgeously complex specialty chocolates did.

One more lusty moan later, Luke teased the seam of her lips with the second morsel he'd chosen. She took the salted caramel rosehip truffle in her mouth and then on a whim, licked his fingers as well, just to see what chocolate-coated Luke would taste like.

"*Holy Hefeweizen*," she purred, shivering just a bit.

The flavors continued to tease her taste buds even as it melted away on her tongue. With one last breathy sigh, she opened her eyes...and found herself looking into a gaze so sultry, it made her skin tingle. Luke's soft brown eyes darkened even more when he saw her blush.

"You do know this work date doesn't count as one of our five dates, right?" she teased deflectively, though even to her own ears, she sounded like she wanted him to disagree.

"Sure. *I* know that," he teased back with a taunting grin, an eyebrow lifted knowingly.

She studied him warily, willing herself not to take the bait. Then he began whistling and cleaning up his workplace as if completely and singularly unaffected. Okay, *now* it was on. Smiling deviously, and knowing she was mostly just trying to delay working on the insurance forms, she approached him with a slither. "Guess I was just trying to remind myself then." She traced a finger lightly down his spine and just barely slid her lips over his ear as she whispered, "Although I'm not sure I was successful..."

"*Foul!*" Luke contested with a heated laugh, ducking away. "Illegal use of wiles."

"No penalty," she decreed, her smile devilishly pleased as she backed up and put an extra swank in her step, knowing his eyes were x-raying her thin yoga pants the entire time. Instead of coming after her to do something about it though, he simply swept a tortured glance over her and then fled to the kitchen, mumbling about them both needing to get work done. Dani sighed and followed him back there. Damn boy scout. "Hey, what does this thing do?" she asked, picking up a random utensil from the shelf as if it were the most awe-inspiring thing she'd ever seen.

"Not going to work, honey. Put down the big spoon and get back to those forms." His voice was comically stern.

An indignant pout warred with her laughing eyes. "But I *really* want to know. Is it for a very big bowl of soup?"

Shaking his head, he sighed. "Okay, how about this? You help me finish up here and then I'll help you with your forms after." He slid a warm hand down her back. "And since you have the attention span of a puppy right now, we can even take a ten-minute break first."

"Thirty," she countered automatically.

"If I'd said thirty, you would've said forty, wouldn't you've? Just for the hell of it?"

Her look pretty much said 'duh.'

He suppressed a grin, attempting to look annoyed instead. "You're so damn contrary."

"No, I'm a businesswoman. I negotiate."

"Well, I'm a businessman so here's my counteroffer: ten-minute break—" His eyes danced when she opened her mouth to reject the offer already. "*And* I cook you dinner tonight."

She was startled. They hadn't had a 'night in' yet. On top of that, he wanted to cook for her? Besides her workers, no one had made a meal for her since...she couldn't even recall when.

His smile was gentle, patient. A dozen reasons why she should say no to such a romantic gesture ran through her head. Half of them were warnings from her heart while the rest were reminders from her guilty conscience that Luke wouldn't be so eager to slave over a meal if he knew it was for a woman who'd tried to put him out of business not too long ago.

But the one reason to say yes was right in front of her. "Deal," she agreed almost shyly.

"Okay, so we'll have dinner and just veg after. TV, video games, whatever you want. We don't even have to call it a date. I just want you to kick back and relax."

Aw, that was sweet. "Oh, it'll count as a date," she assured him softly. Suddenly, the air was no longer playful, and his expression was decidedly hungry now as she slid her arms around him and asked, "So this ten-minute break. What did you have in mind?"

His lips answered without saying a word.

They did eventually get back to work as planned…about thirty minutes later.

———•———

"OHMIGOD, THAT WAS the best ribeye ever."

Luke grinned at Dani's moaned declaration as she fell onto her couch, stuffed.

"It's all in the beer marinade," winked Luke, loving this lazy, languid Dani. "Luckily, I have an in with a hot brewmaster who was able to sneak me some of the really good stuff."

"Which you made absolute magic with in the dessert too." She sighed in bliss. "I ate so much I can't move. I think you might have to be my servant for the rest of the night."

"Works for me." He waggled his eyebrows. "Traditional servants help their naked mistresses into their night clothes before bed, right?"

A throw pillow from the couch immediately went airborne for a brief moment before landing limply at his feet.

He shook his head. "That's just sad. Poor baby. Alright, alright since you're clearly exhausted, I *guess* I'll help you stay upright in the shower too." His belabored expression turned teasingly predatory as he advanced on her.

It didn't register until he was within arm's length of her that she wasn't trying to escape.

"Okay," she murmured quietly after a beat.

He froze. Shit, he should've known better than to play this game with Dani. Who was he kidding? She'd win every time. "Now that's just mean." He backpedaled ruefully. "Wave food in front of a starving man, why don't you."

"Okay," she replied again, her voice now bedroom soft, and when he checked, more asleep than not.

Damn.

He grimaced as he adjusted his jeans and leaned down to slide her hair back from her face. Pressing a gentle kiss to her forehead, he suggested softly, "Honey, why don't you go on and shower so you can get to bed. You're not used to waking up as early as I am; I should've thought about that before planning this dinner. You brewed all day today and you've got the dayshift tomorrow; you need to rest. So get going. I'll clean up out here."

With a groan, she dragged herself up off the couch. "But that's not fair," she managed around a stifled yawn. "You cooked, I should do the dishes."

"Next time. Go on. I'll let myself out when I'm done."

She slowly shuffled toward the hallway, her steps heavy with fatigue. "Don't leave without saying goodbye. Promise?" Her words retreated into her bedroom with her. "Even if I'm out cold?"

His own reply was muted out by the blood rushing in his ears—a reaction he was helpless to stop at the sound of her words getting muffled behind clothing.

Clothing she was taking *off*.

Without him.

No amount of adjusting could stop the zipper tattoo that was forming behind his jeans. Quickly turning on the faucet to mute out any more stripping noises, he started scrubbing the cast iron pan in the sink like it owed him money, damn near making it shine until finally, finally, he heard the bathroom door close and the shower turn on.

But then his imagination got the best of him. The hot water, the dish soap bubbles, hell even the damn rubber dish gloves next to the sink all made him think of sex. And wet, naked woman.

His wet, naked woman.

Not twenty feet away.

What was it about a woman in a shower that could make the male brain turn to mush?

His hands gripped the edge of the sink unsteadily as he counted backward from a hundred, willing his mind to focus on something else.

He was in the single digits when he heard the shower shut-off and quiet, feminine footsteps padding across the hallway. The sound of a door opening, but not closing shut all the way made him almost drop to his knees in surrender right there. He started his silent counting back at a hundred.

It wasn't until complete silence echoed back at him that he leaned way the hell over and finished the rest of the dishes, surprised he hadn't managed to drill a hole in the cabinet paneling in the process. When he felt at least partially sane, but still not at all under control, he headed down the hall to Dani's bedroom to say goodnight.

No dallying, no thinking. Definitely no touching. Just get in and out—

Freak-in-*A*. Poor word choice. Excellent mental image though.

Yeah, definitely none of *that*.

Knocking gently before he pushed the partially ajar door open, he came to a full standstill and just stared. He'd expected Dani to be asleep.

He hadn't expected to find her asleep in her towel.

Hair still damp from the shower, tiny goosebumps across her skin from the cold, and her expression wholly relaxed in sleep, she was the sexiest thing he'd ever laid eyes on. A beautiful sleeping angel.

Wrapped in a towel that was two, maybe three breaths away from falling open.

His legs hurried him closer before her lungs filled again.

He grabbed the right side of her comforter and draped it over her so she was encased from neck to toe.

Statues of his sainthood would be built in honor of him

in this moment years from now, he was sure.

Slowly, her eyes fluttered open. "Luke?" she murmured sleepily.

"Hey, sweetie. I'm going to take off. Just wanted to say goodnight."

She shuffled up a bit toward the left side of the bed.

Thank God he'd covered her up. That didn't stop his eyes from roaming over the comforter as if he'd suddenly developed x-ray vision, however.

"It's late. Don't drive. Sleep here tonight," she offered drowsily, but firmly, one tiny hand reemerging from under the covers to reach out and intertwine their fingers together.

And just like that, he lost the battle before even putting up a fight.

Meanwhile, Dani slipped right back into sleep with a soft smile on her face, her hand holding his.

With a sigh—and a prayer—he laid down on the bed beside her, not even bothering to get under the sheet, what with his entire body running the equivalent of a fever. One hot, aroused fever. He was going to hurt for days after this one.

Smothering another grimace, he undid his jeans to get some strangled blood flow moving back up to his brain. But he left them on. No way in hell was he strong enough to get this close to Dani in bed without at least a layer of denim between them.

Throwing his free arm over his eyes, instead of sheep, he counted his throbbing heartbeats down south until he somehow managed to fall into a restless sleep.

His hand still held securely in hers.

And a contented—albeit strained—smile on his face to match hers as well.

———◆———

THE EARLY MORNING SUN didn't do nearly as effective a job of waking her up as the sound of Xoey's voice did.

"Hey, Dani. Why isn't the coffee started? Breakfast is getting—*OH!*" Xoey dropped the box of bakery fresh doughnuts in shock at the foot of Dani's bed.

Dani estimated the level of Xoey's shock was pretty high up there. Not just because she was still asleep in bed this late in the morning, but more so because she wasn't in said bed alone.

"Get out!" Dani launched a pillow at her.

Xoey shot out of the bedroom. "I'm so sorry!" she shouted as she closed the door behind her. "I figured it was safe! I thought you two were waiting till your fifth date to...hey, wait a sec, did I count wrong?"

"Just stop talking and go wait outside! Or better yet, wait down in the brewpub!" Dani jumped out of bed.

And instantly dropped flat as a pancake onto the carpet.

Good lord, she was *naked*.

And, criminy, she totally just gave herself a carpet burn on her belly.

Where the heck did her towel from last night go?

At the soft whoosh of falling terry cloth landing inches

from her face, she muttered, "Thanks."

"No problem," came Luke's amused reply.

Dani tucked the now dry bath towel around herself securely before peeking just her eyes and the bridge of her nose up from behind the tangle of goose down comforter lined-up like a trench barricade on her edge of the bed.

"Good morning, beautiful."

She popped her head up fully like a prairie dog, and asked the first burning question swirling around in her head. "Did we—"

The heated look he shot her stopped her from finishing that sentence.

"Honey, if we *had*, the trench barricade my soldier is failing to hide behind wouldn't be taller than yours right now."

Oh my.

A quick glance toward the center of her bed had her rising to her feet quicker than the sound of the national anthem had ever inspired. Furthermore, *she* wasn't the one saluting the flag in this case.

Before she could do so much as gape, however, he dragged her back up onto the bed beside him in one easy swoop.

With a sleepy morning growl, he gathered her into his arms and laid warm, rumbly kisses down the side of her neck. "Believe me Dani, the next time you wake up next to me in bed, you won't be *wondering* if we did, you'll damn well know it, remember it, and want more of it."

All evidence in front of her would certainly suggest so.

He nipped at her earlobe. "I can practically see your thoughts, sweetheart. Before you slaughter my control even more than you already have, put some clothes back on me in that pretty little head of yours and go take care of Xoey. I'm going to see how cold I can get your shower to run."

As she rushed out of the room to go demand her spare key back from Xoey, it registered belatedly that Luke had spent the entire night lying next to her, fully clothed and on *top* of her bed spread, just holding her hand.

A total gentleman.

With whom she fully intended to renegotiate the intolerable terms of their pesky five-date waiting period.

Seriously, whose crazy-ass idea had that been anyhow?

Chapter 15

IT WAS ONLY SEVEN P.M. and there was already a line at the entrance to Ocotillos for the night's festivities.

Impressed, Luke followed Dani as she headed up to the roof deck. After a no-holds-barred game of *strip* rock-paper-scissors—the masochistic woman's idea—not only had Luke won all of Dani's clothing sans her underwear but he had also gotten Dani to agree to let him nosily tag along to see what was going on in enemy camp this evening.

He had a sneaking suspicion she threw the entire game on purpose.

Now as he looked around the deck, he had absolutely no idea what to make of what he was seeing. Meanwhile, Dani was practically glowing as she studied his reaction.

There were games of every variety set-up everywhere in little stations of some sort. He did a double take. "Is that a *Twister* mat?"

Dani beamed. "Welcome to our second singles mixer."

He'd heard about their inaugural mixer last Sunday. By all accounts around town, it had been a rip-roaring success, kicking off first with beer tastings where everyone sampled various beer-food pairings before preparing their own unique beer-based recipes together at the couples' cooking stations.

"Some of them were great cooks, others comically disastrous," Dani had detailed joyously the next day. "But really, none of it mattered. It was just a means to get the singles to have fun, connect, and take pleasure in the other's company, along with the fruits of their labor."

Remembering her excitement, Luke smiled and looked around at yet another showing of Dani's creativity. "So instead of cooking stations, this week, you've set out board games?"

"Yep!" Dani led him around the deck eagerly. "Seeing a few of the couples get a little competitive with the cooking last week gave me the inspiration. Aside from the beer tastings again, we set up buffet food along with different games all around the deck so the feel was like game night at a house party. There are a bunch of games to choose from, all of which require pairing as a couple." Her eyes danced. "This way, they'll get acquainted faster."

"*Really* acquainted." Luke chuckled when he saw that Xoey had typed out her own set of adapted, spicier directions and game pieces for *Charades, Taboo,* and *Pictionary.*

She sighed. "That one was Xoey's idea. The English language can be a loaded grenade in Xoey's brain."

He chuckled his approval, and then shook his head

tragically when his eyes moved on to the table next to the board games with his chocolates. Sitting next to blowtorches. "Ah, the chocolate massacre area, I presume?"

Her shoulders lifted in humor. "Yep, the make-your-own-dessert bar of beer fondue and beer cracker s'mores, along with beer-flavored floats and sundaes."

Pausing for a second, she bit her lip and turned a questioning gaze his way. "Does the game theme seem too juvenile? I just thought it would be fun for couples to work together to annihilate the other couples, but..."

He pulled her into his arms. "I'm sure everyone here is as bloodthirsty as you, my dear." Kissing away the worry lines on her forehead, he pointed over to folks amusedly discussing the selection of games. "Look, it's already a hit. I think you've got a winner here, sweetie. Really."

She let out the breath she'd been holding in relief. "You know, even after our little wager is over, I'm thinking of keeping a scaled-down version of all this up here—weekly beer tastings along with some games or activities."

An indulgent grin tilted his lips when her eyes widened, presumably in response to another crazy idea hitting her.

"Dance contests!" she exclaimed.

He arched an eyebrow. "Dance contests?"

"Sure! Some basic, fun partner dances like the Tango or a spicy Latin number. Xoey could teach them and they could all have a dance-off."

"That does actually sound like a fun way to get to know people," he admitted.

She looked at the couples all around. "I just really want everyone to have a good time."

With a tender gaze, he threaded a hand through her hair and looked in her eyes. "You really do, don't you? You just want them to enjoy their dates."

"Of course."

Huh. If it were Quinn at the reins, customer happiness would be important, sure, but their experience would still be congruent to the bottom line. Not so for Dani though—she simply wasn't built that way.

He pulled her in close. "You're amazing. Have I told you that lately?"

"Not in the last hour." Her hand flew up to cover his mouth. "Oh no you don't. If you lay your sweet talk on me, we'll end up doing a lot more than what we did that first night in the storage closet."

Really, the woman was just arguing against herself now.

He tried convincing her without words to take a stroll down to that memorable closet now. She inhaled a shuddering breath and covered his heated eyes with her other hand. "Enough of that too. When you look at me like that, my clothes tend to want to fall off."

Her eyes dilated when his teeth gently scored her palm. "Okay, that's it," she muttered. "Out you go. You need to take your sneaky enemy distractions back to your turf."

He tried his best to look wounded.

"Save that look for after Valentine's Day when Ocotillos declares victory," she poked with oodles of sass. "You *have* seen the preliminary online voting tallies, haven't you?" She blinked prettily with a patronizing pat on his arm.

His gorgeous foe was having the time of her life rubbing it in and egging him on. Yes, according to preliminary feedback online and around town, it did seem Ocotillos had a slight edge in the throwdown voting, but only by a slim margin. "Don't get too comfortable on top, honey because you just gave me an idea for one last romantic promotion that'll be our surprise sprint to the finish this week."

Already, he could see the thrill of the new hurdle in their game already hitting Dani as well. Eyes glinting in challenge, she unconsciously touched the tip of her tongue to one of her canine teeth, almost as if testing its sharpness, the way she did whenever he goaded her. So sexy.

"Okay, well you all have fun with this little event of yours. I'm going to get started on this new idea of mine." He dropped a kiss on her lips and left before she could pry any details out of him. As he headed to the stairs, he could feel Dani's curious, hot gaze on his back.

A few steps down the stairwell, he chuckled when he overheard Xoey's comment to Dani: "You two have the most bizarre form of foreplay."

———◆———

LUKE HOPPED ON HIS office computer to check the shop's blog page to see if there had been any activity since he'd launched his little challenge yesterday.

A smile hit his lips when he saw exactly what he'd hoped to see in the response threads to his post today.

Random acts of romance.

Last night, seeing all that Dani was doing to make magic happen between perfect strangers at Ocotillos had made Luke realize he'd been focusing more on his 'new' Valentine's Day rules and less on the root of the holiday itself, *the people* Dani had been focusing on all along.

Hence, his little late-in-the-game play.

When he'd first come up with the idea, he'd gotten a little high off the holiday spirit, wanting eagerly to spread the holiday cheer of punch-drunk romance far and wide. This intoxicated buzz of his was what had led to the decision that February 13th would see not just this challenge, but every customer getting two free chocolates of their choosing to share with someone special in the spirit of random romance.

A Valentine's Day fluffer, if you will.

He called it the Random Act of Romance challenge. Today, on the day before all the teddy bears, roses, and lace-scalloped gifts, he was challenging folks to take some time to do a simple, random act of romance from the heart. No purchases necessary.

Further, he was encouraging folks to post their stories on the Desert Confections blog in hopes that one random act would inspire another. Of all who posted, five random posters would get a certificate for a couple's massage at a popular Scottsdale spa that specialized in gender-perfect pampering.

Feeling like a postman at the North Pole, Luke grinned

as he clicked open the first entry.

Interestingly, it wasn't an entry, but rather, an editorial post from a sixty-seven year old woman writing about how random acts were what kept her and her husband's romance going strong. She explained how just this morning, her very non-mushy husband of forty years had surprised her by reprogramming all her favorite shows into the blank queue of the DVR box they'd just replaced and taking the extra time to also add a few new shows he thought she might enjoy. Better than diamonds or pearls, his doing this tedious task for her was just one of the many unthinkingly thoughtful ways he always made her feel more loved than any store-bought gift ever had and ever could.

That non-entry post had gotten a flood of likes, and it had clearly set the tone for the actual entries that followed.

From there, the stories ranged from surprise lunch-hour walks to alarm-set text message exchanges on the hour every hour declaring one special thing about the other person.

The one from the man whose young wife was on her second year of deployment had garnered a lot of comments thanks to the video clip he'd provided of him belting out a laughingly off-key, but still very touching rendition of his wife's favorite song by Rascal Flatts *with* the accompaniment of thirty of her fellow service men and women behind her who he'd arranged to join in. The performance, along with her teary-eyed reaction to it all was all captured on video so she could replay it whenever she missed him.

Speaking of which.

Luke grabbed his cell phone and send Dani a quick text.

>> *I miss you...what are you wearing?*

Not a minute later, Dani texted back:

>> *A T-shirt that reads: Chocolate=Good, Beer=Bad, Which do you want ME to be?*

Grinning, he had an answer for her right away, but before he could send it, his phone beeped again. A second message from Dani:

>> *P.S. I miss you too. What say I come over in a bit so we can test out one of YOUR storage closets this time.*

Hot damn, he was head over heels for this woman.

———•———

DANI RE-READ THE text she'd just sent Luke, wondering if right this instant was too soon to make good on her text...

Nope, she decided a second later.

Grinning, she shut her office door and headed out.

Was a part of her wanting to butter him up? Admittedly, yes. Come hell or high water, tonight was the night she was going to tell Luke about the I-tried-to-sabotage-your-shop situation. He deserved to know. She was positive they'd get through this. It was in the past and nothing terrible had come of it. True, he might be upset that she hadn't told him earlier but no matter. Even if they ended up getting into an argument, she didn't want this cloud hovering over their relationship anymore. His trust was too important to her.

He was too important to her.

Yup. Though she'd fought it, she'd gone and gotten attached to Luke, that much was clear.

Looked like she really was her father's daughter.

But being a second generation for this masochist affliction of the heart had its benefits. From here on out, she was going into this relationship with Luke with her eyes wide open, and her heart closely guarded…to protect it from the utter doom her father had gone through.

She just had to keep reminding herself about her and her dad's shared history in that regard. Love isn't always kind to the Dobsons. Simple as that.

There wasn't a rule that said she couldn't enjoy the ride along the way, however.

Starting with a random act to show him how she felt.

Unfortunately, the presence of a local news van parked right outside the front entrance of Ocotillos waylaid her mission before its launch. Puzzled, she walked over to the news reporter, Paul something-or-another from the funny hour-long news at five.

"Can I help you with something?" she asked him.

The reporter glanced from her to a piece of paper in his hand that had her photo and a bunch of notes on it. "Oh good, you're Dani, the owner and brewmaster here right?" She nodded, and he flashed a perfect white grin at her. "I'm Paul Edison. I was just coming in to meet you. Our station heard about this throwdown between you and the chocolate shop next door so they sent me over to see if I could snag a human interest piece for our pre-Valentine's segment tonight. Are you game? It'll just be a few questions."

"Sure," she replied, joining him over by the cameras under the brewpub sign.

Paul had a quick word with his sound guys as a stack of papers got thrust in his face right before his cell phone rang from his pocket. He answered and hung up quickly. "Geez, they're rushing us on this one. Sorry, Dani. You okay to get started?" At her nod, he swiftly explained, "Okay, we've been slotted a few minutes for the segment but keep your replies short just in case they need to cut things down when it airs—" His phone rang again and he silently motioned to her that they'd be ready to shoot in one minute. The equipment got set up in a blur around her and before she knew it, Paul had a wide smile pasted on his face as the cameraman stuck on a headset and gestured a silent countdown with his fingers. *Three, two, one...*

"Thanks, Jane," said Paul on cue. "I'm here in Cactus Creek where some of you may have heard of the battle brewing in the world of romance. Two local businesses—the ever popular brewpub Ocotillos and the new chocolate shop on the block Desert Confections—have been going head-to-head with promotions and activities to encourage romance for the past month and a half. Now, I know what you're all thinking. Chocolate has always been playing in this arena next to flowers, but beer? This Valentine season, Dani Dobson has been showing everyone why beer is now a contender."

Dani waved at the camera.

"So, Dani, we've been hearing about these...let's call 'em atypical promotions you've been having at Ocotillos to inspire romance. Can you tell us a little about it?"

"Sure, Paul. We've set up what we call the 'Meddling Cupids' dating network through our website where friends set their friends up on blind dates." It was an idea she'd come up with, reasoning that since people are always trying to hook up their friends, why not make it bigger, better...and throw in some beer? With the help of one of their regulars, a techie over at ASU, Ocotillos had launched the finished site a few weeks ago. Pulling out her smartphone, she showed the TV viewing audience the *Meddling Cupids* link off the Ocotillos website. "It's like an online dating site but the actual single people don't do any interacting—just their friends. So basically, if you have a friend you want to set-up, you log in and input your friend's info and photo on the site. Then you search the postings and interact with other folks who are also setting up their friends. If both sets of friends think it would be a good match, they arrange for the couple to meet for the first time tomorrow on Valentine's Day for a date totally arranged by their meddling cupids."

Paul glanced at the camera. "You don't happen to have a file on me in there do you? From my mother? I wouldn't put it past her; she's been hinting about grandkids for years," he kidded as Dani laughed alongside him.

"So for tomorrow's meddling cupid dates, are they going to be like the singles mixers you've been having here on Sunday nights? I've heard a lot about them."

"Those were totally different, a lot more laidback. The mixers have mostly been beer tastings and other fun activities that pretty much defy the traditional stuffy blind dates. It's been a lot of fun. We love seeing blind dates go so well."

"You sure the beer isn't playing a role in all that success?" he teased lightly.

She didn't miss a beat. "Well, if you ask me, good beer and good dates *do* go hand in hand."

"That's always been my motto," he winked. "Okay, so then what do you think about this whole two-part Valentine's holiday your chocolate shop adversaries are promoting?"

"Actually—" she paused dramatically before flashing a comically reluctant grin. "I think the idea itself is rather great…even if it was a chocolatier who came up with it," she added with a teasing grin. "I really do love the idea of having two separate days. Plus, it's genius to give guys a month to prepare to reciprocate on March 14th," she chuckled. "Though it pains me to admit it, I think Desert Confections has a winning idea on their hands here."

Suddenly, a small group of random college guys took their five seconds of fame by chanting into the camera from behind her, *"Beer! Beer! Beer!"*

The crowd in front of the brewpub cheered and hooted.

She laughed. "I guess they're not voting chocolate tomorrow."

"Looks like this heated rivalry between you and your neighbor has been great for business in these parts." Paul directed the camera man to take a shot at the now swarming street corner, before firing off another question from his notes, "So can we expect more throwdown action around here for Desert Confections' White Chocolate Day in March as well?"

"Unfortunately, we'll be busy with Arizona Beer Week after Valentine's Day. But, we will be back with our own Asian holiday import on *April* 14th. That's a unique holiday devoted to all you singles out there so you better believe Ocotillos will have something off the wall planned."

"Very cool. Okay, any last things you want to add in the time remaining, Dani?"

"Maybe just a little reminder for folks to come down for the concert we'll be having this weekend to celebrate our crushing victory tomorrow," she threw in for fun.

"Ouch, you're aiming for the gracious win, I see."

Her eyes twinkled at that. "Trust me, my opponent expects nothing less from me."

"Ah, sounds like there's no love lost there between you two. Too bad. A lot of the gals at the station were hoping the online gossip about you and the enemy being madly in love was true," he lamented playfully.

Say what? Where the heck had *that* come from? Dani froze. An uncomfortably long split second stretched past as she attempted to find an answer for Paul. And herself.

A reporter to his very core, Paul's eyes took on a new light as he found the stray thread of a story here and began pulling. "Or *is* it true? You and your archrival falling in love *would* be the ultimate fairytale ending to this Valentine standoff. There something to the rumors?"

There was that made-for-TV laugh of his again.

Tongue-tied over the grating stranger trying to unlock a closet where she'd been shoving her feelings into for a reason, she just smiled awkwardly and said the first thing that popped in her head. "Sorry to disappoint but what you see is what you get. No fairytale love story. This is just a good ole-fashioned pistols-at-dawn duel. All in fun."

She blinked and stared at the camera, replaying her answer in her head, stunned at how the words were making her eyes feel waxy and the air in her lungs sift like sawdust.

What the hell just happened?

"Well there you have it, folks. While love may not be in the cards for this dueling duo, the romance revolution they've started in this throwdown has certainly stirred up love for folks all across Arizona. Of course the question still remains, on this Valentine's Day, which will *you* vote for: chocolate or beer?" Paul flashed his cheesy smile one last time. "Coming to you live from Cactus Creek. Back to you, Jane."

———•———

LUKE WAS RUNNING ON FUMES by the time he made it back to the shop for his evening shift. He'd had so many corporate deliveries he'd been forced to work right though his normal schedule. Worse still, being out all day, he hadn't even been able to see Dani today as they'd planned. *That* truly had sucked since he'd really been looking forward to it.

Checking the time, he reasoned that there was just enough time before the concert for Luke to sneak Dani out for a little random romancing. He grinned and went into Quinn's office to see if she could keep working for just a tiny bit longer.

Quinn jumped about three feet in the air when she saw him. "Luke! What are you doing here?" She propped her hip awkwardly on her desk and glanced uneasily at her computer.

His eyes narrowed. "What's going on?"

"Nothing!"

"You've always been a bad liar." Sweeping her to the side, he went over to her computer screen and found himself more confused. It was just a video news clip.

"You know, I really need to get back to—"

His look silenced her. Pushing her hands away from the keyboard, he rewound the video back to the beginning and hit play.

It was Dani, looking particularly cute as she answered some news reporter's questions for the five o'clock news. Luke's nerves relaxed. Was this all Quinn was freaked out about? More chocolate vs. beer stuff? Funny, he figured Quinn would welcome the attention—

His smile fell apart when he heard Dani's final answer in the interview. Her flippant comment dismissing the possibility that she and Luke were in love slashed him right in the gut. It wasn't just hearing the words that stung. It was seeing the stricken expression on her face that proclaimed the mere idea of being in love so far from any realm of possibility for her.

"Luke, I'm sure she didn't mean that how it sounded."

He remained silent, staring at the blank screen long after the clip ended.

Quinn put a comforting hand on his arm. "Don't blow this out of proportion."

He shrugged her off and headed out the door.

She ran after him. "Luke, stop. Cool down a bit before you head over there."

"I just want to talk to her," he said quietly.

Walking into Ocotillos, Luke didn't know what he was going to say or what he thought would happen when he saw Dani. One thing was for sure—he hadn't expected to see Dani and Rylan up in her office, heads low, voices hushed in deep conversation, arms wrapped tight around each other. Luke's feet cemented in place. Hands fisting, he watched as Rylan gently smoothed back Dani's hair to comfort her while she continued to spill her heart out. What they were discussing, he couldn't hear. But it didn't matter. The harsh reality of what he was seeing delivered a blow to his solar plexus sharp enough that the details would've just been overkill.

She was confiding in him. That was why the current expression on Dani's face was one Luke had never seen. Until this precise moment, Luke hadn't realized how very little he knew about Dani or how surface level their time together had really been. She'd never once let him in the way she was doing now...with another man.

Honestly, Luke thought it would've been better if he'd caught her making out with Rylan instead; at least that wouldn't have been as personal, or cut so deep. The twisting pain he was feeling in his belly was worse than betrayal. It was raw doubt of the loneliest form that came from looking in a window at everything he couldn't have, just inside.

What was it she'd told that reporter dick in the interview? *'No love story here...All in fun.'*

Yeah, that's all their relationship thus far had been. Seeing her with Rylan, a man who clearly had a significant and permanent place in her life, made that fact painstakingly obvious.

Blind frustration soon turned into numb hurt. He felt like the ground around him was cracking, like everything he'd recently started believing in again was slipping away. But why? It wasn't as if he'd expected Dani to feel the same way he was starting to, right?

Vaguely, it registered that Quinn was now standing beside him, seeing what he saw.

Without a word, Luke turned away from them all and left the building.

Chapter 16

THE CONCERT TURNED OUT to be a raging success. Ocotillos had been packed, the musicians had all had a blast, and Dani had been thrilled to see the appreciative crowd of singles and couples alike all dancing and having a great time.

Exhausted, Dani fell into her office chair and spun around so she could prop her feet up on the bookshelf behind her desk. Glancing at her phone, she saw she'd missed a call from her brother Derek. With a tired shrug, she ignored his voicemail for the time being. Really, the only voice she wanted to hear right now was Luke's. But for some reason, she couldn't bring herself to call him, an affliction she'd been dealing with all day. As a result, this was now the longest they'd gone without talking to each other...and the fact that she'd felt every lost minute was an unsettling portrait of how much she's changed in the last month and a half.

Yet another reason to feel discombobulated today.

The news reporter asking her about being madly in love with Luke had really messed with her brain. All day since, she'd questioned everything—and doubted even more. Like the plague, spreading until it consumed her, the doubts and questions mocked her, reminded her that she wasn't at all the woman a romantic like Luke deserved. Her eyes slid to the glaring evidence of that fact sitting on her bookshelf—the Valentine gift she was planning to give Luke.

Her first Valentine ever.

Choosing it had been a weird experience—thrilling-until-you-felt-naked sort of weird. She'd spent more time on this gift than on dozens of birthday and Christmas presents in the past combined. Each possible gift idea she'd rejected before this one had undergone tireless scrutiny and prompted endless unanswerable questions about their relationship.

How did people do it each year? It was ridiculous.

Leaning against the chair, she peeked at the gift again through one eye, seeing the second laughable evidence of her questionable sanity. She'd swathed the gift in red wrapping paper with pink and gold hearts and loads of shining curly ribbon. What had she been thinking?

She *hadn't* been thinking. That was the problem. Lately, she wasn't thinking like herself at all. Stranger still, as lost as she felt lately, when she was with Luke, she felt *found* as well.

Not exactly a less scary revelation.

Picking up the Valentine gift, she peered at it and saw a stranger reflected back at her.

Without knowing exactly why she did it, she found

herself slowly untying the bow, watching as it fell to her lap. She slid her nail under the clear piece of tape next, pulling it off to peel back the bright wrapping paper. Soon, the gift box was stripped bare, totally unadorned.

That was more her, right? No surprises to look forward to but no disappointments either.

"Who's the valentine gift from?"

Dani gasped and spun around.

Luke stepped into her office, his expression growing darker as he watched her shove the book-sized box into a drawer. "Who gave you that gift, Dani? The one you were just opening like it held life's secrets." His voice was raw, gritty.

And hurt.

Her eyes widened in confusion. "What's wrong? Are you okay?" She shot over to him, shutting the door.

"Well, first I saw the woman I'm falling in love with dismiss our relationship on air, and now I see her staring at a Valentine gift that isn't from me. So no, I'm not okay."

She flinched at the stark pain tearing through her chest...until her emotions boomeranged back and changed to shock when she replayed the first part of his sentence. "You're falling in love with *me*?"

His expression turned exasperated. "Who else?"

"I j-just wasn't sure that you...I mean, you've never said..." His sad, stony expression tore at her heart. "I can explain that interview. The guy just caught me off guard."

"Then answer that same question for me. Is it really that one-sided between us? Am I the only one feeling there's

209

something more happening between us here? Something real? Something with a future?"

Shocked, she didn't know what to say. It was too soon. For reasons she hadn't had a chance to explain to him yet.

"Explain it to me," he murmured, reading her mind. He brushed the side of her face with his fingertips. "Please. Just tell me why you're purposely keeping me at a distance. Xoey, Rylan, most of your workers, you let them in in ways you never have with me. Why is that?"

An impossibly long minute passed and Luke just stood there with the most caring look in his eyes, comforting her unconditionally for reasons he didn't even understand yet.

"They've been a part of my life longer," she answered lamely, giving him most of the truth.

"It's more than that and you and I both know it. Hell, I've even heard you make future plans with *Quinn*. Meanwhile, you specifically avoid any talk about us in the future. You act like our being a temporary thing is a foregone conclusion. You actively cut yourself off when you catch yourself making a plan with me that's too far in the future. Why, sweetheart? Why does everyone else have a potential place in your future except for me." He stared at her, demanding her to acknowledge the truth of his words.

"Because none of them will break me," she all but cried out. "I know none of them will suddenly decide they don't want to be a part of my life, tear the foundation out from under me, and leave me unable to stand back up again."

She stopped, her breathing ragged, her eyes no longer

hiding anything as they met his. "None of *them* will steal back the place in my heart I've entrusted to them and leave it so it can't become whole again."

"And you think I will?" Luke looked at her incredulously as he hauled her into his arms.

"No...I don't know. But you're the first person who's gotten close enough to be able to in a really long while."

He said nothing more, just held her patiently. Waiting...

His silence eventually rattled her nerves to its boiling point. "I was perfectly fine with all my hang-ups until now, you know. Then you come barging into my life, being so freakin' perfect and turning my wonderfully comfortable, live-only-in-the-moment life on its ass. And suddenly, I find myself *wanting* to plan a future with you. *That's* why I have to keep reminding myself— *Stop smiling, dammit!* I can feel you smiling!"

He tipped her perturbed face up to his, and then quickly bent down and kissed the frown from her lips. "So you *do* think we could have a future."

She harrumphed and remained stubbornly silent.

His face turned serious then. "Dani, I'm not going anywhere. You can trust—"

"NO," she cut him off in rough denial, her voice firm, distant. "Don't promise me anything like that. Just...*don't.*"

Luke frowned, and she could see him struggling not to pry. She hadn't told him anything about her past relationships. And she wasn't going to.

"Dani," he said quietly, "look at the universe's track record with my life." He shrugged self-deprecatingly. "I know more than most guys that there are no guarantees in life. While I can't make any guarantees, I can tell you what I *do* know. I know how I feel about you. And my not knowing what the future holds isn't going to stop me from wanting you in my life." He turned her face up to his. "What I need to know is if that's enough for you to let me start being a real part of your life too."

Her eyes searched his. "I want it to be," she breathed.

He exhaled raggedly. "That's a start."

"But...it might take time—"

"I'm not in a rush."

"I may screw up a lot along the way."

"I'm sort of expecting that."

Smothering back a smile, she gazed up at him for a few heart-thudding beats.

"I'll try," she said finally.

"I'll take it." He swept her into his arms and kissed her long and hard.

When he finally let her up for air a long while later, she saw it. The unfiltered trust now naked in his eyes where there was once a wary curtain of 'casual' affection showed her just how much he'd been holding back for her benefit.

She couldn't possibly take this relationship one step further without being sure he knew exactly what he was getting into. How broken she was. More than he probably realized.

And also...how she'd very nearly jeopardized his life's work just a few months ago... "Luke, there's something I've been meaning to tell you—" she began softly.

212

"Just one last question—" he said at the same time.

She shook her head nervously. "You go first."

"You sure?" The second she nodded, his words rushed out as if a dam had broken. "Okay, will you *please* tell me who gave you that Valentine gift? It's making my gut burn. I won't get mad, and I swear I won't attack the guy."

Something told her he'd crossed his fingers behind his back before making that declaration. She shifted her eyes from her desk drawer back to him. Back to the drawer.

"I'm faster than you," he assured, correctly judging her intent.

"It's not a gift for me," she said slowly. "It's a gift *from* me."

"For who?!" he demanded at a near growl.

She rolled her eyes.

A light entered his. "Me?" His expression became achingly tender and then utterly confused. "Wait, if it's for me, why did you unwrap it? Are you not going to give it to me anymore?" He frowned. "Wait, this isn't an apology gift is it? Because of that interview with the douchebag on the news?"

Cringing, she looked up at him with regret written all over her face. "I swear, that guy just caught me off guard. I didn't know what to say. I mean I haven't even admitted it to you yet. Why would I say it on air?" she rambled.

Every muscle in his body locked, as a slow, meaningful smile stretched across his face. "You said 'yet' just now."

Her lips became a flat line, to avoid letting any more damning evidence slip out before she was ready.

Grabbing the gift, she stuffed it into his hands.

His smile dissolved and his eyes softened with affection. "Are you sure, sweetie? Honestly, I'll understand if you're not ready to—"

"Oh, just open it."

He took it from her gently, as if it did indeed hold all of life's secrets.

"It's no big deal. It's just a silly—"

He quickly placed his fingers on her lips. "Don't. Let me open it. Let me experience it."

She watched as Luke's eyes widened when he saw what was nestled inside the box.

A photo of the two of them. She distinctly remembered the day captured in the photo, though neither of them could've possibly known a camera was on them. She and Luke had been eating lunch at Ocotillos, and he'd automatically passed her the Sriracha sauce she liked on her sandwiches. The camera had caught the expression on her face when she'd looked up at him in surprise. In that one moment, she'd looked so unguarded, so happy, so…in love.

Seeing the photo again made her heart swell with the same feelings she'd had that day.

"Xoey took that picture with her camera phone one day when we were here," mumbled Dani, shoving her hands into her pockets nervously. "I thought you might like it."

He nodded, still speechless as his gaze shifted to the intricate brushed-steel frame holding the photo. In silent wonder, Luke slid a finger along the carved ridges, instantly identifying the twined images scrolling all around the metal perimeter. "Dani, where did you get this?"

Shrugging, she casually explained, "I had it made. My friend knows a tattoo artist who also does metal etch work so I drew a design and asked him to carve it. It's nothing fancy..."

"It's juniper and hops," he broke in, his voice rough with emotion. "It's you and me."

She blinked past her surprise. "Yes."

"I love it," he said softly.

Embarrassed, she tried to put the cover back on the box. "It's just a little trinket."

"Dani," he rumbled tenderly, "I won't let you keep insulting this amazing gift you've given me." With no more warning than that, Luke brought his lips down on hers, swallowing her gasp as he tugged her into a long, hot kiss that left them both breathless.

"But it *is*. It's just a—"

His eyes gleamed like hot coals before he raided her mouth again.

"—Valentine," she substituted weakly, trembling by the time he lifted his lips from hers.

"One that speaks volumes," he pointed out with rough male satisfaction.

She raised an eyebrow at his possessive tone and swept an investigative glance down south to the now very snug fit of his jeans. A slow, enticing smile lit her face. "This is not *that* big a deal," she argued, her eyes glittering in a silent dare. "It's barely a gift."

Looking both amused and turned on, he lunged forward and caught her around the waist, lifting her onto her desk for another drugging kiss. Before he could go for an extra dose of word exorcising, however, he stopped and looked around. Cursing silently, he then pulled back.

At least he tried to.

The rocking of her hips against his was severely hampering his progress.

"*Jesus*. Why are you forever arguing with me?"

"It's like foreplay," she admitted, pressing her lips to his neck, trying to drive him wild with tongue and teeth, suction and heat. "Know what comes after foreplay?"

Luke groaned and quickly backed away. "Honey, try to remember we're in your office," he reasoned, in a voice that said he was seconds away from forgetting it himself.

Dani closed in on him, tracking him as she pulled her t-shirt over her head. "There are only a few people left here and they're all up on the roof. The walls are plaster, the door solid oak," she replied, her voice thick, eyes hooded. "Soundproof."

"You're not thinking clearly, babe. It's the adrenaline—don't growl at me. I'm trying to be noble here, dammit. We can argue again later and have hot make-up sex. At *home*," he negotiated, looking very much like a man barely holding onto his resolve.

Slowly, she undid her jeans. "It wasn't the arguing; it was watching you open the"—her eyebrows pitched up in playful defiance—"*silly* gift." She grinned when he almost reacted. Then she grew serious. "That was the first time I felt..." Her voice went soft and she shrugged helplessly. "Honestly, I don't know what I'm feeling. All I know is that I want you." Stone-washed denim and a tiny scrap of lacy cotton puddled at her feet. "Right here, right now."

Pure, explosive desire flooded his face.

He hauled her up against him, his hands and mouth roaming every square inch of her body. As if he couldn't taste enough, touch enough.

Then he tore his lips away.

Breathing rough and ragged, starving eyes fixed on hers, he walked backward toward the couch. Silently demanding she follow. *Damn.* Her feet matched his step for step, her eyes drinking in the sight of him shedding his clothes in that masculine tug-and-throw method that was so criminally sexy to watch.

When she saw the condom appear in his hand, seemingly out of thin air, she all but pounced on him.

He caught her hips to keep her standing before him even as he settled back against the cushions, condom already impressively in place. "So, right here, right now, huh?" he repeated her words back to her in a smoky growl as his lips skimmed across her belly. Her knees buckled. But he wouldn't let her join him on the couch. "Because you feel the same way about me as I do about you?" Leaning forward, he trailed a path of soft kisses over her sensitive curves. Lower, and then lower still.

He was trying to torture the admission out of her...and

it was *almost* starting to work. "We covered that already," she replied evasively when she could catch her breath. "I said I did, didn't I?" She broke through his hold and managed to just barely straddle his thighs.

"No you didn't." He halted her final descent at the very last second, leaving her hovering midair. So temptingly close. "You didn't say it."

"It was implied," she sliced out jaggedly.

"Not good enough," he grated through his teeth, his ill-timed stubbornness showing no quarter as he jerked her to him and locked her hips against his torso with one arm, sliding his free hand up over the back of her thigh before slowly slipping his fingers between her legs in a barely-there touch that mirrored what his lips were doing to her nipples. First one, then the other. "Even if you're not ready to tell me you love me, at least admit you're falling for me, Dani."

Her eyes widened. Completely without defenses, she looked at him, straight into his heart, his soul.

The same way he was looking at her.

When he shifted, kissing hot flesh to even hotter flesh, she snapped. "*Fine!* I admit it. Happy?! I'm falling so hard for you that—" Air hissed through her teeth when his hands clenched and drove her down onto him.

Swiftly, he flipped her onto her back and gripped the back of the couch, knuckles strained white. "I'm falling hard for you too," he rasped roughly before surging into her with a force that stole her breath. Eyes locked on hers, he moved with arduously bridled thrusts.

Achingly slow at first, and then harder, mind-wreckingly deep as his stormy eyes gazed down at her with an almost primitive hunger that stole what little breath she had remaining in her lungs.

Soon, she was clutching his shoulders as shivers of electricity shot down her spine, and waves of blinding sensations built to a crest from her core. Her body arched as the unexpected, explosive release charged through her, whipping all around, throwing her into a vortex of twisting pleasure she'd never before felt. It swept through her, jolting her again and again, scattering her until she was soon mindless, boneless as one last current of pleasure pulled her under a tidal wave of bliss.

Never had she come that hard in her life.

"God, I'll never get tired of seeing that," whispered Luke against her skin.

Draped against him, languid and boneless, Dani belatedly realized that he had let her rip through her orgasm without seeking his own. The aftershocks that were ebbing through her were undoubtedly torturing his still savagely rigid arousal, yet he simply held her, letting her body settle into a luscious slumber. She raised her eyes to his in question.

He tilted her chin up to collect an untamed kiss. "Remember what we were arguing about the other day? How I think pro sports officials using video replay more and more is changing the game?" he asked, his voice turbulent as he hungrily explored her ear with his tongue.

She could barely remember her own name, let alone

whatever he was talking about.

"Hmmm?" she managed.

Pretty good effort on her part, considering.

"I decided you're right, sweetheart; *it* can be a good thing." He slid behind her and placed slow, deliberate kisses up her spine.

"It?" she managed to stutter out, the incredible sensations stealing the oxygen required for anything beyond monosyllabic answers.

He gave her a wolfish grin by way of reply as he plunged back into her soft heat to prove just how right *it* could be.

Twice.

Hours later, back at her apartment, snuggled in bed next to Luke, it vaguely occurred to her she was supposed to tell him something. But as her eyelids grew heavy and her brain fuzzy, she couldn't reach the niggling reminder. Even the muffled ringing coming from the living room seemed miles away. Her cordless phone, perhaps? It was probably wedged in her sofa cushions.

The long message being left on her all-too-neglected answering machine was so faint and static-filled, she couldn't even make out the words...

———◆———

"Hey, sis! Man, this is the longest we've ever gone without talking. I miss you! The honeymoon is going great. Vienna was amazing. So were Verona and Naples—hence our lack of calls all this time. It's

been an unbelievable few weeks. I swear, I should have planned for more time in that part of Europe; we'd spend a month just in Italy if we could."

"Anyway, enough about us. Jonathan and I have been hearing all the titillating gossip from Xoey, which I'm assuming is the reason for the lack of calls on your part. We're dying to hear more about you and this Luke fella so you better get ahold of us soon, sister-dear. Although Jonathan says he'll settle for an email if you send a photo of Luke with it. The one Xoey took on her phone is way too blurry. It's like the man didn't know a camera was on him..."

A car horn blares

"Okay, okay, our ride is here. We've been in Greece all week; we're in Santorini now wrapping up our trip. Remember, we're flying back in on Valentine's Day so don't forget to pick us up from the airport. We have a bet going on whether you'll actually remember to get us this time. I'm keeping my fingers crossed that you'll actually check your voicemail this week."

Indistinct laughter in the background

"Oh, by the way, oddest thing, I got a voicemail from Noah the other day. Something about a winery? I have no idea what he was talking about, and since I promised Jon I'd stop checking my phone for the rest of the trip do you think you could swing by Harold's to see if he knows what's up? Who knows, maybe it'll fit in with my new grand plans in life—I'll tell you more about that work epiphany when I'm home. See you soon. Love you."

click

221

Chapter 17

"SHOOT, WHAT'S WITH all this beer? Where can I get some *chocolate* in this town?" boomed an obnoxiously loud man at the bar.

Dani gasped and dropped everything she was holding, almost taking out a waiter around the corner in her mad dash to the front. "Nice entrance," she called out, laughing as she hurled herself into the awaiting arms of her one and only big brother. "Sheesh, you look like hell."

Derek planted a big kiss on her forehead. "Aw, and I missed you too, sweets."

She grinned, looking around. "Where's Jonathan?"

"Exhausted from the flight. We got in early. No worries, he'll be here later." He grabbed a seat with her at the nearest table. "So? What's been going on the last two months?"

"You first. How was the honeymoon? And leave out the TMI parts please."

"The honeymoon was incredible. I'm glad we held out for a longer trip; experiencing Europe like that made it tough to leave." Sighing wistfully, his eyes danced as he looked over at her. "Though I admit it's nice to return to the same old, same old." Tsking, he shook his head with a smile. "You made me lose twenty bucks to Jonathan at the airport today."

Confusion knitted her brow.

He pitched his voice high, in what was presumably an insulting imitation of her. "I swear I won't forget to pick you guys up this time..." He rolled his eyes teasingly. "I left a reminder on your home answering machine and everything. Your cellphone inbox is full by the way."

Her mouth fell open. "Dang it!" She cringed, smiling sheepishly. "That's right. *I* was your ride home today. I'm so sorry, Derek. Things have just been nuts around here lately."

He ruffled her hair affectionately. "We figured. From what I hear, plotting to take down a neighboring business and then falling madly in love with its owner can be very exhausting."

Dani's eyes narrowed into slits. "You know, ever since you became Xoey's gay BFF, all you two do is gossip about me," she huffed, looking around for the perpetrator in question.

"Oh, that's not true at all. Until you met this Luke guy, your life was way too boring."

She punched him in the arm. "I am not boring. Keep up this abuse and the bottles of wine I keep for you in the back are going right down the drain." Her eyes widened in mock dismay. "Then you'll have to drink *beer* with your meals here!"

"You are a cruel, merciless woman," laughed Derek, approvingly. "I've trained you well. Okay, I take it all back. Xoey and I did nothing but talk about you while you were dull as a doorknob but as soon as you got interesting, we didn't gossip about you at all!"

"Actually, that's the closest you've ever come to apologizing to me. Good doing business with you." Chuckling, she called over a waiter and ordered the plate of fancy tapas that Javier always made especially for Derek whenever he came in along with the secret bottle of Spanish wine she'd picked up recently and stashed in the kitchen in honor of his return.

Derek sighed. "I still say it's a crying shame you don't serve wine here."

Dani swallowed back the lump in her throat, startled by her visceral reaction to even the thought of wine in conjunction to Ocotillos now. But she held her guilty conscience in check. Valentine's Day was hardly the right time to tell Derek the sad little tale of a brewpub-winery merger that was not to be. Finding out they'd been closer than ever to achieving his long held dreams but still not nearly close enough would be a hard blow to take...and deliver.

Next week, she promised herself.

Shining a bright smile at him, she laughed as she always did at his wine remark and gave him the response he'd come to expect. "You know where I stand. Beer is far superior for the stronger Latin and Mediterranean flavors on our menu."

"Spare me. You've given me the same beer speech with delicate Asian dishes too."

Very true. She grinned and lifted her palms unapologetically. "That's why I'm a brewmaster and not a sommelier. Honestly, I still can't understand how the beer bug totally skipped over you. It left you completely unvaccinated for that nasty wine virus."

"Oh please, you beer elitist. Don't forget who you're talking to. Remember, I have firsthand knowledge that all Dobsons know their way around a wine cellar too. You may not like it, but your palate rivals that of a seasoned wine connoisseur."

"Shhh! You keep that dirty little secret to yourself!"

"Speaking of dirty little secrets." Derek's mouth tugged up at the corners. "What's this I hear about you having kinky loud sex in the office?"

Dani's hands clapped over her mouth in horror, her cheeks burning. "Xoey is DEAD!"

He laughed and hugged her to him. "Oh, don't go killing Xoey for news I would've pried out of one of the other workers anyway."

Keeping her face buried in his shoulder for a few seconds longer, she asked worriedly, "Did she say she literally 'heard' me and Luke in the office?"

"Actually, she only speculated; you just confirmed it for me. Thanks! Can't wait to update Xoey."

"Older brothers are *evil*," she muttered, lightly jabbing an elbow into his gut.

He chuckled unrepentantly. "Okay, so now that I know you and this Luke guy are at least semi-serious, tell me more about him."

"I've told you plenty."

"Boring facts I could find about him online. I want to know the deep, juicy stuff. Major flaws, skeletons in the closet, plans for world domination. And it *would* be nice to know if I'm going to need a tux and speech ready soon. Details, baby sis. I need details."

Dani conveniently chose to ignore the question she knew her brother most wanted the answer to. "Other than the fact that he's a hopeless romantic? No other flaws I can see."

"Hey, I'm a romantic, and so is Jonathan. Being a romantic man is not a flaw."

"If you say so. How'd you get like that anyway? Dad wasn't romantic at all, and neither am I. How come you're the only one with romantic genes in the family?" After thanking the waiter for bringing the food and wine, Dani slid the plate over to Derek and poured him a glass.

Derek looked at her like she'd already had a few. "Are you kidding me? Dad was the worst offender in the romance division."

"No he wasn't," she scoffed. "I remember mom used to complain about that very fact about dad, that he wasn't romantic enough."

"Dad was plenty romantic, I assure you," defended Derek with an underlying current in his voice. "Mom had just passed the point of being able to see it."

Dani gave him a sidelong glance. "Sounds like you know some things I don't."

His look became hooded, entrenched in secrets. "Comes with being the older brother." He broke eye contact and switched their focus to the plate of food in front of him as he quickly took a bite and groaned at the savory flavors. "I swear, I would give Javier my shares in the brewpub if he could teach Jonathan to cook like this."

At the abrupt, not so subtly dismissed chat about their mother and father, Dani's head clouded with more thoughts than she'd had about her parents' relationship in a while.

"You okay, sweetie?"

Turning her troubled eyes up to his, she attempted to get the words out. "I feel like...like I can't..." She bit her lip, suddenly feeling very much like the baby sister she knew Derek still saw her as. Finally she blurted out, "Do you think I'm abnormal? When it comes to love?"

A weary sigh trickled out of him. "I knew this would come up some day." His expression told her he'd much rather have the birds and the bees talk with her over this one.

She continued to gaze at him until he put down his fork and started talking. "When mom left, it was tough on all of us, but I think it was hardest on you in a lot of ways."

"What do you mean?"

"Well, growing up, you weren't ever really close to mom. You were always more like dad. And right about the time when you should've gotten to bond more with her, she left. At the time when a girl really needs her mom, you know?

Dad and I did all we could, but neither of us could replace that motherly insight into love and relationships you missed out on."

She nodded faintly. "So that's a yes to my being irrevocably messed up?"

"No. Let me finish. You need to hear the whole thing." He gripped her hand. "Do you...do you remember that mom met someone else while she was still with dad?"

Shock paled Dani's face.

"Yeah, I thought you'd made yourself forget that part. You were young, but I know you understood when you and I heard her talking on the phone with that other man one day in the kitchen. I saw the realization in your eyes when you heard mom sounding so different, so happy—it had been awhile. Hearing her so much in love...I don't think I ever heard her talk like that with dad."

Pain darkened his eyes at the memory. "I remember looking over at you and seeing you so lost and upset that I just grabbed your arm and ran us both out of the house."

"So that's why she left?" she whispered. "She was cheating on dad?"

He shook his head firmly. "No, she didn't cheat. Not really, anyway. But her heart was starting to drift, slowly but surely. And dad knew it too.

Now she was shaking her head. "No, he couldn't have. Mom left out of the blue."

"Dad did know, sweetie. Trust me on this. He fought for her too, damn hard. Don't you remember? Toward the end, every night, he came home to try and sweep her off her feet."

Suddenly the memories came bombarding back to Dani and she saw pain fill Derek's eyes as he watched it strike blow after blow.

"Dani, you have to know they tried. But as much as mom still loved dad, she just didn't feel about him the way he felt about her. Not by the end."

"Don't you try and make me feel sorry for her, Derek. There's no excuse for a mother to abandon her family. She didn't just break dad's heart; she broke ours too."

He took her shaking hands in his. "I'm not trying to make you feel anything about this. All I'm doing is trying to help you remember. You need to see the whole picture. When mom left, she'd only meant to leave dad, not us. She actually wanted to keep us as a part of her life. The only reason we weren't is because *you* wouldn't allow it."

"That's because she only wanted us on holidays. She left dad and then had the nerve to ask him to raise us and then spend holidays alone without family?! A bitch is what that made her," spat out Dani in disgust. The floodgates were open now and she just couldn't stop. "Of course I didn't want anything to do with her."

"And you never let her forget it," said Derek sadly. "For years, you sent back every letter she sent you with a 'return to sender, not interested' note slashed across the envelope."

"I had every right to."

"I know. You didn't forgive her. In a lot of ways, I didn't either. But, in some ways I did." He eyed her wearily before expelling a loaded, long-held breath. "Dani, I went to go see mom six years ago."

Dani swung a betrayed glare his way.

Derek was unapologetic. "You were just starting to take over the brewpub then so you were busy enough that you didn't even know I was gone. There was no real reasoning for it but something in me just wanted a chance to talk to her. So I flew up to go see her in Chicago."

Jaw locked, Dani looked down and fiddled with the table settings as conflicting emotions muddled her mind.

It took her a long while, but she finally managed to ask tightly, "So what did she have to say?"

"A lot of apologies mostly. Until I stopped her." Derek looked like he was trying to find the words to explain it to her. "After seeing her, I knew that, though I would never forgive her completely, I *would* be able to move on. And that made us more like strangers meeting for the first time that day. I told her I just wanted to spend the time getting to know her."

He smiled softly. "She turned into a different woman from when she was our mom, Dani. She became a lawyer. A great one, in fact. Well known for defending the little guy. She got married to the man we heard her on the phone with—" He swallowed a lump in his throat. "I didn't want to meet him. But, I did send him a card when mom died in the car accident a year later."

The tears that sprang into her eyes revealed that her heart hadn't totally cut off her mother.

Derek looked solemnly relieved at that. "She was an

amazing woman, Dani. I think you would've been real proud of her had you gotten to know her too. The life she had with her new husband...we'd never have been able to give her that. He loved her the way she'd loved him. The way dad had loved her until his dying day. That kind of love was something she just couldn't turn her back on."

"No! None of that means anything!" cried Dani. "I don't care if she met her soul mate. You don't just walk out on your husband and kids to be with some other guy."

"What did you want her to do instead? Tell me." Derek became almost brutal as he forced her to face the truth. "Did you want mom to stay with a man she only loved as a friend, knowing he loved her more than she ever could? Go through the motions every day and watch that love slowly kill them both? Did you want her to spend her life working in a brewery she never liked to begin with and instead never become the great legal mind that saved countless people throughout her career?"

Derek grabbed her hand to prevent her from turning away. "Did you want her to forego the happy life she eventually found just so she could be a mom for you and me? Because she would have. That would've been the only reason she would've stayed. Not for dad or anything else. *We* were the only thing that almost made her stay."

"Then why the hell didn't she?" Now Dani was tearing up, and it pissed her off since she seemed to be crying more in the last few months than she ever had in her whole life to this point.

"Dad told her to go, honey."

Her gaze snapped back to his. "What?"

"Mom told me it was dad who convinced her she should go and be happy with that other man. He set her free so she could have the kind of love he'd always promised her she deserved."

"*No!*" Dani shook her head fiercely. "I was outside dad's office, I saw him in there reading that awful letter mom wrote him when she walked out on him that night. He was crying so hard. Oh my god, Derek. I watched his heart break right then and there."

Derek shut his eyes and dropped his head down in pain. "Dani, I'm so sorry. I never knew. Why didn't you tell me?" He squeezed her hand. "You were so young—"

"I was ten, Derek. Old enough to remember. Mom lied to you; she left him."

"No. *He let her go.* I asked dad and he told me the exact same things she did, sweetie."

"But that night...the letter."

"That letter had been a thank-you. And a goodbye."

"I don't understand. He was crying so hard."

"Of course he was, honey. She was the love of his life, even if he wasn't hers. Just because he let her go, it didn't mean he didn't love her with all *his* heart. She may not have left like a thief in the night, but she left him all the same. You're right; you did see his heart breaking that night because it was finally truly over."

Dani was dumbstruck, still shaking her head as if

objecting to the truths as they battled the facts she'd based her entire life upon.

"Now let me ask you something," said Derek softly.

She looked up slowly.

"What do you remember about Valentine's Day growing up?"

She shrugged, not seeing how that had anything to do with their conversation. "Not much. I didn't have too many friends growing up and didn't date until college. I never cared about the whole Valentine's thing; the guys I dated were pretty stoked about that."

"Yeah," he interrupted sadly, "*everyone* knew you didn't care about Valentine's Day."

Something in the way he said that made Dani narrow her eyes in defense.

"You left out the part about you working here every Valentine's since you were a teen."

"So?" She measured him carefully, still confused about where this was going.

"Do you remember *why* you started doing that?"

She frowned, never having giving it a thought before.

Derek pressed on. "The year after mom left, when you were eleven, you hatched this elaborate scheme to hook dad up with the divorcee down the street from us, remember? You got me to babysit her kids with you so that dad could go out with her on Valentine's eve?"

Memories lit her face. "Oh yeah. Nice lady, cute kids."

"The next year, it was a teacher from school. And the

year after, a 'dancer' you met."

"What's your *point?*"

"Always on Valentine's, Dani. *Only* on Valentine's. You made it your mission to keep dad happy every February 14th to take his mind off the fact that mom left him on the 13th."

Dani blinked. Only on Valentine's Day, really?

"And the reason dad let you do it every year was simply because it made *you* happy."

She shook that off as an impossibility. "No, he had fun on those dates, I remember."

"Probably. You sure did your damndest to make certain he would. I think that's why, in a way, Valentine's *was* special to him because every year, on that day, you'd show him your crazy, determined love through your matchmaking antics." He chortled. "Gawd, remember after he had his first heart attack? You managed to get him that cute nurse's phone number?"

Her emotional laughter joined his. That's right, she *had* been fixated on a medical professional for him that year.

"A fortunate byproduct to your seasonal scheming is that you found out how much you loved working here," continued Derek. "At fourteen, you started learning to cook, work the brew tanks, and run the business end of things here. You couldn't get enough of it."

"You make that all sound like a bad thing."

"No, it was a great thing. By the time you were twenty-one, you were practically running this place by yourself." His smile was filled with pride. "Everyone said you were just like dad."

"Again, where's the '*but*' in all this memory lane bliss?" She had no idea why she was sounding so snarly. It was like she knew something was coming...

"Dad thought you becoming 'just like him' was your deep-seated fear." Derek ignored the red-hot denial ready on her lips and bulldozed on. "The only reason he let you miss out on Valentine's each year and focus on his love life instead was because he thought *you* needed it."

"What are you talking about?" Now, she wasn't so sure she wanted to know.

"You made Valentine's a day for absolutely everyone else but you, hon. You still do."

"Big deal. So I don't believe in the magic of Valentine's. I don't believe in Santa Claus either." Dani immediately felt contrite, knowing Derek did believe in the magic of the holiday. After all, Valentine's had been the day Dani introduced him to Jonathan.

Fiddling with his wedding band, Derek sighed. "Okay, say for argument's sake it's all that simple. So what do you do now that you can't play matchmaker for me or dad anymore? Why are you so hell-bent on fixing everyone else's love life but your own? When is it going to be your turn for the happily ever after?"

She blinked, not having an answer for him. Or herself.

He hugged her tight. "To answer your original question, no, there is nothing wrong with you in terms of love. You have more love in you than anyone I've ever known. Do you look at love the same way others do? Definitely not. But that's what makes you special."

Dani felt the tears welling up again.

But the unexpected jangling of her phone stopped the deluge from flowing free.

Reluctantly, she read through the urgent text message. "Crap! I'm sorry, Derek. They need me in the back." She gazed at her brother, not ready for their talk to end.

"You better go," said Derek, reading her thoughts.

"If I didn't have to get all these musicians settled..." She lingered on the chair.

"Go on. We'll talk more later, I promise."

Torn between sadness and something she couldn't yet define, she hugged him again, finding it hard to let go. "Give Jonathan a hug for me. I'll send wine and the sweetheart's meal over." She gave him a watery smile. "You two enjoy Valentine's Day double for me, okay?"

"Nope," he replied cryptically, his eyes focused over her shoulder.

Standing, she regarded him quizzically and followed his gaze. Her eyes widened when she saw Luke standing not six feet from them.

"How long have you been there?" she asked in a hushed voice reserved for a ghost.

"The whole time," came his gentle reply.

She turned back to her brother. "Why?"

Derek squeezed her hand. "He deserved to know."

Her phone rang again and she looked down at it helplessly.

"Go," said Luke softly. "Call me. Even if it's late. I'll be waiting."

The weight of the last statement hung in the air, not lost on either of them.

———— ◆ ————

"YOU'RE SERIOUS ABOUT my sister, aren't you?"

"Getting there, yeah," replied Luke simply as they both watched Dani leave.

"Good. She needs that. She needs *you*."

Thank god. One Dobson down, one more to go. Luke sighed. "Can you tell *her* that?"

Derek barked out a laugh. "Nice try. I'm not getting involved in this." He shot him an appraising look. "You're different from what she's used to."

Luke's grin took on a hint of pride. "She hates my views on romance."

"Ah, that she would." He tilted his head. "Has anyone told you she's never gotten or given a Valentine gift? Despite that, deep down, I know the holiday is special to her. Ask anyone around town. She's played cupid for her fair share of couples." Derek pointed to a waitress who'd just winked at one of the assistant managers. "Hands down the most romantic Valentine proposal I've ever seen was the one Dani planned for those two."

Luke believed it. "I've been trying to get her to admit she's a closet romantic."

"*Ha!* Good luck with that. Honestly, it's not Dani's fault that she's the way she is. Considering the whole mom-abandonment thing, she is actually more normal than most. And though I'm sure she never talks about it, Dani has in fact been hurt by love before. Once. But it was enough hurt to last a weaker person several lifetimes to come back from. It's not my story to tell, but you have to know that with everything she's gone through, she just needs time. If you can give her that—"

Luke didn't even have to turn around to know the reason for Derek's abrupt pause. Only the man's husband could make Derek's eyes light up and go hazy with emotion like that.

Jonathan Dobson approached their table and *hmmm'd* Luke up and down with overt approval. "I swear, everywhere I turn lately, there's my husband talking with a gorgeous man."

"Yes, well, the honeymoon *is* over now," teased Derek.

"Why do you think *I'm* noticing they're gorgeous?" taunted Jonathan right back.

Luke chuckled good and loud. These two were characters.

And then it began.

The inevitable machine gun interrogation the pair then launched on him, while mildly invasive, did manage to earn him their avid support in his long-term goals with Dani.

"This was fun." Luke got up to leave at their eventual cease-fire. "Now if you think of any more questions for me, you can find me next door daydreaming about your sister. Or you can also get my number from Xoey," he informed them dryly, well aware who was supplying their grilling ammo. Their resulting burst of laughter made for a pretty grand exit for Luke.

As he made his way out of the dining area, he found it impossible not to look back and smile at the couple one more time. They were so in love. They looked like one of those quintessential images usually accompanying a caption of 'ah, true love' in the Valentine insert of the local paper.

That got Luke thinking.

If it hadn't been for Xoey's paparazzi moment, the candid snapshot of him and Dani together wouldn't be sitting beside his parents' anniversary photo in his office at this very moment. Grinning, he took out his smartphone and got his camera booted up just as Jonathan and Derek started exchanging gifts. The shutter click caught both men in hysterics over what truly was the oddest pair of Valentine gifts he'd ever seen.

But the resulting photo...wow. It was the very picture of love.

Luke was humbled.

Suddenly, he was hyperaware of all the couples around him, some doing Valentine's Day the traditional way, others embracing the 'new' traditions he'd introduced. And of course the token few dancing to their own beat completely. The one thing they all shared in common was that they were blissfully, irretrievably in the moment, that moment Valentine's Day brought about.

Right then, Luke tossed the rulebook out in his mind and made a game-changing decision. He immediately went over to show Derek and Jonathan their inspiring photo and ask if they'd allow him to put it up on the Desert Confections blog amongst others in a gallery of images he'd be dedicating to the celebration of Valentine's Day—new, old, and everything in between.

It would be fittingly romantic.

It would quite possibly unravel everything he and Quinn had done for his shop.

But how could he not? Where once he'd thought he was the unlucky bastard who just couldn't catch a train ride to the altar even with a ticket, he knew now he simply hadn't been heading in the right direction. The diehard romantic he'd always prided himself to be had not even begun to reach the depths of which he was capable. Because every feeling of love he'd felt in every past relationship paled in comparison to what he was feeling now.

Everything was different now. *He* was different now.

And the reason for that change was the very person running around the brewpub doing what she did best.

Chapter 18

LUKE SPENT THAT AFTERNOON wandering through Cactus Creek with Evan in tow as his official photographer for the day, photographing a broad spectrum of special moments around town to capture Valentine's Day in all its multifaceted glory. Surprisingly, when he went up to introduce himself to his photo subjects after each shot, every single one of them knew of him and the throwdown. And over half of them, he discovered amusedly, weren't the least bit shy to admit their allegiance to beer.

When he then went on to ask their permission to upload the photo for a Valentine gallery on the Desert Confections blog, the response each time was the same. Every couple asked to see the photo first. From there, the okay was inevitable because they'd see the same thing anyone viewing the photos would—love, pure and simple.

What more could you ask for on Valentine's Day?

That's exactly the conclusion Luke had come to before he'd begun collecting photos for the blog—before he'd even made the big decision that would affect all the Valentine's Day and White Chocolate Day plans he and Quinn had worked so hard on for the past month and a half. The same month and a half he'd spent placing the entire focus of Valentine's Day on his and Dani's businesses, rather than their relationship where it should've been from the start.

All that was about to change as well.

As Luke began sharing these new plans with the random strangers he met throughout the day, not only did they provide enthusiastic support of his changes, they gifted him with priceless romantic advice as well. Each couple, in their own way, helped him remember how much he loved Valentine's Day. Looking back on his life, he could recall most every Valentine card he'd ever written, every gift he'd fussed over, and each person he'd celebrated the day with. Valentine's had always been a privileged time for him to lay all his emotions out in plain sight for one special person to see, and have that person show him the same.

But Dani never had any of that. Yet she was still the most naturally romantic person he knew.

With that fresh in his mind, Luke uploaded all the photos onto the Desert Confections blog site, putting the starting gate spotlight on the photo of a pair of teens wordlessly cuddling at a bus stop.

Below their picture, he typed the advice they'd had for him, just as they'd said it:

*"Remember to hold hands as much as you can,
for no reason, even."*

Always a good reminder.

The next photo to go up was of a third grade girl giving a boy at the playground a homemade heart-shaped cookie. Luke and the two kids' mothers had thought it just about the cutest thing they'd ever seen. The boy had eaten it right away, after which, he simply asked if she wanted to ride bikes together the next day. When the little girl's mom later asked her why she'd given that particular boy a valentine cookie when they always seemed to fight in the park, the girl replied like it was so obvious:

*"It doesn't matter if the person you like acts stupid sometimes,
you should tell them you like them anyway."*

Talk about profound.

The photo following was the one that had hit him the hardest. It was of an elderly couple walking down the lake path this afternoon. The woman's purse strap had slipped down her arm and her husband, hands shaking in his old age, tucked the strap back onto her shoulder as if he'd done it a million times before. The action prompted a smile between them with a familiarity that simply transcended time.

Luke was racked with emotions when he showed them the resulting photo and listened to the sage advice they gave to him in that half-you/half-me way of speaking that only those lifelong couples who shared everything could.

The husband's advice:

> *"Though your brain may house all your smarts,*
> *your heart's the organ you should listen to about love."*

And his wife finished:

> *"But always remember to go with your gut when it comes to*
> *the timing of following-through with anything your heart comes up with."*

Advice seemingly custom-tailored for him.

The completed photo gallery showcased love in every aspect. Seeing it all together brought him a sense of calm as he opened the Desert Confections blog and started typing:

———— • ————

HOW BEER BEAT CHOCOLATE
ON VALENTINE'S DAY

Yes, it's true. Shocking, I know.

But beer has in fact triumphed over chocolate by exactly one tie-breaking vote.

My vote.

All month, Desert Confections has promoted the "new" Valentine's Day, challenging folks everywhere to change how they celebrate this special day. Now, while I do believe that two separate days for partners in love to spoil each other is still a terrific idea, I've recently been reminded of what I seem to have forgotten a bit along the way.

I love Valentine's Day.

Exactly as it is, antiquated though it may be.

And I'm not alone.

In the photo gallery, you'll see what I saw all day throughout Cactus Creek—folks showing their love for one another through gestures unreliant upon any preconceived rules. All these couples graciously helped remind me of what else I forgot throughout this throwdown: Valentine's Day isn't about chocolate sales.

Occupational hazard, I guess you could say. My fierce throwdown opponent, on the other hand, never suffered the same ailment. As I've seen in countless ways, Dani Dobson has done nothing but inspire romance over the last month in her brewpub without any agenda (well, perhaps the thrill of beating me was a tiny bonus).

It had never been about beer sales for her. Not once. Truly, all she wanted was for people to love and be loved, experience the greatness of romance without antiquated notions or new kitschy pressures.

We should all be so lucky to experience that from her.

I know I am.

What's even more incredible is that Dani was able to show me all the most romantic parts of Valentine's Day, amazingly, without having experienced one of her own. Those closest to her tell me she has spent the last seventeen years never once having celebrated Valentine's Day herself, instead choosing to ensure all those around her created the best memories possible in her place.

And she doggedly insists that she's not a romantic.

I've never wanted to prove a woman more wrong in my life.

So from today, I plan to do just that.

For starters, I'm going to give Dani every one of the seventeen

Valentine's Day memories she missed out on growing up.

The other part—showing her she's a romantic—I'm going to need your help with since, from what I hear, it's no secret that over the years, Dani has inspired more than just me in lessons of love.

So, my request is this: if you have a special story of love starring Dani or her brewpub, please send it to Ocotillos via a Valentine's card so she can be reminded of just how much she and her business have touched all of you. I know your Valentines will mean so much to her.

Okay, with that request, I sign off on this Valentine's Day eve with my official throwdown concession. Though I still think chocolate reigns supreme over beer any day (hehe), I do concede this win to Dani, not just because she did in fact get more town votes, but because—unique though her methods may be—she has clearly proven herself far more of a romantic.

For now. But just wait, honey...I'll catch up.

Happy Valentine's Day, all.

Luke

————◆————

DANI STARED AT HER LAPTOP SCREEN.

No freakin' way.

Luke did not just go and make that outrageously romantic declaration on his web page.

Oh yes he did.

The blog tags showed tons of replies already, all in huge support of both his concession and this romantic crusade of his. A lot of folks posted suggestions for his seventeen

Valentine's Day re-do's while most just gushed their congrats for the 'happy couple'.

When she clicked over to her twitter feed, she felt her jaw drop. *Holy Hefeweizen.* Tweets were pouring in by the second. It was unbelievable.

Why the heck are so many folks online now instead of on their Valentine dates?!

True, it was after midnight but still, she never thought quite this many people cared about the throwdown. As she spent some time reading through the posts and tweets, however, she realized the majority wasn't about the brewpub's victory over Desert Confections, but rather, in giddy response to the news of her and Luke being in a fairytale relationship.

"I think people like us." Luke came up behind her and leaned against her doorframe to her office, looking very much like her very own personal Prince Charming come to life.

"I can't believe you did that," she whispered as she made her way over to him.

"What? Give you the win on a silver platter? I mean, how else was beer going to beat chocolate in—" Amused as the devil, he caught her hand before it socked him in the belly.

Cradling her in close, he said softly, "I did it for all the reasons I wrote," before slanting his mouth on hers in a deep, drugging kiss.

When he let her come up for air, she slowly opened her eyes. Then she shook her head to clear it of lovey-dovey cobwebs. "Wait, stop. Luke...I have to tell you something."

He gave her a suspicious once-over. "You have that

look like you want to talk business."

She winced. "I do...sort of."

"Then I don't want to hear it. No business talks today."

"But—"

He kissed her again. Still holding her in his arms, he nibbled distracting kisses along her jaw. "Stop focusing on work. Give me a work-free night. If you haven't noticed, I did just do a pretty romantic thing."

She ducked her head down and smiled. "I noticed."

He sighed. "But you're still stuck on this my voting for you, throwdown concession thing aren't you?"

She hesitated, but couldn't stop herself. "I don't want any of this to affect your shop in a bad way," she exclaimed, concerned. The man was certifiable. Romantic, but crazy. This couldn't possibly be good for his business. "Luke"—she placed both hands on his chest to keep him at least an arm's length away—"you basically undermined your entire Valentine's Day and White Chocolate Day campaign by admitting you prefer the original solo day Valentine traditions. Because of *me*."

"I know," he said with pride.

Dani was seriously torn between frowning and swooning. "I love what you did and what you're planning for me..." She forged past the flipping of her heart at the reminder. "But shouldn't we be thinking damage control? A backup plan to save White Chocolate Day at least?" Her eyebrows stitched together. "Would you stop with that panty-melting smile?! I'm being serious."

"God, you're incredible." His eyes searched hers tenderly, his expression almost disbelieving. "Damage control is to fix *mistakes*. This wasn't a mistake." His tone was firm, unyielding. "I meant everything I wrote, consequences for my life's work be damned."

If possible, she fell in love with him even more then.

He stroked her cheek gently. "Everything will be fine, sweetheart."

Dani looked away, hidden guilt an arrow through her heart. "What if you're wrong?"

He chuckled at her lack of minced words, his eyes crinkling in mock offense. "I wonder if I should be offended that the two women closest to me *both* think I'm wrong here."

She frowned, puzzled.

"Fear not, my dear. Quinn's already on it. She's doing this whole 'since Luke fell in love with the enemy, we're changing White Chocolate Day to Red and White Day' spiel. No, don't go look it up—you can check her blog later. *Hello,* romantic man sweeping you off your feet here."

Dani nodded in false complacency...before breaking free to run back to her computer.

His unsurprised laughter followed her as she jumped on her laptop to see what marketing genius Quinn managed to spin this time.

Whoa. "This is even better than the original White Chocolate Day idea." Dani was in awe.

"I know. It's the only reason why Quinn hasn't killed me, I think."

"Red and White, as in roses right?" Her eyes narrowed in mild offense at his confounded expression. "Even *I* know red and white roses symbolize love and unity, or some other metaphor to that extent." She held her hand up to keep him from speaking further while she read through Quinn's new pitch. "I get it. I like it. So you're encouraging folks to give everyone special to them—significant others, relatives, friends, whoever—something red and white to celebrate the different kinds of love that unites them on March 14th, in contrast to February 14th, which is only for romantic love." She smiled. "That's sweet."

"Yup, and I'm not just making it just about chocolate this time either. The whole month, while we're promoting Red and White Chocolate Day, I'm going to give shout-outs to florists, bakeries, card makers, *brewpubs*, and pretty much every industry that helps bring people together."

Dani sighed in relief. So he hadn't ruined all he'd been working toward in one insanely romantic gesture. This new campaign was going to be a huge success, she had no doubt.

Now to deal with the matter of the man and his mission... She turned and saw Luke giving her the look that made her skin tingle. Clearing her throat, she stalled for another few seconds to get her bearings. "So, uh, does this mean you're ending your campaign against beer?"

"Sadly, yes." His eyes took on that competitively teasing glint that totally turned Dani on. "Too bad, too." He gave a masculine pout. "The video for White Chocolate Day was all ready to go."

"Yeah? What were you planning?" she asked, slowly feeling her nerves slip away.

"Basically, it would've had a lonely guy, a cold twin bed, a fridge empty except for beer, and a logo that gets slapped across the screen: *Shoulda Voted Chocolate.*"

Dani burst out laughing.

Luke tugged her in close. "Dani," he said soberly, framing her face with his hands, "I meant everything I wrote. I want to give you the Valentine memories you deserve." He put a flat, rattling box in her hands. "Starting now."

Dani carefully unwrapped the gift and stared at it in disbelief when she was through. "Sweetheart candy?" She clutched the pink $2 box of message-inscribed heart-shaped candies and flew her eyes up to meet his.

"You'd mentioned once that no one ever gave you these when you were younger. So, I thought I'd start there." He gazed into her eyes. "Happy first Valentine's, Dani."

Her pulse tripped. Boy, was she in trouble. The wobbly, watery-eyed 'thank-you' she managed to spill out seemed enormously inadequate, but that's all she had for him.

"You're welcome, sweetheart." He hugged her tight. "Now, while I do have a proper corresponding Valentine date for tomorrow that's age appropriate for the year you were eleven, for tonight, how about we do something that's a little more, *ahem,* our age first?"

Smiling through her tears, she leaned in to give him a kiss in agreement when she suddenly fixated on what he just said. Pulling back, she pulled her smartphone out of her jeans.

Luke glanced at it. "What are you doing?" he asked idly as he moved to nuzzle her neck.

"Here, hold the candy instead of my butt," she directed while thumb-typing on her phone.

He didn't seem at all thrilled about the trade, but he complied, his dimples making a flash appearance when she caught him off guard with a sweet, smiling kiss on the cheek.

Her camera shutter went off.

Startled, he asked her again, "What are you doing?"

"Sharing a memory," she answered as she tapped a few buttons to upload the photo.

Luke peered down at her smartphone screen and read the Twitter photo tag she'd typed in:

My very first Valentine...the candy and the man.
Totally worth waiting seventeen years.

Eyes warm, he bent down to collect a long, slow kiss before giving her a doting grin and dropping back to sit atop her desk. Pulling her onto his lap, he promptly raised his hands in surrender. "A deal's a deal. Since a forfeit is technically still a loss, you get to be *on top* and lord it over me."

"No," she said softly, pulling him back up to his feet. "Nothing can top what you've already given me, what I've already won just by having you look at me the way you do every day, not just today." She wrapped her arms around his neck and looked into his eyes. "Happy Valentine's Day, Luke. Thank you for helping me see this day the way you do."

Hours later, after taking their Valentine celebration back to her apartment, Dani was up at four a.m.—voluntarily—kissing Luke at the door and wishing him a good day as he left for work. It was all very domestic, and strangely, she wasn't feeling the normal quicksand of unease that was her normal allergic reaction to anything resembling 1950s marital bliss.

Gliding back into her apartment, she noticed her blinking answering machine. Yikes, *ten* messages—a bigger than usual pile-up this week. She quickly hit play and chuckled as she at last heard Derek's airport pick-up reminder. They both knew he shouldn't have put money on her remembering, but per usual, he didn't bet against her. That's just the kind of big brother he was.

Her smile vanished, however, as she heard the message in its entirety:

"...I got a voicemail from Noah the other day. Something about a winery..."

Oh god.

Chapter 19

_____

"YOU'RE ACTUALLY CONSIDERING my winery idea?!"

"Why do I get the feeling you're not screeching in my ear out of joy, Dani?" came Noah's token always-cool reply.

"Because I'm not!" Dani nearly shouted into the phone. Noah's silence rang out over the phone line while she tried to calm down. "When I didn't hear from you, I thought you'd dismissed my idea as financially unsound. You didn't even have Connor check out the legal aspects or have his investigator do any digging."

"As I said from the start, Dani, it's a very good idea. One I believe will be very lucrative for Cactus Creek. The reason I didn't bother Connor with it was because the man is barely getting any sleep at home with his newborn. I wasn't going to ask him to do things I could very easily do on my own. And I rather enjoyed doing it. The more research I did, the more I saw the extreme potential in your proposal."

Strange how the words she'd been hoping to hear out of Noah's mouth at one point now made her sick to her stomach. "But I pitched it to you *months* ago. Why now?"

"You do realize this is an entire business we're talking about here right? Two businesses, if you include Luke's. I needed time to research, study the investment potential, weigh the pros and cons, check out the competition, consider town impact. And that was around my existing work. You didn't think my response to your proposal would happen overnight, did you?"

Actually, she had. Sheepish now, she sounded almost childlike when she asked, "Okay, but why did you contact Derek about it before talking to me?"

His patient sigh sounded weathered around the edges. "Because I'd yet to hear from your brother at all about this even though he *is* the proposed vintner. His wines are good, yes, but that doesn't necessarily mean he's cut out to run his own winery. I wasn't going to proceed one step further without talking to all the players involved in this proposed business plan."

Damn, his logic was taking the wind out of her sails.

"Noah, I'm sorry, but I've wasted your time. I just don't want to go through with it. Could we just forget I ever mentioned it?"

She swore he was silently counting to ten.

"I'm disappointed you feel that way, Dani. It's a solid plan." Another measured pause. "Is there anything I can do or say for you to reconsider? I'd like very much to help you make your brother's dream a reality."

The man fought dirty. "You'd back this plan at the expense of one of your tenants who's done nothing wrong?"

"Yes." The reply was just like the man, brisk and no-nonsense. Unfazed.

This time, she was the one counting in her head...the number of synonyms for bastard.

"Look, Dani, I know you and half the town think I'm an ass, but really, I'm the one who's been keeping things from changing all these years. I own seventy-five percent of the town commercial real estate even though they're downright lousy investments. Of all my business holdings, my properties in Cactus Creek are by far the most money draining." His voice softened a bit. "Still, I've been steadily buying up the lots where I can to try and keep things how it's always been, the Cactus Creek we all grew up in." He cleared his throat abruptly. "But I can't do that forever."

Dani was stunned. "Noah, I had no idea."

"Clearly." Though she knew it wasn't possible, Noah sounded almost...wounded. "By following through with your winery idea, yes, Luke would lose out here, but based on my research, the presence of a winery would bring in a new customer base that could attract more traffic to the town as a whole. The good outweighs the unpleasant here. Further, if you and Derek take over the lease for the amount you said you were willing to pay in your voicemail, I could keep from increasing the monthly lease of three older businesses who desperately need the help—Gavin's breakfast diner, Dan and

Barb's grocery store, and Libby's ice cream shoppe. All three of those businesses were there from when we were kids, Dani. Do you really want to see them have to close their doors?"

No. She didn't. Still. "Noah, I can't do this to Luke...I can't and I *won't*."

"Fine." His voice hardened over the phone line. "Then I'll bring in another winery that will. After your little tirade in my father's office, I called a few friends in the wine business. They took one look at my building blueprints and told me how ideal it is for a winery because of the layout and the cellar. Location was another big selling feature. Ironically, even if it isn't tied to Ocotillos directly, any winery sitting next to a successful brewpub like yours would apparently do well. And thanks to your little throwdown with Luke, Cactus Creek has sparked a lot of interest with the right crowds. I now have two wineries interested in purchasing the building outright and a third who wants to lease, but is willing to pay far more than what Luke is currently paying monthly." He paused for a beat before adding coolly, "Just like *you* were willing to."

She winced at the reminder. *Damn, damn, damn.* She'd really screwed this up.

"I'm really not the monster here," he maintained quietly, his voice gentling in response to her defeated silence. "Like I said, it's business. Right now, Luke's building is a hot commodity that, frankly, will do the whole town some good. We could help two more local businesses in addition to the three I mentioned earlier—Kim's adult novelty shop, and Jilly's world music school. Kim, who grew up here like us, and

Jilly, who needs the steady income to help pay for the nursing care her mother needs."

He took a deep breath and let it out. "So yes, I do think Luke would be an innocent victim here, but if given a chance to sacrifice one to save five, I'll take it."

"Noah, please," pleaded Dani quietly. "You can't do this to Luke. He loves it here and we both know it wouldn't be as simple as him dusting himself off and starting up again somewhere else. This would cost him a ton to recuperate from. There has to be another way. By what you've explained, you care deeply about all your tenants. So why can't you help Luke out just a little here?"

"I *have* been helping him out, Dani. I've been sending my biggest corporate clients his way. Not to mention the extremely reasonable loan I gave him that few others would even entertain."

Dani did a double take. *Luke's new equipment.* "I didn't know you gave him a loan."

"That's odd." Surprise tinted his tone. "The whole reason why Luke called me for the loan was because you mentioned my helping Lia out a few years back."

For some mysterious reason, Dani felt hurt Luke hadn't told her that he'd gone to Noah for a loan. A double standard considering the conversation she was in with Noah now, but still. Hearing something like this secondhand just made her frustration...erupt. "So let me get this straight. You give the guy a loan that would bury him in debt if he didn't come through and then you pull his shop out from under him? Our whole town is just one big *Monopoly* game to you isn't it? Don't pretend like you're the town's goddamn fairy godfather. All you care about is making more money!"

The very instant her brain caught up to her mouth, she gasped and slapped her hand over her lips, immediately feeling worse than pond scum. "Oh my god, I'm sorry. I'm so sorry, Noah. I didn't mean any of that, I swear." Dani knew Noah had worked damn hard for everything he had. And he was always fair. Nothing she had just accused him of could be further from the truth. "I don't even know why I said it."

"You've changed," he said quietly, simply. A touch sympathetically. "Your heart is involved now. This isn't just business for you anymore."

An awkward moment stretched out over the phone line. She didn't have a reply.

He muttered something that sounded suspiciously like '*the real Dobson curse*' under his breath before producing a deep sigh.

"Dani, the best I can do is offer a compromise. The wineries who want to buy aren't necessarily putting forth multi-million-dollar deals so, if Luke can match the doubled monthly lease the third winery is willing to pay, I'll keep him on instead."

Double his monthly lease? She simply didn't see how that would be possible, not if Luke was already having finance issues. Regardless, it was something.

"And Dani," added Noah quietly, "I was already planning on giving him a one-year deferred payment extension

259

on his loan. I'm not without a heart."

More guilt punched her in her gut. "Noah, I swear I didn't mean what I said earlier. Lia's absolutely right about you. You're one of the good ones. Truly. I'm really sorry if I hurt your feelings."

He simply grunted in response. "I'll call Luke tomorrow and present the situation. Do you want me to explain to him how you and I reached this compromise?"

Dani felt a cold sweat break out over her skin at the thought of Luke hearing Noah mention her part in any of this. Really, this was all her fault…

"No, I'd appreciate it if you didn't bring me up at all when you talk to him."

———•———

AN HOUR AGO, Luke had watched Quinn smile over a text message—undoubtedly sent from Rylan if the now familiar blush on her cheeks was anything to go by—while looking happier than he'd ever seen her.

An hour ago, Luke had belatedly taken inventory of all the other related changes in Quinn over the past few weeks and realized that, miracle of miracles, she was in love…or as close to it as the woman's jaded heart was capable of getting.

Then five minutes ago, he'd been responsible for making that smiling happiness vanish from her face and get replaced by worry.

Worry over the financial problems *he'd* put them in.

"Quinn, I just found out this morning myself. Noah called to explain everything and give us our options." Luke waited for the bomb he'd just dropped to sink in fully. "If we decide to accept his terms and renew our contract, the lease increase he'd be mandating would start in July."

She fell back against her office chair, stunned as she repeated the new 'terms' set by Noah. "*Double* our monthly lease?"

"He said a few wineries are interested in setting up shop here in Cactus Creek and our building is the top choice because of the cellar and the location. Apparently, besides the two who want to buy the building, a third is part of some big franchise offering to pay double what we're paying to lease. But he says he'll stick with us if we can match what they're offering."

"There's no way we can afford that drastic a hike. Since we went with the shorter business loan for the lower interest rate and higher monthlies, nearly all our profits go straight to our payments as is." She shook her head sadly. "Crazy as it sounds, I've grown to love it here almost as much as you, but I honestly can't see us paying that huge sum each month just to stay here."

"It's not as if this space isn't worth it. And we both know the amount isn't unreasonable."

"But it's unfeasible. At least for our business. We'd be lucky if we managed to break even." Quinn banged her fists on her desk. "I can't believe Noah's being such an opportunistic dick!"

Luke sighed. "That's the part you're going to really hate. Noah owns most of the commercial property here in town. Remember how I told you Dani mentioned that some of the mom-and-pop businesses are having a tough time keeping up? Well, by just accepting that third winery's lease offer, he can help five of those businesses from shutting their doors. Folks we'd try and protect if we were in his shoes, Quinn."

"Don't tell me, Dan and Barb's little grocery store?"

"Yep. That's the one he's most worried about. If they shut down, it's unlikely he'd get another tenant given their location on the far edge of town, which would force him to sell the whole lot to keep from losing a ton of his investment. If he did, he thinks a big box outlet store might be the only one to offer. Apparently, they've been sniffing around. Despite my hating the position he's putting us in, I do admire his doing what he can to prevent those kinds of big city changes around here. He won't say it but I think he has a soft spot for small-town life."

Quinn flipped her head back in defeat. "I liked it better when I thought he was an ass."

"Yeah," he nodded. "Me too." Noah was truly a class act. Not only had he offered a more than generous deferred payment extension on the collateral loan so Luke wouldn't lose his recipes whether he stayed or left, but he'd also prepared an extensively researched list of comparable relocation properties if they opted not to renew their lease.

Quinn's gaze fell back down to the ground and stayed there. "Luke...I just don't think..."

"I know," he broke in quietly. There was no way he could ask Quinn to take this sort of risk, this kind of sacrifice. Yet again. "I know," he repeated more to himself. This was an impossible choice before them. While staying would in fact mean operating in the red, leaving would flush the thousands they'd invested in this new shop right down the toilet.

Damned if we do, damned if we don't.

Studying her pained expression, he added with as much hope as he could muster, "But we have a few months to come up with a plan to maybe finding a way around…that." *That* being exactly what they were both thinking.

Luke frowned and looked away. The reality of the situation was staring them both down and winning. Because no matter which route they decided to take, they both knew there could be a shared outcome he never thought he'd ever have to face.

The end of their business partnership.

Chapter 20

DANI'S HEAD WAS a mess—her heart too.

True to his word, Noah hadn't brought her up when he'd informed Luke about the lease increase. Which made it ten times worse when Luke told her about the situation and chalked it up to crappy luck on his part that those wineries just happened to be interested in his building.

She needed to come clean.

And maybe she would have by now if the crazy man wasn't making good on his romantic crusade to give her back the seventeen Valentine's that she'd missed out on. Ever since his blog declaration, every few days, just when the high of the last surprise would wear off enough for her to man up to try and tell him everything, *BAM*, he would veto any non-romantic talk before sweeping her off her feet with another touchingly sentimental gift or gesture.

He was impossible.

And she was falling irretrievably more in love with him every day.

From the valentine where Luke channeled the pre-teen version of himself back in the day to write a hilariously adorable love poem for her, to the romantic mixed CD he'd made of old school teenage power ballads that even had *Xoey* taking a sentimental stroll down memory lane of high school exes past... The man was just so romantically candid, filling all the gaping holes in her heart she never even knew existed with experiences she now couldn't imagine living without.

A surprise picnic at the desert botanical garden complete with the basket and checkered blanket, which she'd secretly melted a little at seeing awaiting them on the lawn.

An outdoor movie night using a borrowed video projector and the gray wall on the far end of the Ocotillos parking lot wall to replicate a drive-in movie—something she'd always wanted to do.

It was all amazing.

But more than that, it was the way he'd carry on in full Valentine mode just for her—as if the entire world were still celebrating February 14th along with them.

Dani sighed and tapped her forehead lightly against the wall. The fact that he was doing all of these wonderful things for her while working so hard to stay positive about his business situation was just compounding her guilt. A part of her wanted to believe that they'd get through this just fine.

But then she'd think about how her talk with Derek had gone the other week and lose her nerve all over again.

Derek. The reminder made her tap her forehead even harder against the wall.

Shortly after her phone call with Noah, she'd gone and visited Derek to explain the messages he'd received while he'd been on his honeymoon. She'd started by describing her entire winery idea in detail...watched her brother's face light up in a way she'd never seen before...and then felt absolutely pummeled in the heart when she'd had to take it all away from him shortly after.

He'd barely said two sentences to her since.

Not anger, just disappointment, he kept reassuring her. Still.

With disappointment like that, she almost wanted the anger instead.

And that's how it would be with Luke. But worse.

So here she was, in true Dobson tradition, dealing with the situation the only way she knew how.

By making beer.

Or rather, failing to make the beer she was now starting to obsess over.

Talk about the Dobson curse.

"*Your order's up, Dani!*" shouted Javier over the brewery intercom that was linked to the kitchen. Grabbing the plate of food she'd requested for her assistant manager, she hurried up to her office to feed the poor man, who was probably starving by now.

"Sorry I made you miss lunch again, Sam," she called out as she rushed in. "I just can't get the lautering right on

266

this new brew recipe. It's driving me nuts."

Sam tugged her ponytail sympathetically. "No worries. It was slow today. And I loaded up on energy bars when I saw not all the steam in the brewery today was from the kettles."

She stuck her tongue out at him. The guys loved teasing her that the extra soundproofing they'd sprung for in the expansion was partly to block her at times, loud and 'colorful' brewing lingo.

He chuckled and grabbed the plate of food she'd brought for him. "I'm going to take my lunch and break together since I only have two hours left in my shift. Holler if you need me."

Dani glanced at the clock—yikes, it was later than she'd thought. "Damn, I'm sorry you worked straight through. You know what? Go on home already. You earned it."

He slammed a finger up to his lips. "Shhh! You know Elle has ears like a bat!" Wary, he stuck his head out the door and cased the hallway to see which waitresses were nearby. "Last thing I want is for Elle to call Terri and tell her I'll actually be able to make it home in time for Jenna's ballet recital. Thanks, but no thanks—my ass is working my full shift to make sure I miss it. It's Terri's turn to sit through the thing and videotape Jenna's three minutes on stage."

Not even attempting to hide her smile, Dani made a zipping motion of her lips and slapped Sam on the back sympathetically. They'd all heard about little Jenna's last recital—it had lasted *five* hours. And since it had been during Terri's shift waitressing, Sam had been on video duty while

Terri had been in Ocotillos, crossing her chest in thanks every time he'd sent her a pained text from his seat in the auditorium amidst a sea of rabid dance moms.

"Hey, what's this?" she asked Sam, belatedly noticing the big file box on her desk.

Amusement twitched across his lips. "Your mail, madam. We eventually had to box it all because it was overflowing your similarly neglected in-tray this week."

Ah yes, that sounded about right. When her head was focused on a new brew, there were times her workers had to club her over the head with day-to-day business things. The year she'd made her award-winning black lager, she'd completely forgotten to renew their logo napkin contract. For a week, they'd had to use picnic napkins—the big country-cute square ones that had no place in a bar—to tide them over until she'd gotten everything straightened out.

That was what had given birth to Sam's '*Dani, open me!*' folder hanging from a string in her office doorway, right at nose-level. She was embarrassed to admit that on two occasions—okay, maybe three—she'd walked face-first into it while she was deep in thought about a beer recipe.

No one said brewing wasn't a dangerous business.

Particularly lately, it seemed that Dani had suffered two more face whacks from the folder just this week. "I'll be better once I fix this recipe, Sam, I promise." Dani opened the file box. "Hey, if you need to hide out from Elle, why not eat here and help me sift through all this mail?"

Sam gave her a strange look and backed away slowly.

"You don't remember, do you?"

"Remember what?" Her blank expression turned more suspicious with every step he took toward the door. She peered in the box to take a look.

And fell into her seat in shock.

There were dozens and dozens of pink and red envelopes in the box. "*No.*" Her voice was hoarse as she picked one of the cards up delicately. "People actually sent us Valentines?"

"A lot of people." Sam's shoulders lifted in a hey-it-was-inevitable way. "Luke pretty much became the most romantic guy in Arizona since his little concession speech. It was just a matter of time till the right people read about his whole 'send a valentine to Ocotillos' request. Hell, all of us here were prepared from day one to get slammed with letters. We've been getting dozens a day for the past two weeks. Hence the box." With that, he quietly moved to the door to give her some privacy.

"Wait, stop! You can't leave me alone with these. You have to help me open them."

"Nooo." He took two more steps back. "Sorry boss, but I'm allergic."

"To Valentine's Day cards?!"

"To the ones in that box? Oh yeah. Remember, I've been working with you long enough to know exactly what kind of stories are going to be in those cards. If I read 'em, my allergies will hit and turn my eyes all watery. Not good. Sorry, Dani, you're on your own." He exited the office quickly.

"Vick!" called out Dani when she saw her headwaiter outside. "Help me out will you?"

Vick started in the door with a smile until he saw Sam shaking his head slowly, eyes closed. Then he saw the box.

"Nuh-uh, no way," he jumped back out to the hallway. "Sorry, Dani, but those letters there are addressed to you and it is a crime, *a federal offense* in fact, for me to open another person's private mail."

Clearly, his acting classes were *not* paying off since laughter was bubbling out with the bullcrap dribbling from his mouth. "And you know how I'm a stickler for the law."

"Are you frickin' kidding me? I'm the one who bailed you out of jail for fighting a few years ago!" she blasted out, smacking his arm with one of the big pink envelopes.

"Yes, and I know you want me to stay on the straight and narrow. What you're asking is what they call a gateway crime." He tsked as if devastated there weren't a better solution.

"Argh!" She pushed past both exasperating men to make a plea to Javier, who'd come over to see what was making Dani have a near meltdown.

When he saw her holding one of the Ocotillos Valentine's Day cards, he skidded to a halt and spun around to run right back to the kitchen.

She caught him by his apron strings. "Javier!"

Slowly, Javier turned and gave her a polite look. "*Si*, Miss Dani?"

"Please, please, you have to do this with me."

His round eyes turned thoroughly perplexed. "*Lo siento, no entiendo. No hablo Inglés.*"

She glared at him. "Really? You don't speak English suddenly?"

He blinked innocently and replied in more Spanish.

Dani's head flipped back. "You guys are just mean!"

"Naw, we just think it's time you saw how great you are, boss," shrugged Vick.

"Plus, it *is* Luke's gift to you," reasoned Sam.

Javier shook his head with a dopey, lost smile, staying impressively in character. Another sentence in Spanish, undoubtedly a beautiful sentiment, came flowing out of his mouth before he kissed the top of her head and pushed her back into her office.

She gave them one last pleading look.

They closed the door in her face.

Now alone, Dani dragged herself over to the box, took a deep breath, and gently tore open the seal of the first Valentine's Day card.

She recognized the name immediately. *Janet Myers.* She and her husband Ken had taken a day trip to Cactus Creek a few years back to celebrate their anniversary. They'd planned to have a vow renewal ceremony in Sedona, but after Ken lost his job, they'd had to cancel it.

After seeing how disappointed they both had been, Dani made them promise to come back to Ocotillos for a special anniversary dessert—on the house—in a few hours after shopping around town, before heading home for the evening. When they returned, just before sunset, she led them up to the roof, where she'd arranged for them to have a small ceremony with flowers, some twinkle lights, Rylan on guitar, and later, a romantic dinner for two.

Needless to say, she was a crying mess at the end of Janet's card.

The hours flew by from there.

From long, emotional stories sent by regulars she'd known for over a decade to shorter, excited notes from couples who'd just met this past month during one of Ocotillos' blind date nights, to letters from folks who had stories about her dad. Every single Valentine's Day card was filled with moving portrayals of love. And every single one of them squeezed the tears right out of her heart.

By the time she got to the last card, Dani was a wreck, a curled-up ball of tears.

She didn't even remember picking up the phone or dialing the number but somehow, Luke answered and swept in minutes later to hold her as she finished crying her eyes out.

She'd simply had no idea all these people had been so touched by what she'd considered such small gestures. Every bit of love they'd shared with her filled her heart so much that it almost hurt.

When she told Luke as much, his eyes turned even more adoring. "Sweetie, you have this gigantic heart filled with a downright inspiring capacity for love. But you've spent all your time giving it instead of letting yourself receive it. So now that it's all coming back to you, your heart's just getting a little overfull is all. Don't worry, it'll make room. It's *your* heart, after all. It knows it has to keep up, simply for what you do for others...and who you are."

Irrationally, that of course made her cry even more, and through her tears, she realized that her heart did feel different.

She felt different.

Like a five-year-old pointing an accusatory thumb, her heart declared unequivocally, "Luke started it."

He really had.

Chapter 21

"HEY, SWEETHEART." Luke tried to keep his tone light as he put away his laptop and the depressing post-lease-increase financial predictions to make room for Dani on the bed. "I saw Derek go into the pub while I was heading home. How's he doing? Any change?"

Dani threw her keys on her dresser and flung herself onto the covers beside him. "He stopped by for maybe a minute to pick up a take-out order for Jonathan. He didn't stay very long. Said he didn't want to talk."

Luke pulled her into his arms, comforting her as best he could. He wasn't sure what was going on between Dani and her brother but as far as he could tell, it had something to do with the brewpub and Derek's recent decision to quit his job out of the blue. Jonathan had advised Luke to just let them work through it on their own.

He kissed her tightly closed eyelids, trying to ease her

tension. "Give it time, honey. Quitting a job he was at for five years to look for a new career path can't be easy on the guy, even if it was his choice."

"That's just it. He's not *looking* for a new career path; he already knows what path he should be on."

That was news to Luke.

But beyond that cryptic remark, she offered no more coherent information. Her voice soon shrank away, getting smaller the more obscure her words became. "I just wish I could help him," she whispered, seemingly more to herself than him. "I should've. Not that I *would've...*"

She trailed off her scattered ramblings and then shook her head, tucking her chin on his chest and ruefully refocusing her eyes on his again. "Sorry, I'm not making any sense. My brain's a little scrambled tonight."

A wobbly half-dim smile edged her lips. "Why don't we talk about your day instead? Rylan was telling me Quinn has a new Red and White Day promotion. How's that going?"

It was a weak attempt at a redirect. Lately, Dani looked like she was dealing with the weight of a boulder on her shoulders. The last thing Luke wanted to do was change the subject. But whenever he'd bring it up, she'd *almost* look ready to talk about it...before sadly smiling away the subject.

What a pair they made.

Since he'd done the same at least a half dozen times when he'd been on the receiving end of her concern, he did what she'd done for him each of those times.

He backed off. For now.

He sighed and waded them over to shallower waters. "The promos are going as good as can be expected, I suppose. We don't have the same traction as we did with Valentine's Day but we're doing well for March."

Still troubled by the sadness in her eyes, he began absently kneading his fingers down her back.

She groaned softly. "You know, I'm getting addicted to these massages you keep giving me. If you're not careful, I'm going to turn all diva and start expecting them every night."

He brightened a little then, chuckling at the impossible notion. "I'm not worried. I think last Sunday alone is proof positive that you going diva on me will never happen."

"Last week?" she peered at him quizzically. "Oh, hehe, the wedding."

"Let's recap, shall we? The day of my friend's wedding, you ran to the grocery store in your PJs to get a last-minute wedding card. When you got back, you took a one-minute shower and then yanked on an un-ironed dress, along with a lovely pair of rubber beach slippers—the only non-sneaker footwear I think you own. You air-dried your hair with the window down in the car on the way to the reception. Once there, you promptly helped the bartender—who you of course knew—run the bar when he got backed up, and snort-laughed when the waiter brought you wine instead of beer to drink for the bride and groom toast. After a fierce game of tag with every child at the wedding, you then sucker-bet me and dragged me out to dance horrifying NFL end zone classics like the Sprinkler, the Dougie, and the Dice Roll as your prize.

Next came my personal highlight of the evening when you tossed whiskey back with my buddies while owning them in NBA smack talk. Finally, on the way home from the hotel, you begged me to get us a deep-dish pizza as a post-wedding snack, but you didn't even let us eat it till it was cold because you attacked me in the living room and had your wicked way with me on the carpet. And then again in the hallway."

Her whole body was shaking in hilarity by the time he was done.

"So no, honey, I don't think you're ever going to go diva on me." He grinned, perhaps even more in love with her now after the Dani highlight reel. "That doesn't mean I won't treat you like one though. I don't think I'm going to be able to stop spoiling you even after the seventeen Valentine's Days. It's too much fun. You may very well have to suffer through more foolishly romantic gifts," he said, completely serious. "Like last-minute drives to San Diego during red tide season."

The reminder made her smile softly. "I still can't believe you did that for me. Seeing that red water turn electric blue at night was one of the most amazing things I've ever seen."

His eyes warmed as he studied her face. "*You're* the most amazing thing I've ever seen."

Rolling her eyes, she snuggled against his chest. "You're good for my ego. I think I'll keep you around to tell me things like that when I'm old and wrinkled."

He felt a sharp tug in his rib cage. Lately, Dani had been letting long-term talk like that slip out more and more, giving him hope that he knew was premature.

It wasn't as if Dani ever got excessively tense or even skittish with the topic. No, she would usually just laugh as if she were on a different page—or more like a totally different book. Take her giving him a key to her apartment yesterday for example—a milestone for most couples. Not so for Dani. She'd matter-of-factly told him that with her late hours, this way, he could let himself in the nights he wanted to come over when she wouldn't get home until after he went to bed. She'd meant it exactly like that, too. Practical and simple.

Meanwhile, Luke had wanted it to be more of a big relationship moment. This thing they had was unlike any relationship he'd ever been in, so simple that it looped back around to being complex. On the surface, Dani had all the makings of a classic casual girlfriend, never planning or overanalyzing things between them. Paradoxically, she also seemed made to be the perfect wife and mother. She was kind of like a sexy girl-next-door buddy and Suzy homemaker rolled into one with her heart on her sleeve and a mild case of commitment A.D.D.

Fascinating yet unnerving at the same time.

Nevertheless, he could see himself with her for the long haul. The way she was handling his whole lease predicament was yet another solid check in the potential-wife column. Ever since he'd told her about his lease predicament, she'd been his rock, going above and beyond the call of girlfriend duty. Beyond just being there for him for moral support, he found out that she'd also begun sending customers his way via food specials for anyone who brings in a Desert Confections receipt. Instead of running in the opposite direction at the prospect of him being broke in a few months, she just threw herself into helping him make his business succeed. It was nice. She was the exact antithesis of the short-haul girlfriend.

And therein lay the root of their relationship complexities.

With their growing fame as Cactus Creek's favorite couple, he was seeing those roots grow into thorny stems—the most recent being when an overzealous neighbor teasingly asked her if she thought he'd be 'popping the big question' for his seventeenth valentine.

That's when he saw it. The discomfort bordering on fear. No, Dani wasn't close to being ready for him to pop any sort of question.

But he was.

Seeing her settle in on 'her side' of the bed—because they had designated sides of the bed now—he felt a sudden, deep need to know for sure.

So he eased into his interrogation. "I always meant to ask, how come you don't bottle your beers? You'd make a killing if you did."

"I swear, I get asked that every day." Her eyes twinkled. "Call me sentimental but I inherited my dad's views on bottling. He always said beer should be fresh from the tap, foaming in a glass at a table with friends," she reminisced with a smile. "I've always thought so too."

"So you don't have grand visions of turning your beer into the next big Sam Adams?"

She shook her head. "Nah. I like how things are now. Luckily, we've been successful just from in-house sales without distributing." She gave him a thoughtful sidelong glance. "What about you? Are you aiming to give Godiva a run for their money?"

"Honestly? No. The financial security would be nice, and it'd be great to give Quinn her own location to run. But really, I've always dreamed of having a crop farm like my folks."

Her eyebrows shot up in surprise. "A farm?"

"Why, can't you see me as a farmer?"

She thought about it for a bit before her lips tilted to one side. "You know, I actually can. You'd make a sexy farmer. Count me in to help during harvest season."

His pulse sped up a bit. "Your turn. If you weren't a brewmaster, what would you do?"

"I'd cook," she said definitively. "Maybe a dive restaurant, something tiny with a grill."

"Yeah?"

"But I don't think I'd ever be able to get rid of the brew bug. I'd have to at least have a small craft brew set-up."

He leaned her back against the bed and began kissing the spot behind her ear that always seemed to muddle her mind. "You know, there are a lot of farmers who have home brewing systems. I also know of some family crop farms that have restaurants on site too."

"Mmm hmm," she hummed, losing track of the conversation.

"We could put both on a farm together."

She went still.

"Don't hyperventilate." He helped slide off her shirt, distracting her from over-thinking his words. "Just do a little dreaming out loud with me. It'll be like playing pretend. C'mon, it'll be fun." His expression was jovial, completely innocent as he nipped at her shoulder.

She shivered at his ministrations. "*Fine*, but you better darn well put out later, mister."

He chuckled against her sternum as he paused in indecision whether to travel right or left.

"Well," she began breathlessly, awaiting his decision as well. "If we had a farm, yeah, I'd want space for a small brew systems setup so our restaurant could serve our own beer."

"And?" He chose left.

Her breath broke on a moan when she felt the hot suction of his mouth. He paused, silently telling her he wouldn't continue unless she did. She let out a frustrated breath and kept talking. "The restaurant would be open from brunch to late lunch, but the crop farm just in the mornings except for seasonal picking in the evenings."

Damn, even half-drunk with arousal, the woman could put together the foundation for a pretty good plan.

For *business*.

"What about kids?" he asked quietly.

A little more coherent now, her voice dropped off a little. "Maybe."

That '*maybe*' twisted his insides, spiked his dreams with doubt. "I think you'd be a great mom," he proceeded carefully. "You basically mother everyone and you're a natural with kids."

"But I'll never be voted head of the PTA. Like mother, like daughter, right?"

He frowned at the bitter twinge of hurt in her voice. "Screw the PTA. Your kids will absolutely adore you, trust me. Their friends will too for that matter. The sports-nut beer mom who cooks—you kidding? You'll be the cool mom well past the college years."

Laugher rippled out of her. "I never thought of it like that." She slid her hands around his waist. "At least I'll be able to keep up with you then. You'll be a wonderful dad."

His heart thumped. *Keep it light.* "Hey, can we have a few dogs in this dream too?"

She laughed. "Of course. Oh, and you definitely need to keep making chocolates. Wow, can you imagine a little restaurant that served lunch with farm-picked produce, beer brewed fresh, and chocolates made on site by a master chocolatier?" Her eyes took on a far-off look.

He could.

Never had a dream seemed so close to reality. "So, folks would come in for crop picking in the mornings and stay for lunch, which would be served with our famous beer and chocolates." His mouth teased over her collarbone. "Our kids would be angels who do all their chores before family time every evening. Then you and I would stay up late having crazy sex." He nuzzled her neck. "That's a great dream, babe."

A suffered sigh, tinted with adoration whooshed out of

her. "You are—"

"I know, I know. A hopeless romantic. Lately though, you make it sound less like a complaint and more like a compliment." He looked into her eyes as he slid his hands down her body, tantalizingly close but still too far from any of the good parts. "Want me to stop?"

"No," she whispered. "Never stop."

He laid a possessive kiss on her lips and beat the world record for getting on a condom, for sure.

Though the sex was always white-hot between them, tonight it was different. Synced on a whole new level. Every kiss felt deeper, every sound sweeter.

He heard his name slip past her lips on a moan and he almost came right then and there.

Gripping her hips like a man possessed, he slid home once more, burying himself to the hilt just as he felt her squeeze him like a vise and the first shuddering waves of her orgasm began pulsing all around him, milking him, making him almost mindless with the primal need to have her.

Keep her.

She clenched around his granite-hard shaft and he only just barely held himself back another brief second before he really began to thrust, taking her, laying claim on her in every way he could. He heard her cry out his name again and felt her second orgasm crash into him even harder than the first. The most exquisite torture he could imagine.

Blinding bliss spiked his blood like a drug, rushing his veins, overtaking every one of his senses as his own release hurtled him into a sea of emotions that shredded what was left of his control, his defenses. His heart pumped hard in his chest, leaving him dazed, capsized to the point where he didn't know which way was up.

Then he felt her arms wrap around his waist and her body cuddle against his, and all at once he felt whole again.

Grounded.

In love beyond belief.

God, this was what he wanted. This right here and so much more.

He wanted the dream.

As he lay holding her while she drifted off into a deep sleep, he felt the panic begin to set in. But for good reason. Even when he'd asked her to dream of a future together with him, he'd felt her holding back, unwilling to commit the words to become an actual dream, which was still miles away from a plan, and an eternity away from a true future.

Then she'd done the most unsettling thing of all.

She'd uttered the word that's been his own urban legend for years now with every confirmed case in his past relationships—hear the word 'maybe' five times uttered by the woman he loved and the boogey man would snatch her away.

He knew without a doubt that Dani was the one he was truly meant to spend his life with, have that forever love with. And amazingly, she wanted the dream too.

Maybe.

Chapter 22

DANI'S HAND COLLIDED with a foreign object on Luke's side of the bed. Prying her sleepy eyes open, she saw he'd left something for her on the center of his pillow. A gift.

Rolling over, she slid the Valentine card out from under the square gift box, tearing it open immediately. Though Valentine's Day was long over and no one carried the greeting cards anymore, somehow Luke found a way to have a new and unique one for each of his gifts and gestures. The hopeless romantic. Goofy smile already launched, she read the card:

> To my beautiful sleeping Valentine:
> Happy 16th Valentine's Day. I tried to find something as dainty as you are but I'm afraid such a thing did not exist. So I had this made—something you can keep on you that'll hopefully make you smile.

Dani didn't know whether to laugh or cry when she saw the delicate little silver anklet with its gorgeous dangling charms of juniper and hops. It was stunning. These weren't generic charms either. They were exact replicas of the design she'd had carved into the photo frame she'd given him. He must have paid a jeweler to handcraft each of the intricate charms.

Smiling, she slipped it on and secured the tiny silver clasp. She'd never worn an anklet before—it was so dainty and feminine against her skin.

She loved it.

———•———

"*SHIT!*" CURSED DANI, spitting out the small sip of almost fully aged beer she'd just tasted. It wasn't horrendous. But it wasn't exactly beer either.

Mike, her main brew manager, cringed. "I tried to tell you. I think something happened to it during the fermenting stage. It came out way too fruity—totally bizarre since I've been keeping tabs on the heat throughout. I didn't think it was going to turn like that."

Granted, the little brew system they used for recipe experimentation, lovingly named the Baby D system by her dad, wasn't equipped with the temperature regulators their newer, bigger fermenters had. Still, the beer shouldn't have turned out this odd.

This was Dobson-curse odd.

Dani glowered at her tasting cup and dumped the rest of the pale liquid down the drain. "I just don't get it. The flavors should've balanced out nicely in this recipe."

"Maybe it's the water?"

Dani shook her head. "I researched the brew logs at an old California brewery for a similar recipe, a rare non-cider European pear brew I tasted once." She checked her notebook to confirm. "Yep. I added the right salt and gypsum formula to the water to match."

Jim, her other brew man, came up behind them. "Dobson curse strike again?" he asked sympathetically when he saw Dani's befuddled expression. He reached over and filled a tasting cup to see the damage. A reluctant swallow later, he grimaced. "Hell, that's like a bad wine cooler."

Dani let out a frustrated breath. "I shouldn't have used Asian pears—too subtle a flavor. I could have another run at white nectarines…"

The men exchanged pained looks, which caused Dani to flop her head back dejectedly. "You're right. That one was worse." Blowing her hair out of her face with a disgruntled huff, she shut the cooling tank down. "Back to the drawing board, boys." She scribbled some notes in her notebook. "So no-go on the pears. Hmmm, I did hear of a new berry that's supposed to fruit late in the spring…"

Her narrowed gaze looked right through the two men as her brain ran through the few spring fruits left she had to experiment with.

Mike patted his bear paw of a hand on her shoulder

encouragingly. "Man, I haven't seen this stubborn look since your dad brewed that crazy recipe he tried back when we did the brewery extension. Remember that one, Jim? Horrible spring beer, just awful. But later that year, he did a one-eighty and made a double red IPA instead." He smacked his lips. "Now *that* was one tasty brew."

Dani's shoulders slumped at the memory. Yet another inexplicable case that could only be explained by the Dobson curse.

Jim nodded at her. "Is that it? You aiming to break the curse this year, baby girl?"

"There *is* no curse." She crossed her arms mulishly.

When the two brewers—lifelong uncles by beer, not blood—said not a word, she leaned against the wall with a weary grunt.

Mike's brows stitched together sympathetically. "Okay, say we ignore all the damning evidence that points to a curse. Could it be that the *kind* of beer you and your dad always try to make in the spring just isn't a good fit?"

She looked up. "What do you mean? There isn't a specific 'kind.' Dad and I have tried all different recipes in the spring. None of them worked."

Jim and Mike exchanged another look. "Baby girl," said Jim pulling her brew notebook from her hands to flip through some old recipes. "Lookit your notes there. Sure the ingredients may change, but you two have always tried for some sorta new fruity pale lager."

Really? Why had she never noticed that before?

"Well, it *is* for spring." She shrugged. "A fruit beer is just a logical choice." The sentence came out more question than answer.

Mike tilted his head. "Remember the other year, how you wouldn't even listen to me when I said you should try to make a barleywine beer with the fruit instead?"

"It wouldn't have been good for the spring. Too intense," she insisted.

Suddenly, Dani flinched at a flashback of her mother making the exact same assertion, only it'd been in reference to the deeper bocks they brewed year-round. She rolled her eyes. Her mother had never liked their darker brews.

Come to think of it, her mother hadn't been a fan of their pale beers either, though she tolerated them marginally better. She'd been a wine person through and through, just like Derek.

Dani blinked in surprise. How weird. She couldn't believe she even remembered all that. How many ten-year-olds knew their parents' drinking preferences that well? Then again, a Dobson kid wasn't just any ten-year-old. Everyone used to say her father had more beer than blood in his veins. Looked like she was born the same way.

"You've never tried a fruit lambic," added Jim, silently challenging her to explain why.

She gave him a narrow look. "Not our style," she bit out. If memory served, the lambic was the *only* beer her mother had ever said anything good about. Figured it wasn't one they brewed.

"Okay, how about fruit *ales* then?" he tossed back at her, his voice nearing exasperation.

Her lips quirked. He had her there. The hearty complexities of ales with their warm top fermenting process—the opposite of lagers—was theoretically a better match for fruits. But, for some reason, her dad had been *determined* to create a fruit beer with the clean, smooth crispness of a pale lager. She never remembered why though; he'd been an ale drinker like she was.

Huh, maybe she *had* inherited her dad's mysterious fruit lager mission without realizing it...

"Hey wait," she recalled triumphantly, "we tried an ale with prickly pear cactus once."

"You did okay by that one, I guess." Jim lifted a non-committal shoulder. "But it was barely an ale, and more citrus than fruit. Plus, don't be forgettin' that beer came after the prickly pear cactus *lager* batch you near-poisoned us with," he pointed out, grinning smugly when her cheeks flushed in remembrance.

He waved his hand at the brew vessels all around, mostly filled with ales, bocks, and stouts. "Face it, you just ain't the light and fruity lager brewer. Not in your genes, honey. The Dobsons brew beer you have to have *balls* to appreciate, to stick with."

Mike nodded in agreement. "He's right. We all love the funky flavor combinations you try out, and all the different beer styles you make are interesting and all, but you know that your deeper brews are where you shine. The darker ones with lots of mellow layers, hidden strong flavors that come at you later. That's more you. Not all our customers go for it but the ones who do sure are happy they did. It might not hit the spot on a hot day in an obvious way like a light beer, but it's more complex, more satisfying."

He thumped Jim in the chest. "Hey, what was it that contest judge said once? A night of deep lovin' versus a quick sexy nooner?"

Jim arched an eyebrow tellingly. "If there's a Dobson curse, that's it. Yours just ain't the people-pleasin' style of beer that folks will grab to tailgate with. To love your beers, a man's gotta have faith, gotta know what he sees ain't what he's gonna get. Then he's gotta get past all that intensity at the get-go and really let it sink in. Once he does though"—Jim whistled—"ain't no other beer that'll ever do."

He nodded over at the small brew tank in the far corner. "I reckon you have the right idea with that secret chocolate batch you've been workin' so dang hard on."

Dani followed his gaze over to the still-fermenting beer she'd been quietly trying to perfect—the unique chocolate ale that her Hail Mary plan to help Luke's business through the lease-increase hinged on.

Figured Jim was the one to find her out—the man had the nose of a bloodhound.

Jim winked and chucked her under the chin. "Don't try to change, baby girl."

Dani just stood there blinking while the two men went off on their merry ways.

Leave it to brewers to give her life and love lessons using beer metaphors.

———————•———————

Dean Henessey shot a nervous glance around Ocotillos and then tried to make his glare penetrate the menu across the table, behind which, his wife Claire was sitting carefree as can be. "Luke is going to kill us when he finds out we're spying on his girlfriend! I can't believe you talked me into this," he grumbled, shoving a hand through his salt and pepper hair worriedly.

Claire sniffed. "It's not spying. We're just eating a late afternoon lunch next to my son's chocolate shop in Cactus Creek. It would've happened eventually on one of our visits. Besides, she'll never know we're Luke's parents since he kept his father's name."

"Well, I doubt she'll ever learn our names but yeah, I guess you have a point."

"Why that's silly. If we can, we should definitely introduce ourselves. Oh, that reminds me." Claire reached in her bag and pulled out one of their pick-your-own-crops postcard invitations. "I'm going to leave an invitation to the farm here for her as well."

"What?" he hissed.

"*Shhh!*" she quieted him as a waitress came over. Polite as can be, Claire asked about the beer selections before ordering a glass of IPA with the vegetarian paella.

Dean put in his order of the pistachio-crusted salmon over swiss chard and leeks with a glass of porter, and then tried to gently shoo the waitress away quickly after. But Claire, being Claire, began charming the young lady with the gentle grandmother way that worked equally well on lulling their crops as it did on people.

Soon, the waitress was singing like a canary, answering all sorts of questions about Ocotillos—and more importantly, the owner, Dani.

"Darling, why don't you let this nice young lady get back to work?"

"Oh, of course," replied Claire. "I'm sure you're very busy. Thank you so much for taking the time to talk to an old bat like me."

Dean rolled his eyes.

"It's just not every day I get to hear about a female brewmaster. I'm fascinated is all. Do you think I'll get a chance to meet her?" she asked the waitress innocently.

Dean choked on his water.

"Sure," replied the waitress, smiling like she was talking to her own grandma. "Dani loves talking to the customers. I'll go see if she's free."

"How delightful." Claire practically glowed. "Thank you. We can't wait."

Dean was too busy coughing water out of his esophagus to stop the madness.

"What. Are. You. *Doing?*" he finally choked out to Claire when he managed to pull oxygen back into his lungs.

"Isn't it obvious? You were in the military—it's called recon, dear."

About halfway through their meal, a sweet voice tinkled in greeting. "Hi, folks. I'm Dani. How are you enjoying the food and beer?"

Remembering what Claire had said about recon, Dean tried to take hold of the situation before she could. "I'm so sorry my wife called you over. We know you're busy so—"

Claire kicked him in the shin, stopping his attempt at a tactical strike.

Dani didn't even seem to notice. "Oh gosh, you're doing me a favor. I've been doing paperwork all day, so meeting you two gave me the perfect excuse to get out of my office. I hear you two are crop farmers up north. What brings you to Cactus Creek?"

With a smug smirk, Dean raised his eyebrows at Claire, daring her to field that question.

"Just wanted to do some shopping," replied Claire in a half-truth. They *had* gone to Luke's shop to get chocolates; Quinn just hadn't let them actually pay for it.

"Oh, that's nice," smiled Dani. "Hey, so what crops do you folks grow? We use local produce in all our food and beers here. I'm a firm believer it makes everything taste better."

Dean studied the exchange between the two women as they launched into an animated discussion about their favorite crops and the newly created fruits that have been hitting the local farms the past few years.

Oh boy, from the looks of it, if Luke didn't make Dani

a part of the family by marriage, Claire would bring her in anyway by adoption.

Throughout their conversation—which seemed harmless enough—Dean kept a low profile and focused on enjoying his beer. It was damn good beer too. Perhaps the best he'd ever tasted.

So good in fact, it made him miss the moment Claire slipped the farm invite to Dani.

Dammit.

"I'll be there!" nodded Dani enthusiastically. "Oh hey, I know someone whose parents have a pick-your-own crop farm too. Maybe you know them? His last name is Bradford."

For the second time that day, Dean coughed on his drink.

Claire shot him a look. "I don't believe I know any crop farmers named Bradford," she evaded smoothly before smiling in that woman-to-woman way. "Is this man your beau?"

Good lord, the way the woman could question was actually an art form.

"Okay, enough prying into the woman's life," interrupted Dean sternly. "You have to excuse my wife. She goes a little overboard when she gets to chat with others since she's only got boring ole me to talk with day in and day out at the farm."

Dani's laughter chimed in the air. "Aw, I'll bet she counts herself lucky to have that."

Well shoot, that sounded absolutely genuine. Dean couldn't help but be charmed. Before he knew it, he found himself seconding his wife's invitation to the farm. "I sincerely hope we see you at the farm soon, young lady."

"I promise...on one condition." Dani looked at her watch. "I insist you try a sampler selection of our fruit beers along with some desserts. The fruits are all from local farmers like you. You can even enjoy them on the roof deck while the sun sets. We're getting ready to switch over to dinner soon so there's no one up there right now."

"Why, that sounds lovely." Claire looked at Dean, the recon mission now forgotten as her eyes softened over the promise of romance.

He nodded his agreement. "I think that would be an absolutely wonderful way to end the day with my wife."

Smiling, Dani walked them up to the rustically romantic roof deck adorned with an open-weave wooden arbor covering the dance floor. At closer look, Dean realized it was dried Ocotillo, not thin wood reeds, providing the shading. How creative.

After seating them on the west-facing end, Dani looked out at the scenery with wistful eyes. "This is my favorite view of the town from when I was a kid," she revealed softly. "You see that rooftop?" She pointed out the Desert Confections building to them. "When I was younger, that building was a Mexican restaurant, and the family who owned it used to have these amazing parties up on the roof."

Her eyes crinkled softly. "My parents bought this brewpub when I was just a toddler and spent years working so hard to make it successful. We all made sacrifices. For me and my brother, that meant less time making and keeping friends; for my folks, that meant less time for us. But we made do. Thrift store buys, pretending our dinners here were fancy restaurant meals, stealing family time on the slow nights, that sort of thing."

She slid her gaze back to the neighboring rooftop, her eyes sparkling with memories only her mind could see. "My brother once caught me up here to spying on a little girl's party that was happening on top of that building. Apparently, I was laughing and dancing around this rooftop all alone, living vicariously through those kids."

Abruptly, she cleared her throat and quickly blinked the past away, along with the mist that had gathered in her eyes. "I have no idea what made me think of all that," she chuckled, embarrassed, before looking thankfully at the approaching waiter. "Oh good, here are your dessert and beer samplers."

When Dean took out his wallet to pay, she gave him a firm headshake. "It's on the house since it was my idea." When Claire tried to object, Dani didn't give in. "Nope. For local farmers, it's my pleasure, really. Plus, I love seeing couples up here at this time of day." Her eyes drifted across the landscape once more. "Well, I better get back to work. You two enjoy." Then somehow, she slipped away while the desert sunset stole the couple's attention.

After she was gone, Claire said softly, "I like her."

"Me too. She's perfect for Luke." Dean frowned sympathetically. "But she's scared."

"You think? She seems to wear her heart on her sleeve."

"So did you, remember? And it took me *two years* to wear you down, what with all the walls you built to protect yourself."

Claire thought about that for a few seconds before her expression became mulish. "Well, I don't want Luke and Dani to wait years. They deserve happiness now." She flashed a determined, enchanting little pout at him.

Oh no.

"I want grandchildren while I can still run after them."

He sighed, long and slow. "I don't think I like the sound of this."

"I have a plan," she informed him brightly.

Shaking his head, he reached for one of the little sampler beer glasses and was tempted to toss it back like a shot. "Of course you do, dear."

Chapter 23

DANI WALKED INTO Desert Confections just before eight p.m. to meet Luke for their date, only to find a sign awaiting her with a giant arrow aimed upward printed on it. Rissa, who was manning the register, simply grinned and pointed to the old rear stairwell behind the kitchen.

After getting no further clues or hints of any sort, Dani gave her a gee-thanks nose scrunch and warily climbed all the way up the creaky steps to the rooftop. Nothing but darkness greeted her.

"Luke?"

"*SURPRISE!*"

Frozen, Dani could hardly believe the sight before her. One by one, tall floodlights surged to life all around her to reveal an extravagantly decorated rooftop and a swarm of people rushing forward to greet her.

Two strong arms wrapped around her waist.

"Happy birthday, sweetheart," said Luke in her ear, the big smile he was wearing plain as day in his voice. When she turned to face him, completely speechless, he laughed and put a sparkly cone-shaped party hat on her head. "By that mouth agape look of shock, I take it you like this little birthday shindig we put together?"

This 'little shindig' was every kid's ultimate dream, decked out with decorations, game booths, a piñata that was obviously handmade, cotton candy, and enough food to feed an army.

It was beautiful. Everything about the party gave her the same feelings she used to get watching the parties held on this very rooftop when she was a kid. Only this time, she was invited. Even better, she was the guest of honor.

Her first birthday party.

A river of emotions overtook her as her mind worked to crystallize everything around her like snapshots to fill the empty places in her memory album.

Derek came up and swung her up in a giant bear hug. "Happy birthday, sis."

Momentarily too astonished to speak, Dani just flung her arms around him and gripped him tight. He looked so...happy. She couldn't have been more shocked if she'd seen him drinking a beer for once.

Interrogation time, definitely.

"What's going on?" she asked bluntly, weeks of guilt, loneliness, and hurt making her impatient at best. "Just last week, Jonathan had to practically trick you into coming to the

LOVE, CHOCOLATE, AND BEER

brewpub. Now you look...geez, like a different guy. Talk to me, Derek. What's going on?"

Derek flicked a glance over at Luke who'd gone over to talk to his friends so Dani and Derek could chat. "Last week, I was still questioning my sanity over quitting my job on a whim, and a part of me—the dumb, irrational part of me—had you smack dab in the middle of that decision. Took me a while to take my head out of my ass and realize I quit partly because of you, yes—" When tears welled up in her eyes, he clarified quickly, "But in a good way. You're a doer. Just like Dad. You go full-throttle, balls-to-the-wall to make things happen."

"Don't remind me," she muttered. History was a big enough reminder in that regard.

"Dani, don't you see? You inspire me. You never would've spent five years at a job you didn't love. You would've been out there going after your goals. I've always admired that about you."

It was possible she was even more bowled over now than she'd been when everyone shouted, "*Surprise!*"

"I just needed a swift kick to start following in the footsteps of my amazing baby sister."

Oh man, here came the waterworks.

He pulled her into a hug. "The reason why I look so happy is because I'm finally doing exactly what you'd be doing right now if you were in my shoes. I'm not going to let life just pass me by and make excuses anymore. I'm *going* to get my winery." Barely contained enthusiasm tipped the corners of his mouth up into a mysterious grin. "And I'll tell you all about my plans after your birthday weekend is over."

She latched onto his wrist. "No, wait. Don't run off with that cliffhanger. Tell me now," she pleaded, so over the moon at seeing Derek like this that she could hardly contain herself. Threats were not beneath her at this point. "I'll tell Javier never to cook for you again unless you give me a hint."

He chuckled. "Ah, see. Where you and Dad had all the drive, I was blessed with all the patience. So now it's your turn to take a page out of *my* book."

She shot him a look that said she'd rip out that page and bury it given half the chance.

Kissing her forehead gently, he stuck to his guns. "Nope. There will be no thunder-stealing today. Just enjoy your party, sweetie." He gave her a soft smile. "By the way, look around. Have you noticed that this is way better than that lame kiddie party you saw up here in the first grade?"

Dani felt her heart squeeze and a different kind of tears ready to start flooding. "It is, isn't it?"

"I'll take about twenty-five percent of the credit for how it turned out." He winked. "But the rest was all Luke. That's a good guy you've found, sweetie. I'm happy for you." He kissed her cheek again and then thumped Luke on the shoulder before disappearing with Jonathan into the crowd.

Luke was back at her side moments later, tucking an arm around her while a group of what looked like the entire town of Cactus Creek shuffled forward via some invisible cue and began singing Happy Birthday at the top of their lungs. She gasped at the sight of the giant birthday cake they carted over. Colorful frosted decorations, candied confetti, and *her name* written in icing.

Her heart leapt up to her throat, and all of a sudden, time seemed to slow.

The symphony of singing voices became echoed as the twenty-eight flickering candles turned into a soft glow that lit a haze all around as a new image ebbed in and out her mind. Materializing…just out of reach. Too fuzzy to be a memory, too real to be strictly fantasy.

A dream, more like.

In it, she and Luke were singing Happy Birthday to a child. *Their* child.

Dani blinked and the scene disappeared. But her reaction to it remained. The dreamy images lodged her breath in her chest, right over her heart. And as if Luke were dreaming of the same future, his hand gave hers an emotional squeeze. She went up on her tiptoes and tilted her head up to catch his mouth in a feather-light kiss.

"I love you," she whispered against his lips.

———◆———

LUKE'S LIPS KICKED UP; he was positive he had the look of a man so far entranced he was just holding on for the ride. Hearing her say the words could always get him there in an instant. He pulled her into his arms until they were touching shoulders to knees.

303

Looking into her eyes, seeing all her unspoken words, he almost forgot there were guests all around them. Almost.

"*Get a room, you two!*" shouted someone from under the giant tent. Luke chuckled and put some distance between their bodies—one inch, at least—before leading her to a table with a gigantic bowl in the center. Then he just waited expectantly for her to look down. She didn't disappoint.

When she realized that was fresh caramel corn in the bowl, Dani gasped and grabbed a handful to inhale as if her life depended on it.

Luke had heard the story, knew how the flavors she was groaning in happiness over right this minute were the tastes of her childhood that only her nose had been privy to from a building rooftop away.

When she turned her shining eyes to him in gratitude over such a small thing—a handful of popcorn—Luke felt his heartstrings tug tight.

"I can't believe you did all this," marveled Dani, after finally coming up for air when half the bowl was in her tummy. "Every game, every treat, it's all perfect."

"Derek helped a ton. I followed his suggestions on every detail." Luke cleared his throat. "Sans one, that is."

Curious, Dani asked, "What suggestion was that?"

"Your brother wanted to setup *Spin the Bottle* for the guests. In fact, he was pretty adamant about it."

Her cheeks turned a deep scarlet. "That little twerp!"

He nodded sagely. "With the way Derek had been laughing when he suggested it, I knew there was a backstory

that would ensure I slept on the couch tonight if I gave in."
He patted himself on the back. "Okay, so tell me what's the
deal with *Spin the Bottle*."

She ducked her head down. "Well...there was this
middle school party..."

"Middle school? Why, Ms. Dobson, I'm shocked"

Her cheeks burned brighter. "I didn't actually do
anything! When it was my turn at the bottle, I bolted, making
some excuse about my curfew. I ended up sneaking into
another room and calling Derek to come pick me up early."

"Are you telling me you never got to make out at a boy-
girl party before?" He was doing a terrible job sounding
sympathetic about the fact.

And Dani knew it. She turned laughing eyes his way,
mischief ebbing out the embarrassment in her expression.
"Since you're all about giving me experiences I missed out on,
are you going to go looking for an empty bottle now?"

He gave her a hell-no headshake. "Are you kidding?
Way too many guys here who can't keep their damn eyes off
you." He swept an appreciative glance over her in the casually
ultra-feminine, white flowing dress with her token Dollar Store
white rubber beach slippers to match.

Dani just laughed the flattery off and pointed to a group
of nearby guys. "Hey, what about your friends over there?"

His horrified look at the particularly houndish set of his
fantasy football buddies she had picked out made her
giggle...then break out in a sprint in their direction. She
swiped an empty wine bottle off the table on the way. "Hey,

you guys want to play *Spin the—*"

He ran after her and threw her over his shoulder, tickling her mercilessly as he led her a safe distance away from his friends, all of whom were enjoying the comical exchange.

"Honey, you can set that bottle up right here. I'll be the first to spin," needled one of Luke's buddies, his eyebrows bobbing just enough to heckle Luke.

"That's the *other* reason why we aren't playing any big kid party games tonight," grumbled Luke. "A few of my so-called friends have made it very clear that they wouldn't mind terminating our decade-long friendship if it meant a chance at dating you."

Two of those 'friends' had their fingers up to their ears in a motion for her to call them.

"Awww," said Dani, genuinely touched.

"That *wasn't* a selling point on their behalf. Trust me, each and every one of those guys is a purebred alley cat."

"Unlike you and your suave caveman techniques of throwing women over your shoulder," she laughed, wiggling even more now.

With her shimmying giving him all sorts of interesting, wholly inappropriate ideas, he reluctantly let her down—only because the alternative was just not rated for this party.

She kept on with those impish fairy giggles though, and he couldn't help but steal a kiss. He just couldn't get enough of her. And soon, their kiss, which may have started off playfully chaste, became a claiming so complete, he got completely inebriated off her.

That is, until his brain recognized the sobering voices coming closer by the second.

"*Great*," he muttered, though a reluctant smile peeked through. "Okay, pause button on the mind-numbing kisses. My parents are at three o'clock and closing so let's pretend to behave." He winked and kissed the tip of her nose affectionately. "Hey, that reminds me. How come you never told me you met them the other day—"

Looking utterly confused, Dani whirled around and did a double take when she saw the elderly couple approaching them. "You're *Luke's parents?*"

Luke whipped a glare at his folks. "You didn't introduce yourselves at Ocotillos?!"

His dad immediately pointed at his mother and took a step back as he mouthed, *"It was all her."*

His mom batted her lashes. "Of course we didn't. How covert would our recon have been if we had?"

Luke rolled his eyes. His life was a circus. "Dani, I'd like you to *officially* meet my parents, Claire and Dean Hennessey. They're actually the ones who suggested this party."

Dani laughed and hugged them both. "You know, I'm not surprised at the intel they managed to get. They did the whole 'good spy, bad spy' routine. Hella-crafty interrogators."

"Glad you approve of our methods," delighted Claire, deadpan. "Because we want to invite you up to the farm tomorrow morning for a second helping."

"Really?" Dani looked positively tickled.

Claire glanced up. "Oh, Luke dear, you can come too."

"Gee, thanks Mom."

Laughing even harder, Dani teased, "If he can't make it, I'm sure one of his friends—"

Luke bumped her hip and proceeded to 'save' her from tripping. "Poor li'l thing is toe-up drunk. They make that caramel corn strong here. So, what time tomorrow, mom?"

Claire chuckled. "Nine o'clock works for us. We can have a nice brunch outside."

With that settled, his folks merrily wished Dani a good birthday and headed off to enjoy the party, alternating between whispering to each other and laughing the whole time.

"They're so cute." Dani murmured, smiling at the pair.

"Nauseatingly so," agreed Luke, grinning as well. "Now you see where I get it."

She twined her fingers with his. "With a happily-ever-after like that right in front of you growing up, I'd be more surprised if you weren't the romantic you are today."

"That's the first time you've ever said 'happily-ever-after' without rolling your eyes."

"I know. I think you and your parents are contagious. And my immunizations are wearing off."

Seeing her smile when she said that made a flicker of hope come alive in his heart.

———◆———

THE NEXT MORNING, Luke awoke Dani with a kiss.

Not on her mouth.

Head still under her pillow, she grouchily mumbled a complaint about a four-limit max. But not before lifting her hips up toward his lips with a soft, heated moan...which she quickly extinguished and rolled over to play possum.

He smiled and trailed kisses down and up her smooth back. Strategically.

She remained impressively silent.

Didn't the woman know this was the equivalent of a dare? When he got to the ticklish base of her spine, he paused for one just-to-mess-with-her second before continuing with just the tip of his tongue. Lower, and lower...until she broke and flipped over, propping herself up on her elbows to grouse, "You need a reverse-Viagra."

So saying, her eyes licked over him like a slow, hot flame that lingered on the biggest evidence supporting her argument, which was confirming rather shamelessly that yes, it was indeed morning.

And that she was unimaginably sexy.

"You're one to talk, babe. You about killed me with that last run before we passed out."

Her gaze turned frisky then. "I've actually never tried that position before last night. In fact, I'm not even sure we did it correctly. We better practice that one again to be sure," she said solemnly, dragging the layers of bed sheets off her body, one erotic inch at a time.

With a regretful frown, he put one hand over his eyes and used the other to swat away her curious ones as they set out to convince him to play.

"You're killing me. We're supposed to be at my parents' farm by nine this morning, remember? If we don't leave in fifteen minutes, we'll never make it."

She sat up and swiftly wound the sheet around his chest and arms before pushing him back down onto the bed. Kinky. He felt like a tightly bound half-covered mummy—with a very alive lower half aching to be buried somewhere infinitely tighter. She blew a soft breath up first one rock solid thigh and then the other as she started outlining some sort of math word problem for him.

Yeah, like he could even add one plus one right now.

"If it takes two people five minutes to get ready..." Her fingers lightly grazed his happy trail. "Will ten minutes be enough to..." A slow glide of her tongue filled in the rest of the equation.

His hips shot forward, arching him up off the bed. "Keep that up and I won't last the next five," he growled, lust playing havoc on his vocal chords.

"Really?" she hummed, her mouth promptly interpreting this as a goal, not a warning, as her decadent ministrations kicked into high gear.

He groaned, low and tortured, quickly yanking himself out of the sheets to free his trapped hands. What he was hoping to do with those hands now, he wasn't at all sure...until he caught sight of the unabashed pleasure in her expression.

Damn.

His fists clenched in the sheets to keep from sliding into her hair and taking control. His head slammed back down to the bed, his body strung tighter than a crossbow. "T minus four, babe," he rasped.

Her deep, throaty laugh didn't help his cause one bit.

Neither did her wandering hands as they stroked, cupped, and basically drove him out of his mind.

In fact, the feel of it all along with a few other diabolical skills she sprung on him with lips, tongue, teeth, and throat sped the clock up drastically.

But before he could alert her to the fact, she let out a long, soft purring moan.

And swallowed.

Just like that, the countdown was over.

He'd probably shouted. Hell, he might've even passed out. Eyes shut, body convulsing with each crashing wave of release, he barely had the presence of mind to keep breathing.

Eventually, the storm dissipated and his little temptress slowly kissed her way up his body like a satisfied cat while the roar in his ears took an extra minute or two to subside.

As soon as she lifted her long lashes to meet his gaze, however, the roaring returned with a vengeance and his body corded with a hot hiss.

The pure, raw hunger he saw in the depths of her dark honey eyes stole his soul and sold it to his raging hormones.

But for some reason, she didn't ask him to return the favor. Instead, she just quietly laid her head against his chest and stroked his overheated skin with trembling fingers.

"We better get going," she said finally, her voice trying to cover up the fact that she was literally shaking with need.

"Dibs on the shower." After one more soft love bite on his bicep, she rolled off the bed.

And got exactly two steps away.

Silly rabbit.

He caught her around the waist and flipped her back onto the bed. "We still have two minutes. Plenty we can do in that time, love," he reasoned, glorying in her body's instant, rampant response to him. "Plus, be sensible. You can't possibly leave in this condition. Do you know how rocky the ride to the farm is? You'd be like a powder keg going through a mine field."

She started giggling helplessly at the ridiculousness of his comment.

All part of his master plan.

While she was distracted with the image he'd painted, he quickly shouldered apart her legs and gave her another good morning kiss.

They didn't leave for the farm until well after nine.

Chapter 24

DANI STEPPED OUT of Luke's car and took in the farmhouse before her like she was staring at a painting. Her soft smile and wide eyes told Luke how beautiful she thought his childhood home was while her measured breathing clued him in on just how nervous she was to be there.

Adorable woman.

As he rounded the car, Luke saw her look at her phone at the '*10:01 a.m.*' time he knew was flashing at her. He hid his smile when she stared intently at the phone screen as if she could turn back time with a glare. When he reached down to hold her free hand, she whacked him in the stomach with the other. "I still can't believe you let us be this late!"

"Let us? Honey, I wasn't the one who instigated the morning b—*oomph*!"

She gave him a murderous glare and he ducked before she could sock him a third time for laughing.

"Wow, you're really anxious." He kissed her forehead comfortingly. "They're just my parents. Relax."

"I've never met a boyfriend's parents before, okay?"

"Oh, so *now* I'm your boyfriend? But I told my parents we're just casually—" Luke had the good sense to make a run for it then.

Dani chased him all the way up the dirt walkway he'd ridden his bike on everyday as a kid. He wasn't at all surprised to hear the twin hyena laughs coming from the porch.

"Don't stop on our account, dear," called out Claire. "Whatever he did, I'm sure he deserves the beating you're about to give him."

"Gee, thanks, mom!" he hollered back at her, not missing a beat. "She'll do it, too, you know! She has a right hook like a wrecking ball."

"And that's why we like her so much," cheered Dean, continuing to drink his coffee as he passed a small plate to his wife. "Try the gooseberry scone, Claire-dear. It's delicious."

"It's a wonder why I ever come back to visit you two." Luke leaned down to kiss his mom on the cheek and hug his dad. "You'd think my getting my butt kicked by a girl was like a breakfast show for you two."

"Yes, well, we were getting a little bored out here for the last hour," replied Claire with a smile only he could see. She was teasing of course. He'd texted that they were running late.

"Oh yeah, sorry about that, mom. You see, Dani—"

Dani shoved him off the top step with a hard bump and

stepped forward to greet his parents formally. "We forgot to set the alarm," she lied politely before her eyes shot wide open at the way that sounded...to his parents. "Our own alarms...I mean separately...that is..."

Luke snorted in quiet laughter.

Dean lightly smacked him upside the head. "Did I raise you to laugh at your woman?"

He shot his dad an incredulous look. "If not, you did a *really* good imitation of it."

Dean pondered that. "Okay, I'll give you that. But your mom just makes it so hard *not* to laugh at her when she says some of the things she does. When you think about it, the fact that I hold my tongue as much as I do is a real testament to how much I love her," he ribbed.

"Like you're not a walking punchline," retorted Claire with a sniff, turning to Dani and holding a conspiratorial hand up in a stage whisper. "The tales I could tell you about this man..."

Eyes dancing with delight, Dani looked at the three of them like they were the nuttiest comedy act she'd ever met, for which, she was all ready to buy tickets to the next show.

Luke was ready to give her a lifetime membership.

His heart ballooned to crazy proportions again; it was starting to become quite the affliction. He cleared his throat and directed Dani toward the house. "While the cackling comedians here are finishing their coffee, which they only just started a few minutes ago, *not* an hour ago"—he gave his mom a mock-stern look—"I'll show you inside."

Though she looked disappointed to leave the laughter his parents were still sharing through digs and zingers, Dani happily followed him into the house. Seeing an old bookshelf filled with family photos, she rushed right past him, leaving him in the doorway. With the squeaky screen door slapping him on the ass, Luke just stood there and watched Dani pore over all the various mementos of his childhood like the youth soccer team photos that memorialized his chubby years and his many hockey 'participation' trophies. She touched them all with fingers that could've been stroking fine china.

Then he heard her breath hitch when she discovered the black and white photograph of him when he was just a baby, being held by a man he'd only had a few precious years with.

"You look just like your father," she whispered, her voice cracking with emotion.

"Lucky for him," said his dad from the doorway, sounding as reverent as he always did when he talked about Neal Bradford. "All the Bradfords were always more handsome than the Hennesseys," he joked, his eyes sad as he looked at the photo of his childhood friend.

Dani spun around to look for the source of the fatherly teasing, seeking its warmth like someone coming in freezing out of the cold. Her eyes looked wistful when she found his dad. Then her expression became confused. "Wait a sec. Dean, did you know Luke's father?"

"I actually knew Neal even before he met Luke's mom. We were great buddies all through high school. He was my only childhood friend who still kept in touch with me after I'd joined the military. The only one who'd make a fuss whenever I'd come back to town for a visit."

Dani smiled. "Oh, so that's how you met Claire."

"Actually, no," said Claire as she slid into her husband's arms. "Dean and I didn't meet until a few months after Neal passed away."

Dean took another sad look at the photo of Neal Bradford. "After getting stationed out in Virginia, I did two tours back-to-back. Got married too. But we ended up divorcing after eight years—it came as more of a surprise to me than her. With both my marriage and my time in the army finished all at once, I just packed myself up and headed back to Arizona to start fresh. Since Phoenix was expanding pretty rapidly at the time, it was easy to get a job, though it took me a little longer to get settled. When I finally did, I went to go look Neal up...only to discover I'd missed saying goodbye to my old friend by just under a few months."

Claire patted his hand comfortingly. "I actually don't even remember meeting him then. The first few months after Neal passed were so hard; I'd been living life on autopilot."

"But as luck would have it," smiled Dean, "fate let me meet her all over again at the little grocery store she used to manage just a little ways from here. I'd been getting concrete-restless in the city so I'd decided to come out here for a little country air. In the produce section of that grocery store, a mountain of pumpkins decided to avalanche and attack me." He grinned at the memory. "Just goes to show Cupid doesn't always use an arrow. Claire came running over, all sweet and beautiful, apologizing for the accident. And I swear to you, I took one look at her and felt like a whole new pile of pumpkins had just fallen on top of me, this time on my head."

Dani took in a girlish breath and put her clasped hands up to her heart.

"He guilted me into dinner," declared Claire, chuckling.

"It was warranted. I was a man suffering from a pumpkin injuries and a bad case of love at second sight," he grumbled back.

"And two short years later, he eventually wore me down," she finished, leaning over to smack a kiss on Dean's cheek.

Though he'd heard the story a hundred times, Luke's mouth still tugged up at the corners when he heard the happy ending. Suddenly wanting to have Dani all to himself for a bit, he glanced over at his mom. "Is there time before brunch for me to show Dani around outside?"

Claire looked over at them and smiled motheringly. "Brunch won't be for awhile. Go on, take your time. And Luke honey, don't forget to show Dani which rocks are the best to scare away those thieving birds that keep attacking my crops, alright?"

The corners of Dani's mouth curved up and she shook her head in silent laughter.

"And don't go hogging her all morning. Your dad and I still want to get a chance to interrogate...I mean, get to know her."

Luke rolled his eyes. "You did plenty during that non-sanctioned ambush at Ocotillos."

"I like to be thorough, dear," replied Claire, deadpan.

By now, giggles were attacking Dani's midsection.

Luke laced his fingers with hers and pulled her out back.

Once outside, she stopped and tugged him gently back to her. He folded her into the hug she was wanting as she looked out at the lines of crops all around them. "It's amazing here."

"Yeah." He kissed the top of her head. "You ready for the tour?"

"Can we stay like this for just a little while longer?"

He tucked her closer. "Take all the time you need."

———•———

DANI SAT DOWN next to Claire Hennessey on the porch bench and the two of them watched Luke and Dean head around the corner of the farm to see a dog about a bird. "Thank you again for inviting me to brunch in your home."

"It was our pleasure. I just hope you enjoyed our food as much as we enjoyed the food in your restaurant. Oh, and that beer. My goodness, Dean can't stop talking about your porter."

Dani wrinkled her nose in regret. "These are the times I wish I bottled my beer." Her mouth twisted to the side in thought. "I could send you two a keg if you'd like."

Surprised laughter split the air. "Oh my, we'd be the

most popular farm in town. We'd never get rid of the neighbors." She patted Dani's knee. "That's alright, dear. Going into Cactus Creek to eat and drink at Ocotillos will give us a nice second reason to get out there."

Settling back into the old, faded wooden seat, Dani felt the surreal country scene wash over her. Claire was like the mom Dani had always wished for, and their sipping tea on the porch was a page from a dream she'd stopped allowing herself to have back when she'd written her own mother off...which was much later in her life than anyone would've guessed.

"Something on your mind, Dani? You look sad." Claire tilted her head, concerned.

Dani hesitated, but something in Claire's eyes made her feel safe. "Do you think true love can happen more than once?" she whispered, surprising herself with her candidness.

Claire glanced at her for a moment before answering thoughtfully. "You know, I didn't used to. But I do now. Or rather, I understand better the definition of true love."

With another look around, Dani murmured, "I can see why. Your life is perfect."

"I was twice blessed in that way, I guess." Claire smiled wistfully, explaining, "I had the perfect life with Neal as well."

"But how can that be?" frowned Dani. "Doesn't the whole idea of 'the one' mean one person forever, even if that person is taken from you?"

"I'm afraid I don't have the all answers you're looking for, Dani." Claire peered over at her sympathetically. "All I know is how life happened for me. I didn't see Dean when I'd stopped believing in love. But when he started helping me believe again, there he was."

Dani frowned. "That never happened for my dad." Her gaze dropped down to her left hand, wondering if she'd be following in her dad's footsteps there as well.

"Did he believe?" asked Claire gently.

She thought about that for a long second. "I think he did," she said sadly, lowering her head as she felt a tear roll down her cheek. "But I just don't think he had any of his heart left to give."

Another father-daughter Dobson curse.

"Oh, my dear," soothed Claire, patting her on the hand, "you and my son are so much more alike than you two seem to think. Love is hard; it isn't perfect. And it certainly can't be outmaneuvered. Searching for it like my son does won't make it come, and avoiding it like you do won't make it stop existing. When it comes to love, you don't know if you'll land on your feet or splatter on the pavement...but either way, fall you must. To be *in* love, you and only you need to know whether or not you want to take that step, regardless of the outcome."

Dani took a deep breath and admitted quietly, "My...reservations when it comes to love and my trust issues aren't just about my mom."

"I know, dear. Broken hearts tend to be worn on our sleeves without our consent." Claire sighed, looking out in the field, over at her son and her husband, who were now running after a dog who was stalking the cat they'd wanted to keep around to chase away the birds. "Like me, Luke stopped believing for a while too, after his wedding that never happened. Oh, we watched him go through the motions of life—dating, throwing himself into his work, being there for his friends. But, he no longer seemed himself. The Luke that had always believed in the type of love he wanted so desperately to have and keep, not just always give...*that* Luke disappeared. We truly thought he'd become broken at that point."

"How did he recover?" Dani asked softly, wanting, needing to know how a person could overcome the thing she feared most—a heart not just shattered, but ripped completely out from a loss so severe, a hole remained in your chest where all your hope and trust once was.

"He met you."

Dani blinked in surprise.

"Sometimes when you're ready to believe, love appears, but sometimes, life gets it backward. It doesn't matter. The result is still the same."

Claire didn't have to say it. Dani already knew what the result was.

Because that's what she wanted too.

Chapter 25

LUKE HIT HIS HEAD on the roof of the chocolate display case when he saw her approach.

Angela Prichard stepped forward and peered into the glass case. "Hi, Luke."

Memories slammed through him. Four years since she'd stood him up a day before their wedding and her voice was still exactly as he remembered it.

"Hey, Angie." He hurried out from behind the counter. "Thanks for coming."

"Thanks for calling." Grabbing a seat at the nearest cafe table, she tucked her purse on her lap and looked across at him nervously. "Um, so how've you been?"

"Good. Busy."

She glanced around the shop with a soft smile. "I can see that." Eventually, her gaze collided with his and held. "Your new shop is amazing."

Thank god history was a good icebreaker. "It's nothing like the one in Mesa, huh?"

"I'll say. You and your shop have become quite the household name." The admiration in her voice was genuine. "I always knew it'd be like this for you one day."

The familiar comfort of being around her returned like welcome rain and he finally smiled his first real smile. "You always did believe I had it in me."

She tilted her head. "Why'd you call me, Luke?"

"Were you surprised?"

"Try shocked." Her teeth caught on her lower lip. "Was it because you heard about—"

"Uh, yeah, I actually did hear about your divorce. I'm sorry." The sorrow in his voice was genuine. "But that's not why I called," he admitted awkwardly.

"Then why? I didn't think you and I had anything left to say."

"Oh, we did; I just didn't want to hear it. I do now. Tell me what went wrong with us."

Her mouth fell open, startled. "But I told you—"

"No, all you said was that you didn't want to marry me." He couldn't raise his eyes to meet hers. "But then you went and got married really quickly to the next guy who came along."

"I am so sorry, Luke," she said softly, her voice filled with remorse.

Blinking slowly, he finally looked at her. "I'm not trying to make you feel bad. Really. I just want to know why it is that my not-so-happily-ever-after highlights include being stood up a day before my wedding, dumped a week after getting engaged, and nicknamed the rare species of male serial monogamist who can't get a woman to commit to him."

Angie looked stunned.

"Is it me?" he asked quietly. He didn't use the past tense.

"Luke, of course not. You're an amazing man who pours his heart and soul into love."

His expression became even more hooded. "You make that sound like a bad thing."

"No, it's an *incredible* thing. Just... I think not everyone loves the way you do. Even though I think we all want to." Her lips tilted down at the corners. "Tell me something."

He glanced up.

"You loved all your girlfriends, right? I'm not talking about Quinn and the girls you just dated, but the three others like me that you were serious about. You loved us each, right?"

"Of course."

"The woman you were engaged to before me, did you love me more than you loved her?"

Luke' mouth fell open in shock, but no words came out.

"Since you wanted to marry her, by your blessedly romantic Luke logic, she was 'the one' that you'd love through space and time, right? Well, after you two split up, I came along and then I was 'the one' for two happy years. So then what does that say about her? About me?"

Uncomfortable now, he avoided giving a complete answer, mostly because he didn't have one. "The love part wasn't, isn't quantifiable like that. You and I were more compatible, so the future I saw with you was just different from the one I saw with her."

"And there it is," said Angie with a wistful headshake. "When you're serious about a woman, you look into the future and see an entire life with her. You can't imagine what it's like for the other person, if they're *not* there, *not* able to see the same future."

He was beginning to.

"So with your husband?" he asked. "You saw..."

"Yes, I saw the same future he did. That's why I married him and not you."

It all settled around him like a swift, dismal cloud. "And still you two got divorced."

Her expression turned fierce. "Nuh-uh, no way. I didn't spend two years having you turn me into this giant romantic who believes in forever love, only to see *you* lose it now. It exists Luke. I think I even had it for awhile." She rubbed over the empty spot where her wedding band had once been. "Now *holding on to it* is another story though."

A bitter laugh sifted out of him. "It's a wonder my parents ever found and kept 'it'. The sort of love that stays the course, builds stronger and brighter without an expiration."

"You always were searching for that type of love, weren't you, Luke?"

Of course. Everyone knew that—it might as well be on his business card.

"So why'd you give up for the last few years?"

Startled, he looked up. "What do you mean?"

"After we split up, I've had the 'pleasure' of running into Quinn a few times—you know, while she was out cruising around Tempe on her broomstick."

Luke snickered. After she'd left, Angie had seen the true Wicked Witch in all her glory.

"Last she and I talked, she told me you'd been focusing on work and not on any lasting relationships. Friday night flings and the Saturday sleepovers, I think she called them."

"For awhile." He shrugged. "I guess I was just trying it out—"

"That's not you."

"Maybe, but with no one to ask to marry me, I stayed hurt free."

She made a face. "No rhyming, Luke. Lord knows you never were a poet."

His lips quirked, remembering as she probably was, the awful first few drafts of his vows.

A little bit more of the old Angie peeked out then. "Stick to your strengths, Luke. You're not a play-the-field bachelor. You're more like dun-dun-na-NAH *Romantic Man* whose superpower is hopeless romanticism. Your bat signal would be a big red heart over Gotham."

What a god-awful, asinine description. He half-glared at her. "Gee, if *that's* my superhuman power, what the hell is my kryptonite?"

"That's you too," she replied softly.

He stiffened.

Angie lifted one shoulder sympathetically. "The part of you that can look at something so utterly spectacular and wonder if it's a mirage, the part of you that *expects* it to be. That's your kryptonite." She studied him carefully. "What I've always wondered is why it even exists."

His eyebrows drew together bitterly. "What's not to get? Look at my track record."

She blinked in surprise as if finally realizing something. "Luke, you should know better than anyone that futures change. That we shouldn't ever stop looking for 'the one' for us."

"So we're back to my failed relationships."

She shook her head, annoyed. "No. I'm talking about your *successful* ones."

The flagrant disbelief on his face mocked that notion.

"I'm talking about your parents, Luke."

He looked up sharply.

Angie put a gentle hand on his face. "Your mother loved your father with all her heart. And from what she's told me, he loved her with all of his. But one day, that same heart of his stopped beating. Call it fate, or life, or just plain cruelty from the universe. But as awful as that was, your mom survived and received the amazing gift of finding love again. And *you* got another parent who you loved as much as the one you lost."

She looked into his eyes. "Your mother and father didn't get to the forever part of their love because it simply wasn't destined in their futures. But it is there with your mother and your stepdad. Luke, I think you and I were similarly meant to love, but just not for forever."

He let that sink in. "Did you think you'd found forever with your husband?"

"Yes. It took me awhile but I know now that we were also meant to love exactly as we did—deeper than what you and I had, but for no longer in length."

The pain in her eyes reflected in his frown. "I'm sorry," he said again.

"Don't be. I'm not. I'll find it someday." She smiled at him. "What about you? You dreaming about a wedding with your beer woman yet?"

Well...

She chuckled lightly. "Yeah, that's what I thought. Where there's a rumor that Luke Bradford's ready to walk the white plank, it's usually true."

"Haha," he retorted, humor returning to his voice.

"For what it's worth, I'm really happy for you, Luke. Now you can finally have it all."

His gaze faltered. And then his lips were moving without any assistance from his brain. "There's a good chance I won't have Desert Confections on that list," he revealed softly.

Incredulous, her gaze snapped up. "What? Why?"

Luke gave her the abridged version of his lease situation. "Quinn and I have crunched the numbers over and over. Even with us knocking it out of the park with March sales from all the Red & White promos, if we'd have been operating this month with the higher lease amount, we'd have been in the black, yes, but I wouldn't have been able to pay Quinn even close to her normal salary. And God knows, she needs—and deserves—every penny of that." He scrubbed a tired hand over his face. "More and more, it's looking like our only option will be to bow out before June."

Angie shook her head, refusing to accept that as the only option in the stubborn way he'd always loved. "Don't give up, Luke. You can just move again and turn Desert Confections into as big a success in a brand new location. You've gained a huge following from the throwdown. You can—"

"No," he said quietly. "Not if I sell my recipes too."

Saying it aloud for the first time was like a knife to his gut; and by the stunned, appalled look on Angie's face, he knew that she knew what this decision was costing him.

"What do you mean? Why in the world would you—"

"Quinn invested nearly as much as I did into the relocation. I've thought about this every which way. I can't... I can't drag her down with me. Not with everything she has on her plate." Exhaling slowly, he met Angie's sympathetic gaze. "Most of my homers would probably sell easily—a few premiere shops on the east coast have made offers over the years. And I can likely sell off my third basers to a company that specializes in chocolate gift sets for high-end department stores," he rambled off emotionlessly.

All the while, Angie just kept shaking her head in denial, her expression stricken. "Luke, you can't do this. I know you. I know what those recipes mean to you."

"People are more important than recipes." He patted her hand in a show of calm he wasn't really feeling. "I can always create more."

Knowing exactly what she was wondering, he said simply, "My five best aren't in the bunch I'm selling." At her relieved look, he clarified grimly, "They're actually being held as collateral for the loan I took out for all my new equipment. I'm still weighing my options on what to do there as well. Worse case scenario: I'm unable to keep up with the loans even if I do manage to get back on my feet again, and I end up having to give the recipes up as collateral payment. Then I really would be starting over again with nothing."

"Who would give you a twisted loan like that?" she asked, visibly angered.

"Noah Jameson. My landlord."

Her hands curled into fists. "What a slimy bastard. I have half a mind to—"

He halted her rant. "I knew what I was getting into when I signed that loan. Noah's not at fault here. In fact, he offered me a fairly long no-penalty deferred-payment extension due to the circumstances. But I just..." He sighed. "I don't want to keep putting Quinn through this. A part of me feels like I should just close out the loan and buy Quinn out. Either way, everything I get from selling my recipes and dismantling the rest of the shop is going straight to Quinn to return her investment, proportionate to the number of years she's been with me, and give her a hefty severance package. Smart as she is, she's way better off in some big corporation anyway."

Angie studied his impassive expression. "Easy as that?"

"Yep," he said blandly, his eyes avoiding hers.

"And where do you fit in all this? How much of what's left goes to your future?"

His eyes grew more hooded. "Not enough to open up again on my own right away," he admitted. "But that's okay. I'll start over. Make new recipes. Resave. I did this whole thing once. I can do it again."

"This is a huge decision, Luke. All of it, not just the closing down, but the forfeiture of your five best recipes… What does your girlfriend think about all this?"

"I haven't told her yet. She's not exactly…future-oriented. I don't want to scare her."

Frowning at the dismal look he was undoubtedly wearing, Angie placed her palms on either side of his face and sighed. "Luke, the future is just a path. For two people to be on one path together, all they need to do is head in the same direction—at the same time—and want to take the same turns and exits together. In my case, my path eventually veered away from my husband's. In yours, it might be as simple as you waiting a little longer for her to catch up."

"Sometimes I wonder if she'll ever get there."

"Want me to light the heart signal in the sky?" asked Angie, straight-faced.

He pinched her side, laughing despite himself. "I forgot what a brat you are."

Angie squeezed his hand. "Even if it takes time, don't settle for less than you deserve." She shrugged sagely. "If we'd stayed together, that's what we would've been doing—settling."

"I still would've gotten the better deal," he said honestly, stroking her cheek.

"Damn straight. I'm a freakin' prize," she preened. "So now stop feeling sorry for your mediocre self and get that girl to marry you so I can stop feeling bad about leaving your ass."

He laughed and hugged her tight. "I'll do my best."

Closure—as liberating and eye-opening for hindsight as it was for foresight.

Placing his forehead against Angie's, he finally said goodbye to the woman who'd ensured he now had a future with Dani by breaking off their engagement the way she had. "Thanks you. For doing what I probably wouldn't have had the foresight, or balls, to do—"

Suddenly, a quick motion outside drew Luke's attention away from Angie.

Only, there was no one there.

There *was* something on the ground outside his shop, however.

An uneasy feeling crawled through him as he walked over to the door, hoping that his eyes were wrong.

They weren't.

It was a piece of chocolate…a carefully crafted, intricately decorated truffle.

Fallen out of the hands of the woman who'd made it for him.

Chapter 26

DANI RAN INTO her office and locked the door, taking in deep gulps of air, failing miserably at stopping the useless flow of tears.

She ignored the worried, heavy knocks on the door of first Javier and then the lighter ones, probably from Xoey. Ignoring them all, she sank into the big leather chair that had once belonged to her father.

And just cried.

Her nails clawed at the piece of duct tape holding together the biggest rip in the seat's leather. The chair was so old and worn, she sometimes wondered why she didn't just get a new one. After all, it was an awful reminder of the worst moment of her dad's life. And hers. He'd sat in this very chair reading that note from her mom. Dani still remembered the desolate look on his face, the tears that had run without end, the quiet anguished sounds of his heart breaking.

Curling into a ball, she tried to shut herself off from the suffocating pain seeping in.

Until the fierce pounding on the door rattled the walls all around her.

"*Dani, open this door!*" Luke sounded...furious.

His voice seemed to waver as the seconds ticked away and still she refused to let him in.

"Please, sweetheart," he said softly, "talk to me. Whatever you think you saw at my shop, it isn't what you're thinking." The heavy sadness she heard made her hand slowly turn the doorknob.

She wasn't at all prepared for the sight before her.

He stood there looking as crushingly sad as he sounded, his hands clutching the chocolate that had slipped through her fingers while she'd witnessed Luke's reunion with his ex-fiancée.

It was almost unrecognizable now, coated with street dust and debris.

"You gave up on us," he whispered, his voice bleak.

Dani stared at the chocolate in his hands and started crying again.

Luke stepped in quickly and shut the door behind him. "Please don't, Dani. I swear, what you saw was nothing like what you're imagining. She's just—"

"Your ex. The one who left you at the altar."

"A day before the altar," he corrected before blinking, confused. "How did you know?"

"You always have the same look on your face when you

talk about her." She took in a shattered breath and shrugged with forced nonchalance. "She's pretty. I can see why you wanted to marry her."

"Nothing happened," he insisted.

"Looked like something."

"I swear, you can ask her yourself."

"It's okay, Luke." She tried her best to put on a brave smile. "You and I were going so fast; it was probably time for us to slow down anyway. If your ex wants to get back together, you should give it a shot. With me and my commitment issues, you're probably better off—"

He yanked her to him and placed a searing kiss on her lips. "Don't you dare finish that sentence. I'll never be better off with anyone else."

She clung to him for a hopeful second before pulling away. "No. You can't say that. You can't have it both ways, Luke. You can't be this hopeless romantic who believes in old school love, and then say your feelings for me somehow replace feelings you used to have for someone you'd proposed to—a woman you'd wanted to have a family, a life, and a future with." Her gaze dropped to the floor. "The fact that *she* ended your engagement doesn't erase all that either."

He gently put the chocolate down and slid the curtain of hair she was hiding behind away from her eyes. "Dani, she's a part of my past. *You're* my future."

With unyielding doubt, she shook her head. "I saw you two together. It's clear you two loved each other deeply." Her voice cracked. "And that you still do."

"Of course I still love her. I always will. You're right, I did want to spent the rest of my life with her at one point. She was important to me." His eyes searched her face. "But what I felt for her *pales* in comparison to what I feel for you."

"How is that possible? You spent years with her. You were engaged to be *married*. And again, *you* didn't end it; she did. Meaning even though she broke it off, *you* still wanted a future with her."

He cradled her face, forced her to meet his gaze. "It's not about time, or who ended what. All that matters right now is you and me."

"That's not true. How can you say you want a future with me when you were ready to spend that same future with her? *You can't have forever with more than one person!*" Her agony raged with frustration.

"My mother did," he reasoned quietly.

"So did mine," she replied bitterly. "But my *dad* didn't."

He hissed in a breath in belated understanding of where her thoughts were taking her.

She gripped her fingers into his shirt. "My dad only got to love once. And he spent the rest of his future alone after she left. He never got to love again, never got to heal his broken heart...something I know a little something about."

He covered her crumbling heart with his hand. "Sweetheart, I don't think you realize your heart got broken long before your relationship with that unnamed asshole you still can't bring yourself to tell me about. Your heart shattered when your mom left you and your dad and brother. And it never truly got fixed. How could it? You watched your dad continue to love your mom his entire life, even though that love never came back to him. So your heart was already vulnerable before your ex all but destroyed it. I know seeing my ex with me today must've done even more damage to your still unhealed heart, just when you'd started to trust that I would never do what either your mom or your ex did. I know the situation seems like one you should avoid entirely to keep from getting hurt."

Gathering her close, he whispered, "But what if you and I *are* each other's forever? Don't you and I deserve a chance to find out?"

Fresh tears glittered her eyes.

"I know it's a risk to think that way, to hope that way. For you *and* me, Dani. Look at my life; I'm a realist about how things never work out the way we expect. But even though loving you may end up crushing me to pieces, I'm not going to stop believing in the future or the possibility that you'll be the one sharing it with me."

He drew in a slow breath and stroked a hand through her hair. "Loving you is something I can't *not* do in the same way I can't just stop needing oxygen. Not knowing how long I'm going to keep breathing isn't going to stop me from taking my next breath."

The more he spoke, the harder she hid her face against his chest, her tears soaking his shirt.

"So maybe I'm not that guy from the movies who knows without a shadow of a doubt that he'll get the girl and they'll end up happily ever after. Or the one that can stand here and promise you your heart will never ever feel pain again." He wrapped her up in his arms. "But I am the guy who loves you so much that, even without any guarantees, I'll love you uncontrollably anyway."

Her heart just about burst out of her rib cage at his words, and she couldn't help but respond...though it came out as a rumbled purr against his skin that paused his hand mid-stroke in her hair.

"What was that, baby?" he asked.

More inaudible words went into hiding in his shirt.

"Woman, the *very least* you could do after I declare my hopeless, undying devotion to you is speak loud enough for me to hear your response."

She jerked her head up and mock-glared at him. "You're so pushy! And unbelievably moronic if you think you're not even more impossibly, ridiculously romantic than any guy in any stupid movie."

She tried to maintain her composure as a sexy, happy grin transformed his face from handsome to gut-punchingly magnificent. "And those aren't even your worst qualities! You're sneaky, old-fashioned, and...insatiable! I have no clue why I already love you without any guarantees, but I do. Even when I saw you with your perfectly beautiful ex, faces pressed up against each other, I *still* continued to love you."

At the undoubting elation she saw lighting his eyes, she sighed. "Forget my heart, clearly it's my *head* that I need to have examined by a doctor."

"Well," he sighed, "not the most romantic declaration of love, but then again, you are Dani Dobson. Don't worry, I'll teach you how to do it better."

She stomped on his foot, blocking his efforts at a kiss.

Laughing and nursing his now bruised foot, he fell backward onto her office sofa, pulling her down with him. "God, I love you, woman."

Smiling, she curled up against him and finally gave him the kiss he'd been seeking.

"Again," he urged, moving on to nuzzle her ear. "I want to hear the words once more."

"You're pushy and unbelievably moronic—"

Dani halted with a laugh when his teeth nipped her earlobe in warning. "And I love you. Without any guarantees."

A pleased, *primal* male sound hummed out of him. Gathering her in close, he tipped her head back. "I'm sorry seeing me with her made you drop the chocolate you made for me."

Shrugging, she answered truthfully, "I'll just make you another one. A better one."

"You hopeless romantic."

She rolled her eyes then grinned mischievously as she reached for the chocolate in question. When she turned back to him, she put on the best puppy-dog expression she could muster without giggling. "But then again, I did pour my heart and soul into this one. You're not going to deprive me of seeing you taste it, are you? I worked so hard on it." Blinking, she held up the dirt-covered chocolate to him expectantly.

He didn't even hesitate. He snapped the chocolate up in his mouth, her fingers and all.

"Stop!" she yelped, not letting go of the chocolate. "Spit it out! It has dirt and who knows what else all over it from the ground. *Stop!* I was kidding!"

He held on stubbornly with lips and teeth, eyes dancing in that I-called-your-bluff way.

"I told you, I'll make you a new one. A better one."

His eyebrows lowered, demanding she up the ante.

In response, she settled against him much more snugly, enjoyment flushing through her veins when she saw—and felt—him light up like a fuse. "I'll make you a hundred more, and serve them to you naked, each one after a marathon sex session where I satisfy your every carnal fantasy and then fan you with a palm leaf while whispering the glories of your astounding—"

His mouth let go of the dirt-coated chocolate and sought her lips instead.

After a few hungry kisses, he sighed. "You always manage to turn my win into your own." He tried to sound put-out, but failed, his smile caressing her ear amusedly.

"Lock that door and I could be persuaded to *let you* win one for a change."

He almost knocked her down as he lunged for the door.

She screeched out in laughter and pounced on his back to stop him.

But he was quicker, stronger, and clearly hornier.

The loud click of the lock echoed in the room, and with

one arm, he reached back and flipped her around in a wide arc until he caught her against his chest and held her against him. He lowered his lips to start collecting his just rewards right away.

Dani closed her eyes to bask in the kiss, in the feel of Luke gently loving her.

Without any guarantees.

———•———

ENROUTE BACK TO HIS SHOP, Luke was glad he'd had the foresight to ask Rissa to come in early for her shift the moment he'd seen that truffle on the ground.

Since he, Quinn, and Rissa often had solo shifts throughout the day, they kept a "Be Back in Twenty Minutes" door sign on hand for emergency errands.

They did *not*, however, have a "Be Back in Two and a Half Hours" sign.

He grinned. In a rush, vivid images of just how he'd spent those last few hours flooded his brain.

Soundproof offices. Gotta love 'em.

Before he could get totally sidetracked with memories of spectacular vertical sex with Dani, however, his ringing phone broke him out of his thoughts.

And the frantic sobbing that came over the phone line froze him in place.

"Quinn, hold on. Slow down. What's wrong?" Luke gripped his phone as he listened to Quinn's devastated voice on the line attempt to string together a coherent sentence. "Sweetie, you're freaking me out. Please. Stop crying and tell me what's the matter. Where are you?"

Cooper's doctor's office.

Luke felt a terror-filled rage when he heard the news.

Another surgery.

Little Coop needed yet *another* surgery.

Luke listened to the details with growing rage at the injustice of it all. Various areas of scar tissue from the respiratory complications and resulting half dozen surgeries Cooper had endured as a newborn were now blocking a large portion of his airway and hindering his ability to breathe even in normal day-to-day function. So that hadn't been mere asthma attacks that he'd been suffering through the past few weeks.

Quinn cried even harder as she explained how Cooper now needed an entire airway reconstruction surgery—a complex procedure that would be multiply invasive, require months of difficult recovery, and of course, cost thousands even after insurance.

Luke almost crushed his cell phone in his hand.

Damn it, hadn't the universe been hard enough on that boy? On Quinn? Luke tried desperately to console Quinn even though he himself was silently raging inside.

The kind of money Quinn needed to pay out of pocket for the surgery was enough to bankrupt her as is, and that was *on top* of the thousands she already owed in medical loans. His hands fisted in emotion.

There was no doubt in his mind anymore. Quinn and Cooper were more important to him than his shop. He wouldn't draw out this decision any longer.

He knew what he had to do.

One by one, he began slowly cutting every emotional tie he had to everything he's worked for over the years as he searched for Noah's phone number.

Simply giving up the shop in Cactus Creek wasn't going to be enough.

He had to give up his five best chocolate recipes too.

———◆———

"JAMESON."

Dani took in a deep breath and expelled out in a rush, "Hi, Noah. It's Dani. Please just keep an open mind over what I'm about to propose."

Aside from a small tired sigh, an acquiescing silence echoed back at her.

"I know you said you need to go through with either the lease increase or the sale of the building to one of those big wineries, but what if you had a third option?" Pausing to gulp in some air, she took comfort in the fact that Noah hadn't interrupted or hung up on her yet. So far so good. "Derek and I share equal ownership of Ocotillos; I'm willing to sign over half of my half in exchange for fifty-one percent of the Desert Confections building. *Just* the building."

"Dani—"

"It's more than fair and you know it," she defended before he could argue. She couldn't bear to hear him say no. Something had happened when she'd thought she'd lost Luke to his ex; some dam in her heart had burst open. And with the ensuing flood of emotions, came this crazy idea. An idea she'd never have even *considered* before Luke, would never have considered for anyone *but* Luke.

"Noah, the twenty-five percent of Ocotillos I'd be giving you would be of the brewpub *and* the brewery, as well as my apartment, and the lot itself, which is easily five times the size of the one Desert Confections is on, and worth ten times as much."

"Yes, but what you're asking for is *controlling* percentage of my building," retorted Noah. "Presumably to keep Luke's monthly rent down, correct? Why would I agree to that to only have a quarter ownership of yours?"

"Because the profit sharing you'd get as twenty-five percent owner of my business combined with the portion you'd still make off Luke's lowered monthlies would be more than you make off Luke's lease alone. And let's face it, you and I both know that what I'm offering is a far more valuable business holding."

"There's still the matter of the other flailing businesses in town—"

"I've thought about that too. I haven't worked out the details yet but I think I can help them with their revenue. I've drafted vendor contracts to present Dan and Barb for produce and Libby for ice cream. Truthfully, I'm not sure why I hadn't thought to do that before this but no matter. It'll be mutually beneficial. As for Kim, I can work in a distribution deal for her novelty products—discreetly behind the bar of course. That should do well with the college crowd that comes in. And I've already talked to Rylan for his music expertise on how to help Jilly." She gulped in a breath to slow down her racing monologue. "For Gavin, to be perfectly honest, I have no idea how to help his diner yet but I'll come up with something, I'm sure of it."

"*Now* you're starting to sound like the businesswoman responsible for making Ocotillos what it is today," Noah replied gruffly, sounding noticeably impressed.

"So do we have a deal?" She held her breath.

Sitting through his long contemplative pause was an exercise of patience. Not really her strong suit.

"Dani, your ideas sound all well and good, but to be honest with you, it doesn't sit well with me to make business deals of this nature. Not when there are more emotions than sense involved. You shouldn't give away part of your business and real estate for some guy."

"I'm not. Giving it away, that is. I'd be getting something out of this too. And besides, why do you care if I'm doing it partly to help 'some guy?'"

"Because I know what your business means to you, what it meant to your dad. What happens if you and Luke don't work out?"

Flinching at the prospect, she rushed to fire back. "Then I'll do what you're planning on doing anyway—kick him out and have Derek open his winery." *LIE.*

By the derisive snort from Noah, she knew he was calling bullshit on her big talk.

Noah sighed. "Look, I think what you're doing is noble, romantic even. But take it from me—no good comes out of mixing your business and personal lives. I speak from experience."

Dani's eyes rounded in surprise. "Wait, what? *You* let a woman interfere with—"

"I'm not saying no, Dani," he said, ignoring her question and bulldozing right along. "But I'm not saying yes either. You're right, this would be a good deal for me to take and I'd be a fool to pass it up; yours is one of the most successful businesses in Cactus Creek, with the kind of staying power I'd normally pounce to invest in. *However*, I'd be just as big a fool if I accepted without giving you a bit more time to think about it. I think we've established that you tend to jump into these things ass first, brain second."

The man did have a way with descriptions.

"I'll go ahead and have my assistant draft some paperwork," he continued. "But in the meantime, I suggest you evaluate this from all angles once more. Since we're still vetting the wineries interested in Luke's building anyway, that'll give you another few days to think this through some more."

"But I don't need any more time."

"I don't care what you *think* you need. Take the few days," he ordered brusquely. "Also, though I'm pretty sure you're going to disregard my advice, I still say you should talk to Luke about all this before you make your decision. Trust me on this; he needs to know what you're trying to do here. I really don't want this turning out badly for you."

She remained silent. It wasn't that she didn't *want* to tell Luke and Derek what she had planned; she just didn't want to 'pull a Dani' here and fail as epically as she has been known to before. No. She'd do a grand reveal *after* Noah signed on the dotted line and all chances of failure were eliminated. "Fine. I'll take the few days but be sure those contracts are ready for me to sign at the end of those few days," she said, using her best Danica Dobson voice, the one that have shriveled the balls of men nearly as imposing as Noah.

Noah muttered under his breath about irrational romantics and ended the call with an exasperated, "I'll be in touch."

Dani looked over at the photo of her dad on the wall.

You'd do this for mom, wouldn't you?

She took his big, teddy-bear grin as a clear hell-yes.

For once, following in her dad's footsteps regarding love didn't quite seem so bad.

Chapter 27

"HAVE I MENTIONED that my folks can't stop asking when I'm bringing you back to the farm again?" Luke tugged Dani down into bed with him. "I think they kind of love you."

"I love them too," she replied, propping against his chest. "They're great."

"*You're* great." Even he could hear how fuzzy his voice was sounding right now. He *probably* shouldn't have had that last beer. Or was it the two shots he'd downed at the bar when Dani had been in the restroom?

All very foggy.

She leaned back to study his expression, chuckling. "*You* are drunk, mister. You drank more than I did tonight. You've been drinking a lot all week, in fact. What's up with you lately? Nervous about something?" she teased.

If only she knew.

If only he had the balls to tell her what a failure he was,

how he'd soon be a broke loser with nothing.

Except her.

His heart dropped to the pit of his stomach and his eyebrows dropped down a telltale notch at the mere thought of losing her.

Instantly, her face sobered, mirroring his own no doubt. "What is it? What's going on?"

"Nothing bad; it's something good, actually. A start to new beginnings, I think," he said cryptically, feeling the multiple meanings in that statement as he reached over to open the nightstand drawer. He might be losing his shop, but with Dani at his side...

Suddenly, he felt more high than drunk, the significance of what he was about to do sobering him up in an instant.

"I owe you one more Valentine gift." His heart gave a little thump at the smile lines crinkling around her eyes; they'd appeared when he'd said the word Valentine—such a contrast to how she would've reacted just a few short months ago.

All the worry left her voice, her tone softening. "You're a chronic romantic. You know very well you gave me all seventeen already."

"Those were to make up for the past," he reasoned. "This year would've been your eighteenth Valentine's Day. Remember? The Valentine gift I gave you last month was the first of your seventeen Valentines. I didn't actually give you a gift for this year's Valentine's Day yet."

"Yes you did," she said, her voice a loving timbre as she held his face in her hands. "Everything you've done, every moment together since that day has been a gift."

His eyelids lowered tenderly at that. "Well then consider this a supplementary eighteenth Valentine gift then." He turned his hand over to reveal a very distinct little gift box.

Dani gazed at the velvet cube. "What is it?" she asked in a voice he hardly recognized.

"Open it and find out."

Unable to meet his eyes, slowly, she shook her head in a silent no.

Pain. He'd never known that, until this point, pain wasn't something he'd even remotely experienced. Not this pain. What he was feeling now robbed him of breath, of strength.

It was worse than the sickening feeling he'd felt injected into his veins when he'd made the call on Monday to tell Noah that he was opting to give up his five best recipes to close out the collateral loan.

At least that pain was resulting in a $50,000 severance check he could give Quinn to help pay for Cooper's upcoming surgeries.

But *this* pain that he was feeling right now...it just bred more pain that gouged at his soul and hollowed out his heart.

A hot tear fell on his hand. He opened his eyes and looked at it. "Don't cry, sweetheart."

Her tears came anyway, words powerless to stop them.

"The gift isn't what you're thinking," he said gently. "It's not the ring you're so deathly afraid of." He took the thin red ribbon off the box and flipped it open. There was a tiny chocolate inside with gold message stamped on the bottom.

She read it slowly, hands shaking, eyes welling up more. "You said you never make promises."

"No, I don't make guarantees. *This* is a vow."

"That you'll always love me?"

"Yes."

Her voice shrank. "How can you possibly know that?"

"How do you know that you'll always love Xoey, or Rylan, or your brother?"

"I just do," she shrugged, unable to put it into words.

"Exactly. Try not to think about it; it makes it easier." He arched an eyebrow wisely.

She let a reluctant half grin appear. "Simple as that?"

"Simple as that." He gathered her into his arms. "And it is. That simple, I mean. I just know without a doubt I'll always love you. No matter what."

"Even if I say I don't want us to live together?" she asked quietly.

His jaw clenched back the stab of hurt. "Of course."

She focused her eyes on the center of his sternum. "You've been hinting at it."

"Yes I have. Because I want us to live together."

"Why?"

Dozens of reasons swam in his head, but knowing Dani, he picked the most logical. "I sleep here all the time as it is. Hell, my pile of belongings is getting big enough that I only go back to my apartment once a week, if that." It was true. For the last month, he'd been staying at Dani's almost the entire time. With their hectic, often clashing schedules, this way, at least they were able to spend a few hours together on the days one of them was sleeping while the other was working. "It's practical, and it works for us."

"Try again," she whispered, leaving out the 'bullshit answer' part that was his usual line.

He took a while to regroup. "I love you. I love how things are with us. Don't you?"

"You know I do."

"It's not like I'm asking you to marry me. I want to keep things exactly how they are...just more officially." He tried adding more rational reasoning. "Besides, it doesn't make sense for us to both have apartments. If I move here, I can help pay the rent for your apartment."

"My apartment is part of my building so I don't pay rent."

"Then I'll pay for all the maintenance...and the food."

"Just stop. I'm not quibbling over money here." Frustration spiked her voice.

"Then what? What's so wrong about my wanting us to live together?"

"Nothing, except for the reason why."

"I've told you why."

"The real reason, Luke. Tell me the real reason."

Exasperation expelled out of his lungs. "Because I want to start down a path toward a future with you! Is that so bad?"

"No," she said softly. "It's not bad at all." A sad smile overtook her lips. "But that's not all you want." Her eyes held his, daring him to prove her wrong.

"I have no idea what you're talking about. But since you seem to think you know more than I do about what I want, why don't you enlighten me?"

She didn't waver. In fact, she pushed back. Hard. "You want a guarantee. Even though you say you don't have faith in guarantees, that's exactly what you're looking for. From me. Why? Because you want to assure yourself that this wondrous, *magical* oasis of forever love you've been trying to reach for so long actually exists. That it's not just some mirage." She shook her head. "Life may have made you strong enough to recover losing those you loved, but you aren't nearly strong enough to face the possibility that the entire idea of forever love with one special person out there just for you might in fact be a complete fantasy—something you dreamed up and made unattainable."

Every emotional fiber in his being reared up in thunderous denial over such a claim.

Even though, logically, he knew what she was saying was true.

"Luke, I can see how it scares you to think you might finally reach it, dip your hands into that crystal blue water for a drink, only to feel dry sand touch your lips. Admit it. You want a guarantee that I can deliver the future you've been dreaming of all this time... That I'll finally be the person *you want me to become.*"

That last part stunned him to his core. "You think I want you to change?"

"I know you do," she sighed. "Yes, I know you love me as I am, but I think you also love a version of me that only you see. The person I believe myself to be deep down really doesn't see what the difference is if we *officially* live together or not. In fact, sometimes I wonder if I'm skeptical about marriage as a whole too. Truthfully, I've never really thought about it until now because I never got close enough to anyone to need to. And now that I am, honestly, I feel *rushed*. Rushed to figure out things that other, normal people have spent years thinking about."

She was on a roll now, absent of filters, undaunted by consequences. "So I'm not normal. So what? Why should I be? Fate will do whatever the hell it feels like doing anyway, without rhyme or reason, regardless of what we plan or dream." A bitter laugh shot out of her. "Your life is a prime example! Love a woman and plan for forever until it doesn't work out. Too bad, so sad. But look, there's another who could 'really' be the one. *Oh darn*, no go with that one either. Guess what though? There's a broken brewmaster who needs fixing next in line. Yeah, well, what's to say the next woman after me isn't who you're truly meant to be with?"

His face hardened savagely in defense. "Don't start saying shitty things to me to try and push me away, Dani. It won't work."

"You're pushing me to protect your heart; *well I'm pushing right back to protect mine!*"

Jesus Christ, this was the mother of all impasses.

She raised her eyes to his. "You think I don't notice, but

I see you holding back at times because you're afraid I'll bolt. Even after we have an absolutely perfect night, I see the questions in your eyes mercilessly torturing you, making you wonder if what we have is really just an elaborate mirage." Frustration slashed across her features. "You can't keep living your whole life walking through the desert just trying to reach this damn delusional oasis!"

"And you can't think that wasting your life playing day to day with your head hidden in the sand is actually living!" he shot back.

Breathing hard, they stared at each other, blurry emotions masquerading as anger.

"Are we over?" Dani's voice broke softly.

His shocked gaze flew down to her shattered expression. "What? No! It's just a fight."

"But look at what we're fighting about. There's no resolution. I feel like you look at me and see someone you think I'll become, in a future that I'm simply unable to see."

"Sweetheart, I look at you and all I see is you. I look into my future and I see the same thing. I don't want some fictional you, I swear it."

She shook her head skeptically. "But you and I are so different. You're such a hopeless romantic, and I'm just...not."

An incredulous groan tore out of his chest as he dropped his forehead down onto hers. "Oh. Dear. *Lord.* For the last time, you are one of the most diehard romantics I know. Re-read those cards. Ask anyone who's met you. Everything you do outs you as a closet romantic." He kissed her eyelids gently. "It's one of the many things I adore about you."

"But you're right, Dani." He gently wiped the last of her heartbreaking tears away. "I *can't* live just looking for and waiting for the future. I've done that in the past and I don't have much to look back on. It wasn't a life. Not really. But being with you *is*, and it's the life I want." His speech might have begun as a means to comfort her, but as the words tumbled out, he knew he spoke the naked truth. "Honestly, all I need—all I want—is to have you by my side and to be by yours. For as long as fate—or you—will have it." Sliding his hand down her cheek, he warned, "Even so, that doesn't mean I can just make myself stop dreaming of something a heck of a lot more permanent than a chocolate vow in that box you're holding."

She placed her head on his chest. "I know, and I love that," she admitted softly.

"I am a hundred percent invested in this relationship— long or short, I want to see what the future holds for us." He gazed into her eyes. "Question is, do you?"

"I do," she said without any hesitation.

His heart soared. He hoped to hell and back he'd be hearing those words from her lips again one day. To a far more important question.

His arms tightened around her. "Then dream with me," he rumbled softly in her ear.

Feeling her stiffen, he brushed a kiss against her lips. "No plans or promises, just dreams," he reassured gently. "No stressing about the future. No torturing ourselves with our pasts. We do it your way and just live day to day. *But* each day, we agree to dream my way...big and endless."

Closing his eyes, he forced himself not to push too hard. "We can stay together as long as our dreams still have the other in it—no more commitment than that. What do you say?"

Breath held, he stroked the tense muscles of her back for agonizingly long seconds.

She looked up into his eyes. And then shot her gaze away.

His stomach plummeted.

Thankfully, the sound of Dani's landline ringing in the living room saved him from having to come up with a casual response to that train wreck.

They each pretended like their sole purpose in life was to stand there like statues and listen to the phone ring. Ditto when the answering machine switched on.

But hearing Dani's cheerful voice say. "I'll get back to you when I can," on the recorded greeting just served to put a serious chink in his composure.

...Shortly before the message following took a wrecking ball to it.

"Dani, this is Noah. Sorry to call so late but my assistant said you already signed the paperwork and call it a wild guess but I'm pretty sure you haven't talked about your plans with Luke yet. There are things I can't disclose to either of you so I'm in an

awkward position here. I don't like doing business like this. Not telling him your connection to his lease increase was one thing, but this—"

Dani ran and slammed her hand down on the answering machine.

Luke watched the guilt blanket over Dani's pale expression.

So much for the hope that he'd been misheard that message.

Seeing that she wasn't going to be the first to break the silence didn't help him keep his calm. "What the hell was he talking about, Dani?"

"That's what I've been trying to tell you for weeks now, actually, months really if you count the beginning," she whispered, keeping her head down, avoiding his eyes.

Months?

He tipped her face back up and studied her tortured expression, saying in a voice that sounded clipped and foreign to his own ears, "So tell me now."

"I asked Noah not to renew your lease contract."

Ice filled his veins. "You did *what?*"

"*Before!* I asked him before we met, right after Quinn had done all those interview attacks outside of the brewpub." The words rushed out of her so fast he had a hard time keeping up. "I was just so angry; I went to see Harold to vent about it. And that's when I ran into Noah. You have to believe that, in the beginning, I was just complaining about what you all did that day. But somehow—you know how my brain and mouth can be—that turned into my saying business owners who purposely slander other businesses in town have no place here in Cactus Creek, which led to my blurting out that maybe Derek and I could lease out the building instead and turn it into a winery that would partner with Ocotillos..."

His eyes hardened. "*Winery.*" Unbelievable. "So *you've* been working with that Noah this whole time behind my back."

He couldn't even look at her.

———•———

DANI GRABBED HIS HANDS. "Please, don't shut me out."

He shot her a look so frustrated, so *hurt*, she released her hold on him immediately.

"Luke, I swear I didn't plan for that to happen. I didn't go searching for Harold with the intent to oust your shop. It just sort of...happened. I'd never even thought of leasing your building before, nor had it even occurred to me to turn Ocotillos into a brewpub and winery. It all gushed out of my mouth faster than my brain could process, really. I mean, I'm not going to lie and say I didn't get caught up at the time. This *is* Derek's dream after all, and I really wanted it for him—"

"So you threw my dream under the bus to get it."

"NO! I never wanted that. In fact, after I hung up the phone, I felt sick to my stomach about it. And that was before I even knew you were the owner."

"But we had our formal intros the next day, didn't we?

What happened after that?" His voice was brittle. Cold. "Doesn't sound like you jumped on the phone to undo everything. In fact, it sounds like you and Noah got mighty cozy making back table deals at my expense!"

She recoiled as if he'd just slapped her. Hot tears flooded her eyes. "Do you really think I'd do something like that behind your back?"

"How the hell should I know? Before today, I didn't think you'd ever do *anything* behind my back, let alone something like this. You kept who knows how many things from me for months. Against Noah's advice to tell me the truth too, apparently. My god, the entire time he was working with me on shop matters—" He flipped his head back, laughing bitterly. "The man must think I'm a total idiot." Shaking his head, mortification tinted his tone dark and ugly. "When I first told you how I might lose the shop, you just stood there *pretending...*" His eyes narrowed suspiciously. "Were you even going to tell me before Derek opened shop? Or were you planning on dumping me before then so you wouldn't have to?"

"You've got it all wrong! It wasn't like that at all. What I've been working with Noah on is a way to *help* you, I swear. Luke, the only reason I didn't try to undo everything right after you introduced yourself was because I didn't think there was anything to undo. I thought Noah had dismissed the idea because he never called to follow-up. That is, not until later..."

He gave her an annoyed look. "Don't stop now. You're

on a roll. Spit it out. Have the guts to do what you should've been doing the whole time. Tell me the truth—when later?"

She swallowed thickly. "Valentine's Day."

His razor sharp flinch cut her just as deep. She closed her eyes miserably. "That's when I found out Noah had contacted Derek. But it wasn't until the day after that I learned how my hasty proposal had started an avalanche effect—the wineries that made offers on your building only did so because Noah had been calling around to follow-up on my idea." She sank further into her disdain for herself. "After that, it felt like I just couldn't ever find an appropriate time to tell you."

"Right, because I was so busy being a Valentine schmuck, making it impossible for you to bomb that news on me." Luke's jaw was clenching in measured beats, as if he were forcibly restraining himself. "Then what?" he barked.

"Well, then I broke Derek's heart a little." Now Dani was the one sounding bitter. "I got to first describe, then yank my brilliant plans away from my big brother, the person who has shoved all his dreams of having a winery onto the backburner just so I could keep running my brewpub. Just so I wouldn't have to suffer through all my failures that put us in this situation to begin with." Suddenly, she felt so young, so stupid. "I failed him yet again."

His angry gaze faltered a bit, concern for her softening his glare. With one last glimmer of hope, she tried to grab hold of that lifeline. "I know it was way late in the game, but I *did* tell Noah I couldn't go through with it. Not at your expense."

He averted his eyes and threw out flippantly, "You know, if you'd just trusted me enough to be honest with me, you could've saved yourself a whole lot of guilt." His jaw ticked. "And you wouldn't have had to waste all your time 'helping me' so much."

"None of that was out of guilt," she shot back forcefully.

With a disbelieving snort, he countered stonily, "You mean to tell me you don't feel a smidgen of guilt over being responsible for what Quinn and I are going through?"

Her heart tore at the seams at the betrayal she saw in his eyes. "Of course I do. I know this is all my fault." She reached out but stopped herself from touching him. "I'm so sorry."

Silence filled the room and all emotion disappeared from Luke's expression.

Dani felt her legs almost give out when Luke reached forward and slid his hand along her jawline, cupping her face tenderly as he wiped the tears running down her cheeks. "I know you're sorry, Dani." With a low, tortured sigh, he leaned forward and buried his lips in her hair for the briefest of moments before whispering, "But I think I need some time away from you right now."

Then he left the apartment without another word.

Chapter 28

AS FAR AS REFUGES for escape go, his shop wasn't exactly the most clandestine, but Luke didn't care. He knew Dani wouldn't come after him.

The look she wore when he'd shut the door behind him was burned into his retinas.

But he just hadn't been able to remain there another second.

Glancing at the clock, he was surprised to discover how long they'd been fighting.

Midnight.

Usually the only time of night he and Dani could be asleep in bed together—the few nights a week she wasn't scheduled to close—before he got up to make his four a.m. chocolates. This would be the first night in weeks that he wasn't going to be there to see her open her eyes and sleepily wish him a good day at work.

If it were up to him, he'd never miss another morning like that for the rest of his life.

That still didn't erase what she had done though.

Regardless of how much his heart wanted to forgive her, his head just…couldn't. Quinn and Cooper were paying the price, and he was about to lose everything he'd worked years to create and achieve.

His mind couldn't help but replay all the instances over the past months where Dani had to have lied to him—white lies or lies of omission, it didn't matter. Regardless the reason, or the clean-up that followed, like a barrage of bitter bullets, every little memory, even to the tiniest detail, pelted at him. Pissed him off. Made him hurt even more. Mostly because they were secondary wounds that were simply adding new pain to the already gaping hole in his heart that she'd torn out of him by the betrayal of trust. Not his trust for her, but rather, the opposite.

She should have trusted him enough to tell him the truth. Trusted that he'd continue to love her. Trusted their relationship enough to stop hiding from him.

This whole time, he thought he'd been making progress, building a foundation for the future. But tonight, it was obvious—she still didn't trust him.

His phone chirped just then.

An incoming text.

He couldn't get himself to open it.

Two more chirps about five minutes apart, and then a chime. A voice mail.

That was odd. Dani never left him voicemails. Pulling out his phone, he scrolled through the messages and felt his heart stop.

The texts weren't from Dani. They were from Derek.

>> *Get to the hospital just off the north exit. My sister needs you.*

Then ten minutes after that:

>> *Look, I know you two had a fight but you're never going to forgive yourself if you're not here.*

And the last one was time-stamped a mere five minutes after that:

>> *Swallow your damn pride and get down here you stubborn ass!*

Holy shit. What the hell was going on? Luke grabbed his keys and ran.

The fastest, and slowest, ten minutes of his life later, he was rushing into the emergency room to find Derek and Dani talking to a doctor at the far end.

Seeing Dani standing there, and not lying in some gurney on the way to surgery, hit him with a wave of relief so strong, he felt sucker-punched.

When he got near enough to hear their exchange with the doctor, however, the next sucker-punch he felt was one of sheer shock.

"We managed to stabilize your father for now," explained the doctor, "but you two will need to make a decision shortly. We can transport him back to the care home but really, we don't advise it given the circumstances. I know this isn't an easy one to make but you really do need to consider all I've told you about his quality of life from this point on."

Luke had never been more confused in his life.

Dani and Derek's father was still alive?

Not wanting to barge in, he held back and watched Dani follow the doctor through the double doors that led to the ICU.

Derek turned and looked up, relief blending with the concern etched in his expression. He headed over to sit next to Luke in the deserted waiting area.

"Thanks for coming, man. I just really thought you needed to be here. You and Dani are both so stubborn—"

"Derek, what in the world is going on? I thought your dad passed away from a heart attack a few years ago."

"He did have a heart attack, which resulted in a massive stroke that sent him into a coma shortly after. Dani would never have told you our dad died. Most folks just assume he did. And you wouldn't have heard otherwise from any of us that know differently because frankly, none of us will ever talk about it." Luke saw the stark pain streak across his face. "Dani blames herself for our dad's heart attack." His voice was rough with long-held sympathy for his sister. "Every spare dime she has goes right into his life support and the care home he's been in for the past three years. And at least once a month, she's right there at his side. Apologizing. Praying for him to come back. Begging him to forgive her for failing him so badly."

Luke felt icy dread prick across his skin as each memory of her little personal jabs about how she'd failed in the past came rushing back.

"Dani has been blatantly ignoring the doctors who've been telling her for years that our father is almost assuredly never going to wake up, definitely never as more than a vegetable even if he did. Still, she simply won't let him go. And I have no doubt that she'd sooner bury herself in debt then be the one to pull the plug on him. So she just tortures herself by keeping him alive at the care home and going through her weekly rituals of apologizing for being the one that put him in there all because of her misguided trust."

Trust.

Shit. He should've known there was something more to it. He should have forced her to talk about it. The mere thought of Dani going through this maimed him. He couldn't possibly imagine being the one experiencing it.

"Why does she blame herself?" he asked finally.

"Because it was all my fault," she said simply as she came up behind them.

Turning, Luke was struck mute by how devastated she looked. Broken.

Her dull voice turned hollow as she continued through gritted teeth, "Because I made the stupid mistake of trusting a man who stole my father's most prized accomplishments, who nearly destroyed our family business, and who I was foolish enough to believe loved me as much as I loved him."

Instantly, Luke's hands fisted with rage. Not in jealousy. In pure, deadly fury over the man who would have done this to her—betray her to such a vicious degree. He destroyed her. Her heart, her ability to trust, her faith in love.

This was what Derek had been talking about on Valentine's Day. Luke had thought it was a bad break-up, akin to his being left at the altar by his ex. But nothing, *nothing* had prepared Luke for the magnitude of how badly she'd been hurt.

Dani walked over the rest of the way and stood just out of arm's reach. "Starting about six years ago, my dad began finally making a name for himself in the craft beer world, taking home trophies and creating brews that distributors were offering small fortunes to bottle. But like I told you before, bottling was never his thing. He turned all the offers down. And there were many. One more persistent than the rest."

The last glimmer of life in her eyes dimmed then. "After his first heart attack four years ago, I took full control of the brewpub. Dad stayed on to brew occasionally but all decision-making became mine alone. That's when it all began tumbling downhill. The day our dad decided to choose me as his successor instead of Derek."

Derek broke in with a sharp, "That's *not* true and you know it, Dani. You were born to that position in ways I never was. And as far as your decision-making, you ran into a string of bad luck. It happens. Hell, we both saw how much bad luck Dad used to have to overcome. And just like him, you did. You got us through it all."

"Except one," she argued back weakly.

This version of Dani standing before him was breaking Luke's heart. Even her arguments held no fire, nothing but anguish, and suffocating guilt.

Over what, he still didn't understand.

Derek gripped her shoulders. "The sheer amount of Dad's hospital bills would have crippled most small businesses, Dani. You did what you had to do." Turning to Luke, he explained, "Our dad didn't have more than the bare minimum health insurance. Before the first heart attack, he'd been healthy as a horse. He rarely even came down with a cold. In our toughest years, shortly after our mom left, he cut back on a lot to make ends meet, his health insurance being one of the first to go on the chopping block. And none of us knew."

Anger leapt into his voice. "Those vultures who'd been trying to distribute dad's beers had done their research. Because they knew exactly how much we owed when they came knocking on our door with their offer."

A bitter, self-flogging laugh drifted out of Dani. "And I opened that door wide open for them to come right in and take everything our dad worked his entire life to build, to be proud of, to leave behind as his legacy."

When Derek started to object, a small spark of life ignited in her voice. "No! You don't get to play this off. This was on me. I knew dad didn't want to bottle his beers and I took the meeting anyway. A guppy thinking she could play in the same tank with the sharks. What's worse, I did it without *hiring* a lawyer."

That last statement had Derek's mouth snapping shut, his jaw clenching harshly as if holding back a tidal wave of words.

This time it was Dani who turned to give Luke an explanation. "I didn't hire a lawyer, I just trusted him is all. After finally convincing our dad that bottling was our last option, I had my boyfriend broker the deal for us." Her eyes narrowed, her voice taking on a hateful edge he'd never heard her use before. "Eric was a corporate lawyer working in one of the biggest firms in Phoenix; deals like this one were child's play for him. And when he refused to let me retain his services fully, I thought he was just being Eric. The great boyfriend he'd always been. The one man I'd allowed myself to fall in love with and actually trust."

Her shoulders fell with the weight of utter disappointment her memories brought. "It wasn't until long after we had no legs to stand on did I discover the real reason he hadn't wanted us to retain him officially was because he'd already been retained...to negotiate on behalf of the bottling company, who'd apparently also given him an exorbitant finder's fee to set the whole thing up. To set *me* up."

At Luke's hiss of disbelief, she looked away.

In shame.

And that enraged him even more. "Dani, you couldn't

have possibly—"

"*No.* I don't want to hear you trying to put it all on him. Yes, Eric was the lowest of life forms for what he did, but he wouldn't have been able to do it if I hadn't stood back and let it happen." Her hands curled into her stomach as she detailed just how badly Eric had screwed her and her business over. "I trusted him based on love and love alone. Even when my gut was telling me something sounded off about the 'branding clause' in the contract. Even when his generic, non-descript answer to my questions about it had given me pause as well. We didn't know until the week that the first shipment of bottled beer was scheduled to be distributed around the country that they had changed the name of our beer and erased all connection to our brewery on the label via their 're-branding' rights. And *my signature* was what had allowed them to do it. Legally, in an iron-clad contract we couldn't get out of."

Disgust filled her expression. "At least I'd been correct in thinking he was the best to negotiate this deal. He was. There wasn't a single loophole in that contract. And believe me, I paid good money in legal fees to try to find one. By the time we could fight it, they'd already begun selling the beer like hotcakes. When we tried to terminate the deal and retain sole ownership of our brew recipes, they threatened to sue us for breach of contract and losses—which was close to a million in start-up expenses alone."

With a tired sigh, she continued with barely any emotion at all, "And in the end, they turned around and sued us for groundless public defamation and damaging press. We'd played into their plans perfectly. And we couldn't afford to fight it. We couldn't even afford to start the *process* of fighting it. So, we ended up giving up *all* our rights to my dad's six award-winning beers to make the whole thing go away."

She glanced sadly at the double-doors she'd emerged from just minutes ago. "After weeks of stress, that was the final straw that caused his heart attack...on Valentine's Day three years ago," she finished softly.

"Instead of sitting in front of a fireplace in the log cabin up in Flagstaff I'd booked for Eric and I to spend the first Valentine's date I'd ever allowed in a relationship...instead of cooking him the perfect meal I'd spent weeks thinking about and preparing for...instead of starting to plan the wedding I'd finally let myself begin to dream about, with the man I'd told my heart it was to safe to dream with..." Her crushed gaze fell on Derek. "Instead of getting to see my big brother marry the love of his life two weeks later...I was *here*. Here in this exact E.R. watching the doctors jolt my father's body over and over again to try and re-start his heart."

She tilted her head and looked into Luke's eyes. "Do you see now why I couldn't see Valentine's Day the way you saw it until you showed it to me? All I've been able to see for the last three years was my father start to die in front of my eyes, just hours after having felt my own heart get ripped from my body from the one man who'd sworn he'd love and protect it above all else when he'd proposed to me the month before."

Tears filled her eyes and anger beyond understanding filled her trembling voice. "I let myself believe in the fairytale, only to have it turn into all of my worst nightmares. And everyone I loved *paid* for my mistakes." She slid the inside of her wrist over her eyes to wipe away her tears, her hands balled into fists so tight her knuckles were white. "Eric will no doubt go straight to hell for what he did, but until the day he does, *I'm* the one living here on earth with what I've done. Dad was able to overcome every hardship flung his way by the universe, heal after losing the love of his life; and in the end, it was *my actions that killed his heart.*" The last she raged at herself in a whisper as deafening as the most blood curdling shout.

She crumbled right there before him when she brought her gaze up to clash with his. "The worst part of it all? I turned around and did the same thing to you." Her hand started to reach for him before she pulled back. "I don't blame you for not being able to forgive me, Luke. What I did was unforgivable. And I'll spend my whole life living with those regrets as well. I know my apologies mean as much as Eric's did, so I won't even insult you with them."

Refusing to meet Luke's eyes a second longer, she turned to head back to the double doors before Luke could even formulate a response that could break through the lonely despair trembling out of her in waves.

He went to follow her, with every intention of dragging her back to listen to him until she could finally hear him.

But her next words stopped him in his tracks.

Uttered so quietly Luke could barely hear them, the words were directed to Derek, "I'm sorry I've been holding onto dad so selfishly all these years. His life insurance was always supposed to go to you, to your dreams. I know you saw his living will too." Tears filled her voice. "I never meant to keep you from your dreams all this time, Derek. I just...couldn't let him go."

Hand on the door, she whispered brokenly, "But I signed the forms five minutes ago. They're waiting for us to come back in so they can shut off his life support."

And with that she walked away from them both.

A near stranger to Luke now.

Chapter 29

LUKE FELT RABIDLY HELPLESS.

He'd watched as Derek and Jonathan all but carried Dani back to their car so she could stay at their house. At her request. She hadn't been able to look at him once.

Not wanting to be the selfish jackass that pushed her on the night her father died, he let her go. He watched the woman he loved drive away from him, broken-hearted and just plain broken.

He rammed his fist into the wall. Dammit, he wanted to kill that Eric guy. Make him suffer the way he had made Dani suffer. Drag the asshole out from whatever hole he'd crawled into and—

And what?

Nothing could undo what had happened to Dani; nothing could return all she'd lost.

Thankfully, before another frustrating wall of despair

could slam into him, however, a Hail Mary thought hit him first. Grabbing his cell phone, he dialed his friend Connor's number.

"H'lo?"

Shit. It sounded like Connor had been dead asleep. Luke glanced at the clock. Well, no wonder. It was five in the morning.

Hearing Connor's wife in the background—her voice filled with soft concern right next to the receiver—had Luke's jagged emotions spinning even further out of control.

He wanted what Connor had found.

He wanted Dani's voice murmuring right at his side, ready to face anything life threw their way together. He wanted to be the one Dani turned to, not the one she drove away from when life seemed cruel and impossible.

"Hey, sorry to wake you. I didn't realize how early it was," he apologized. "I'll call again later."

Connor said something reassuringly to his wife in the background before coming back onto the phone line. "It's fine. I need to get up soon anyway. What's up? Everything okay?"

Where to begin?

Might as well start from his first suspicion. "Tell me the truth. Do you know the guy that Dani dated a few years ago? The one that screwed her and her dad over?"

Silence.

And then a slow, weary, "Yeah. I know him."

He thought as much.

"Luke, listen man. It wasn't my history to tell. I would have told you if…shit, if it all hadn't played out as badly as it had. But the way things went down—"

"No, I get it," Luke said tiredly. And he did. It pissed him off to no end that everyone had kept so much from him, but he understood the difficult situation they'd all been in.

What he *didn't* understand, however, was how his friend had allowed the fucker to get away without jail time at the least. Connor didn't have many friends, and the few he did, he protected almost ruthlessly if it came down to it.

"The fact that you haven't had him arrested tells me there's more to the story," guessed Luke, unsure whether he even *wanted* to be right about this.

"A lot more," agreed Connor quietly. Another measured pause passed before Connor finally dropped the first bomb. "Dani doesn't know this but Eric is actually one of the senior partners in the firm Victoria and I started up last year."

That Luke hadn't been expecting. Not by a longshot. It occurred to him then that aside from Connor's good friend Victoria, he didn't have a clue who else was in the Pierson Sullivan firm. Knowing the man that had hurt Dani was still linked to their circle of friends made his protective instincts go on full alert.

He barely managed to keep the calm in his voice as he asked the most obvious question, "What in God's name were you thinking hiring a man like that?"

Connor sighed. "He's a great lawyer, and despite all

evidence to the contrary, a good guy as well."

Shit. Even though every enraged, rabidly possessive cell in his body didn't want to hear any context in which a man like Eric could be *a good guy*, Luke couldn't leave well enough alone. He had to know. "Is this another one of those things that isn't your story to tell?" he grunted, fully prepared to drag the story out of Connor somehow.

Connor paused for a long moment before relenting, "No. This one I can tell you. Because I think you need to hear it."

The silent suggestion for Luke to sit down hung there at the end of the sentence like an ominous warning, so Luke sat. And listened.

A half hour later, he wished to hell and back that he hadn't asked.

———◆———

HE WAS OUT OF HIS MIND.

Luke pulled up to the apartment complex address Derek had texted him and took another minute to think about what Connor had told him, and what he was getting ready to do with that information.

This wasn't a gamble.

This was a risk, plain and simple. But a necessary one.

Dani deserved to know the whole story about the man she'd once loved in the very way she was afraid to love now.

Even if it meant Luke might end up losing her to him.

He rang the doorbell and waited. Prayed he was doing the right thing. Prayed that even if it wasn't the right thing for him, it would mend the scars on her heart that she had never allowed to heal.

"*Luke.*" A red-eyed Dani dragged the door open in surprise, her voice gut-wrenchingly tattered around the edges. "What are you doing here?"

He'd rehearsed this in his head—the band aid-ripping approach he'd had all planned out. But one look at her and all he could do was drag her into his arms and hold her until she finally stopped fighting. Until she dissolved against him and allowed herself to be held, comforted. Loved.

God, I can't lose her. Don't let me lose her.

Luke helped Dani sit down and said softly, "Honey, I know nothing can take the pain away right now. And no amount of talking will make the loss of your father any more fathomable or manageable." He knew from experience. "But I'm hoping this will help you with some of the anger, confusion, and hurt that's tied into it all."

She pulled back and looked questioningly at the print-out of the information he'd found online shortly after talking to Connor. It took a mere second for her to see the relevant names that would effectively rewrite history for her in one fell swoop.

"Luke, why are you showing me Eric's mother's obituary notice?"

This was the first time he'd heard her say that name without disdain and resentment.

Which simply served to multiply his worries ten-fold.

"Sweetheart, look at the date Eric's mother died."

"February 15th. Three years ago," she whispered as her eyes shot back up to find answers to questions Luke knew she'd never known to ask.

Luke sat on the coffee table in front of her to tell her the side of the story Connor had been unsuccessful in getting her to listen to. Not that anyone blamed her for not wanting to even hear the man's name mentioned. "Honey, Eric's mother had been diagnosed the year before with an aggressive blood cancer, which he'd apparently cleaned out his savings and sold anything of value he had to pay for the bone marrow treatments she needed to stay alive."

Dani blinked and murmured, "He used to live in this tiny studio apartment in Phoenix." A slow dawning look of understanding crept across her face. "And I remember one of his friends asking him once why he was driving a piece-of-shit car instead of a car worthy of a junior partner at the second biggest law firm in the city."

She shook her head. "I just thought he was down-to-earth, unlike his other lawyer friends. And I'd appreciated him all the more for it."

Luke gripped the edge of the coffee table and pushed himself to keep going. "But even after spending hundreds of thousands of dollars that year on her treatment, his mother's condition still worsened. She didn't have much time left, and the only option remaining was gene therapy, which again, his mother's insurance wouldn't cover."

Dani's eyelids fluttered shut in pain. Three deep breaths sawed in and out of her before she asked hoarsely, "So you're telling me that Eric did what he did to try and save his mother's life?"

"Yes."

With a quiet headshake filled with hurt and a completely new variety of confusion, she asked, "Why didn't he tell me? He never even talked about his mother. All I knew was that his mother lived out East."

"I don't know, sweetheart." He grit his jaw, barely managing to force out the words, "And honestly, there's only one man who does know."

Her head snapped up in disbelief. "You think I should go talk to him?"

Luke clenched his teeth and shoved aside the voice inside his head that had instantly yelled, "*hell no*," so loud his brain hurt. "I think you should do whatever you feel you need to do to get the answers you deserve. The answers that might even help you forgive him."

A soft gasp slipped past her lips at the prospect of forgiveness. He watched her eyes glide out of focus as she stared at the ground, or rather memories from her past that he wasn't privy to.

"How do I do that?" she asked, genuinely mystified. "How do I even begin to forgive him for what he did?"

"The same way I forgave you," he replied softly.

Fresh tears filled her eyes. "You forgive me?"

"Sweetheart, I think I forgave you the moment you

came clean. Just as importantly, I *understand* why you did it. That's why I wanted to tell you about Eric's mom."

With a sigh, he spoke from his heart, even though every male fiber in his being was calling him the biggest fool in the world. "Just because you forgive his reasons, doesn't mean you dismiss his actions, honey. I'm not saying you should forgive *what* he did. But maybe by talking to him, you'll be able to find the peace to forgive *him*—the person, not the action. And more importantly, the peace then to forgive yourself."

"I don't know if I can."

Seeing the lost expression in her eyes, he asked gently, "*Do* you forgive the reasons behind what Eric did? Or at least empathize?"

She thought about it for several long, silent seconds. "*Yes.*"

Hell, he did too. Honestly, Luke didn't know how differently he'd have handled things had he been in Eric's shoes.

"Then start there," he offered quietly, leaning forward and pressing his lips to her forehead, wishing he could do more, wishing he could read her mind right now. "Do what you need to do to find that peace, sweetheart. Take your time."

And then come back to me.

The last, he hoped, she could read in *his* mind.

383

Chapter 30

DANI SAT IN THE SAME spot long after Luke left. Questions were now jumbled in with her grief, confusion smeared into her anger and sadness. She felt ungrounded, untethered. Not just as if she'd lost the things that had been tying her to her past and all that she knew, but that she'd been *released* from those very things as well.

As evening turned into night, she attempted to process how her entire world had shifted so dramatically in a day's time.

She was now an orphan.

Eric was no longer the soul-less villain she'd relegated him to be three years ago.

And Luke wanted her to forgive herself...the same way he'd forgiven her.

She looked at the blank spot on her ring finger where Eric's engagement ring had once sat and wondered if she would've forgiven him back then had she known what she did now.

Probably.

She'd certainly loved him enough.

For hours, she sat and asked herself questions she'd never even considered the answers for, played out dozens of starkly varied scenarios of how her life would be right now had things been different.

And then, irony of all ironies, she compared what Eric had done to her and her business against what she'd done to Luke and his business.

It was a sobering comparison.

Picking up her cell phone, her fingers dialed the numbers out of rote memory, the voice answering on the other end slamming memories into her like a freight train.

"Hello?"

"Eric?" she said softly.

After a stark silence, his voice returned with confounded shock, "*Dani?*"

Try though she did, she couldn't separate the anger from her memories. Not yet. She simply wasn't that evolved. Just hearing him say her name brought it all back—the good and bad—in one overwhelming wave of emotion saturated with fury more than anything else. And Eric, being Eric, just let her sit there and silently rage.

In retrospect, that's how their fights always used to be as well. Not nearly as satisfying as fighting with Luke, she mused then, out of the clear blue sky.

"Why didn't you tell me?" she demanded finally, the mere thought of Luke calming her like nothing else could. "We were engaged to be married. Why didn't you ever tell me about your mother?"

Eric sounded older, more regretful than she'd ever heard him. "Because I was ashamed."

What? "What on earth for?"

"I'd been a crappy son. I went off to law school and got so caught up in being this big deal attorney making the big bucks, I pretty much ignored my mother. I went from calling her once a week, to once a month until I got the job in Phoenix. Then, I was lucky if I remembered to call her on her birthday and holidays." Shame and loss of equal measure blanketed his words. "I didn't even know she had cancer until months after she'd been diagnosed. I never checked my messages." A self-flogging laugh escaped his lips. "Can you believe that? My mom had to tell me on my answering machine that she had cancer. And I actually screened that message, shoved it into the memory as soon as I heard her say hello."

"Eric, I'm sure she understood. You were just starting out in your career."

"That's what made it worse. She *did* understand. She didn't call back after that because she didn't want to 'bother' me. If one of the interns at her hospital hadn't mistakenly called me instead of her actual emergency contact, I might have never known she was sick until it was too late." He sighed. "So I didn't tell you because I was ashamed. I thought you'd be as disgusted with me as I was. And I didn't want you to see my worst flaws; I didn't want to lose you over them."

More similarities they shared.

His tone changed, softened as he asked her a question in return, "Would you have gone through with the deal if I had told you about my mom from the start?"

One of the many questions she'd already asked herself.

"I think I would have. And just as importantly, I think my dad would have, too." Though she was being the pot to his kettle, she said candidly, "You should have trusted us. Trusted that we would've done what we could to help you. Everything might have actually worked out."

The measured pause on his end primed her for the question she knew was coming.

"Everything? Would you have stayed with me? Married me like we'd planned?"

The answer no longer freaked her out anymore. "Yes."

His quiet curse had her smiling in surprise. Eric never used to curse.

"Would you still marry me now?"

Ah, now that sounded more like the old Eric she knew.

Her chuckles turned into outright laughter. "Do you really want me to answer that?"

"*Yes,*" he rumbled immediately, before following-up with a sighing, "No."

Something told her he already knew about Luke.

"Are you happy with him? That chocolate shop guy?" His tone was sincere, though it sounded like he was gnashing his teeth over the word 'chocolate.'

"Yes. Surprisingly, really. He's nothing like you."

"Yeah? Like I-still-have-a-chance different?"

She could almost see his green eyes brightening at the end of that question mark. God, she'd forgotten why she'd fallen in love with the man in the first place. He was an outrageous flirt. In a sweet, 'come meet my labrador' way.

But there was also something in his voice that made her consider her answer carefully. "Luke was the one who told me about your mom. And he's the one who encouraged me to call you...and forgive you."

"Damn. Of course he had to be a friggin' saint."

She didn't know who this new Eric was, but she liked him. Didn't love him. But could definitely see being friends with him. One day.

"Do you?" he asked quietly. "Forgive me?"

"No." She had to be honest. Even though the pain she heard in his near silent exhale made her hurt as well. "But I want to," she added softly. "And I think I will. One day."

"That's more than I deserve, frankly." His voice flooded with sorrow. "Sweetheart, if I thought it would help, I'd spend the rest of my life apologizing to you, and every day of it trying to make things up to you somehow—"

"Then I'd spend the rest of mine telling you it wasn't your fault," she broke in, the truth of that statement seeping into her skin, settling into her bones.

She could hear the question marks in his patient silence. A silence she knew he'd never be the first to break.

Again, so different from Luke.

"I said I don't forgive you; I didn't say I still blame you." Her words snagged in her throat as she replayed the final, paradoxically heartbreaking look of peace on her father's face just before the monitors flatlined—simultaneously imagining Eric having gone through that same final moment with his mother. Alone. "You did what you needed to do for someone you love, Eric. The only fault there is in loving that person beyond all reason and ramification. So no, I don't blame you for what happened to my dad. Not anymore."

"Dani..." He sounded shocked. Out of sorts. "You *don't* have to do that. I told you, I don't deserve it."

"Well, you're going to damn well accept it, you stubborn ass," she huffed, smiling when she heard the stunned pause followed by the surprised chuckle ringing out from his end.

It took him a moment to get his bearings, and when he did, the Eric that returned was definitely not the same man she'd been engaged to. Just as she was no longer the same woman.

"Wow," he said in something close to awe. "You really have changed."

"Yep." Pride—and thoughts of Luke—filled her then. "Haven't you heard? I'm all hardcore now. I issue throwdowns, kick ass, and take no prisoners."

His chuckle deepened. "I *have* heard."

"I also collect on debts owed to me."

"Yeah?" Amusement and curiosity battled for dominance over that one word.

"Uh-huh." She took in her first deep, unstifled breath of the night before throwing out lightly, "After all is said and done, the fact is, mister, you owe me for everything you've done. Big time. And just so you know, the day I forgive you will be the day I'll start collecting. So be ready."

He was smiling now, she could hear it, and the sigh he expelled was rich with fondness. "I've missed you, Dani. You tell Luke I said he's one lucky guy." Humor and admiration lit his tone. "One very lucky, very brave guy."

Aw, that compliment just got the guy one step closer to debt-collection day.

———◆———

LUKE WAS READY TO LOSE IT.

It had been two whole days since he'd broken the Eric news to Dani and the woman hadn't called him. Not once, dammit.

Well, to be fair, it was only a *day and a half*, really, considering it was four in the morning right now...

Okay, okay. Their talk had been late in the evening and she *had* texted him before she'd gone to bed the next morning to thank him for coming over. So *technically*, mathematically, it was really more like a day.

Longest freakin' day of his life.

And it wasn't helping one bit that he was sitting in his soon-to-be-closed shop, unable to do shit about that situation either.

As he stared out the window across the pitch-black side lot that led to Ocotillos, straight out of left field, Luke remembered the story that waitress had told him and the guys months ago—about how, even when they'd been looking at closing their doors for good, instead of wallowing, Vince Dobson had thrown everything he had into one last brew. One final recipe. To go down swinging, and leave it all out there on the field.

Huh.

One last chocolate. One final recipe.

Yeah. *That*, he could do.

Moments later, his hands were already pulling ingredients off the shelves, seemingly independently from his brain. While his heart rarely got involved in the chocolatiering process, it was clearly calling all the shots today. And he wouldn't have it any other way. Within minutes, Luke was a man on a mission, tempering the butterless couverture white chocolate before adding the rich cream that would thicken it.

The logical part of his brain knew that making a new chocolate now was just going to be painful since it'd only have a home in this shop for maybe another month before they shut everything down for good. He didn't care. This one was just for him.

And Dani.

Time zipped by as he created a layered center firm enough to cut, but still soft in texture, reminiscent of his whip fillings. While it hardened in the cooler, he focused on the design, heating red cocoa butter to liquid and brushing it onto a sheet of food-safe mylar in random geometric patterns—one of the first tricks he'd learned to transfer deco art designs onto chocolates. Dipping the now-cooled centers into newly tempered white chocolate, he then pressed the coated chocolate onto the dried mylar sheet design. And just like with those kiddie tattoos, voila, the red cocoa butter patterns transferred onto the chocolate squares.

As a final touch, he carved out an organic design around the swirls with a tiny blade and sprinkled vanilla-infused red crystallized sugar into the grooves.

Then it was done.

A new chocolate. Fittingly, a *red and white* one.

And for the first time in his chocolatiering career, *Quinn* wasn't the first person he wanted to taste it.

As he gazed down at his final chocolate, Luke decided then and there that if Dani didn't call him today, he wasn't just going to sit back and wallow. Nope. Shop or no shop, she was his future. And as soon as she woke up, he was going to stomp over there and demand that the stubborn woman marry him already so they could get started on that future. Start adding more dreams to that future so they could both—

A loud rapping noise broke into his thoughts.

Startled, he noticed the sun was now out. But it was still early.

Who would be here at this hour?

Heading out to the storefront to investigate, he was beyond surprised at who he saw standing there on the other side of the glass.

"Hey, man." He quickly unlocked the door to let Derek in. "Is Dani okay?" Puzzled by the man's smiling, almost giddy energy, Luke put aside his worries and amended his guess. "Or is this a chocolate emergency? You planning something for Jonathan?"

Derek grinned and shook his outstretched hand. "No, nothing like that. I actually have something I wanted to show you."

"Have a seat." Luke pointed to the nearest table. "Want some coffee?"

The almost frenzied shuffling of papers he heard in response made him look back over at Derek. Seeing Dani's brother, one of the most easygoing people on the planet, looking so nervous made him forget the coffee pot altogether. The guy obviously didn't need any caffeine at the moment.

"You okay, man?" Luke sat down across from him, now back to being worried.

After a deep breath, a now very serious, very formal Derek slid a portfolio across the table and stated, "Luke, I'd like us to go into business together."

Luke did a double take.

Having no clue how to even process that sentence, Luke simply looked down at the elegantly scripted folio cover while trying to turn his brain right-side-up again. "Desert Confections Chocolates *and Wines?*" His gaze snapped back to Derek's. "You want to open your craft winery with my chocolate shop instead of the brewpub?"

"Ah, so Dani finally told you. Good. Then I can skip the

forgive-my-sister part and get right to my spiel."

The fun-loving Derek was back, visibly teeming with excitement and a very Dobson-esque confidence as he explained, "I've been thinking about this for weeks now and I really think turning Desert Confections into a chocolate shop *and* winery would be the perfect pairing—product-wise, business-wise, and location-wise."

Like a kid in a candy store, Derek looked around the shop excitedly. "This is a spectacular space for a winery. Harold told me about the huge cellar you have downstairs, with both an internal and external entrance from the kitchen. Seriously, you couldn't get any more perfect of a set-up for an add-on winery. I could do every step of the vinting process down there and you'd never even notice our presence since I hear you don't even use that space."

It was true, they didn't even need it for storage.

Now equally excited, Luke flipped open Derek's detailed prospectus and scanned some of the highlights.

Meanwhile, Derek quickly walked over to the walls on the west end of the shop. "As for the shop itself, if we line this bare wall with bottle display shelves and shift everything over a little, it wouldn't take very much room to showcase the wines. And since you only use display tables for your boxed chocolates, it wouldn't impede on your space at all. You'd barely notice our presence—"

"Stop talking like you'd be in the way, Derek," cut in Luke. "What you're proposing is a good idea. Hell, a great one. And an equally profitable partnership from what I can see so far. If we do this, we'll split the space. The bottles don't have to be isolated to the shelves; we can pair it with the chocolates in our displays and put it in combined gift baskets too."

When he flipped to the next page in the business plan, Luke grinned when he saw Derek had been thinking along the same lines.

"Check out the computer-generated sketches Jonathan and I did. On the last page specifically." Derek's voice was brimming with barely contained glee. "I got this idea while we were up on the roof planning Dani's birthday party."

Pointing out features on the illustrated page, Derek described what he envisioned for the roof deck. "If we go with a garden setup with vine-covered pergolas to protect the entire area from the elements, we could put comfy patio oasis seating and turn the deck into a trendy little tasting area for customers to hang out. We'll get even more bang for our buck if we arrange everything so it's designed with weddings and parties in mind as well. That way, we can rent it out as an event venue with a gazebo corner that can also double as a party/wedding planning café that houses all the food and drinks." He looked at Luke hesitantly. "What do you think about serving food up there regularly?"

"I think that'll finally make good use of the chef's kitchen this place came equipped with." A wry grin stretched across his face. "And it'll definitely draw in more customers. It's an excellent idea."

Derek exhaled in relief. "I've already asked Javier to

help me think of dishes to pair with chocolate and wine for a small menu. It would be classy but easy things—finger sandwiches, appetizers, desserts—things he could train a part-timer to put together without any fuss."

Luke skimmed over the plans for the cellar layout and frowned. "Wait, where are you planning on doing the wine bottling if not in the cellar?" He didn't know much about wineries but he knew they needed to be bottled and he definitely didn't have the space for that.

"There's not enough room for it down there," confirmed Derek. "One option is to bottle by hand. Quite a few small wineries do. But I was thinking, since I *am* partial owner of Ocotillos, bottling in the brewery might be a possibility. I haven't discussed any of this with Dani, but I think she'd go for it. We could easily clear some space to put in a small bottling unit or even do an expansion if business picks up enough for us to need bigger bottling and labeling equipment."

Quickly reading through the final pages of the proposal, Luke saw more and more green lights with each page. Eventually, he closed the folio. "I'm sold. I mean, I have to discuss it with Quinn, but seeing as how she *loved* that wine you made her last week—"

He blinked, and then understanding—and admiration—hit him. He'd *wondered* why Derek had dropped off that bottle specifically for Quinn.

Derek gave a proud shrug. "What can I say? I'm a businessman. I work the people as well as the problems."

Grinning, Luke shook Derek's hand. "You call your bank; I'll call Quinn and Noah. I can't say for certain, but I think Noah might actually crack a smile over this one."

At that impossible prediction, Derek laughed. "I said I had a great idea, not a miraculous one. But I do think Noah would get on board with this. Let me know if he gives you any hassles and I'll go talk to him as well."

After scheduling a time for Derek to meet with Quinn later that day, Luke was ready to climb out of his skin. He couldn't wait a second longer; he needed to see Dani. Share this new development with her. Kiss her. Hell, just hold her in his arms.

Shackle her there if he had to.

He raced to clean up his work area, all the while glancing back over at the chocolate he'd made earlier. With considerable effort, he did everything in his power to remain pragmatic and not get his hopes up prematurely but nothing could stop the thought that had begun drumming in his head the moment he'd realized the potential in Derek's business plan.

Maybe this wasn't his last chocolate after all.

Ignoring the intermittent beep coming from his cell phone the entire time, he shoved his phone in his back pocket and boxed up his new chocolate. Everything could wait until after he kissed Dani awake, until after he convinced her that he was there to stay in her life and that she was his for good. His life, his future, his...everything.

He wasn't sure how he was going to accomplish the

latter if she put up an argument but he figured there would be some convincing bouts of sex involved.

Along with his new red and white chocolate fed to her in bed.

The perfect start to the rest of their lives, as far as he was concerned.

At ten to eight, Luke dashed out to his car, barely pausing to give Quinn a fast high-five hello when she came in to open up shop. His beeping phone was driving him crazy, putting a serious buzz-kill on his grand plans. Digging it out of his pocket to silence it, he stopped in his tracks when he saw that the persistent reminders were for a text from Dani.

>> *Could you meet me at Ocotillos this morning? I need to show you something.*

Shit. The text had come in over an hour ago. He didn't even stop to lock his car back up; he just spun around and raced over to the brewpub.

Seeing another text come in mid-sprint, his heart flipped over when he read it.

>> *I'm going to sit and wait for you, damn it. I'll even shut down the brewpub for the day if I have to.*

Well, hell.

That was just about *the* most romantic thing that Dani could say. That brewpub hadn't been closed since the day it opened its doors, as far as he knew.

Christ, he loved the hell out of that woman. He was so going to kiss her silly the second he saw her. Smiling now, he yanked open the back door.

And got blown ten feet back into the alleyway.

———◆———

SON OF A BITCH! Coughing, Luke rolled to his side with a loud groan, pushing up from the dirt, wondering what the hell had just happened. It took him a second to realize he was in the lot next to Ocotillos and there was black smoke billowing out all around him. His head whipped to the brewery. Already the sound of folks on the street screaming confirmed his worst nightmare.

There'd been an explosion.

"*DANI!*" Luke ran at a dead sprint. Inside was a horrific scene from a movie—the corner tank wall of the brewery looked like a bomb had detonated right through it. Debris was everywhere with blackened metal shards littering the ground. Beer was still shooting from the pipes above one of the brewing tanks like a liquid firework show.

Luke screamed Dani's name again.

His heart plunged when he saw her finally, lying in a heap next to the spot where a full tank used to stand, not just the metal remains that looked like the pit of a jagged cauldron.

A few other men raced in behind him but he got to Dani first. She was eerily still; he wasn't even sure if she was

399

breathing. "*Dani!* Oh my god. Wake up sweetheart." He didn't want to shake her, not knowing what her injuries were. Pulling a large metal panel off her body, he just kept talking to her, praying for her to be alive, demanding that she be okay. He stroked her char-smudged face. "Please, please. Just open your eyes for me—"

Shaking erratically now, he smoothed her hair back to check her pulse. It was faint but there. Why the hell wasn't she waking up? "Dani, honey, can you hear me?"

Strong hands tried to pull him away from her body.

He shoved them to the side and pleaded, begged for Dani to come back to him.

Soon, more people appeared and forcibly hauled him out of the way as firemen swarmed over Dani's body to give her first aid. The voice shouting in his ear to let the firemen do their jobs washed over him, went through him numbly.

He fell to his knees helplessly as they took Dani, lifeless and limp, away on a stretcher.

Chapter 31

LUKE SCRUBBED HIS FACE with his hands, furious that the goddamn hospital assholes still wouldn't let him see Dani. She was his...no, not his wife, which was why they wouldn't let him go to her yet.

Only family they'd kept repeating to him.

When they'd asked who he was to her, 'boyfriend' didn't seem nearly strong or true enough an answer. Still covered in the blackened blast dust he'd found Dani lying in, he stared back at them, unable to speak.

Patiently, they rephrased their question, this time asking who she was to him.

"She's the woman I'm going to spend the rest of my life with," he whispered back.

The nurse looked stricken, sympathetic, but still, no one would let him through.

Minutes later, Derek ran in and shouted for someone

to tell him where his sister was. He ran up to Luke and grabbed him by the shirt. "Is she okay?" he demanded.

"They won't let me see her. Only you. Go. The doctor is right there."

Nodding shakily, fear in his eyes, Derek rushed over to the doctor and they swept him straight into the back. Derek's husband Jonathan stood next to Luke. Silently, they both watched Derek disappear behind the swinging doors.

Then they waited.

Quinn and Rylan arrived at the hospital soon after. Xoey and the entire bartending and wait staff came next. A little later, all of the workers from Ocotillos joined them, along with many other concerned business owners, vendors, and friends.

The waiting room was soon packed. And for the next two hours, they all sat there and heard nothing. At hour three, finally, the doors opened.

Luke looked up.

"She's awake."

He felt a wave of dizziness as blood rushed into his heart for seemingly the first time since he'd found her unconscious. Relieved cries echoed throughout the room.

Derek came straight over to him. "She's asked for you."

Luke rose up on legs he was amazed were still working.

He looked back and saw the friends and family that had known Dani for so much longer than he had. Suddenly, he felt gut-wrenchingly awful for them that they couldn't go see her this instant. Just to see that she was okay. His step faltered, his emotions cementing him in place.

"Go," said Xoey, her voice hoarse with lingering terror. "We'll get our chance. You go now and tell her we all love her and that we're all here. You just be there for her. For us."

Luke nodded once and then walked the most emotional hundred yards of his life.

Oh god. His hands fisted in fury at the universe when he walked into her hospital room and saw her. His heart and soul was lying there before him on the hospital bed—bruised, battered, and broken.

"*Dani.*" Hot, angry tears ran down his face as he went to her side.

She cracked her eyes open. "Hi," she said softly, her voice gritty and pained. Reaching for him with weak fingers, she laced her fingers with his.

"I thought I'd lost you."

She tried to shake her head, but it came out as a weak head tilt. Opening her lips, she tried to speak again, but a serrated sound scraped out of her throat instead, causing her body to flinch.

"Shhh, don't talk." Luke swept the tear rolling down her cheek. "They said your throat is going to be pretty raw for a while."

Her eyes snared his, and even though she didn't— couldn't—say it, he heard her.

"I love you too, Dani. So much." He stroked her cheek gently, watching her eyelids flutter closed again as the pain meds overtook her. "Sleep, baby. I'll be right here, always right here. And everyone is outside waiting too so you have to get better soon, you hear me?"

The silent room was his only reply.

———•———

"YOU GUYS ARE ALL being ridiculous. I should be able to go home already." Dani tried to reason with everyone in her hospital room. "I'm not even that badly hurt. Sheesh, it was just a little steam explosion."

Luke apparently didn't think he could've heard a more absurd comment out of her mouth. And he told her as much.

She rolled her eyes. "I was just in the wrong place at the wrong time when that tank over-pressurized. A freak mishap with a faulty valve—it happens. Luckily, it was Ole Betsy and she'd been empty. If it had been one of the active brew tanks or the bigger systems, then I'd see your concern. But it *wasn't.*" She smothered her wince when she shrugged. "Really, I'm just glad no one got hurt."

"Besides you!" growled Luke, looking so pained by the memory. "A damn elephant could stick its head in the hole that got blasted through the building, Dani. You got knocked out by metal debris the size of a frickin' desk that hit you with the force of a car. It could've sliced you in two! You're lucky it just put you in a coma." He fluffed her pillow roughly. "Derek and I already talked about it; you're staying in the hospital until they kick you out."

Dani groused in response, but her eyes shined with love. She turned those eyes to him, and he gave her a growly kiss. They'd been doing this song and dance all week.

And she was all ready for another go.

"At least hand me my phone. If I don't call for bottling equipment quotes before Derek does, the stubborn ass is going to finagle a way to make it so I can't pay a cent to help."

A few days into her recovery, Derek and Luke finally got a chance to tell Dani their winery/chocolate shop partnership idea. She'd been so elated over the beautiful plans that she'd nearly cried. Then when the topic of using part of the brewery for bottling came up, she had cried—a bizarre byproduct of the hospital meds, she'd declared.

"Plus, there's so much to do with the insurance," she continued on a rolling grumble. "The tank manufacturer, the building repairs, the contingency plan during renovations," she counted off her fingers when Luke snagged her phone and shoved it in his pocket.

"All taken care of," interjected Xoey from the corner of the room.

Everyone in the room turned to gape at her, mostly in shock, though Dani's shock turned quickly into a huge smile beaming with intense pride. And hope.

"Oh cut it out," sniffed Xoey. "It's not that big a deal. My uncle's a contractor. As far as the other stuff, it didn't take a brain surgeon. The numbers are right there on the bills; I just picked up a phone." She glared at her. "Quit looking at me like that."

"Like what?" asked Dani, innocent as can be.

Xoey's eyes narrowed. "Like you're going to try and

extend your little stay here in the hospital. This is just temporary, you hear me? I'm *not* going to be your general manager."

Dani's hand shot to her side, her groan splitting the air.

Everyone gasped and rushed to her bedside.

"I dunno, Xo," she moaned on a theatric grimace of pain. "It may be a really long recovery for me." Of course, her acting had always stunk so she couldn't keep her smile hidden for long.

Xoey glared at her something fierce. "Evil!"

Dani raised a shocked eyebrow when she saw it was Isaac holding her back from charging the hospital bed. *Wait a minute. Are they holding hands?* A quick blinking eye-rub confirmed that no, she hadn't been blinded by the blast, and yes, that really was Xoey holding Isaac's hand.

Amazing. She'd never known Xoey to actually do that. Sleep with a guy? Sure. Contemplate a long, extravagant life together? Of course—if he was worthy. Hold hands with him for no reason? Hiss, boo, holy cross.

Aw, she really liked him. And not in the whirlwind Xoey-in-love-within-the-first-minute way either.

Dani directed a pointed look at the hand-holding and gave her a not-at-all-subtle thumbs up.

Xoey replied with a blushing eye roll and then spun on her heel to make a quick exit, practically dragging Isaac out the door. Once outside though, she stopped and stuck her head back in. "I'll be back tomorrow. You better be walking by then!" With that, her stilettos clacked away.

After seeing the time, Javier and Sam hopped up to head on out as well, handing Dani some contraband Ocotillos food along with the many get-well cards that had begun pouring in from customers. "Business in the pub half hasn't been affected at all, and the brew boys are working around the clock to get things functional on the brewery end," reassured Javier.

Rylan spoke up from where he was decorating Dani's arm cast. "Yup, and Quinn is already planning a grand re-opening hoopla."

Dani shifted her gaze over to Quinn and all thoughts about the brewpub vanished when she saw the clouds of suppressed worry in her friend's eyes. "Hey, how're you holding up? Is everything on schedule for the first stage of Coop's surgeries? How's he doing?" With her injuries looking about as bad as they felt, Dani hadn't gone upstairs to the pediatric ward to visit Cooper yet as she didn't want to alarm or upset him before his surgeries. But she'd been getting updates from everyone ever since he was admitted for pre-op procedures a few days ago.

Quinn gave her a reassuring—albeit tired—smile. "The doctors are optimistic that everything will go according to plan next week. So far, everything has been swinging in our favor, and they're thinking the reconstruction might not be as problematic as they'd first anticipated. And as far as Cooper's concerned, this has been the best week of his life. His hospital room is filled to the brim with new toys, books, and video games. All your workers and Rylan's guys have been spoiling the boy silly."

Rylan stood and slid an arm around Quinn's waist. "The kid's easy to spoil. And it's not just us. He's got the nurses wrapped around his little finger as well." He quirked an I-shit-you-not eyebrow at Dani. "I didn't believe it till I saw it but even Noah sent Coop a gift."

"Will wonders never cease," called out a gruff voice from the hall.

They all turned their astonished gazes to the door, where Noah was standing with two envelopes in hand, one addressed to Luke and the other to Dani.

Though curiosity was painted all over Quinn's face, Rylan dragged her away so Luke and Dani could chat with Noah in private. Bypassing all preliminaries and how-are-you-feeling small talk, Noah got right down to business, handing Luke his envelope first without a word.

Peering over Luke's shoulder, Dani saw Luke pull out a triplicate document labeled ADDENDUM from the envelope.

"Luke, given your promising new business partnership with Derek, as well as his financial assets via his part ownership of Ocotillos, I've found your business to be solid enough not to require your patent collateral for the loan I gave you. We can revert it to a standard business loan. You can come by my office this week to sign those."

He handed Dani her envelope next, a much thicker one. She slid open the seal, already knowing what she would find.

"And Dani, given Luke and Derek's new business partnership, I've found our agreement for you to sign over a percent partnership of Ocotillos to be completely unnecessary. And frankly, just as foolish as I told you it was to begin with."

Her envelope contained the contract it had killed her to sign last week.

Ripped in half.

Noah shook his head at them. "I honestly don't know how you two are so successful at your businesses." His lips twitched to the side. "But I *can* see why you two are so perfect for each other."

Funny, though that statement came out as both compliment and criticism, when she looked up at his face, Dani saw a flash of...envy that made her wonder if it was more the former than the latter. But the peek into the mysterious inner workings of Noah was gone a second later as he turned to leave the room without another word, leaving them stunned silent in his wake.

"He's like a very dramatic cross between the fairy godmother and a suit-wearing Dirty Harry," muttered Luke.

Chuckling lightly through the shards of pain across her body, Dani just dropped the envelope and pulled him down next to her in the hospital bed.

———•———

HE COULD'VE LOST HER.

Every day since the explosion, that's all Luke kept thinking about. How he'd been so close to losing her. It ate at Luke's gut to see her like this. His breathing was ragged as he stroked her non-broken arm, needing to keep touching her to know she was okay—banged up, but alive.

"Dani," he began slowly, turning carefully in the hospital bed so he didn't aggravate any of her injuries, "I know I said I wouldn't push, and I'm not going to, but I'm worried about you. I want you to live with me at my place until we know for sure your apartment is safe. And whether you like it or not, I'm taking care of you until you're fully recovered. Don't freak out, alright, sweetie? It's just for a few weeks."

Dani's fingers covered his lips lightly. "Luke, do you want to move in together?"

He stared at her in disbelief.

She let out a slow, beautiful grin that devastated his heart, made it spin in his chest as a tattered breath deflated his lungs. "You drive me insane, you know that?"

"Is that a no?"

He looked at her as if she'd lost her marbles in the blast. "Like I'd actually say no." Then his eyes softened. "But you don't have to do this now, honey. I'm not going anywhere. We can discuss this again when you're fully recovered." He sighed. The universe could be so cruel—scaring a commitment-phobe enough to start planning for the future, and scaring him enough to almost, almost accept. Gripping her hand, he gave her a reassuring smile. "Besides, I don't want our relationship to move forward because of an explosion I'd just as soon forget."

Leaning her head against his cheek, she said simply, "I decided before."

His face tightened skeptically.

"I did. Ask Xoey. I woke her up the morning of the explosion to talk. Of course, when I told her about us moving in together, she went on and on, reminding me about *all* the other gorgeous fish in the sea." She giggled at the annoyance flitting across his face.

He caught Dani's chin to look into her eyes. "Why? What changed your mind?"

"I woke up alone."

The hope he was feeling crumbled. "And I'll live with that for the rest of my life. I'm so sorry, sweetheart. I never should have left you after our fight." He dropped his head into his hands. "If I'd just stayed in bed with you that night, you wouldn't be lying here like this in the hospital—"

"Stop." Dani smoothed the agony from his face with gentle fingers. "That blast was an accident waiting to happen. Plus, it was my day to open; I would've gotten hurt no matter what."

He shook his head. "The explosion happened well before you normally go in to open and you know it. You would've been safe if you hadn't headed in early to arrange that surprise for me." With hands that trembled, he traced the deep bruises on her face and neck, the lacerated skin all along her chest and arms. "Face it, I'm the reason you almost died."

"Luke, no. I was there because I wanted to be. I wanted to show you the two new brews I'd made from your chocolates. They're the first of six different chocolate beers we'll be selling as Ocotillos' inaugural bottled beer set." His utter shock lit a smile on her face. "*That's* why I knew all about bottling equipment when Derek mentioned it for his winery the other day."

Luke simply had no words. After her horrible history with bottling their beers, the fact that she had been willing to do this for him...

"That was the brilliant plan I'd been working on. Even after I'd struck that final business shares deal with Noah, I hadn't been able to stop working on 'em." She smiled softly. "I was inspired, I guess. I was planning to split the profits with your shop but now that you're going to be fine lease-wise with Derek partnering in, I decided to have the money go to Quinn for Coop's surgery expenses." She cradled his face in her hands. "So, yes, I had something to show you that morning. And maybe if I hadn't been all crazy in love and wanting to surprise you with this whole 'look how good we can be together' metaphor, I'd have just told you without this whole romantic gesture thing at the brewpub. A few months ago I would've. With anyone else, I would've. But for some reason, I find myself wanting to do things differently now with you."

A slow smile overtook his lips.

"Instead of just simply telling you, I find myself wanting to show you how I feel. I'm constantly thinking of ways to make those two dimples of yours appear."

His smile turned into a full-blown fool-in-love grin.

The corners of her lips lifted. "Yeah, like *that*." She sighed with mock despair. "Okay, alright? My name is Dani and I'm a complete and utter romantic. My vice of choice is fluffy feelings. And apparently, my boyfriend brings it out of me in a flagrant fashion because I'm so dang in love—wait, wait, stop," she laughed, covering his lips. "Don't go kiss-crazy just yet."

She cocked her head to the side. "You didn't let me finish. I didn't mean I was upset that I was alone that morning. I meant I felt alone as a whole. Like something was missing from my life. So, I closed my eyes and found my mind wandering over to those dreams we talked about once." Her gaze met his. "And the more I dreamed, the more right I felt. All I could think about was how much I wanted to reach that life in my dreams—really live, you know?"

He did know.

"Luke, I've never really thought of the future because there was never one there in front of me that I wanted to dream about. But with you... When I think of you, I see a future, not the other way around. That means something, doesn't it? That I don't just picture a fantasy future with any Joe Shmoe edited in, but rather, I can't see a future unless I think of you first?"

She looked down, embarrassed.

He swiftly extinguished that embarrassment with an all-consuming kiss that burned with every emotion he was feeling.

Not until she looked sufficiently dazed and as high as he felt, did he finally stop to answer, "That's a yes, by the way. Yes, on us moving in together."

Epilogue

TO LUKE'S UTTER FRUSTRATION, less than a month out of the hospital, and Dani's stubborn-ass bullheadedness was back and badder than ever.

"You're being unreasonable," bit out Luke, obstinately. "Just wait a few more months to brew. The brewpub is doing fine without it." He stood his ground. "I know you don't fully believe in the Dobson curse, but I sure as hell do. You were in here last month trying to make a new spring beer and *your brewery blew up*. Uh, hello? So, again, I repeat, NO."

"First of all, the chocolate beers weren't spring beers. Secondly, I'm not asking for your *permission* you lug nut." Dani folded her arms and glared at him. "I'm NOT waiting!"

"Why now?" he exploded. "Why do you *have* to make this beer now?"

"It's a spring beer," she shrugged matter-of-factly.

"Make it a summer beer."

"No."

He fumed in frustration. "Why? Why can't it be a summer beer?"

"It's the one spring beer I've always refused to make because of my mom." She took his hand in hers. "I want to do this, Luke. Or I'll never know if I can get past what she did." Her eyes took on a suspicious little light then as she added, "And that's the last thing I want to be wondering about come next spring when we get married."

His entire body went completely still.

Smiling like a devilish angel, she walked right past him to the brew tanks.

She was three steps away before he picked up his unhinged jaw and spun around to pull her back to him. "Wait a minute. You can't just drop a bomb like that and walk away."

Amusement dancing all over her face, she tilted her head and waited for him to continue.

"You want to get married?" he demanded roughly.

Smooth, Luke. Real smooth.

Apparently, she thought so too. Because she laughed.

Her eyes slid down and saw that his hands were shaking. Big time. "Have I ever told you how much I love making your hands shake?"

She leaned over and kissed him, long and deep.

Every inch of him hardened. But he stayed the course. "Stop distracting me and answer the question. Do you want to marry me?"

She sniffed like a diva and glanced at her nails. "Not if

415

you ask me like that."

Great, *now* her acting improves. The woman didn't paint her nails.

Hanging on to his sanity by a very thin thread, he rephrased his question. "Are you saying you want me to ask you to marry me?"

She thought about it for a torturous second before popping a kiss on his mouth and giving him a saucy wink.

"*Maybe,*" she teased as she turned and did her signature Danica walkout.

Luke slapped a hand over his chest to stop his heart from busting out of it.

Never had a single word sounded so sweet coming from the woman he loved.

The End

———◆———

Up next in the CACTUS CREEK series,
RYLAN & QUINN'S story:

LOVE, DIAMONDS, AND SPADES

Includes a <u>bonus</u> 5,000-word Luke & Dani short story:

"LUKE & DANI'S WEDDING"

———◆———

OTHER BOOKS BY VIOLET DUKE

The CAN'T RESIST Series
The acclaimed New York Times bestselling series, an emotional, heartfelt Top 10 Bestseller both in the U.S. and internationally.

RESISTING THE BAD BOY
FALLING FOR THE GOOD GUY
CHOOSING THE RIGHT MAN
FINDING THE RIGHT GIRL

The CACTUS CREEK Series
The laugh and cry USA Today bestselling small town series with strong heroines, romantic heroes, a quirky cast, and inter-series cameos galore.

LOVE, CHOCOLATE, AND BEER
LOVE, DIAMONDS, AND SPADES
LOVE, TUSSLES, AND TAKEDOWNS
LOVE, EXES, AND OHS

The FOURTH DOWN Series
The fun and sexy USA Today bestselling sports romance series starring three sweet and incorrigibly alpha heroes, from Random House Books.

JACKSON'S TRUST
BENNETT'S CHANCE
DONOVAN'S HEART

The UNFINISHED LOVE Series
Four brothers fighting for their second first chance at love. Years be damned.

BEFORE THAT NIGHT *(Caine & Addison, Bk 1)*
EVERY NIGHT WITHOUT YOU *(Caine & Addison, Bk 2)*
BEFORE THAT KISS *(Gabe & Hannah, Bk 1)*
EVERY KISS GOODBYE *(Gabe & Hannah, Bk 2)*
BEFORE THAT PROMISE *(Drew & Skylar, Bk 1)*
EVERY PROMISE UNSPOKEN *(Drew & Skylar, Bk 2)*
BEFORE THAT CHANCE *(Max & Kennedy, Bk 1)*
EVERY CHANCE WE LOST *(Max & Kennedy, Bk 2)*

The JUNIPER HILLS Series
An emotional new small town series from Montlake Romance

ALL THERE IS
WHERE YOU'LL BE

Made in the USA
Lexington, KY
14 December 2018